THE SECRET
PURPOSES

THE SECRET PURPOSES

David Baddiel

WILLIAM MORROW

An Imprint of HarperCollins*Publishers*

This book was originally published in Great Britain in 2004 by Little, Brown, an imprint of Time Warner Book Group UK.

FIRST U.S. EDITION

Printed on acid-free paper

Library of Congress Cataloging-in-Publication Data

Baddiel, David.
    The secret purposes: a novel/David Baddiel.—1st ed.
      p. cm.
    ISBN 0-06-076582-8 (acid-free paper)
     1. World War, 1939–1945—Great Britain—Fiction. 2. World War, 1939–1945—Germany—Fiction. 3. Germans—Great Britain—Fiction. 4. Jews—Great Britain—Fiction. 5. Concentration camps—Fiction. 6. Women translators—Fiction. 7. Refugees, Jewish—Fiction. 8. Isle of Man—Fiction. I. Title.

PR6052.A3126S43   2005
823'.914—dc22   2004063125

05 06 07 08 09 RRD 10 9 8 7 6 5 4 3 2 1

To my grandparents, Otti and Ernst, survivors;
and to my great-uncle, Arno

'I can see God in the creature, but the nature, the essence, the secret purposes of God, I cannot see there.'

John Donne, Sermon, St Paul's, Christmas Day, 1629

PART ONE

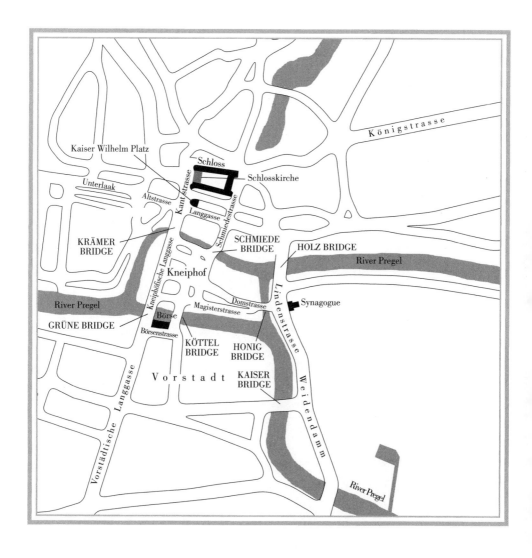

Königsberg, 1934

'The jewes are not the men who will be blamed for nothing.'

Jack the Ripper

It always pleased the Reverend Isidor Fabian that he had only to step out of his synagogue on the Lindenstrasse and there it was, the first of the seven bridges. In fact, he simply had to walk across the road, in a straight line from the synagogue's wood-panelled double doors, and already he was on the Honig Bridge, and into the first chapter of his regular Sunday journey. As he stepped through the doors on this particular morning, sun-bright and clear as February days often were in Königsberg, he felt the heaviness in his heart lift a little in anticipation of the reassuring pleasures of the walk: the smell of the sea-laced air, the sight of the beautiful medieval houses lining the waterfronts, the sound of the gulls crying as they swooped low over the fishing boats, and, most importantly, the feel of his soul cleansing, as underneath each bridge the River Pregel washed his sense of sin away.

Isidor based his weekly walk on Leonhard Euler's 1736 paper 'Solutio problematis ad geometriam situs pertinentis'. The great Swiss mathematician, while crossing the German states by post-wagon in the 1720s, had become interested in a puzzle long discussed by the good burghers of Königsberg – which was: could it be possible, on a single walk, to visit all of the four separate land-masses of the city, crossing each of the seven bridges only once? The burghers had for years tried to solve this puzzle in practice, by end-less Sunday walks around the city, but Euler solved it by throwing away the scale map and replacing it with a topological version: in one stroke proving that it was indeed impossible to visit every part of the city crossing each bridge only once, and inventing modern Graph Theory. Isidor, when in conversation with other senior mem-bers of the Königsberg Jewish community, was wont to mention often his acquaintance with the 'Solutio problematis', partly because reading a mathematical paper published two centuries ago marked him out as an intellectual, but mainly because it carried the

3

implication that he had read it in the original Latin – and therefore that Isidor was not just an intellectual but, in Jewish terms, a radical: a rabbi prepared to learn the holy language of the Other.

Isidor had to wait for the no. 14 tram to pass before he could cross the street to the bridge. Its slow rumble past took the edge off his improved mood a little, reminding him that, although Jews were not yet banned from using public transport in Königsberg, he knew of no one in the community who would use the trams any more: you were stared at so violently now, especially by the young men, and there was a story going round that Reuben Fischer had got on the no. 37 outside his shop on Kaiser Wilhelm Platz – as he had done every day for sixteen years – and the driver had refused to take his money, indeed refused to drive on at all until Reuben had been forced to turn and walk back to the street. Isidor kept his head down until the tram had continued past some yards away, in case there should be boys at the back window making obscene gestures towards him.

The tram gone, the bridge beckoned, towards the Kneiphof, the densely populated island in the middle of the Pregel around which Königsberg had concentrically evolved, and from which five of the seven bridges shot out – two to the north, two to the south and one to the east, making the island look on a map like a huge scorpion dropped into the centre of the city. Isidor crossed the street, his eyes fixing on the rising Gothic towers of the cathedral, the most prominent building on the Kneiphof. He had always felt that it spoke of his city's tradition of tolerance – the *Königsberger Verhältnisse*, the Königsberg Way – that the synagogue and the cathedral were built so close to each other. Admittedly, the cathedral faced away from the synagogue, as if disavowing its spiritual forefather, but Isidor still remembered the speech made by the old Mayor in 1896, on the inauguration of the synagogue, the synagogue that Isidor, nineteen years old then, knew he would one day inherit:

It is a savage time we live in today. Long rotten but deeply rooted ideas dare to come to daylight again. Thus, this day appears to me like the morning sun announcing better times. Here, in Königsberg, adherents to all religions and persuasions live next to each other in peace and harmony. To this, the local Jewish population has contributed to no small extent. Stronger than anywhere else, among them the bonds of family and friendship do work; receptive to any progress of humankind, glowing for the arts and sciences, filled with true and genuine humanity, at the same time obedient to the laws of state and faithful to its king, this . . .

And here Isidor recalled that the Mayor paused, looking up at the great dome, the reflections of one hundred and eighty menorah-mounted candles glistening like a constellation on its copper interior (Isidor knew it needed cleaning now, but did not know who would be prepared to take the job, Hartmann and Co. having not renewed their contract); he paused, long enough for it to seem as if his rheumy eyes must have caught sight of something there on the roof, before looking down again at the six hundred or so luminaries seated in front of him:

. . . this is how the same Jew who once was burnt now stands before my eyes, and not mine alone.

But that was nearly forty years ago, thought Isidor, stopping his walk for a second. And then, before the melancholy of time and age could settle on him: so *much for progress*. The internal shrug that came with the epithet punctured his reverie, reminding him that he was nearly halfway across the bridge, and had not even considered the present condition of his pride.

For this was Isidor's secret weekly project: each of the seven bridges of Königsberg represented, for him, one of the Seven Deadly Sins. As he walked across each bridge, he would force himself to contemplate his own participation in that particular sin; and then feel how that contemplation, allied to the consequent sense of repentance which sprung up inside him like a reflex, would somehow free himself of the taint of the sin as he walked. He imagined it falling off him like the discarded skin of a reptile, off him and over the sides of the bridge, to be swallowed up and carried away by the river, out into the freezing Baltic Sea. Sometimes, he would consider also the sins of his family, or even of members of his congregation, feeling that in some way it might help to lift evil from them, too; that it was part of his calling as their rabbi to use his cleansing process for their benefit, like a prayer on their behalf. His route each week did not necessarily follow the classical order of the sins – pride, covetousness, envy, anger, lust, gluttony, sloth – but instead was based on whichever sin was uppermost in his mind, which, as a matter of self-discipline, he would always leave until last.

Isidor tried to focus on his pride for the remaining twenty yards or so of the bridge, but it was difficult, as his mind, meditative, as religious men's are, was whirring at the moment, destabilising the rigour of his self-scrutiny. Pride, he thought, forcing himself to disregard the other voices in his head, when recently have I fallen victim to it? Concentrating hard, he remembered feeling a glow of self-satisfaction following his sermon last Shabbos, delivered on one of his favourite passages from Deuteronomy:

> Since you saw no form when the LORD spoke to you at Horeb out of the fire, take care and watch yourselves closely, so that you do not make an idol for yourselves, in the form of any figure – the likeness of male or female, the likeness of any animal that is on the earth, the likeness of any winged bird that flies in the air, the likeness of anything that creeps on the ground, the likeness of any fish, that is in the water under the earth. And when you look up to the heavens and see the sun, the moon, and the stars, all the host of heaven, do not be led astray and bow down to them and serve them . . .

He had always liked this passage because, theologically, it was so *modern*: he always felt while reading it, or reciting it out loud in the synagogue, that in it one could hear religion as we understand it today being born, individuating itself from all the tribal fantasy-narratives that preceded it, with their multiple animal and planetary deities. The primitives were people who just looked around them, he had said, naming whatever frightened them as gods. But this *imagination* of God, as he remembered daringly putting it, as a

6

formless thing, invisible but omnipresent, was a precise historical moment: the creation of the cornerstone of all modern religion, faith – religion as the worship of what you could *not* see.

The rabbi was over the bridge by the time he'd finished reciting the words in his mind, and then felt a little embarrassed and confused, knowing that what he had intended as a searing indictment of his pride had ended up simply as a – rather pleasant – contemplation of something he had been proud of, his sermon. The replaying of his words in his mind had left him feeling not abashed but rather pleased with himself – exactly the opposite of what his ascetic endeavour was supposed to achieve. He looked behind him, back towards the synagogue, and considered starting again; but he felt that to do so would be, as it were, breaking the rules. And, besides, time was getting on – the entire walk, which used to take him only an hour and a half, now took him nearly three, and he had promised Eleanor that he would be back by noon: she was making salt cod and latkes. Any lingering doubts were made up for him by the arrival of two uniformed men – SA, were they? Isidor wondered: he could never remember which paramilitary group was which in the new regime – who began erecting some sort of platform at the Kneiphof end of the bridge. He hurried on into the island.

Isidor was of course aware that in an Orthodox sense this whole undertaking was a sin: the Seven Deadly Sins were a Christian invention. Technically, sin itself was a Christian invention, a mistranslation of the Hebrew word *chait*, meaning an error, a mistake. In the original text of the Bible, Adam and Eve's eating the apple of knowledge was *chait*, which makes sense, as Isidor had once pointed out in another sermon, since how can you deliberately do anything without knowledge? Knowledge allows you to discern what is good and what is evil. Before knowledge, all sin can be only *chait*. Some Talmudic scholars whom Isidor had studied liked to believe that this demonstrated a greater generosity of spirit on the part of Judaism, allowing for the idea that human beings are often passive in their failings: the evil they do is not always their fault.

Well, Isidor thought, true though that might be, it seemed to make little difference to God, not at least when it came to punishment: I mean, what would He have done to Adam and Eve if they *had* eaten the apple deliberately? It was just semantics. The Old Testament was all about the dynamic of transgression and chastisement. As a liberal, Isidor was interested in how that dynamic could be made a bit more human, or rather, humane; and, for him, the key was the most Jewish value, atonement. *What is the fate of the transgressor?*, Leviticus asks. *He shall bring a guilt-offering and it shall atone for him.* His walk over the bridges was his guilt-offering. The sins were a way of packaging his transgressions. And because there were seven of them, they appealed to the Kabbalist in him, the numerologist: seven was the most significant number in Judaic lore, after three. God made the world in six days and rested on the seventh, hallowing it. He was sure, historically, that the reason Pope Gregory had originally placed the Deadly Sins into a list of seven went back to this root.

He often chuckled to himself, wondering what Esra Munk, the leader of Adass Israel, the ultra-Orthodox section of the community, would do if he knew of his musings: try to have him excommunicated, no doubt. Adass had already insisted on separate prayer-meetings, following the decision – pushed through by Isidor soon after he took office in 1912 – to install an organ behind the synagogue altar. For a while, it looked as if they might come back, but then he had gone further – too far, even for some of his liberal colleagues, who had left to join Adass – with the introduction of women into the choir. Isidor won this battle, though: synagogue attendance was up nearly three hundred seats by the end of his first two years in the job. And this was why he was unashamed of his small heresy; he knew that the survival and augmentation of the community required modernisation, and any modernisation in religion inevitably involved borrowings – what were the organ and the gorgeous sound of the women's voices floating above the chazan's on Kol Nidre night if they were not, stylistically, Christian? Besides, Isidor felt that, by accepting into his spiritual core some small trappings of Christian ideology, he was only living up to the Königsberg Way, the way epitomised by the Mayor in his speech that day. As he continued his walk down Domstrasse to the Köttel Bridge, he remembered the words on the grave of Königsberg's greatest son, just behind these cathedral walls, overlooked by the university beyond: *Der bestirnte Himmel über mir, das moralische Gesetz in mir*. 'The starry Heavens above me, the Moral Law within me': so Kant had said in the *Critique of Pure Reason*. Isidor felt proud – sinless pride, just as he should at this point in his journey, devoid of self-congratulation – to be part of the intellectual culture that clustered around these words.

Approaching the Köttel Bridge, he found his thoughts once again magnetically drawn back to the pressing issue in his life. Leave it, he thought, leave it until the last bridge; leave it until you want to feel anger. The Köttel Bridge, like the Grüne Bridge two hundred yards beyond it, overlooked the Börse, the enormous, palatial Königsberg stock-exchange. This had served Isidor rather well on previous walks, as it allowed for an easy contemplation of envy; he had only to imagine the greed-charged traders inside, making their sweatless wealth, their pockets – as he conceived of them – overflowing with notes conjured there by the strange magic of the market, and he would feel the sin immediately, as a physical sensation, a hot flush of envy. He had done that too often before, though, and his response had become Pavlovian. As he stepped onto the bridge today, not knowing exactly how to catalyse envy within him, the idea suddenly came to him that his interest in Christianity might be a form of envy. He was so shocked by this idea that he paused, holding on to the iron side-railings of the bridge. But perhaps it was true. He had to admit it – he envied Christianity. He envied its simplicity – a few proscriptions, rather than 613 fidgety laws to obey; no complicated dietary regulations; no inscrutable prayer-regulation – and he envied its iconography. A man on a cross. What could compete with that as a central image? Such *power*. What was Judaism's central image? A star. And not a heavenly body, but a topological representation of a star, drawn as if by Euler himself, like the religion, abstract, mystical, disconnected from human experience. Isidor felt these ideas rush in on him, and a panic begin to seize his inner self, but they would not stop. At heart, he knew, he was interested in religious *success* – those three hundred seats were still his proudest achievement – and it seemed to be coming to him, all at once, the reasons why Christianity was so successful. The

9

cross-breeding of God and man – Jesus – was such a brilliant conceit, creating a worship that was a kind of empathy, a unique combination of adoration and identification.

Luckily for Isidor, his train of thought was broken by a hooting alarm sound, announcing the arrival of a tall fishing boat immediately to his left, and the consequent opening of the bridge. He moved back, off the lifting middle section. Marvelling at the way the concrete arched slowly up towards him, like a palm commanding stop, his mind calmed a little: perhaps it was just the times, he thought reassuringly, that had made his thoughts screech so against the grain of his own faith. He felt slightly awkward, though, standing among the small group of people gathered on the bridge waiting for the boat to pass. It made him realise how much his walk, in recent times, had unconsciously started to exclude rest; how preferable, out on the streets, now, it was to keep moving. Those around him all seemed like ordinary Königsbergers – a young couple, arm-in-arm, a stout older man carrying an umbrella, an upper-class lady in a fine fur coat, two children in school uniform, like small sailors in their suits – but Isidor, even with his head down, could feel their eyes on him, sizing up the length of his beard and the blackness of his Homburg. He could sense their discomfort, their inarticulate uncertainty about how to deal with this sudden enforced proximity to a Jew.

The ship passed through, and the two halves of the bridge came back together again. As they began to dock, Isidor wondered if this opening and shutting mechanism could be incorporated into his allegory, in terms of the bridge representing the sin: the opening and closing of the envious heart, perhaps? Although did that make sense . . . ? Before he had time to think it through, the bridge halves had closed, and the crowd around him had moved off. Watching their backs hurrying away, Isidor felt the intricacy of his thoughts slacken a little. I just envy *them*, he thought, restarting his walk: their normality, their complacent impunity. I just envy the fact that they can walk the bridges of Königsberg without fear. He held this thought as he moved behind those who had shared his space a moment before, and as others, similarly free, came towards him from the other side: for a moment, repentance was not forthcoming,

10

until he remembered that therefore what he envied about his fellow citizens was that they were not Jews.

Off the Köttel Bridge, Isidor turned right into Börsenstrasse, which ran along the river the length of the Börse, and then right again into the Vorstädtische Langgasse, which led directly on to the Grüne Bridge: gluttony. It was his simplest sin. Isidor had always loved his food; like many Jews, it was his primary pleasure. When Tussel, the old Shidduch, had first presented Eleanor to him, her head shyly bowed, her hands clasped in front of her virgin's smock, his heart had fallen a little, he remembered – she was no beauty. Her eyes were a touch crossed, and she had clearly inherited her father's nose – the young Isidor could not help imagining, briefly, her nostrils overflowing, like his, with grey, spiky hair – but his spirits had picked up when Tussel, perhaps sensing Isidor's initial reaction, had said, a little pleadingly: 'She's a splendid cook.' It was true. At the first mouthful of her lokshen pudding, Isidor's eyes had begun to moisten, and it was all he could do to stop himself turning to her to say: 'This more than makes up for the nose.' Nice noses, he knew, were ten a Deutschmark, but lokshen pudding like manna – where would he find that again?

Lokshen pudding, home-marinated schmaltz herring, gefilte fish, sweet, sweet red cabbage, still-warm-from-their-black-oven chulah, borscht the colour of blood, chopped liver as smooth as you like, boiled salt beef, kibbeh, kneidlach – she could make them all, and Isidor often found himself fantasising about her food, as other men might have done about their wife's – or mistress's – body. Still now her food remained luxuriously good, because Stein the grocer kept all the ingredients especially back for her, despite the shelves in his shop being half empty these days, what with most of his suppliers refusing to trade. As Isidor stepped onto the bridge, he was already, aided by the smell of fresh fish rising from the boats moored beneath, tasting in his mind the salt cod, soaked by Eleanor not in water but in lemon juice, making the cooked fish sharp and sweet at the same time; and the latkes – oh, her latkes! – nothing else he'd ever tasted did so literally melt in the mouth, like butter, like the softest, silkiest butter. He felt the saliva collect in his jaw, and his spirit settle easily into gluttony; and, lost so deeply in the daydream

11

of Eleanor's cooking, was nearly over the bridge before he'd even considered repenting for the third time today. This was a common problem for Isidor on the Grüne Bridge, not just because he so quickly found himself spellbound by latkes, but because he was not entirely convinced that gluttony was a sin. Did not the Lord say to Adam: *Everything that lives and moves will be food for you?* This same Lord who rained bread from the heavens for our people in the wastes of Sinai? It was a big difference between the religions, between the cultures, Isidor thought. Jesus was a Jew, yes, but we should have known something was not quite straightforwardly Jewish about him when he decided to *fast* for forty days and forty nights.

None the less, more to fit in with his schemata than for any deeply felt spiritual reasons, he managed to cobble together some vague feelings of guilt about the over-indulgence of his taste-buds – feelings that were sharpened by remembering how many families in the community were unable now to get hold of kosher meat at all – and the last ten yards or so of the bridge were taken up in an attitude of demure atonement. Once over the bridge the Vorstädtische Langgasse became the Kneiphöfische Langgasse, a long road that ran the length of the central island; incorporating as it did the Grüne Bridge to the south and the Krämer Bridge to the north, it was the only road directly to connect the three main land-masses of Königsberg. Isidor passed the Catholic church, St Katherine's, and, only a little further on, the Lutheran church with its tall, thin steeple. The houses here, on the crammed space of the island, were packed high and narrow, most of them four or five storeys, hiding elegant courtyards through which Isidor would never walk. He imagined their central fountains, their high, over-looking galleries, their cloistered lawns. Further down the street, the ground floors of the houses had been converted to elegant shops: fashionable ladies' outfitters, expensive delicatessens, exquisite florists. Isidor did not need to look into their windows, knowing that he could not afford to buy any of their products, and preferring not to notice if they had *Wir bedienen keine Juden* signs up.

He was glad when he saw the first sight of the river and the Krämer Bridge; it was so much easier to focus the mind once on the bridge. Lust, however, was not really one of Isidor's priority sins. He and Eleanor had five children, four girls and a boy: not a huge family by rabbinical standards but enough to demonstrate that he had followed the Lord's most fundamental commandment fully enough. He had tried his best to be a good husband to her in this regard, knowing that intercourse was one of the three basic provisions a man must make for his wife, along with food and clothing. Latterly, though, she seemed little interested, tending to go to bed before him and be asleep – sometimes Isidor thought she might be pretending, but he wasn't sure – by the time he came up from his night reading. Spiritually, this did not cause him pain. Now that she was past child-bearing age, Isidor did not consider their abstinence an offence against the Law, as it would have been twenty, even ten, years ago. In fact, he sometimes wondered, in his more abstruse theological contortions, if abstinence was in fact the only path available for them under the Law considering that *sh'chatat zerah* – destruction of seed – was never permissible, and, frankly, spilling his seed into Eleanor these days was as good as destruction. He knew that *sh'chatat zerah* generally referred to certain other processes by which seed got destroyed, but still, technically, it meant any case where ejaculate could not physically end up in fertilisation. He wondered if God, a stickler at the best of times, would consider sex with Eleanor a version of the sin of Onan; whom God had killed for his act.

Physically, too, the withdrawal of sexual intimacy caused him little pain; long ago, he had sublimated all that desire into food and theology. Thus, the falling of the flesh on her face, and the rising of it on her body, had not, as with some men it does, caused him to turn away from her, towards younger women. Once, or twice, in the last few years, he had caught sight of women looking at him from the upper gallery of the synagogue – a young girl rapt, as it seemed, by his words; or a widow, gauging him through her veil – and the thought had crossed his mind: What if? He knew there were clergy of all denominations who abused their position for just such reward. But it seemed such an emotional *shlep*, for Isidor, to go to that place, for pleasures he had never really known and now was too old to begin learning about.

13

It was a quandary for Isidor, this bridge. He found himself in the invidious position of having to drum up sinful thoughts he didn't actually feel just so he could repent of them. He could, of course, have missed it out, but, like all religious Jews – it is an autistic creed – he needed order and regulation; walking six of the seven bridges just because he didn't particularly indulge in one of the sins would have felt incomplete. So he forced himself to imagine one of these synagogue women approaching him after a service, and inviting him back to her house, and plying him with wine, and food, and more food, and somewhere in the convergence of his excitement about food and the idea of it being served to him by a woman not his wife, he managed to create a feeling inside that served well enough as illicit lust. He imagined it, duly repented of it, and left the Krämer Bridge behind.

He continued up Kantstrasse, into the more heavily populated northern part of the city, and then turned right into Kaiser Wilhelm Platz, dominated in its centre by an imposing bronze statue of Bismarck, pointing skywards, ringed by fountains, the epaulettes on the Imperial Chancellor's uniform turning green. The square was busy with traffic, and, as Isidor paused, waiting to cross the road, he noticed he was standing by the granite cube which marked the tomb of Hans Luther, the eldest son of Martin, the reformer. A phrase came into his head – *Bleibe im Lande und nähre dich redlich* – 'Stay in the land and make an honest living'. He had heard it a lot lately from people in the community, particularly those who thought themselves most German and least Jewish; it had become almost a motto for them, a badge of honour, a manifesto, of their decision not to emigrate. It was funny, he felt, because they thought it was a typically German proverb, but Isidor knew that it was from Luther's translation of the Hebrew Psalms, the deranged theologian's typically puritanical mistranslation of the original, luxurious, 'Dwell in the land and truly you shall be fed'. Last time Solly Weinstein, who was particularly fond of *Bleibe im Lande*, had quoted it at him, Isidor had replied with another of Luther's sayings: 'In Prussia, there is an infinite number of evil spirits.' A clever reply, but pointless, Isidor knew, as Solly just looked confused, and besides, in principle, Isidor agreed with him anyway: he had no intention of leaving Germany.

The cars and carriages subsiding for a moment, Isidor crossed the square, towards the Schloss, the palace built by the Knights of the Teutonic Order when they made Königsberg their fortress in the thirteenth century. Isidor had visited the Schloss as a child, on a school day-trip; on entering the quadrangle, he thought he had never seen a space so vast, somehow all the more so for being enclosed. It was a good trip, he remembered, as he walked past the lofty Gothic tower that grew out of the Schlosskirche, built into the quadrangle's southern corner. He remembered the Prussia Museum, with its towering portraits of Wilhelm II and Frederick the Great, in gilt frames which he had thought spun of real gold; he remembered the coats of arms emblazoned on every wall, a black eagle crucified by its wings on a yellow cross; and he remembered his mix of horror and fascination on being shown the *Blutgericht*, the old torture chamber, converted since into a wine-room but still exhibiting some utensils of pain: it reminded tiny Isidor of his uncle Joseph's carpentry workshop, full of strange, unknowable wheels and levers. He passed a banner strung along the outer wall announcing the arrival of a new exhibition inside – *Health, Strength and Beauty: A Celebration of New German Art* – but paid it no attention: since the New Year, the Schloss had been closed to Jews.

At Schmiedestrasse, he turned right, back towards the Kneiphof, and the fifth bridge of his journey (in the old days, he used to extend his walk further north, up Königstrasse as far as the old city walls, but a combination of age and the sudden remembrance that the street was about to be renamed Hermann Goering Strasse drained him of the energy to do so now). Despite the bite in the air, it was bright enough for tables to be laid outdoors at some of the cafés, and Isidor caught the burnished smell of Viennese coffee and pastries as a waiter's tray went past towards a group of seated young women, laughing, he hoped not at him. The Schmiede Bridge lay ahead, and he put the scene out of his mind, concentrating on his covetousness. He always used this last section of the Schmiedestrasse to try to separate clearly in his mind the difference between covetousness and envy. As far as he understood it, envy represented the more destructive urge: whereas covetousness meant the desire to possess the fruits of another's success for oneself, to the point of wanting to steal them, envy was the active hatred of another's success, to the point of wanting to destroy it. As he stepped onto the bridge today, however, this distinction, which had seemed entirely clear to him in the past – his theological mind loved nothing better than such fine separations of meaning – appeared suddenly muddled: taking possession of someone else's wealth, for example, would always involve the destruction of it *for them*, and so could be motivated by either envy or covetousness. Surely, in fact, there could be no envy without covetousness, and no covetousness without envy? In which case, was there any need for two sins? Was not the existence of the two sins just the product of the early Christian thinkers' desire to overload sinners with the weight of their own wrongdoing? Or perhaps just to produce seven, because it was a holy number? These thoughts distressed him, ruinous as they were to the pattern of his walk, and, at heart, he knew they were themselves the products of anger, the sin he was putting off, because they were irritated thoughts, sparky and chafing. He was still smarting from what on the Köttel Bridge he'd realised in himself was a certain captivation with Christianity.

Standing at the entrance to the bridge, he took two or three deep breaths, drawing the salt wind down to his lungs. He needed to rein in his mind, he thought. Anger is propelling my thinking out of control. To calm himself, he said 'Covetousness' out loud, gravely, as if beginning a sermon: it drew a startled glance from a small urchin boy sitting on the bridge wall, who ran off scared. He walked onto the bridge. Going back to basics, with each step he rehearsed in his head the words of the Ten Commandments: *Thou shalt not covet thy neighbour's house, thou shalt not covet they neighbour's wife, nor his manservant, nor his maidservant, nor his ox, nor his ass, nor any thing that is thy neighbour's.* He wondered if he did covet any of those things. At the moment, most of his neighbours' possessions were being taken away from them, bit by bit. Soon there would be nothing left to covet anyway.

Then he remembered that Oshor Finkel, the lad whose family owned the old brick factory, had come to his office in the synagogue last Monday and told him that he had obtained a visa for America: visas for his wife and young child, too. It had cost him his stake in the factory in bribes, but he had them now. He fanned them out like playing cards on Isidor's little oak desk. Oshor wanted to know if the rabbi could absolve him in some way, because they would have to travel on Shabbos, but Isidor was hardly listening – he was staring at the small squares of card on his desk. It was the first time one of the community had definitely decided to leave, and it made Isidor realise at once how serious the situation was, and how there was no possibility of such escape for him. Oshor was . . . what? Thirty-five? Thirty-seven? Young enough to start afresh in the skyscrapers. All Isidor knew was Königsberg. All Eleanor knew was Königsberg. And besides, if – *when* – things got very bad, the people who stayed, who stayed in the land and tried to make an honest living, would need their rabbi.

But none the less, in that moment, staring at the visas on his desk, Isidor knew that he had felt the purest, most distilled covetousness. He coveted Oshor's documents – his visas, his passport, his tickets. He coveted his new life in America, a land he had seen only in postcards, but knew to be a glimmering place, set on the sea, rising to the sun. He coveted Oshor's journey into the future, into the modern age, leaving him behind here in a past crashing in on itself. He coveted Oshor's possession, in these small squares of card, of something that, locked into his destiny, Isidor had never truly tasted, even well before the present regime curtailed it: freedom.

Walking along the Schmiede Bridge, Isidor felt the keen cut of this covetousness again, almost as he felt the east wind whipping off the Pregel towards the sea. A part of him was pleased: it had been a troublesome and difficult walk, with none of the clarity of thought that accompanied his normal Sunday routine, and now at last he felt he was getting into his stride. He had remembered a clear instance of sin, fresh, alive in his mind, for which he could precisely atone. A prayer came to his mind, from the Psalms, the one he always called up when reminded of his sin, but which he had so far held in reserve today: *Be gracious unto me, O God, according to thy loving kindness; according to the abundance of thy tender mercies blot out my transgressions. Wash me thoroughly from my iniquity, and cleanse me from my sin. For I am sensible of my transgressions, and my sin is ever before me.* He murmured the words as he walked, in the quietest whisper, partly because prayer is private, and partly because he was frightened of being heard to speak Hebrew in public.

Over the Schmiede Bridge, he had to walk all the way back through the Kneiphof, back across the Köttel Bridge, and into the Vorstadt, the southern section of the city, to get to the Kaiser Bridge, which was set apart from the others by some two kilometres. It was always a trek, and therefore Isidor had marked it out to represent sloth. Today, as ever, he felt the pull of sloth well before the bridge was in sight, a voice inside telling him that his legs were tired and his feet were hurting, and that perhaps the best way to embody sloth was not to bother going to this bridge at all. He was always quite pleased to hear this voice, as it warmed him up well for the spiritual process of the bridge.

He went via the old synagogue. This took a little longer, but it was worth it to feel still that slight swell of pride – unsinful? Isidor wasn't sure – about the fact that a whole street in Königsberg was named after one of his community's places of worship. He knew there had been talk in the city council about renaming it – one of the ruling Nazis had said at an urban planning meeting that it brought shame on the entire Vorstadt – but at least for now it was still there, the street sign, not yet defaced: *Synagogenstrasse*. Passing the building itself, with its three rusty Russian domes, he noticed that a number of the stained-glass windows were broken, but it mattered little, as the community tended to pray as one now at Isidor's temple, the times not allowing them the luxury of splinter groups. Initially, this had of course swelled Isidor's congregation, and he remembered a Sunday walk about a year ago when he had had to use this Honig Bridge to atone for the pride automatically induced by the increase in numbers. He still felt ashamed about that now, even when the congregation had fallen back to below its previous size, with so many people too frightened to attend.

The sight of the old synagogue, fallen into disuse, propelled Isidor out of his momentary delight at the street sign. For a second, he felt his soul slip, and his body seize, as if a stone hand had been laid on his chest. As the Kaiser Bridge hoved into view, he wondered if this feeling, which he'd felt increasingly in recent months, should change his understanding of sloth. It was normally quite a straightforward sin. He would think about some work he had put off, some minor *mitzvah* he had not performed, some domestic chore that Eleanor had had to nag him about to get him to do, and that was that: sloth, thought about, repented of, finished already. But latterly, he had found himself in the grip of a different kind of sloth, not laziness, or indolence, but real sloth, as he knew Aquinas defined it, *acedia*, from the Greek *akedos*, careless, meaning that state where the ability to care about anything seeps from one. He had felt it, a form of torrential despair, and knew this was the place a man went when he was furthest from God. This sin caused him real fear: it would not wash off him on the bridges.

It was strange to relate this feeling to sloth, because of the fear. He had always thought of fear as a manic, electric thing, a thing that makes you jump. But this fear – it wasn't so staccato: it was like a blanket in which he didn't want to be wrapped, wet and heavy and never drying out, and rather than make him jump, it exhausted him. It was like a debilitating illness, like fear was in his blood and its symptom was *acedia*.

Touching his foot to the bridge, Isidor put these thoughts from his mind. His walk was a project of self-castigation, and required, at times, unblinking introspection, but this was something he could not face today, not with all he still had to think about at the next bridge. Instead, he went back to the earlier, easier idea of sloth. Waiting for dinner last week, he had asked Else's husband Chaim to help him carry the wood in for the fire, and then let him do it on his own, because the combination of the armchair in their tiny front room and a glass of red wine had rendered him too comfortable to move. Else hadn't minded anyway – she was such a good daughter, unlike some of his children – but when Eleanor had nudged him in the ribs he pretended to have fallen asleep. Isidor allowed himself a small smile at the memory, before settling into his vigil of self-reprimand and prayer.

Sloth slipped from him quickly as he turned left on Weidendamm, even as his body reacted against the thought of the long walk back to the northern half of the city. It was a wide, busy road that took him back along Lindenstrasse and some way east along the river-bank, through the fish market; as invisibly as he could, not wanting to be spat at, Isidor wove around the burly hordes of herring-heaving men stepping in and out of the fifty or so small boats clustered along the shore. The bustling noise and smells helped him keep his thoughts away from a premature immersion in anger. He was nearly there now; there was no point in letting it all out too soon.

With the Holz Bridge in sight, however, he hurried his pace still further, like a man carrying a full bladder might up the pathway to his house. He was bursting for the psychological relief of the bridge; and, with his first step above water, his thoughts scrambled out in an angry flurry, like the fists of a drunken man in a street brawl. Why did Isaac have to do this to him, now, with everything else bad that was happening? What kind of son would do that to his father? He would never speak to him again. He would cut him off without a pfennig. With each step, Isidor became angrier: he imagined, even though Isaac was now twenty-four, beating his son hard with the belt that his father, God rest his soul, used to beat *him* with, woven leather with a heavy metal buckle – something that Isidor had never done even when Isaac was younger, too present had been the searing pain in his mind to revisit it on his own children. He imagined slapping Isaac across the face, repeatedly, until the scale of his outrage registered in the redness of the marks on his face.

He stopped in the centre of the bridge and looked out to where the river curved away to its wider water, feeling its current rushing in tune with his fury. Isaac had married a *shikshe*. He said the phrase again in his mind, each word another turn on the ratchet of his rage. His eldest son had announced, at Friday night dinner no less, that not only had he been, for the last year, secretly courting this – he felt his mind spit – hussy, this *schreiach*, this *Lulu* – but that they had married, in secret, in a register office, last week. Isidor had nearly choked on his pickled cucumber. Through his coughing and spluttering he was aware of his youngest, Rosa – the other daughters were all married and at their own Shabbos tables, thank God – asking Isaac if he was pleased, now that he had killed his father. Isaac just grimaced and came over to slap Isidor repeatedly on the back, until eventually he cried out, 'All right, stop hitting me now; I'm fine.' In body, if not heart.

He had taken a sip from his silver cup of watered-down red wine; cleared his throat; assumed an air of grave dignity, falling back first on his knowledge of himself as a rabbi, rather than the more ticklish area of himself as a father.

'The practice of not intermarrying,' he had said, trying to keep calm, aware of Isaac still standing behind him, 'is one of the oldest features of Judaism. It dates back to Abraham telling Eliezer his servant not to find a wife from the Canaanites. It continues with Isaac's command to his son Jacob not to marry "the daughters of the land". It is part of the covenant the Jews made when they rebuilt the temple after the Babylonian exile.'

'So what?' said Isaac.

'*Isaac*,' said Eleanor, looking up from her plate. 'Don't speak like that to your father. And at the Shabbos table, too.'

Isaac's eyes, black at the iris, chocolate brown at the penumbra, lowered a little, whether in defiance or shame Isidor could not tell. A surge of hope rose in his chest on momentarily perceiving his son's usual expression – open, engaged, a little sorrowful – behind the scowl of controlled bullishness he was presently wearing.

'Well . . .' he said, less aggressively, coming round to face his father, 'quoting the Bible at me is not going to make any difference. And anyway, I thought you were supposed to be a liberal rabbi.'

Isidor took a deep breath. 'Yes, Isaac, a liberal rabbi. A liberal Jew. That means I have respect for other cultures and other religions. But I don't want my grandchildren to belong to them.' He searched for Isaac's eyes in the light dancing around their cramped kitchen from the Friday night candles. 'Otherwise they will not *be* my grandchildren.'

'Izzy,' said Eleanor, 'must you do this now? It's not a good time to do such a thing. I have heard that in some villages they have marched through the streets Jews who have' – she struggled for the decorous word – 'consorted with German girls.'

'Is she a communist?' said Isidor.

'Why do you ask that?' said Isaac.

'Because I assume that's where you met her. At one of your meetings.'

Isaac resumed his seat at the table. 'Does it matter? She's not a Jew. She's Catholic. That's what bothers you, not her politics. Would you prefer she was a Nazi?'

Isidor put down his knife and fork. 'Don't you speak to me with that tone, young man. Don't sit at my table—'

'Isidor,' interrupted Eleanor. He shot a glance at her. 'Rebbe . . .' she continued, in a meeker voice, 'correct me if I am wrong, but it is a sin, is it not, to argue over the Shabbos candles?'

Isidor blinked, and swallowed. A half-hearted approximation of a smile flickered across his face. 'Yes, Eleanor. It is against the spirit of Shabbos, if not the letter.' His face went to his food; his attitude became, he hoped, benevolent. 'We will talk about it tomorrow.'

But they hadn't. Tomorrow had been Saturday, and Shabbos was not over until sunset, by which time Isaac had gone out; and this morning Isidor thought it best to go for his walk first, to allow him to mull over the issue. Truth be told, Isidor hated confrontation; it made his guts ache, the thought of an impending row. He had hoped the walk across the bridge would sluice him of his rage, but, rather, it had forced his anger to an apex, and stare as he might, he could not see beyond it. Knowing that he had the walk, and specifically this bridge, in reserve, he had bottled up his anger until this moment, but now all the bottles were broken and the well of it seemed infinite.

He stayed put in the centre of the bridge, in a state of some spiritual confusion. He did not want to cross another bridge without having achieved, at some level, catharsis; he wanted to reach the other side at least partly cleansed of anger. But it would not move. Below him, away to his right, the fish market had begun to close down for the day – trestle tables were being folded up and the fishermen were shouting out reduced prices for their herring. It reminded him of his impending lunch, and, through a supreme effort of will, Isidor forced down his anger, or at least changed the texture of it to something more like self-pity. *What have I done to God,* he thought, *that my only son should treat me like this? My only son, Isaac, whom I held in my arms when the mohel's knife cut off his tiny foreskin, and held him still until he stopped crying, and although I knew it was right and good, the tears welled up in my eyes too for his pain.* The tears came to him again, blown sideways across his face by the river wind. He felt the eyes of passers-by on him more than ever now, and saw himself as they must, an old Jew crying for his misfortune.

Spots of rain began to fall, ticking on the brim of his hat. He took out his pocket-watch, that was his father's and his father's father's: nearly half-eleven. With going back to the synagogue for a final blessing – he always did that, as a kind of spiritual coda – he was going to be late home. Self-pity wasn't exactly atonement, but it would have to do. He muttered a catch-all *Hear O Israel, The Lord is God, The Lord is One*, and moved off, face down, along the remainder of the bridge, holding the rail for support. His mind was blank.

He decided to retrace his steps past the fish market, then into the Kneiphof, taking the Honig Bridge again back to the synagogue: the distance was about the same and it was a more pleasant walk. The rain was slight, the type of rain that falls when the sun is shining. Somewhere there will be a rainbow, Isidor thought: perhaps at the Schlossteich, the lake that cuts the northern half of the city in two. Couples walking in the surrounding pleasure gardens would look up and see it. Or maybe it would appear out towards the beaches at Samland, where once he had picked up a rust-red stone, glowing from the surf, and his mother had hidden it for him, because it was amber, and illegal for private visitors to collect. He remembered her soft hands wrapping the stone carefully in a napkin – taken from one of the beach cafés where they had had ice-cream and poppy-seed cakes – and placing it in her handbag. Isidor worried that it was still wet and would drip onto her important things. She had closed the clasp on her handbag, and put her finger to her smiling lips: *Shush. We won't tell your father even.*

Lost in reminiscence, as a man will when the present is comfortless, Isidor hardly noticed that he was already back at the Honig Bridge. He didn't notice at all until he heard the voice:

'Hey! *Rabbi!*'

Its tone was not good: sarcastic. Best to ignore it, Isidor thought, carrying on, but then his way was blocked by a brown-shirted arm. It pushed him roughly back off the bridge. Isidor wanted to continue looking down, but his face was pulled upwards by the beard. One of the SA men: not older than twenty. The left side of his face had shaving nicks below the ear.

'Can't you read?' he said. 'Or are all you Jews illiterates as well as thieves?'

'And he's supposed to be one of the learned ones!' This was the other: older, darker, with a heavier set to his face. He was leaning, with his arms crossed, against the sign that they had been putting up when Isidor had crossed the bridge earlier in the day. His remark made the younger man smirk, but it all felt somewhat forced to Isidor, the sneering, the bullying: like it wasn't quite natural to them yet; like they were still learning.

The darker SA man uncrossed his arms, revealing in his right hand a cosh. Isidor flinched, waiting for the blow. Instead, he pointed upwards to the sign.

'Read, Jew. I know you can.'

Isidor looked up. The words were written in Gothic script and followed by an exclamation mark. He read them out loud: 'Honig Bridge: Strictly Forbidden To Jews.'

'Sorry, Jew,' said the SA man, cupping his ear. 'I can't hear you.'

Isidor felt the humiliation, already a customary emotion. He raised his voice: 'Honig Bridge: Strictly Forbidden To Jews!'

'That's better.'

'Now you know,' said the blond one. 'So fuck off.'

Isidor paused. He could see the synagogue at the other end of the bridge, complacently beautiful, oblivious to this outrage. That was why they would have chosen this bridge, of course. Isidor turned away, and looked up to the sky, for guidance, for that rainbow, but saw only the Gothic towers of the cathedral, which this time brought to mind not the Mayor's speech opening the synagogue in 1896, but Hitler's, on 4 March two years ago, his final plea to the electorate, broadcast to the nation from Königsberg. As the speech ended, the cathedral's bells had rung out, blending with the sounds of the 'Niederländische Dankgebet', the 'chorale of Leuthen', associated with Frederick the Great's victory over the Austrians in 1757, which they had played at full volume on speakers placed all around Kaiser Wilhelm Platz. That, now, was the Königsberg Way.

'Didn't you hear me, Rabbi?' said the blond SA man, jabbing at Isidor's chest. 'I said, *Fuck. Off.* Or are you wondering how you're going to get to your disgusting synagogue now you can't cross the bridge?'

Isidor looked at the young man, his eyes as full of sadness as the other's were of hate. In part he *was* wondering that. He, and the rest of the community, would not now be able to get to the *shul* from the Kneiphof. They would have to take the longer, less scenic route via Lindenstrasse. His walk, which he had done every Sunday for fourteen years, was over. But in the main he was wondering what sin *this* was, and whether a bridge would ever be built wide enough and long enough for men to walk and repent of it.

PART TWO

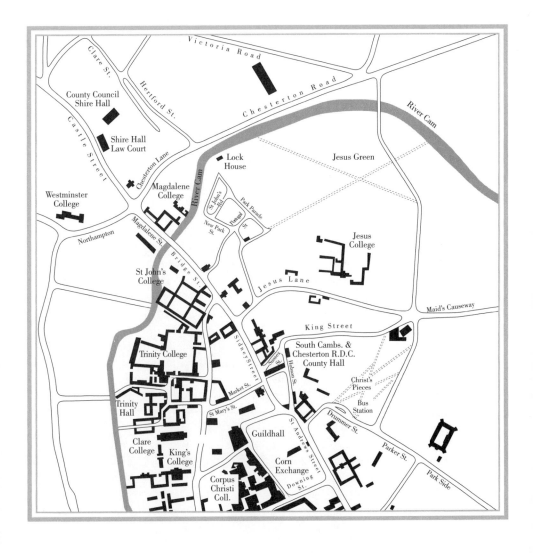

Cambridge, 1940

While you are in England . . .

HELPFUL INFORMATION AND GUIDANCE FOR EVERY REFUGEE

The Jewish Community in Britain will do its very utmost to welcome and maintain all Refugees, to educate their Children, to care for the Aged and the Sick – and to assist in every possible way in creating new homes for them overseas. A great many Christians, in all walks of life, have spontaneously associated themselves with this work. All that we ask from you in return is to carry out to your utmost the following lines of conduct. Regard them, please, as *duties to which you are honour-bound*:

Spend your spare time immediately in learning the English language and its correct pronunciation.

Refrain from speaking German in the streets and in public conveyances and in public places such as restaurants. Talk halting English rather than fluent German – *and do not talk in a loud voice.* Do not read German newspapers in public.

Do not criticise any Government regulations, nor the way things are done over here. Do not speak of 'how much better this or that is done in Germany', even if it is true.

Do not make yourself conspicuous by speaking loudly, nor by your manner or dress. The Englishman greatly dislikes ostentation, loudness of dress or manner, or unconventionality of dress or manner. The Englishman attaches very great importance to modesty, understatement in speech rather than overstatement, and quietness of dress or manner. He values good manners far more than he values evidence of wealth. (You will find that he says 'Thank you' for the slightest service – even for a penny bus ticket for which he has paid.)

Do not spread the poison of 'It's bound to come in your country.' The British Jew greatly objects to the planting of this craven thought.

Above all, please realise that the Jewish Community is relying on you – on each and every one of you – to uphold in this country the highest Jewish qualities, to maintain dignity and to help and serve others.

Issued by The German Jewish Aid Committee, London, 1939.

Sometimes, looking up at the spires of the chapel from the windows in the college kitchens, Isaac could convince himself he was still in Königsberg. When they had first arrived in Cambridge, waking from an uneven slumber on the bus from London, he had for more than a minute been certain that he was indeed back in his home town; the long brick chimneys and filigreed iron window-guards along Pembroke Street made the houses look enough like the houses on Börsenstrasse to make him wonder what had happened to the houses on Börsenstrasse, something about them was not quite right. Then he had looked across the seat and seen Lulu, slumped against his shoulder, and Rebekka, fast asleep on her lap, and remembered: they were refugees.

He had felt guilty many times about destroying Lulu's life, but never so poignantly as then. *She* would never describe it so, of course, but the fact was, if it wasn't for him, his wife would still be living in her parents' more-than-comfortable apartment on Königstrasse, studying anatomy at the university, and looking forward to marrying maybe one of the junior officers soon to be back from the war. Looking at her slim, pale face half buried in his scratchy black overcoat, her cheeks hollow with lack of food and lack of sleep, it struck Isaac for the first time how *Aryan* her features were: how she would have had to pass no stringent physical examination, or provide no elaborate genealogical escape clauses to confirm her racial status. It would not have even been an issue, if it hadn't been for him.

'Oy! Prof!'

Isaac looked round, catching as he did a fresh wave of the thick smell of frying meat that always seemed to overhang the kitchens, whatever was cooking. Jimmy Bailey was coming towards him with a tray of dirty crockery. He was overdoing the carrying of it, zigzagging back and forth, as if its weight were enormous.

29

'I'm not gonna make it, Prof!' he said, mock-strangled. The roll-up that was always somewhere in his mouth was perched precariously on the fleshy part of his lower lip. He danced elaborately around the pudding-cook, who was sleeping on a chair propped up against his pastry board. 'I'm not gonna make the sink . . .' Jimmy toppled forward as he reached Isaac, letting the plates and bowls fall into the soapy water. They bobbed up, grease sliding off them and staining the water tea-coloured. The pudding-cook stirred briefly from his slumber. 'Oh! Just got there!' said Jimmy, coming up from the floor. He handed Isaac a blue sponge mop. 'Lunch. First sitting.'

'Thank you,' said Isaac, wiping suds off his apron.

'Thanks,' said Jimmy.

'No, thank *you*,' said Isaac, thinking that Jimmy was being excessively polite, as he knew Englishmen were.

'No,' said Jimmy, taking the mop back. 'When a mate gives you something, you just say, "thanks". Not "thank *you*". You only say, "thank *you*" if it's Mr Pritchard or someone like him who's given you something. Because he's the boss. Or if he's told you off, when you leave, you have to say, "Thank you, sir" as well.'

'*Aberbut*—' said Isaac, saying the German and English words together, as he was prone to.

'Or when you're a kid and it's your mum or dad who's given you something. Then, I s'pose, you'd say, "Thank you". But when it's your *mate* . . .' and here Jimmy stood on tiptoe and pointed to himself; with his other hand he offered Isaac the mop again, '. . . then it's just "thanks".'

Isaac looked at Jimmy. He hadn't understood everything the young man had said. Jimmy had what Isaac was just starting to understand was a cockney accent, although why, he didn't know, as cockneys were supposed to be from London, and Jimmy had lived his whole life in Cambridge. But he spoke very fast, and there were lots of words in there about which Isaac was still unsure. *Boss*: this is what Jimmy had called Mr Pritchard, but when Isaac had been assigned the job, Mr Pritchard had referred to himself as the supervisor, a word Isaac understood, like the German, *Aufseher*. In English there were so many different words for the same thing.

German was much better, with the way it made new words by compounding other words; so much more economic, so much less confusing. Did 'boss' just mean the same thing as 'supervisor', or was it Jimmy giving Mr Pritchard a joky name, like he called him Prof because Isaac wore glasses and once had brought a book to work with him? If so, maybe Isaac should not call Mr Pritchard 'boss', in case it was inappropriate.

And the central word in Jimmy's diatribe, 'mate', that too was confusing. Isaac gathered from Jimmy's beaming smile that this was a good thing to be called, although he knew that when some of the other kitchen workers called him it – 'hold this, mate', 'got a fag, mate?' – it sounded less friendly. He had looked it up, but could find only a rather peculiar meaning, until he realised that the Collins pocket dictionary which the Refugee Committee had given him on arrival in London translated it only as a verb. That dictionary was all he had to work with, that and a phrasebook – a wrong-way-round phrasebook, for prospective English visitors to Germany – called *What You Want to Say and How to Say It in German*, by W. J. Herman. Every day he tried to memorise four phrases from it. Today, from the chapter 'About Town', they were: 'Will you show us the town tonight?'; 'Can you prove to us that you are trustworthy?'; 'Show us everything'; and 'Do not take us to any vulgar places.'

Isaac hated his linguistic disability. Words were his strength. It was he who had written the pamphlets for the Young Communist League at Königsberg University – the scholarly ones, at least. While others had titles that could be waved above the crowd – *Stop the State!* and *Red Tomorrow* – Isaac's tended towards the arcane: *Workers Councils and the Establishment of Proletarian Power*, *A Brief History of the First International*; *Marx and Hegel: The German Dialectic*. It was one of the things he loved about communism, its wordiness, its intellectual density.

He took the mop. 'Thanks.'

Jimmy slapped him heavily on the back. 'That's *better*! We'll make an Englishman of you yet! Tomorrow, we'll work on pronouncing it properly, like I do.' He leant forward, exaggerating a gurning mouth-shape. He seemed, to Isaac, to be missing every other tooth: you could play chess in his mouth. 'Fanks. With an F.'

'Will you shut your fucking gob for a minute, Bailey? Just for one minute?'

Isaac looked over. Henry Fitch, the grill-chef, was standing on a footstool, trying to tune in the kitchen radio, a great Bakelite arch that sat on a shelf above his hot plate. Henry was delicately adjusting the dial, holding his ear close to the speaker, like the radio was a safe he was cracking. The crackle of the static mingled with the sound of the sausages spitting in the pan below.

'What do you want to go and teach him words like that for?'

'Shh!'

The radio popped and snapped angrily, gaining the attention of the entire kitchen, except for the Irishman, Willie Gallagher, who stared steadfastly at the enormous pot of mashed potato it seemed forever his job to stir. Eventually, through the white noise, a voice emerged:

'. . . station Bremen on the 31-metre band. You are about to hear the news in English.'

Isaac stacked a newly washed plate carefully on the side of the sink. He had heard this voice before on the kitchen radio, and knew that even though he couldn't always understand what it was saying, there was something about its tone – creeping, manicured, insinuating – which had an effect on him, on a level below meaning.

'Oh no, not this cunt,' said Jimmy Bailey. 'Again!'

'Oh, "cunt" is it now?' said Henry Fitch. 'And I thought we weren't supposed to be saying cuss-words in front of the foreigner?'

'The last week has been supremely eventful in the history of the world. It has witnessed the climax of the first great German campaign against the forces of the Allies. And as for the result, there can now be no doubt. We were confident of victory from the very moment when our forces entered Holland and Belgium. But the capitulation of Holland within five days was not something we would have ventured to predict.'

'Who is this speaking?' said Isaac.

'Lord Haw-Haw,' said one of the college serving ladies, coming through from the dining-room. 'More mash, Mr Bailey.' She produced an empty metal tray from beneath her unfeasibly large bosom and handed it to Jimmy who flushed, uncertain if her repri-manding eye sprung from having heard his swear-word earlier. He took the tray over to Willie, who monotonously spooned into it shapeless clumps of grey-white mash, like clouds in an English sky.

'And this week the King of Belgium, the head of the Belgian armed forces, announced an unconditional surrender to our forces of the Reich, in order to prevent further unnecessary bloodshed.'

'Why is he saying "we"?' said Isaac. '"Our"?'

'The map-makers cannot keep pace with the stride of events.'

'He works for the Boche,' said Willie. Then, just flicking his eyes a tiny bit upwards towards Isaac: 'No offence.'

'He's posh, but with German blood in 'im,' said Jimmy, handing the tray of mash back to the serving lady. 'Like the King!'

'That's enough of that, Jimmy Bailey,' she said, cutting short his phlegmy laughter. 'People hang for treason in wartime, y'know.' She turned on her heel and exited, back through to the Great Hall. Isaac noticed that even the large tray of mash seemed to disappear somewhere within her.

'Only a few days ago, the egregious Bassett said that the British Tommy had shown his superiority to the German soldier wherever they have met. You must interpret this remarkable claim as best you can. How the British Minister of Information can utter such asinine claims, so obviously contradicted by facts, is not intelligible . . .'

'Why do we have to listen to him, anyway?' said Jimmy. 'It's depressing.'

'A sensible man makes it his business to know all sides of the story,' Henry Fitch said, still standing on the footstool, the stento-rian nature of the remark somehow consolidated by the bit of extra height. 'And besides, he's from Dudley. Last week he mentioned Allbright and Wilson's.'

'Allbright and Wilson's?'

'It's the smelting works at the end of my road.'

'You live in Newmarket!'

'The road where I grew up, you idiot.'

'But then the British Ministry should rather be called the Ministry of Misinformation. Recently they have been warning British women and girls of the dangers of splinters from German

33

bombs. Most women have reacted to this suggestion with a laugh, by requesting their milliners to shape their spring and summer hats out of very thin tin plate, covered with silk or other draping material.'

'What did he say about Allbright and Wilson's?' said Jimmy Bailey, disconsolately.

'He said that they were going to blow it up,' replied Henry Fitch, proudly. 'He said, "People of the West Midlands, you should know that the German air force will soon be dropping a bomb into the stack at Allbright and Wilson's."'

'Do you think that's true?' said Willie.

Henry Fitch came thoughtfully down from the footstool, stroking his chin. 'That's a difficult one. It's quite a big factory, and it used to be lit up at night, but not now, with the blackout. There's one particular chimney that does mark it out, though, especially if you're coming from Smethwick.' Henry picked up a new string of sausages, and began cutting them into the pan: he stopped after the third one, and nodded, sagely. 'Yes, that would probably mean that a Junkers or a Messerschmitt could pick it out.'

'No,' said Willie, rather nervously. 'I meant . . . about the ladies' hats.'

'And now the world waits for the next fateful stage: already many French generals have been lost to their own cause. Beyond France, the coast of Britain has been evacuated to a distance of up to twenty miles. Defences have been erected that will prove as cardboard and papier-mâché to the might of the Blitzkrieg.'

Henry Fitch, who had stared hard at Willie to see if he was taking the mickey, looked down into his sizzling pan; Jimmy Bailey coughed. For a second, the only sounds in the kitchen were those of cooking. Isaac emptied a new load of dirty plates into the sink, but could not find the energy to begin mopping them. Outside, students passed by his window, laughing, running, reading. The pudding-cook's head, he noticed, had somehow become dusted with flour, making him look older than he was.

'Ah,' said Jimmy, to no one in particular, 'he says stuff like that every week.'

'*And what of Churchill, the providential leader who was going to lead Britain to victory? What a miserable, pathetic figure he cuts today. No one with half a brain thinks any more that this darling of Jewish finance could really challenge the might of National Socialist Germany.*'

'What's Churchill got to do with the Jews?' said Willie.

'Nothing,' said Jimmy, quickly, not quite knowing why.

'They control a lot of people,' said Henry Fitch, turning the radio down a little.

Isaac turned to look at him. Henry's face was impassive, not even especially looking at Isaac, as if perhaps he'd forgotten that someone in the room was Jewish. It was the first time Isaac had heard him say anything like it. Then, he realised, no – it was the first time he had *understood* him saying anything like it. For all I know, Isaac thought, he's been reciting Oswald Mosley's speeches verbatim every day.

'What do you mean, Fitchey?' said Jimmy. 'Control? What's that supposed to mean?'

'Just what it says,' replied Henry, calmly cutting a knob of butter off the heavy slab in front of him.

Isaac had been amazed, initially, at the way that the college seemed not to have been affected by rationing. He knew that some of his work-mates stole food from the kitchens as a result, but he was too worried about his refugee status to break the law.

'A lot of the people behind the people in power – the people you don't see, the ones pulling the strings – are Jews.' Henry looked nonchalantly at Isaac. 'You wouldn't disagree especially, would you, Fabian?'

Isaac shrugged, and pulled awkwardly on the fingers of his washing-up gloves, too unsure of his words and, more importantly, his place in the kitchen hierarchy to take him up on it. Henry Fitch grunted approvingly, feeling his position confirmed. As he reached back up for the radio, Isaac silently classified him as a *narodnik*, Lenin's term for a worker who feels himself to be above his fellows – a good example of Isaac's overpoliticisation, as Henry Fitch was in truth simply one of those people who feel themselves to be above *everyone*, and whose method of demonstrating this is to apply to all things a kind of naive sophistication: a naive belief, that is, that everything is more sophisticated than it appears. As far as Henry was concerned, all agendas were hidden, all motivations secret: it was the way he marked himself out as intelligent, by suggesting that all those who took life at face value were fools.

'*The Old World is tumbling about the ears of the reactionaries who sought to destroy the New. When Germany declared herself independent of their caprice, and threw off the shackles of gold, they resolved upon her destruction . . .*' The voice rose to a climax: '*But thanks to God and the Führer it is not Germany who is confronted with destruction today.*'

A wave of static replaced Lord Haw-Haw; then, a voice, possibly his, possibly someone else's, said, '*That is the end of our talk; thank you.*' Henry Fitch moved the dial. Anne Ziegler singing, '*Say it's only a paper moon, sailing over a cardboard sea . . .*'

'Well, I'm glad that's over,' said Jimmy. Holding his arm out like an impassioned serenader, he glided over to Willie Gallagher, and sang: '*But it wouldn't be make-believe, if you believed in me.*'

Willie continued looking down into his pot of potato, his stirring hand moving just a tiny bit quicker.

Another serving lady came in and called for pudding. The cook regained consciousness and began working seemingly instantaneously, his hands reaching for the flour and sugar on waking. Isaac turned back to the window, letting his arms float in the tepid water. The last section of the speech had enraged him. It wasn't the easy anti-Semitism – he was used to that now, the nonchalance of it, the link between race and money presented as a fact – as much as the appropriation of the language of revolution. He repeated the words in his head, sneeringly, 'The Old World is tumbling about the ears of the reactionaries who sought to destroy the New'. This was his lexicon, Marx's and Trotsky's lexicon, being turned against itself. It was the cleverest thing about fascism, the way it used the discourse of Marxism without any of the difficulty. It was sound without sense. How was fascism a New World, when the world it wanted to create was the oldest one, based on fantastical and ancient racial myths? But such contradictions hardly mattered: the fact was that somewhere in the 1930s, the Right had stolen the modern ground. That was what attracted the young, and the intelligentsia: fascism's sheen of modernity, its clarion call of change.

Isaac moved his hands along the bottom of the sink, searching for the mop. He felt a hand on his shoulder: it was Jimmy Bailey's, bony, claw-like, the hair around the knuckles so black and wiry it looked like insects had been squashed on his fingers.

'Don't worry, Prof. It'll be all right,' he said. His face was moulded into his best approximation of sympathy and seriousness: Isaac thought he had never seen anything so jowly. 'They'll never make it over here. Our navy's too much for 'em.'

Isaac peered into his blue, bloodshot eyes. The Nazis are threatening to invade this man's country, he thought, and yet instinctively he comes to sympathise with me, the refugee. Instinctively, he knows, he is not the target. I am. Jimmy play-punched him on the shoulder, and winked. Too many gestures, Isaac thought, but that was another thing about the English, they were always *playing*, over-playing. As if nothing was serious.

'Thanks,' said Isaac. Thanks: for a mate. He tried to return Jimmy's crooked smile, but found himself suddenly coughing, as if something were making him gag. He had to support himself on the draining board. Maybe it was the kitchen's deeply non-kosher smell finally catching up with him, so *traife*, the scent of uncloven hooves.

Mrs Randolph Fricker saw no reason to change her name once her husband died. When, in 1911, she had married Randolph, a man with no hair on his body who had smelt faintly of gas, she had of course taken his surname – the then Sally Soames had not heard of the possibility that there were women who might do otherwise – but she had also taken the rather more unusual decision of embracing her full married title in her everyday life, which meant that people who had known her previously as Sally had to start calling her Randolph. This caused considerable confusion in their domestic world, particularly during their brief acquisition of a telephone – 'Is Randolph there?' 'Speaking,' she would say – which was eventually accommodated by her becoming generally known simply as Mrs Fricker, by everybody, including Randolph. Any further confusion was thankfully sorted out once and for all by her husband's death.

She was, perhaps unsurprisingly, a woman whose instinct in life was for duty rather than pleasure, and so it was that she responded very quickly to the local council's request for householders to take in, as lodgers, Jewish refugees. Mrs Fricker had never met a Jew before, but she saw no reason, as she told Mrs Spinks next door, 'to be frightened of them'. Her rules, given to Isaac and Lulu on the day of their arrival, were simple: no visitors, no smoking and, as much as possible, no German. If they must speak their own language, it must only be to themselves, and then in whispers: 'I don't want to hear all that "ach! ach! ach!" coming down through the ceiling while I'm doing my knitting,' she'd said.

'*Entschuldigung?*' said Isaac.

Mrs Fricker's house was a tiny Victorian terraced cottage in Hertford Street, a steep hill of a road just on the outskirts of the university town proper. Isaac, Lulu and Rebekka were dropped off by the driver of the bus from London at the bottom of it, with the two large cases they had managed to find of the five that had been loaded onto the SS *Bodegraven* at Königsberg harbour a month earlier. They had been in London for two weeks, sleeping on the floor in a converted church, before the rabbinical-looking man from the Jewish Refugee Committee had informed them that, due to the city being already crammed with refugees, they would have to be relocated elsewhere. 'It'll be safer for you wherever you go, anyway,' he said, not looking up from his clipboard. 'The Germans are going to bomb this city to pieces.' Isaac was so tired from the endless days of travelling and not sleeping that he couldn't carry the cases up the hill and instead just pushed them, their brass corners scraping against the uneven pavement. It took them nearly half an hour to reach Mrs Fricker's house.

They had one room, for which they paid Mrs Fricker fifteen shillings a week. It was wallpapered in a flowery brown print, and laid not quite to the skirting-boards with what had once been a matching carpet. Against one wall were two single beds, bursting, almost pregnant, with bedding; between them, a quite deliberate act of separation, stood a single wooden chair. The fireplace, Lulu said, was the narrowest she had ever seen; its width was easily beaten by the painting above it, of a village green. In the bay window, over-looking the street, two grey armchairs were pressed tight against a tiny round wooden table. The window itself was quite expansive, and would have let in a lot of light, were it not for the enormous blackout curtains encroaching three feet on either side; the curtains were black – unnecessarily – on the inside as well as on the outside. In one corner was a sink, which was the Fabians' main washing facility, although the extended version of Mrs Fricker's rules allowed them to use the house bathroom once a week, as long as no one filled the bath above the line she had drawn on the inside of the tub halfway down in black paint. Next to the sink, on a trestle table, were their cooking provisions: a single-ring gas stove, flanked by a kettle, a milk saucepan, two cups, two plates and two pairs of knives and forks. In the other corner stood what she considered her outstanding display of generosity to the Fabians: a Victorian crib, carved out of burled walnut, with handles the size of doorknobs for swinging. 'It was mine,' she announced proudly. Isaac smiled gratefully at her, concealing his inability to imagine that Mrs Fricker had ever been younger than fifty-eight. Lulu refused to put Rebekka in it for the first month, thinking it must have woodworm. Isaac laughed, saying that if it came down in mid-swing, maybe baby and crib would go straight through the ceiling to land on top of Mrs Fricker doing her knitting and keeping an ear cocked for German.

The day of Lord Haw-Haw's broadcast, Isaac took a different route back from King's to Hertford Street. Usually, he went through the town, even though seeing the walls of the colleges could often make him melancholy – they made him feel his exclusion from the university, from the intellectual life. Other days, however, the architecture made him feel at home; in every curve and lip and frill of stone, there was history, and scholarship, and thought. Even though he could not enter their libraries – and even if he could, would not have been able to understand most of the words printed on the pages lying therein – he could still feel it: he could still breathe the bookish air.

That day, however, the twisting streets felt different. The atmosphere of war had taken a while to seep into Cambridge, it not being an industrial centre, and therefore not especially adaptable to the war effort, nor an obvious target for German bombers. But since the fall of Denmark and Norway, and with the German army hovering like buzzards on the borders of the Low Countries, towns and villages throughout Britain that had previously slept through the war were waking up, scared and sweating, to the possibility of invasion. And with threat came paranoia: Isaac had already this week noticed people looking at him more sharply, narrowing their focus through the rifle-sights of their eyes, when they heard his accent. Today, even without opening his mouth, he felt watched; he felt that people on the streets could smell his nationality – German, whatever Hitler had done to strip him of it. He wondered to himself what that smell might be. Sauerkraut and sausages as far as the English were concerned, he thought, and chanced a smile to himself.

When a porter came out of Sidney Sussex's gates and stared directly at him, Isaac decided to take the alternative route home, across Jesus Green. As soon as his face felt the less claustrophobic air of the park, he relaxed a little, and looked up. The sun was half in, half out of the clouds – that Venn diagram weather which always seemed to characterise this climate. In the distance, he could hear the rushing of Jesus Lock under its bridge over the Cam. When first crossing the bridge, he had been exhilarated by the lock, the way the high water poured into the low so fast and full it turned on impact as white and creamy as shaving lather. The rushing became louder as he walked further down the path which cut across the green, but his attention was distracted from the white noise by a man's voice, at a volume loud enough to be described as shouting, although his tone was placid.

The man was standing at the edge of the river, talking to a group of about twelve men and women. Isaac could not completely understand the man's words, but assumed, correctly, that he was doing some kind of guided tour of Cambridge. He had heard about these tours – the local representative of the Refugee Committee had suggested, a little strictly, that they go on one – 'a.s.a.p.,' he'd said, which was lost on Isaac and Lulu – as part and parcel of their assimilation into local life.

'So this stretch of land we're standing on now is Jesus Green . . .'

40

Isaac stopped with one foot on the bridge, listening. The man was in his late fifties, wearing a tweed coat and a large flat cap. His voice was straining against the whoosh of the river. Jesus Green, Isaac thought, what a peculiar name for a park it is. Two colleges named after their god, Jesus and Christ's, and because of that there are places in Cambridge named like no others in Northern Europe: as far as Isaac knew, like no others in the world. There were no Christ Squares, no Jesus Plazas anywhere that he knew of. But in Cambridge – Jesus Green, Christ's Pieces – Isaac couldn't understand why these names didn't sound blasphemous to the English; when he first saw them on their standard-issue street map, he laughed, asking Lulu if the Christian Messiah had perhaps come to Cambridge once for a stag party. She had looked cross, though, and reminded him that, although not a believer, and although accepting of what Marx said about religion, she had still been born a Christian.

'It was on this spot as well,' the man was continuing, breaking Isaac from his reverie, 'that Queen Mary had the Protestant John Hullier burnt. Townsfolk are reported to have stripped the body of remaining identifiable parts afterwards to provide relics.'

A – trifle contrived – murmur of horror and astonishment went round the tourist crowd. The man, clearly thinking that he'd got them hooked with this, the racy section of the tour, warmed to his theme.

'Oh yes. Religion wasn't the only subject that could get you into trouble at this time – several women were hanged on Jesus Green for alleged witchcraft in the reign of Elizabeth, one of them for owning a frog thought to be her familiar.' He paused, a smile playing about his lips. 'What happened to the frog is not recorded.' A ripple of polite, middle-aged laughter greeted his joke. The man nodded his head, receiving his due. 'And now, if you'd care to follow me, we will move on to Magdalene College.'

Isaac watched them go, shuffling along the river. He wondered about calling them back to query the man's point – if he'd understood him correctly – about religion not being the only subject that could get you into trouble at that time: as if being burnt for being a witch was somehow a non-religious persecution. But he knew that he wouldn't be able to explain himself clearly, and besides, because of his accent, they might suspect his motives. Transparency was not an option for him any more. 'Show us everything,' he said to himself instead, walking up the footpath to the bridge. 'Do not take us to any vulgar places.'

On the mantelpiece above the narrow fire, Lulu had placed two photographs, the only two she had managed to keep from Germany. The one on the left was a picture of herself and Isaac walking through the streets of Danzig, a trip they had made just after their wedding, to attend a congress of the Eastern European section of the Communist International. In the photograph, they were both smiling, but not at each other or at the camera: just individually smiling, as if in twin, self-contained contentment, at being in love and in the Free City in spring. Mrs Fricker, in fact, had remarked, on lifting it up to dust, that it looked as if they didn't have a care in the world, which was accurate, in terms of the photograph, but not in terms of their actual situation, two intermarried, left-wing Germans in 1934.

It had been a strange honeymoon, Lulu thought now: memories of Isaac's body shifting in the dark mingled in her mind with long afternoons listening to bearded men outline resolutions supporting Bolshevism in Spain, cries of ecstasy with calls for workers' freedom. But Isaac's politics had always been part of his attraction for her. When she had first seen him, he'd been talking politics; or rather, when she'd first heard him, because his voice came to her first, a siren call amid the sea of voices in Königsberg University's refectory. She remembered it clearly, as her best friend Sophia had fallen in love, and was telling Lulu all kinds of prized, secret information, breathlessly, of course, almost in a whisper; Lulu had had to concentrate hard on her words. It had been working – she had only asked her friend to repeat herself once – when her ear had been drawn away by a male voice, up the table to her left. Not because it was shouting – even though the speaker was clearly involved in some kind of argument, his voice was not raised – but because of its timbre, low and definite, reverberating in the air like a cello note. She wanted to turn round and see who was speaking, but Sophia had fixed her in her gaze, and so she just listened to the voice, nodding and smiling and frowning whenever Sophia nodded and smiled and frowned.

'A true dialectic,' the voice was saying, 'goes further than the supposition that for every thesis there is an antithesis . . .'

'Out of which comes synthesis . . .' another voice added.

'Out of which comes Fabian's Jewish arse!' said a third.

'Thank you Mittelmann. You are indeed the true spiritual descendant of Kant himself . . . A true dialectic, as I was saying, does not deal in static abstractions. Rather, it celebrates the continual oscillation of thesis and antithesis.'

'But Hegel—'

'Oh, we all know what Hegel said.'

'That's true, actually, Mittelmann, we do. Which is why the Marxist dialectic – dialectical materialism – has moved on. Away from abstractions to specifics: not just capital versus labour, but capital at a particular stage in the development of capitalism versus labour at a particular stage in the development of labour. The fundamental flaw of crude thought . . .'

'Who are you calling crude?'

'. . . lies in the fact that it wishes to content itself with motionless imprints of a reality which consists of eternal motion. Dialectical thinking gives to concepts, by means of closer approximations, corrections, concretisations, a richness of content and flexibility. Trotsky—'

'Oh, *Trotsky* is it now?'

'Fabian's not content with quoting Marx at us – now he's actually quoting a Bolshevik! One who's not even dead!'

'Yes, unbelievable I know – a political science student at Königsberg University quoting a political philosopher who lives and breathes . . . Trotsky calls this . . . this *organic* quality of dialectical thought, a "succulence" – that's brilliant, don't you think? A succulence which, he says, brings concepts close to living phenomena.'

Lulu, still intently responding to the movements of Sophia's face, felt her head swim with the words. She didn't know why exactly – politics was not at this stage an interest of hers, although she had

43

known for years that she would have to find an alternative path into life than most of the women she knew, which was why she was studying anatomy at the university – but somewhere in the phrasing – in the way the voice loved speaking its strange pseudo-scientific vocabulary – she heard a poetry.

'. . . and that's when I let him kiss me, twice!' said Sophia, her hands grasping Lulu's to emphasise the climactic nature of this information.

Her touch brought Lulu back into focus. 'That's wonderful!' she said, and hugged her friend, knowing that was what was wanted of her. In the midst of the hug, she heard the backward screech of chairs, indicating that the group of young male students was leaving. A sudden panic, a dread of missing one of life's main chances, came over her like a sweat: she knew she at least had to identify the speaker. Lulu was confident enough of her own charms to know that, if she could find him, she could make him interested in her. Twisting her neck round the back of Sophia's head, she saw them heading in a cluster towards the door, and knew instantly which of the three had delivered the lecture: the dark one, in the centre, with the messy, curly hair. In years to come, she would think it ironic that this initial recognition of Isaac was, in essence, racial.

The other photograph was of her sister Martha's wedding, a good one to have, in terms of what photographs are meant to do – map the landscape of memory – as it showed every member of her extended family. There were not enough chairs to seat everybody in the picture and so the younger ones were sprawled on the floor in front of the married couple, giving it the look of a photograph taken late in the night, like a survivors' photograph the morning after an aristocratic ball, whereas in fact it had been taken at the start of the reception. Martha had, in what Lulu had come to think of as conventional terms, married well: to Gerhard, whose family owned a brick factory on the outskirts of Königsberg.

When Isaac arrived home following his brief interlude on Jesus Green, Lulu was holding Rebekka up in front of this photograph, taking the twenty-month-old girl through its cast of characters:

'. . . and that's your great-uncle Christoph, with the big eyes and the big moustache . . . that's Grandma Frieda, with the flower in her

44

dress and the lovely smile . . . that's Cousin Ewald . . . doesn't he look splendid in a dinner suit? He would have been only nine then . . .'

For a while, Isaac watched his wife, who remained unaware of his entry into the room. His feelings always went into conflict over this photograph, as he had not been invited to the wedding, even though he and Lulu had already been married for six months. He knew that Lulu's parents had been as unhappy as his own about their marriage, but even so, he had been surprised and hurt at the snub. In his heart, he wondered whether his absence at the wedding had less to do with Lulu's parents' continued anger at their marriage and more to do with the immediate history of the brick factory, its part owners, Finkel & Sons, having just been forced to sell their share to Gerhard's father at an absurdly knocked-down price. Or maybe it was simply that Lulu's parents considered themselves law-abiding citizens and by the time of Martha's wedding the law considered Isaac and Lulu's marriage illegal. Whatever the reason, once it was clear that he was not to be invited, Lulu had immediately said to Isaac that she would not go; but he had insisted, knowing that she loved her sister.

But more than the memory of his exclusion, he found it hard not to feel that, in the juxtaposition of these two photographs, Lulu was making a point – a point about the difference between their wedding and her sister's, and perhaps about the difference between their two consequent lives. He knew he should not feel this, as they were the only two photographs she had, but there were days when he could not help taking the display on the mantelpiece as a rebuke.

'And that's Auntie Ida and Auntie Hannah . . .'

'Hello girls,' said Isaac, his customary greeting for the two of them.

Lulu spun round, holding Rebekka in front of her stomach. 'Look, little one – it's Daddy!'

Rebekka looked at her father with a searching but deadpan expression on her chubby face for a second, as if he were just another one of the flat black-and-white figures from the photograph that her mother was insisting on naming. But then some primeval recognition cog turned, and her mouth opened really wide, her own version of a smile. Sometimes, when she opened her mouth like that, Isaac felt as if she were trying to fit his heart in there.

'Hello, Rebekka,' said Isaac, picking her up and holding her above his head; instinctively, she spread her arms like a pair of wings. 'How's my little Bekky?' It felt all right, now, saying her name, although it had not at first – at first it felt like a stamp across her – because they had been forced to choose it from a list of pre-scribed names for Jewish children. He remembered scanning the names on the piece of paper handed to him by the registrar – Frommet, Brocha, Driesel, Peirche, Zipora – and wondered whether the point of this prescription was not so much to flush out Jews whose race might not otherwise be identifiable from their name (a contradictory need, as Nazi propaganda insisted that the Jew is always instantly identifiable by his indeterminately degenerate fea-tures), but rather simply to force upon a whole generation ugly names. Later, it transpired that they could have called her some-thing else, because Rebekka qualified as a *Mischling* – a half Jew, a tainted Aryan – but Isaac and Lulu had not realised this in their fear and confusion about the new laws.

'How's she been?' said Isaac, handing her back to his wife. He spoke quietly, knowing that Mrs Fricker was downstairs dusting, on alert for the merest whisper of Teutonic vowels.

'Not bad. She slept for a few hours this afternoon. I took her out for a walk at lunchtime.'

Isaac nodded, and kissed his wife, trying to convey thanks in the kiss. Her mouth was soft and accepting.

'Where did you go?' he said, taking off his coat and laying it carefully on the back of one of the armchairs; Mrs Fricker had not provided them with a coat-hook in the room, and they were not allowed to use the ones in her hallway.

'Not far, just round the park. Mrs Goldman's pram is so heavy . . .'

The Goldmans were a middle-aged couple living two streets away, who had been ascribed, by the Refugee Committee, with the task of helping Isaac and Lulu acclimatise to life in Cambridge. Their commitment to this task was, however, more than a little ambivalent, partly because, like most of Anglo-Jewry, they were concerned that an influx of refugees would lead to increased anti-Semitism in Britain, and partly because Mrs Goldman was convinced that the Fabians were peasants. She had, however, managed to procure a pram for Rebekka, a vast vehicle in which every wheel was the size of the big one on a penny farthing. There being no room for it inside Mrs Fricker's house, it was stored in the Anderson shelter in the garden.

Lulu put Rebekka into her crib, smoothing down her wild baby hair. She turned on their one tiny table lamp, and drew the enormous curtains. 'But it was nice. We went to the shops and . . . come and look!' Lulu took his hand and led him to the wardrobe. She glanced a little coyly at Isaac in the mirrored door, and then opened it. Inside, hanging forward from the main bulk of their clothes, was what at first sight appeared to be a map of Europe. Looked at again, though, it was clearly clothing of some sort – Northern Europe appeared to be the shirt, and Southern Europe the trousers.

'Are you going to a fancy-dress party? As the world?' he said.

'No! Stupid.' She lifted the outfit from the wardrobe. 'It's pyjamas!'

'Pyjamas!'

'Yes! You know how cold you get at night. And the fire's so small . . .'

'Where did you get them?

'The corner shop at the end of Alpha Road,' she said, holding a sleeve against his cheek. 'They're cotton. They recycle them from prints used by the army.'

'God . . .' said Isaac. 'It's true then. Necessity really is the mother of invention.'

'And they're big – I could cut enough off the trousers to make a night-shirt for Bekka and you could still use them. And look here . . .' She pinched a section of the right shoulder between finger and thumb, crumpling together Scandinavia and the Soviet Union. Isaac squinted towards it.

'Königsberg . . .' he said, smiling.

'Yes. Actually marked on the map. On the pyjamas.'

Isaac looked down at her eyes, eager that he should be pleased. Her wheat-blond hair, unloosed, curling a little at the ends, had fallen over the right side of her face. Sunlight on her features would bring out a light dust of freckles, but in the muted glow of the lamp, they melted into one another, shading her face copper. His gaze grew fond.

'So . . . whatever happens in the war, it seems we can sleep in Königsberg again.'

She laughed, and wrapped her arms around his waist. 'That's clever,' she said. 'My clever boy.'

'Were they cheap?'

Lulu clicked her tongue. 'No, I thought the one thing we could afford at the moment was expensive pyjamas. Of course they were cheap. That's the point of them. But I think they're rather chic. Don't you?'

Isaac took a step back. Lulu smiled, and, placing her hand on her hip, catalogue-model style, held the pyjamas against herself. Europe fell from her face; and even though he felt delight at her pleasure, and at the sweetness of the moment, Isaac could not prevent his mind, for a second, picturing Hitler's armies sweeping across her body towards Britain at her neck.

Isaac was not allowed to own a bicycle. He needed a police permit to travel beyond the boundaries of Cambridge. He had only been able to listen to Lord Haw-Haw's broadcast at the college, as personally he was not allowed to own a radio. In bed, two nights after that broadcast, he remembered that he was also not permitted to possess a map, and wondered whether the pyjamas counted.

He knew these things from a Home Office pamphlet, delivered through the door and handed with some ceremony to him by Mrs Fricker, entitled *Information for Aliens*. It also informed him, in an accompanying official letter, of the date on which he and his family were to attend one of a series of nationwide tribunals, set up to assess whether they, as Germans presently resident in the United Kingdom, posed a threat to national security.

The tribunal met in the Cambridge Corn Exchange, a cavernous hall used occasionally before the war for concerts, but now only for various forms of civic meetings. Behind a wooden table in the centre of its wide stage, holding four clipboards like black shields against possible alien contamination, sat four men: Sir Stanley Farrow, a decorated First World War veteran and High Court judge, Rear-Admiral Charles L. Holloway (retired), presently chairman of the Cambridge & District Civil Defence Committee, Superintendent Peter Grout, head of the Cambridgeshire Constabulary, and the Very Reverend Christopher Chamberlain, Bishop of Ely. At the side of the stage sat an elderly woman at another table, piled high with paperwork. When Isaac, Lulu and Rebekka arrived, the committee was in the process of interviewing a young man wearing elegant slacks and a college scarf. They were told to hand in their passports to the elderly woman, and then directed to some seats in the hall, where a number of others were waiting, watching the proceedings onstage, like an audience.

'And what college are you at?' the centrally seated Sir Stanley Farrow, his eyes on his clipboard, was saying.

'Corpus, sir,' replied the man, in what sounded to Isaac like a cut-glass English accent. Sir Stanley looked back from his clipboard; a small, knowing smile curved his thin moustache upwards. 'Enjoying it?'

'I should say so, sir. Best college in the varsity!'

'Good man.'

'Studying?' said Superintendent Grout.

'Classics, sir.'

'Excellent,' said Superintendent Grout, with just the merest sense that he wasn't entirely clear what kind of studying that might involve.

'Where did you go to school?' said Rear-Admiral Holloway.

'Ampleforth, sir.'

'Really?' said the Reverend Chamberlain. 'That's a Roman Catholic school, is it not?

'Yes, sir.'

'Are you a practising Catholic?'

'Most of the time, yes, sir.'

Sir Stanley smiled again at this. He scanned his notes, breezily: 'So your father was the German Ambassador to Dublin between . . . ?'

'1921 and 1927, sir. At which point he retired from public service.'

'And the family settled in Ireland?'

'Yes, sir. Although I was born in Germany.'

'Yes.'

'Hmm. One imagines the maternity hospitals are rather more modern there than in the Emerald Isle, don't you, Sir Stanley?'

'No doubt, Charles. Well.' He checked his clipboard again. '*Max*. Do you feel any sympathy with the present regime in Germany?'

'No, sir.'

Sir Stanley leant forward, threading together his fingers. 'Do you feel any sympathy with Germany . . . at all?'

For the first time, the young man appeared to falter. 'Er . . .'

'Be honest with us now.'

'Well . . .' He looked at the floor, and then up again. 'My aunt and uncle still live in Germany. And I have some other relatives there. So sometimes I do feel sorry for ordinary Germans, yes. Living under the yoke of National Socialism and all that . . .'

Max halted at this. He had gone very red: to Isaac's eyes it looked as though he was trying not to cry. Sir Stanley nodded, his face a mixture of gravity and friendly condescension. The four interviewers moved together to confer, at which point the young man coughed.

Sir Stanley looked up. 'Yes?'

'Excuse me, sir. I . . . I have a letter. A reference. From a friend of my father's.'

Sir Stanley beckoned him forward; Max came, holding the letter in front of him. During the reading of it, Sir Stanley's face appeared to clear. He passed it on to Rear-Admiral Charles L. Holloway, who took one look at it and nodded approvingly. The others followed suit. The committee seemed to take a breath.

'Well, Max, I think if you'd said earlier that you had a personal recommendation from Lord Carnegie, we could have saved ourselves a lot of time,' said Sir Stanley, handing back the letter. He turned to the elderly woman to his right: 'Category C.'

She began stamping some papers.

'Sir?' said Max. 'What does that mean?'

Sir Stanley turned back to him with a munificent air. 'That puts you in our lowest category, danger-wise. It means you hardly have to put up with any restrictions.'

'Thank you, sir,' said Max, beaming.

'Don't mention it, young man,' said Sir Stanley, extending a hand. Max shook it vigorously. 'If it were up to me,' Sir Stanley added, *sotto voce*, 'you wouldn't be categorised *at all*. Now, be off with you.'

Max continued to beam as he took his papers from the elderly lady and left the stage. The lady stood, holding a roll of paper. 'Mr and Mrs Fabian,' she read out.

Isaac and Lulu glanced at each other nervously; Lulu gathered Rebekka, who had fallen asleep on her lap, into her arms. They walked up some stairs by the side of the stage, and towards the committee's table, haltingly, uncertain where to stop and stand.

'That'll do,' said Sir Stanley. 'Now: do you speak English?'

'A little. Not very well,' said Lulu.

'Charles?' said Sir Stanley.

'I'll have another stab,' replied Rear-Admiral Holloway. '*Meine man. Was gibt du für seine* . . . oh, what's the word . . . job?'

Lulu and Isaac looked confused.

'You know.' He coughed. '*Was hat du in Deutschland ge . . . fahrt? Für Geld?*'

Sir Stanley gave him a heavy stare. 'Why did you tell this committee that you could speak German?'

'Well, I used to be able to. I cracked a number of Boche codes during the Great War.'

'That was a long time ago, Charles.'

'Just like riding a bicycle, I thought.'

'Sir . . .' said Lulu. 'I think I speak enough . . . to understand.'

'Right. Well. Good. I shall speak slowly for you.' Sir Stanley consulted his clipboard. He made to address Lulu, then turned back to Rear-Admiral Holloway. 'The Boche codes . . . were they *in* German?'

Rear-Admiral Holloway blinked. 'How do you mean?'

'Well, surely they were in code?' Rear-Admiral Holloway opened his mouth to reply, and then shut it again, stumped. Sir Stanley sniffed, and turned to face Lulu once more. 'So: you are Isaac and Lulu Fabian, correct? And this is your daughter Rebekka?' Lulu nodded. 'You travelled here on the SS *Bodegraven* from Königsberg in August of last year. You resided at the Jewish Temporary Shelter in Whitechapel for two weeks before being transferred to a residential address here in Cambridge, where you still . . . are. Yes?'

'Yes, sir,' said Lulu, a little uncertainly.

'In Germany, you worked for some time as a laboratory assistant, and Mr Fabian . . . he has worked part time in a bookshop?'

'Yes. But Isaac – Mr Fabian – he has enough qualification to be – I don't know the word – someone who works at the university—'

'A don. An academic.'

'Yes, in political science. But Jews are not allowed to work . . .' She concentrated hard, squeezing out the words, 'to hold – hold? – university posts in Germany now.'

'I see. Meanwhile, here you have been given a domestic cleaning and housekeeping position at . . . Mr and Mrs Lambert's, 56 Hamilton Road, while your husband has been given work in the kitchens at King's College.' Lulu nodded; Sir Stanley's eyes scanned the rest of the page quickly. 'Blah, blah . . . You have been granted a visa to emigrate from this country to the United States . . . ?'

'Yes. But yet we do not have the money to go. And with the war there are no boats . . .'

Sir Stanley nodded, and dismissed the need for the rest of the sentence with a slightly fey wave. He turned to the other members of the committee, with a sense of opening out the discussion.

'Can I just clarify something?' said the Reverend Chamberlain, looking up from his clipboard. 'The lady. You are not Jewish?'

'No.'

'So you yourself were not subject to the racial laws passed by the Nazis?'

'Sorry, sir . . . I do not understand – not subject to?'

'You yourself are not affected by the laws. Just your husband.'

Lulu looked to Isaac, uncertain as to how to answer.

'Ah . . . it's difficult. Yes, I am. By the new laws the marriage of myself and Isaac is not legal. We are forced – they would force us, the laws, to – how do you say? – *scheiden lassen*. When a husband and wife go apart.'

'Divorce.'

'Yes. To divorce.'

'And . . . you were not prepared to do that?'

There was a pause; Lulu looked taken aback. 'No . . .' she said, eventually. 'We . . . no.'

'What's happening?' said Isaac, to her.

'Perhaps we can cut through all this, Reverend,' said Sir Stanley. 'Save us all a bit of time.' He turned back to Lulu. 'Just tell us exactly: why did you leave Germany?'

'What are they asking?' said Isaac.

'They want to know why we left,' said Lulu.

Isaac looked perplexed. 'Don't they know that?'

'Could you answer the question, please?' said Sir Stanley.

'Yes . . . *Entschuldigung* . . . sorry . . .' said Lulu, struggling. 'We left because the Nazi Party and the . . . new laws . . . have made life in Germany . . . too hard for me and my husband.'

'In what way?'

Lulu looked blank. 'In what way?'

'Yes. Apart from the difficulty for your husband of getting an academic post that you have already told us about. You see, we have heard so many different stories from all the Jewish refugees that we're just trying to form a realistic picture of what's going on there.'

'Absolutely. You can't believe everything,' said Superintendent Grout.

Lulu shook her head, not knowing where to start. 'Our home. The windows are smashed. Men shout at me in the street. Women too. *Pig. Whore.* Isaac is arrested, last year. For no reason. The police, they hit him, they give him no food for three days. They burn down his father's synagogue, and then his father, he is sixty-seven, he must clean it up. On his hands and knees, he must clean it up. My family, they are too afraid to speak to us because . . .'

'What are you saying?' said Isaac. 'Why do they need all this information?'

53

'I don't know. I think it's because they think we might not be genuine refugees. That perhaps we're secretly Nazis.'

'How can they think that? What do they need to know? I am a Jew. I am a communist. How much more of an enemy of fascism do I need to—'

'Excuse me,' interrupted Sir Stanley, sternly. 'What did you say? What was that about communism?'

'Yes, he said he was a communist. Definitely.'

'Yes, thank you, Charles. Even without your command of the language, I can make out *"Ich bin Kommunist."*' He turned back to the couple. Rebekka woke up and immediately started to cry. 'Now, Herr Fabian. I know you don't speak much English, but you can understand me well enough to tell me this: are you a communist?'

Isaac knew that this question was being asked threateningly; he knew, from the man's tone, that the safest answer was no. But he didn't want to say no: he followed his godless creed with all the fervour of a man inculcated with religion. He didn't, though, just want to say yes. He wanted to say that although, yes, he was a communist, he did not support Stalin, the Borgia in the Kremlin who had betrayed the revolution and, incredibly, signed a pact with Hitler, but Trotsky, the poet of Marxism, preaching permanent revolution while waiting for death in Mexico City. But he knew that such complexities were beyond his linguistic capabilities, and besides, Rebekka's crying was cutting his mind in two. And so, in English, he said: 'Yes. I am a communist.'

One of Sir Stanley's furry eyebrows arched upwards; he wrote something down on his clipboard, moving his pencil heavily across the paper.

'Do you have links with any communist organisations in this country?' said Superintendent Grout. 'Have you met with other communists since you have been here?'

'I don't understand.'

'Mrs Fabian, perhaps you'd care to translate.'

'Surely we should know if she is a communist too?' said the Reverend Chamberlain.

'Yes. Absolutely. Are you a communist too, Mrs Fabian?'

Lulu felt hemmed in. She looked to Isaac for help, wanting to say the right thing, not wanting to say something that would constitute a betrayal. He shook his head, signalling some abdication, the significance of which she could not grasp. She turned back to the committee.

'No. But some ways, yes. For some things, some ideas. I have some sympathy. Bekka, shush. It's all right, darling.' The child's cry had moved up to a wail, a long, seemingly unbroken by breathing, note of frustration and rage. 'We do not know any other communists here. We have not met them.'

'Mrs Fabian . . .' said Sir Stanley, raising his voice partly to be heard above Rebekka and partly to suggest that his forthcoming question was in some sense climactic, '. . . could you ask your husband if he would be prepared to fight for this country against Germany?'

Lulu nodded. 'Isaac . . .'

'I understand the question,' said Isaac. '*Ja*. Yes. I would.'

Isaac's certainty took the wind out of the committee's sails for a second; Rear-Admiral Holloway looked almost disappointed. Bored by interviewing hundreds of aliens easily classified as safe, finding one who was a communist was exciting; it had given them a policing energy.

'Well, good. That's good,' said Sir Stanley.

'Ah. But what about fighting for this country against the Soviet Union?' said the Reverend Chamberlain.

'Yes! Absolutely! Good point, Reverend!' said Rear-Admiral Holloway.

'I agree,' said Sir Stanley.

'Sir . . .' said Lulu, pleadingly.

'Would you ask your husband that question, please, Mrs Fabian.'

Lulu turned to him. 'Oh God. Isaac. They want to know if you would fight for Britain against the Soviet Union.'

Isaac's face took on a dazed expression, like a boxer hit with a surprise blow.

'But why do they want to know that? Britain is not at war with the Soviet Union.'

'I don't know why, Izzy!' said Lulu, her face contorting towards tears. 'Just tell them you would.'

Isaac felt his spirit tighten. 'I can't,' he said, looking down.

'Of course you can.'

'I can't. I can't agree to fight ordinary workers.'

'What if Stalin sends his armies in to support Hitler?'

'He won't. It's a non-aggression pact. Hitler will never—'

'You don't know! You don't know what might happen! You and your stupid Marxist certainty about history!' Some of the other refugees seated in the hall looked up at the raised German voice. 'Where did Marx say that Germany would want to rid itself of Jews? Where was that in his predictions for the future of capitalism?' The tears came from her now, furious tears, tears of loss for her lost life. 'Where did he say we would end up here now, in Britain, answering stupid questions like this, refugees?'

'Mrs Fabian. Please. Calm yourself,' said Sir Stanley. 'Or I will have to ask for you to be ejected.'

Through a film of tears, Lulu looked back to the committee's table. Sir Stanley Farrow's expression was not unkind: a whorl of sympathy ran though the grain of his well-weathered features.

'I am . . . I am sorry.'

Sir Stanley gave her a measured nod. He turned to the rest of the table, flipping a page on his clipboard as he did so. 'I think we have seen enough, gentlemen. Clearly Mr Fabian cannot give us an assurance of his support in the case of a conflict with the Soviet Union. It's possible to suggest that this – in addition to his extremist political views – is enough to constitute grounds for a Category A classification, and therefore immediate internment.'

'No!' said Lulu.

'What is he saying?' said Isaac.

'However,' said Sir Stanley, 'in view of the extreme hardship which Mrs Fabian has told us they have suffered at the hands of the Nazis, I am prepared to accept that under the present conditions of the war, Mr Fabian does not constitute a threat to national security. Therefore I would suggest that we classify him as a Category B. Does anyone disagree?'

'A little lenient, in my opinion, Sir Stanley,' said Superintendent Grout.

'You are entitled to that opinion.'

There was a pause, during which the superintendent looked at the rest of the committee, waiting for them to back him up; that support not being forthcoming, he coughed and said: 'No, actually, I think B is about right.'

'Good. Reverend? Rear-Admiral?'

They both nodded in agreement. 'Category B,' said Sir Stanley to the elderly woman, who started her form-stamping duties immediately.

'B?' said Isaac. 'B?'

'And what about Mrs Fabian, Sir Stanley?' said Reverend Chamberlain.

'I think C will be fine for Mrs Fabian,' he said, looking to Lulu with something that he clearly considered a roguish twinkle.

'Thank you, sir,' said Lulu.

'B?' said Isaac, furiously. He wanted to overturn tables, to throw paperwork in the air: he felt like Jesus, spurred to throw the moneylenders out of the temple. 'What does that mean?'

'Sir . . .' said Lulu. 'What is Category B? What does it mean for us?'

Sir Stanley gestured to the elderly lady, who was now holding out two sets of papers for the Fabians to collect. 'Mrs Watson will give you a chit which explains all the restrictions. Weekly reporting to the police, not allowed to own certain possessions, that kind of thing. Not too draconian.'

Lulu moved to pick up the forms, holding Rebekka, whose tears seemed to have been stopped by her mother's own starting, on her hip. Isaac walked behind her, in silence: he did not know what to say to her. Her outburst was the first time that she had come close to blame: to blaming him. He wanted to tell her that that was fine, he understood, but he did not want to say it to her back and she would not look at him. A new German came forward to stand in front of the committee. Isaac, watching them begin their questioning again, remembered: Category B. He felt there had to have been some sort of misunderstanding, something further that could be explained: perhaps Lulu's English had not been good enough. How could he have been put into a dangerous category? He had just escaped from a hell of categorisation – a place where every day there was a new classification, a new demarcation, a new segregation of human from human. Mrs Watson, a very thin woman in whose high forehead the Corn Exchange stage lights were blazingly reflected, held out his new papers, stamped across the top with the letter B, like a headmistress waiting for a pupil to pick up a particularly bad report. With her other hand she held out his and Rebekka's passports, across which – even next to the little baby photo of Bekka – another letter had been stamped: J. Wherever Isaac looked, language seemed to be narrowing.

June Murray was tired. She had worked all day translating the leaflet, and the words were starting to bounce off her eyes. Outside the window in her cramped office at Electra House, the sky was dimming, but the lamp-posts along the Embankment would not come on: a third night of bombing was predicted. She wished she was still at Woburn Abbey, where she could walk home at any time of the day or night without keeping her ear cocked for the opening slow note of the siren's whine.

The leaflet she was translating – from English into German – had been written by a group of men, whose names she was not allowed to know, but who worked directly for Rex Leeper, the head of SO1, the branch of Special Operations Executive responsible for the preaching of subversion to enemy-occupied territories. It was the third in a series called 'From the Clouds', in German *Der Wolkige Beobachter*, a play on the title of the Nazi newspaper, *Der Völkische Beobachter*. The draft of this edition contained articles proclaiming that inflation was now rife in Germany, that the *Graf Spee* had been sold for scrap and that America would soon enter the war on the side of Great Britain. Dropped from the skies by ten RAF Whitley bombers, nearly six million copies of the first two editions of the *Der Wolkige Beobachter* had already landed in Poland, France and Holland. Their effectiveness as a morale-loosener for the German troops stationed there had yet to be reckoned.

Taking off her glasses, June leant back in her chair and stretched her fingers above her head, creaking the wood in the pencil strung through them. A phrase in the English copy she had been given was bothering her: 'wrong-headed'. In the middle of what purported to be a mother's letter to her soldier son posted in Czechoslovakia came the phrase 'I wouldn't want to see you killed fighting for such a wrong-headed cause'. Why did Leeper's men make this stuff so colloquial, when they knew it had to be translated? She could go for *unrecht*, which simply meant 'wrong, morally wrong', or *ungerecht*, which had more of a sense of unjust; but neither got the twist of misguidedness that 'wrong-headed' carried. The German for misguided, *töricht*, however, felt too piffling, not sufficiently accusatory. Unable to decide, her mind wandered, as it often did, to whether translating propaganda was exactly what she had envisaged for her future when she graduated from Birkbeck College with a degree in modern languages. A car went past on the Embankment, its illegally unhooded headlights sweeping over her typewritten page, reminding her simultaneously that she had another paragraph to do and that it was getting late. The picture came into her mind of her one-bedroom flat in Camden Town, lit red by the bars of her electric fire; if she got on with it, she might still be back early enough to listen to her new gramophone record – the latest from the Tommy Dorsey Orchestra – before the old curmudgeon upstairs started banging on the ceiling. She let out a suppressed sigh, before jotting down *eigenwillig*, literally 'wayward'. It wasn't quite right, but it would have to do.

'Finished yet?' said Michael, coming into the office without knocking, as he always did. June looked up: his face was curved around his ever-present half smile. She knew that Michael was interested in her, but wondered whether every woman in the department thought the same, as the half smile made him look constantly flirtatious.

'Nearly,' she replied, turning back to her page, trying to stop her mouth mirroring his.

'Nearly enough for me to hang on so that we can go for a drink?'

June glanced at him. He was wearing a herringbone suit, with a plain grey tie, and smoking. Michael always looked like a second-string matinée idol, and, although she did find him attractive, the way he carried this knowledge about himself put her off.

'You've done the cartoon?' she said.

'See what you think,' he said, producing a sheet of card from behind his back. It was a pen-and-ink drawing of a hillside, over which a sun was rising.

On top of the hill stood a small gallows, from which hung a

black swastika. Underneath it, in bold capitals, were the words 'IT WILL COME'. June looked at it through the plume of smoke rising from Michael's cigarette, which gave the image a peculiarly three-dimensional air.

'It's not exactly Giles, is it?' she said.

'No,' said Michael. 'But our brief isn't to raise a laugh. We do the heavy, portentous cartoons. Anderson and Spilling do the funnies.'

'If you think a drawing of Hitler tripping over a bulldog is funny.'

'That was one of their best,' he said, his half smile widening to full.

She looked back at the drawing. 'Your idea or Stevenson's?'

Michael adopted a mock-hurt expression. 'Hey. I'm the creative genius in that partnership. Jack's' – he adopted his colleague's spread Yorkshire vowels – '"just a pen-and-ink man", as he always says himself.'

He laid the sketch down on June's desk, oblivious to the fact that in doing so it covered most of her paperwork. She let out a small, reluctant sigh, knowing that he was going to leave her no choice but at least to chat to him for the duration. She pulled out a drawer in her desk.

'Have you been sent these?' she asked. She put a sheaf of papers and pamphlets in front of him.

He flicked through the top copies. 'Yes, more or less the same stuff. Obviously, we're just meant to compare the illustrations.'

'What do you think?'

He pursed his mouth, a tad self-consciously. 'I think that the German propaganda machine works along the same lines ours does.'

'Their tone's a bit more . . .'

'German?'

'Yes. Frantic. Insistent.'

He held up an orange leaflet. 'I wouldn't know. I don't speak German.'

'I know.' She took it from him. 'But that's Dutch. Picked up on the road between Rotterdam and The Hague. Although actually it does include lots of German.'

'What does it say?'

She raised her eyes to heaven. 'Do you really want to know?'

'Of course. We've been sent this material so as to keep up to snuff with the enemy, haven't we?' The half smile was stretching again. 'Or is Dutch not one of your strong suits?'

She tutted. Her mother had a word for men like this, men who could make every conversation sound as if it were a tug-of-war into bed: *twinkly*. He really was too *twinkly* for her. '*Warning!*' she said, reading, trying to avoid making her voice too melodramatic: she didn't really want to play his stupid game. '*To the civilians of Holland! Do not take part in sabotage against the German army! You can't stop the German army! This is not your war!*'

'Bit staccato, don't you think?'

'Hold on. *Civilians captured during sabotage actions will be . . . punished by death.*' She put it down. 'It goes on in much the same vein . . . *Britain is our real enemy, your country is already occupied,* etc.'

She looked up at him; his expression was still amused. What strange things men and women are flirting over these days, she thought.

'So?' he said.

'So, as well as translating the next edition of the *Wolkige* in time for its drop by the end of the week, I'm also supposed to précis this lot into English for the entire SO1. In order that we, as you say, keep up to snuff with the enemy.'

'I meant, so are you coming for that drink?'

She laughed, lifting his sketch from her desk to reveal all the paperwork beneath. '*And* I've got overtime to do.'

'What overtime?' he said, taking the opportunity to lean in towards her, ostensibly to take a closer look at her work. He smelt of tobacco and Brylcreem: pleasantly manly, she thought.

'This overtime,' she said, removing the top few sheets of paper to reveal one typewritten manuscript. 'An eyewitness report from Poland. Grim.'

'Grim?'

'About a massacre there by Nazi troops.' She picked up the

manuscript, and replaced her glasses, the thought nipping across her mind as she did so that she had perhaps consciously left them off for this conversation. 'Terrible. Eight hundred and eighty Jewish prisoners, supposedly marching to the Soviet border, shot outside Lubartow.'

Michael squinted at the manuscript. 'To go into the *Wolkige?*'

'Hardly. It's extracurricular. For the boys at the Ministry of Information. They clearly don't have enough translators down there, so they've been sending over quite a lot of stuff. That's why I'm so bogged down. I'm not really supposed to work on material for the Home Front.'

Michael continued to look at it. 'Jews, you say?'

'Yes . . .'

'Hold on,' he said, putting down the manuscript and making for the door. 'Don't go away.'

June watched him leave, smiling in spite of herself at his impulsiveness. Her smile faded, however, as her eyes were drawn back to the words on the page, which she began instinctively to translate in her mind. *Men, women and children dragged screaming through the mud . . . bodies tumbling into ditches . . .* She shuddered, and forced away her eyes. It wasn't the first time she'd read such reports.

Michael returned, holding a large brown envelope, marked with the official stamp of the MoI. He drew out of it a six-page block of official-looking paper, stapled together.

'Haven't you got this?' he said, handing it over.

Her eyes scanned it: an internal memo to all departments of the Ministry of Information, including Special Operations. She checked her in-tray, located at the far side of her cluttered desk. In it was the same envelope, half opened. 'Oh yes. It arrived this morning. Hmm. Signed by Alfred Bassett himself. Must be important.'

'Yes.'

'Funny signature, isn't it? That massive B . . . and the rest of it just looks like a little scurrying rabbit.'

Michael laughed, and, seizing an opportunity to impress, scribbled a copy of the Minister of Information's signature onto a notepad. June picked it up.

'Hey. Pretty good,' she said, flicking her eyes up to him. 'Could you do it with a signature that doesn't look like a cartoon?'

'Stop changing the subject, Translator Murray. I presume, of course, you read this memo as soon as it arrived on your desk.'

'Do you know . . . I was just about to, and then – unlike some people – I realised I had some proper work to do.' She switched her sarcastic eyes back to the memo. 'It looks like it's got about a thousand different points on it.'

'Yes, it's very long. But . . .' He wetted his finger, and flicked over the first page. 'Ah. I thought so: here.' He held it down for her, pointing with his hand. It was item 6b, a sub-section of a main clause dealing with the content of any anti-German propaganda produced by the Ministry. 'Horror must be used very sparingly,' it said, 'and must deal with the treatment of indisputably innocent people. Not with violent political opponents. *And not with Jews.*'

June read it once. Then she read it again. Michael walked over to the window, throwing his cigarette into the rubbish bin beneath. The room fell silent, enough to hear the sound of muffled typing from adjacent offices, other propagandists busily plying their trade.

'I don't understand,' said June, eventually.

'What don't you understand?' said Michael, still smiling, but with just a ripple of irritation beneath the surface of his relentless smoothness.

'How can they put out this memo? It doesn't make sense.'

He made a tiny noise of exasperation. 'How so?'

'*Horror must be used very sparingly . . .*'

'Yes, I've read it.'

'Well . . . don't you see? It assumes that there is something inherently guilty about the Jews. It's saying, essentially, that Jews can't be considered in the category of the –' her eyes searched for the phrase – '*indisputably innocent.*'

'Well – yes, I suppose so . . .'

'Michael. Do you know what the reports are like?' She held up the one from Lubartow. 'Human beings massacred – shot like animals . . . look at this bit here: *a crying baby silenced with a shovel – in front of its mother—*'

'I don't know, June,' said Michael, interrupting, his exasperation surfacing more fully; he had no room in his world for this kind of information. 'I just brought it in to show you that you don't have to do your overtime; so we could go for a drink.'

June looked up from the report to him. He seemed suddenly small and peevish – insubstantial – like a child having a tantrum because they have been told their friend can't come out and play after all. She had been oscillating up to that point, eager to respond to his attention – but, abruptly, like a side of her coming to a halt, she discovered she didn't find him appealing at all.

The Right Honourable Alfred 'Chips' Bassett, Minister of Information, was composing a love-letter. He liked to write a love-letter to his wife every Monday, ever since he had wooed her from the trenches during the Great War, sending off to her each week a volley of poetic prose that rang louder in his heart than the boom of artillery across the fields of Picardie. He knew that the love-letters which he wrote these days did not quite have the same fire as those written in mud and blood from so long ago, and sometimes it concerned him that his practice was becoming rote, but he knew he would forever continue to write, as otherwise Diana would be disappointed, and, of course, it made him feel better about having a mistress.

Writing the love-letter always soothed his spirit. It had been an irritating morning. He had presided over a meeting of the Home Publicity Division, about means to counteract civilian panic resulting from the Blitz. Lady Grigg had said that the most comforting thing – at least where women were concerned – was to have a cup of tea and talk things over. Before Bassett could interject, they were all agreeing that this was a most valuable suggestion and that an appeal should be made to householders to supply tea to anyone in their neighbourhood whose own cups, strainers and/or pots may have been destroyed in an air raid. Professor Hilton had added that sugar was especially useful for steadying the nerves. Bassett had sunk into his chair, feeling weary and thinking of lunch, when he could perhaps get out of the office for an hour and meet Emily at the Waldorf, or, if they were being more cautious, upstairs at the Coach and Horses.

Your beauty has been my rock, he wrote, in pencil, and then crossed it out, thinking that the geological metaphor was perhaps not right for feminine beauty – it perhaps implied a certain hardening of feature in his wife's appearance, which he had indeed noticed in her over the last few years, and would not want to highlight. Best, perhaps, to avoid the immediately physical, he thought, and wrote, *Your love has been my rock*.

There was a knock on the door. He tutted, and withdrew his pad, placing it in the drawer of his desk. 'Come in,' he said.

Nigel Henderson entered, looking as ever, Bassett thought, somewhat over-assured. Although his parliamentary secretary was naturally his inferior, both socially and professionally, Bassett always sensed in Henderson a conviction of his *intellectual* superiority, presumably because of his marriage to a member of the 'Bloomsbury Set'. Not that it was much of a marriage, if the rumours were to be believed.

'Hello, Nigel,' said Bassett. 'Is it that time already?'

'I'm afraid so, Minister,' said Henderson, sitting himself down in the red leather chair opposite Bassett's desk. Most secretaries would have remained standing for longer, thought Bassett.

'What's pressing?'

Henderson took some notes from a leather folder. 'A meeting with the Home Secretary . . . you need to check through those new pamphlets about Civil Defence . . . the Prime Minister has called for increased civilian awareness of spies, which I think perhaps we need to make some sort of official statement about . . . and, oh yes – that young woman from SO1 that I told you about – we said we would see her today. This morning, in fact – I believe that's her outside waiting . . .'

'What young woman?'

Henderson squinted above his notes with just a hint of clerical frustration.

'June Murray. You remember?'

You do remember, don't you, Minister would have been more appropriate phrasing, thought Bassett. He shook his head. She must have just arrived. He was not likely to miss a young woman outside his door.

'She's a translator from Electra House. Works on the leaflets that we've been dropping over Holland and France telling the Germans how badly everything's going for them.'

'Well, very good . . .' Bassett took off his glasses and pinched his nose; he felt tired.

'Last week, she applied for a meeting to talk about that memo we drew up last month about German atrocity stories.'

Bassett opened his desk drawer, and pulled out a sheaf of paper from underneath his love-letter. 'This one?' Henderson nodded. 'What about it?'

'I'm not entirely sure. Something about the directive on Jews.'

Bassett replaced his glasses and peered at the memo.

'Seems plain enough . . .' he said, looking back up at Henderson. 'Do we have to see her?'

'Well . . . it's part of department policy that all members of staff have the right to apply to see the minister if they have a problem about something.'

'Can't your office deal with it?'

'She specifically said she wanted to see you. But I'm happy to sit in on the meeting and' – he hesitated – 'deal with anything that might come up.'

'Jump in if there's anything I don't know about, you mean.'

Henderson made a demurring face, but said nothing. He handed Bassett a file. 'This is the basic gen on her. Graduate, London University, modern languages. Worked for a publisher before the war – in Special Operations since the turn of the year.' Bassett flicked through the information, more detailed on the page. 'Unmarried,' said Henderson.

Bassett looked up and caught in the other man's eyes just a tiny suggestion that the proffering of this last piece of information had been calculated. Oh well, he thought, let's at least see what she looks like. You never know. 'Send her in,' he said.

Henderson nodded to himself. He got up and opened the oak-panelled door. 'Emily?' he said.

'Yes, sir?'

'Would you tell Miss Murray to come in now?'

Bassett stood up, composing himself. His fingers played about the edges of his moustache, straightening it. Henderson backed away, and the woman entered. Hmm. She wasn't really his type. Bit old for a start: thirty at least. And brunette, when really Bassett felt that all women should be blonde, or at least aspire to be. Her skin was olive enough, and her nose long enough, to make Bassett wonder if she could be a Jewess herself, although Murray – no – that wasn't a very Jewish name. When she turned to face him properly, her eyes were dark and slightly feline.

'Good afternoon, Miss Murray,' he said. 'Do sit down.'

'Thank you, Minister,' said June. She smoothed her black flannel skirt over her knees. Bassett made a mental note that women translators' ration coupons clearly extended to real stockings.

'Cigarette?' He proffered a silver box.

'No, thank you, sir.'

He nodded, taking one himself and reclining in his high-backed chair. 'I do apologise if we've kept you waiting. I know how busy you people are in SO1.'

'Really, it's fine. Thank you.' Her voice, shaking a little with nervousness, betrayed a slight lower-class accent. Midlands, Bassett guessed.

'I believe you have already met my parliamentary secretary, Nigel Henderson.' He had remained standing.

'Yes, I know Mr Henderson, sir.'

'You're doing a fine job up there at Electra House. Latest reports are that the last leaflet drop really got to 'em.'

'Thank you, sir.'

An awkward silence set in. Bassett looked out of the window; the sun was breaking through the clouds, throwing a sparkling line across the Thames. For some reason, it made his heart ache a little.

'So . . . Miss Murray,' said Henderson, breaking his reverie. 'Your issue with memorandum INF 1/251?'

'Yes,' she said, and seemed to adjust within herself, as if her next words had been committed to memory. 'I wanted to check if I understood the wording correctly.' She opened her handbag and took out the memo, folded in two.

'Yes?'

'Er . . . the instruction here. About how horror must be used very sparingly. Only in the treatment of innocent people.'

'Yes,' said Bassett. 'I dictated the memo myself, after discussion with Mr Henderson and some of my officials. Not with violent criminals. And not with Jews. Correct?'

'Yes . . .' June paused.

'You are aware,' said Bassett, before she had a chance to continue, 'that the memorandum is principally for the instruction of the Home Publicity Division. I'm not entirely sure how it concerns your work in SO1.'

'It doesn't, sir. Not directly. It's just I've also been doing some work for Senate House, translating reports. About what's been happening to the Jews. So when I read the memo, I—'

'You weren't sure if you needed to do this work?'

'No! No. It wasn't that I wanted to get out of the work. I just wanted to understand . . . I – sorry, I'm probably being very stupid – but I don't quite understand how the Jews are not innocent people.'

Bassett frowned, and looked to Henderson. Henderson seemed to smile a little.

'Sorry,' said Bassett. 'Could you just run that past me again?'

June cleared her throat. 'Well . . . sir . . . the instruction, as far as I understand it, is that we should be absolutely clear – in any stories put out about them – that the Germans are being' – she briefly struggled for the word: a part of her wondered if she would be able to find it quicker in another language – 'beastly.'

'Yes. That's a good way of putting it.'

'That their actions are always unjustified,' said Henderson, help-fully.

'Yes. So I can see how it makes sense that we shouldn't make any mention of when they have meted out terrible punishment to violent criminals, because . . . well . . .'

'It clouds the issue.'

'Yes. Because perhaps the criminals deserved it. But the Jews . . .'

'Ah,' said Bassett, 'I see what you're saying.'

'Yes,' said Henderson, 'so do I. But I think perhaps you have forgotten the exact wording of the memo.' He held his copy out towards her, one of his long, feminine fingers pointing towards a single word. 'There. You see. What word is that?'

June looked at him sharply, for a second wondering whether to say, *I'm not a child*. She thought better of it. 'Indisputably.'

'Exactly.'

'Or rather indisputably.'

'How do you mean, Minister?'

'Erm . . . indisputably the word is "indisputably".'

Henderson looked blank for a second. Then, the realisation coming upon him, he laughed. 'Oh, I see. Very good. Anyway, Miss Murray, the point is that the memorandum has been put forward to make sure that we – the Ministry of Information – come away from any propaganda we might put out as, to use the word again, indisputably the white men. We don't want anyone pointing a finger at us and saying, "Well, you say that, but perhaps, when they did such and such, the Germans had a point . . ."'

'Absolutely,' said Bassett, feeling that the discussion was rather escaping his control. 'Which is why we used the phrase "indisputably innocent". You see?'

'Yes,' said June, although she didn't.

'Because, although the Jews may not be as culpable as violent criminals,' interjected Henderson, 'there are still many people who believe that they have brought a certain amount of their woe upon themselves.'

June nodded, trying to process this information. 'People in Germany?'

'People in Germany, obviously, but also people here.'

June nodded again. 'Do you think that, sir?'

Henderson leant back against the mantelpiece. He seemed to be choosing his words carefully. 'I do, in fact. Individually, a Jew may be a fine man. But *en masse*, wherever they have attached themselves to another culture, they have infiltrated too many of the parent culture's important institutions. In Germany, before Hitler, there were too many Jewish doctors, lawyers, financiers. Particularly financiers. And in that sense, some of his original measures were, I would say, purely corrective.'

'Now, of course, he's gone too far,' said Bassett.

'Of course. But from the point of view of our – I don't like the word myself, but I will use it – propaganda, the arguments against the Jews are strong enough to justify excluding their case when it comes to Nazi atrocity stories.'

June looked to Bassett. 'Is that your position, Minister?'

Bassett coughed. He had been a little thrown by how polished Henderson's argument had been. 'In general, yes. Although government policy is determined by other issues, too. We have to consider whether the stories about the Jews are definitely true.'

'They are a very imaginative people,' said Henderson.

'Indeed,' said Bassett, glancing at him, something in his tone telling him to be quiet, it was his turn to speak now. 'Remember our original directive, set out in my "Aims of Home Publicity" pamphlet: "by the dissemination of *truth* to attack the enemy in the minds of the public".'

'Yes . . .' interrupted June, and Bassett looked a little put out, because he was just warming to his theme, 'but the thing is, sir . . . I can read these reports in their original language. I just know that they're true.'

Henderson didn't exactly snort, but made a noise that was essentially a genteel version of a snort. 'Come now, Miss Murray,' he said. 'I'm sure your linguistic skills are exemplary, but I don't see how you could possibly know such a thing.'

'I have to say I agree, Miss Murray. What is it about these reports that makes you so sure?'

June looked from one man to the other: at Bassett with his bald pate and greying moustache and glasses, sitting forward at his desk with one hand on top of the other; and then at Henderson, standing with his left hand in his pocket, slightly smirking, his hair neatly parted at the side. She felt like an errant schoolgirl in front of the friendly headmaster and flashy prefect. She looked to the window, where across the rooftops she could see the dome of St Paul's, undamaged by the bombing so far, a view she had always loved, but which looked in the context of present-day London like a huge ARP helmet offering scant protection for its treasures beneath. She could feel the sun from the window falling across her face; something about its warm caress made her feel calmer, more sure of herself, a woman who had a first in Modern Languages from Birkbeck College and had read Proust in the original.

'Because they're written so blankly,' she said, turning back to the two men. 'I know propaganda. I translate it every day. Even the stuff that's true, it's still – the style is inflammatory, hectoring, rhetorical. Like a speech, or a call to arms. These reports aren't like that. They're numb. As if the writer himself can't believe what he's writing.'

There was a pause. Bassett, taken aback by the sudden shift in the quality of June's articulation, looked to Henderson, and opened his hands, expectantly.

'Well, it's a moot point,' said Henderson. 'Maybe he doesn't believe it. Surely if everything these reports say is true, they would be *suffused* with sadness and rage.'

June shook her head. 'I don't think so. Or at least . . . they are. There is sadness and rage in them. In the silence. In the blankness. So much silence and blankness. As if –' and here she turned back to Bassett, fixing him with her eyes, trying to touch the element of truth-seeking she could feel in his manner – 'as if adjectives – superlatives – as if *description itself* has failed.'

Bassett held her gaze. For a few seconds, the intensity of her eyes triggered in him a clutching feeling in his stomach – a sensation he had not felt as sharply since the first day of the Somme, when a combination of fear for his own life and a sense of his own involvement in history had precipitated an overwhelming physical anxiety, an anxiety whose prime motor was the need to make snap decisions and for those decisions to be absolutely the correct ones. Then the ornate gold clock on the mantelpiece chimed, a tinkling bell, signalling noon, and he remembered that he was no longer a young officer with a rifle and a bayonet and over a thousand men under his command but a late-middle-aged politician whose chances of lunch with his mistress were fast fading.

'Well, well . . .' he said. 'As Henderson says, it's a moot point. And even if they are true, we have to consider whether the country will believe them. There are people who remember all the stories about Belgian babies with their hands cut off from the Great War. They know that that was all trumped-up nonsense about the Germans, and they might think that all these reports of massacres and so forth may be, too. And lastly, we do have to be careful not to inflame anti-Semitic feeling in Britain.'

'But how would telling people that Jews are being slaughtered like cattle – how would that make people anti-Semitic?'

Bassett clicked his tongue: he was a man who liked always to remain courteous to the gentler sex, but this one was starting to annoy him.

'Surveys conducted by Mass Observation,' said Henderson, smoothly interposing, 'suggest that there is a fair amount of anti-Jewish feeling at large in the country, Miss Murray – not helped by the fact that there are more than a few Jewish racketeers operating in the black market. There have also been reports in the popular press that Jews are always the first into the underground shelters during the air raids. Some of the public even feel that the war itself is something we are fighting not on behalf of ourselves, but on behalf of the Jews. Therefore, it would not necessarily be politic to highlight the "suffering" – as you perceive it – of the German Jews, as it could run counter to both the war effort and to generating sympathy for Jews in this country.'

An awkward silence fell into the room following this speech. Eventually, June, looking out of the window again, said, in the tones of one who knows there is no point: 'The German Jews . . . and the Austrian Jews, and the Czech Jews, and the Polish Jews, and the Hungarian Jews, and the Romanian Jews and now the Dutch Jews and then the French Jews.'

'Yes,' said Henderson, a touch uncomfortably, for some reason not completely able to give the word the undertone of *have-you-quite-finished?* that he would have liked.

'So how's things with the missus and bairn, Prof?' said Jimmy Bailey, as he put a pint of beer in front of Isaac, who looked at its flat, warm, headless contents with a certain amount of distaste. He didn't like English beer, and he didn't really like the atmosphere of English pubs, but there was always an afternoon hour during which the kitchens were down, and on this one Jimmy had managed to persuade Isaac to join him and Willie Gallagher at the Eagle.

'Bairn?'

'The baby. It's a Scots word.'

'But you are not Scottish?'

Jimmy wiped his mouth and put down his glass. 'Stop being such a stickler. Bugger me, one thing Hitler's really got wrong about you Jews is the idea that you aren't true *Germans*.'

Jimmy roared with laughter at his own joke; even Willie Gallagher snorted through his nose.

'They are fine enough, I think,' said Isaac. As ever, he noticed people around him – three men on a table to their left – look round, ears cocked, at his accent. Their squinting eyes were packed with suspicion. Isaac understood their distrust: with Holland and Belgium now under German control, and the Blitzkrieg sweeping through France as if its defences were ghosts, the movement of the Nazi military seemed almost *too* fast, almost as if the ground *must* have been prepared in advance.

'Fine enough, yes . . .' he repeated, doing his best to sound as English as possible, an attitude made more difficult by some lack of confidence in the truth of the statement. Since the day at the Corn Exchange, Isaac had felt the seams that held together his and Lulu's shared self, if not coming apart, at least fraying: he felt it walking round the room in Hertford Street, as fractures in the body of their household, tiny twinges, odd silences, the occasional half-returned embrace – all standard in most marriages, at most times, but for a couple as in tune as

74

Isaac and Lulu were used to being, these discordant notes reverberated long and loud in the gap opening up between them.

What disturbed Isaac most was the realisation that they had argued while under attack. That made no sense to him, because their love had been forged in the bunker; in his mind he and Lulu were at their best under fire, holding fast like a tiny phalanx, each of their bodies providing for the other a shield against the bricks and stones falling around them. Which is not to suggest that he was unaware of differences between them; long ago, he had accepted that Lulu was not, in fact, a communist – she had always assented to Isaac's politics rather than absorbed them – but he had put this intellectual discrepancy out of his mind, confident that her emotional unity with him would always cover over that crack. This assumption turned out to be misplaced: he had not articulated the thought in his mind, but still he knew that she, in that moment in front of the tribunal, had moved just slightly aside, making it clear for the first time that though she might fight for ever for their love, she would not for his beliefs.

'Where does she work again?'

'At a house in Hamilton Road. Cleaning,' said Isaac, who had told Jimmy all this four or five times before. He had realised by now that Jimmy was always more or less drunk, and so communicating with him was essentially a matter of endless repetition.

'Oh yeah. I remember now. So where's the bairn when she's at work?'

'There is a nursery not far away. In the church. Rebekka goes there until Lulu has finished work.'

'How can you afford that?'

'It is free. It is set up mainly for mothers who are working for the war.'

A rather awkward pause; all the men drank; then conversation again. That, Isaac had learnt, was the social rhythm of the English public house.

'And *your* wife, how is she?' said Isaac, remembering his rules of politeness.

'I'm blowed if I know,' said Jimmy, slapping Willie on the back, although this didn't go down as well as his previous remark. 'I'm at work all day, I come home, she's either already fast asleep or round at her mother's complaining about me.'

Isaac nodded, although he knew that there was one clause in this sentence – 'I come home' – which wasn't entirely true: had Jimmy substituted the phrase 'I go to the pub' then no lawyer in the land could have proved him a liar. Isaac had seen Jimmy's wife once, waiting for him in King's Parade: a thin-lipped woman, her forehead high in her headscarf, with the shield face and hard, flat gaze of the female for whom disappointment is as everyday as bed-making. The thought of her made him feel grateful again for Lulu, and allowed him to put out of his mind his creeping sense of unease about their relationship.

'Why do you not have children, Jimmy?' said Isaac, after another pub pause.

The clown-set of Jimmy's face melted away for a second, replaced by a vacant gloom. 'I dunno, Prof. It's not like we didn't want 'em. But times have been hard these last few years, and besides, the wife's had her fair share of problems, y'know – downstairs.' This confused Isaac for a second, thinking that Jimmy's wife's fertility problems were perhaps due to some kind of subsidence in their basement, but Willie Gallagher's instant blushing and downcast face were enough to let him in on the obscure meaning. 'Still – more trouble than they're worth, half the time, aren't they? Kids?'

Willie laughed, with some relief, and Jimmy's face went back to its normal mask of constant affability.

'Not really,' said Isaac. 'Sometimes, when things are bad, I think about Rebekka, and it – it keeps me strong. Because the love a man feels for his child – it's different than the love he feels for his wife.'

'I should hope so!' said Jimmy, with a wink at Willie.

'No . . . I mean – I love Lulu. Very much. But the love I feel for Rebekka – it is . . . ach . . . It is too difficult to explain in English.'

'You haven't been paying attention to me lessons, old son,' said Jimmy.

Isaac nodded, but knew it wasn't true; his English was becoming adequate enough. But the point he wanted to make – that the love a man feels for a woman will always be, in some sense, sexually dependent, and therefore in flux, whereas the love he feels for his child, being, as it were, platonic, is stable, as fierce as sexual love but stable – even if he could have expressed it perfectly in English, probably would have been met only with incomprehension from Jimmy and Willie. There was more to Isaac's sense of isolation in Cambridge than the linguistic.

'Do you have children, Willie?' said Isaac.

Willie looked startled, as if no one had ever asked him a direct question before. 'No. I'm not married.'

'Right woman's never come along, have they, Will?' said Jimmy.

'No, you're right there,' said Willie, laughing.

'More than a few wrong 'uns . . .'

'Leave it out, Jim . . .' Willie laughed again, but then looked into his beer, sagely. 'Nah, women. I dunno. They're a puzzle, sure . . .'

'Too right.'

'A puzzle,' repeated Willie, shaking his head.

'When did you get hitched, Prof?' said Jimmy.

'Hitched?'

Jimmy's face tightened as he drew on his roll-up. 'Tied to your nearest and dearest. Attached to the ball and chain. Married.'

'Oh. Five years before. When I was twenty-one.'

'You threw in the towel early then.' He leant in conspiratorially. 'Ever been with anyone else?'

Isaac looked shocked. 'No! No.'

'Really? Not even a young thing of easy virtue from the back end of the village?'

Isaac sighed. 'I have told you, Jimmy. I am not from a village. Königsberg is a big town. One of the biggest ports on the Baltic.'

'Oh, a port, eh? So there must have been a few . . . houses of ill repute knocking about? To service the sailors. You know what sailors are like, Willie.' Willie nodded, slyly, as if he had been handed a secret password. 'You understand what I'm saying, Prof? Places where . . .'

'I know what you mean.' As a student, before any experience of love, he had occasionally after drinking sessions followed friends to the streets around Schiffsquartier, where every other house shined a deep red light out of its front window. But when his friends entered these houses, Isaac would make his excuses and leave: though he was in rebellion against his spiritually exact upbringing, something would not make him turn that further corner. Once, he came close, when a woman approached him in a bar while he was waiting for two of his friends to re-emerge, and it transpired that she was Jewish, too. Or so she said: she had a room, just off the main street, which was lit both by the red light and, on Friday nights, by a menorah. Isaac believed her, but then found himself feeling pity for her, because he knew in an instant the precise lineaments of her guilt: he knew exactly how her guilt would work on her, what words it would speak in her head. Empathy made him unable to exploit her, even though it was what she wanted.

'But I never went to any of those places,' said Isaac.

Jimmy sniffed. 'Pity. Man's got to sow his wild oats, I reckon, before he settles down.'

Willie grunted in male recognition, although Isaac wondered how much wild-oat sowing Willie had actually done, considering he was so shy that speaking out loud often seemed to cause him physical pain.

'How's your ma and pa, Jim?' said Willie, after another pause. It always astounded Isaac that Jimmy's parents were still alive, as he imagined from appearances alone, that his workmate must be approaching his late fifties.

'Same as ever,' said Jimmy. 'Me dad's got the bad back, from lifting at the steelworks . . .'

'Yea, I know . . .'

'So he goes on at me mum a lot. Sits in the chair and smokes his pipe and moans. And she just makes his tea and cleans up after him, and he's saying "you cow this" and "you cow that", and it's like she can't hear him! Like she's deaf! But if I'm there, I says to her, "Ma – can I have a cup of tea?" and suddenly she's "Why of course, dear" – but before that, I'd swear you'd think she was deaf as a post!'

Willie coughed with laughter; Isaac smiled, because he knew he was supposed to.

'But, Prof,' said Jimmy. 'Do you ever hear from your ma and pa? Back in Königsberg?'

He pronounced it *Kornicksbag*. Isaac looked at him: his leathery face, settling into its most serious mode, seemed as sunken as a doctor's bag. But he was thankful for Jimmy's enquiry. He knew that even though Jimmy's understanding of Isaac's situation was slight, his concern was deeply felt and genuine.

'My mother, my last letter I got from her was near a year ago.

And my father, I have not heard anything about him. But . . . you know . . . my father, he was not really speaking to me before I left. For three years.'

'Oh. Why was that?'

'Because he did not like that I married Lulu.'

'Why?' said Willie. 'She seems like a lovely girl.'

'She is. But she is not Jewish.'

A pall settled over the proceedings for a moment; Willie looked somewhat shifty.

'What, is that a big problem? In Germany?' he said, eventually.

Isaac wanted to laugh. 'Well, in a way. But no, it is a big problem for my father. Because he is a rabbi.'

'A rabbit?'

Jimmy nearly spat out his beer. 'Oh, Willie Gallagher! For fuck's sake, man! That's great! Please God, let me remember that!' Willie looked pleased that he'd made Jimmy laugh, although still confused. 'Yes, the Prof's dad's a fucking March hare!' He guffawed. '*Rabbi*. You must have heard of it. It's like a Jewish priest!'

'Oh,' said Willie, shaking his head. 'A Jewish priest.'

'So a Jew marrying a Christian . . . specially a rabbi's son . . .' continued Jimmy, coming down from his laughter into serious explanation mode, 'that's like a one of you left-footers marrying a Prod. See?'

'It happens,' said Willie, grimly.

'Yeah, but people get all worked up about it. Don't they?' He adopted a cod-Irish accent. 'Back in the old country, beejeepers?'

'I did see him, though,' said Isaac.

Jimmy was momentarily thrown. 'Who?'

'My father. We were both held in the same police cell, after Kristallnacht.'

'*Crystalnakt?*'

'It means Night of the Broken Glass. In November 1938, when Nazis smashed up many Jewish homes and shops and synagogues.' He had a sudden vision of the Jewish prostitute's window. Would it have been shattered too, on Kristallnacht, because it contained a menorah? And would the red light have poured from it then, like blood? 'And the Gestapo arrested many, too.'

'Just you and your father, in the same cell?'

'No, there were a lot of men there. All Jews. Maybe thirty-five of us in this small room. I already had been there for two nights. I was sitting on the floor in the corner, when I saw him. Three Gestapo – three Gestapo, on an old man – throw him in. They were . . . *gestandetish* . . . making fun? Mocking. They were mocking his hair and his beard and his clothes. And my father, he just stays on the floor – on his knees – saying the Shama, over and over . . .'

'The what?'

'Praying. The Lord's Prayer. But then one of them comes up to him and pulls him up and says, "Shut your filthy prayers, Jew." And spit in his face. So I get up to stop them – they would kill me I know, but I did not stop to think – but there are too many others in my way, and by the time I get to him, the Gestapo man has thrown him to the ground again and gone.' He took a sip of beer, not this time because of the pub rhythm, but because his mouth was dry; the liquid tasted as sour as his mouth sometimes did on waking. 'I go over and pick him up. He is looking at the ground, just saying *Shama Yisrael Adonoi Ahed*, over and over. And I pick him up and look him in the eye but his eyes are closed and he is still saying it. I had not seen him at this time until three years before.'

'You hadn't seen him for three years?'

'Yes. That's what I mean. Well, I see him, of course – on the street, and my mother comes to my house and tells me about him – but I do not go to talk to him because he is too angry, about Lulu, he won't speak to me. And then still, even when Rebekka is born he does not come, only my mother and sisters. And they cannot come too many times, because it hurts him that they come.'

Jimmy looked to Willie, who was staring fixedly at his glass, wanting to hear the story, but not dealing well with the unprecedented turn the pub discourse had taken.

'So anyway, I go over and lift him up' – Isaac mimed the action – 'by the arms, you know? And I say, "Papa. Papa. It is me. Isaac." And he just says the prayer louder, and louder, and then because there are others in the room who are Jews and he is a rabbi, they start to say the prayer too, but not too loud, so the Gestapo won't come in again. And then I shake him a little – I am angry, almost, because I think he can hear me but he is pretending he can't – but then I realise he is not pretending, he is in a – how do you say? – *Traum*. Like a dream.'

'A trance . . .' said Jimmy. Willie looked up, shocked by this unusual word falling from Jimmy's lips. But Jimmy was concentrating on Isaac.

'Yes. And then suddenly, he opens his eyes and he stops and he sees me: and it is like, for a second, the whole thing with Lulu and the three years, it never happened. For a second, he sees it is me, he is so happy. He smiles and – his face, his old face with his grey beard, it is like a baby's, it is like Rebekka sometimes when she sees me or Lulu.' He shook his head, the lump that for a while had been forming in his throat grown large enough now to hinder his speech. 'Such a smile. I will never forget.'

Jimmy laid a bony hand on his shoulder. 'Don't worry, Prof. Don't carry on if you don't want to.'

'Well, it is nearly over, the story,' said Isaac. 'Then – just as suddenly as he seems to forget everything, and everything was fine, he seems to remember everything, and it is all bad – not just that he was angry with me, but that he is in jail and his synagogue is in flames and the Nazis are smashing up our lives and all the rest . . . and then he bursts into tears, and cries and cries. I hold him for an hour, I tell him that I love him, that I am sorry – I tell him that though I have married Lulu, we still light candles in our house on Friday night; he is just crying. And then the Gestapo come back and they separate us, the old men from the young, and that is the last time I saw him.'

Jimmy took a deep breath, then let it out slowly through puffed cheeks in a long whistle. Willie swilled the remaining few dregs of beer in his pint glass around a few times. When he looked up, his bloodshot eyes were moist.

'And did he say anything at all, Prof? Nothing?' he said.

Isaac nodded. 'Something in Hebrew. As they pulled him away, I tell him again that I love him and he says to me, "*Ye simcha Elohim k'efrayim v'che-menasheh.*"'

'What's that?'

'It's a blessing. The blessing you give to your children every Shabbos.' When they look confused, he said: 'Friday night.' Then

81

he hesitated, before adding: 'The blessing Jacob gave to Joseph's sons before he died.'

There was the longest pause so far of the afternoon, then Jimmy said, 'Willie, I believe it's your round' – and the words were like a spell restoring normality and Englishness to the air.

But when they returned to the college, things were not normal. The three of them were merry, as if Isaac's story had taken them through some form of joint catharsis. Isaac himself was fairly drunk, and Jimmy and Willie were teaching him 'Hitler Has Only Got One Ball'. It was taking a while, not least because they had to have quite a long argument first about which version was correct, Jimmy plumping for the one that goes on to number the testicles of most of the senior members of the Nazi dictatorship, namely Goering, Himmler and Goebbels, whereas Willie was insistent that the mother/dirty bugger/Albert Hall folio was the official text. Eventually, Isaac, who had been listening for while, settled it by starting to sing a bastardised version of the two, which went:

> *Hitler has only got one ball*
> *Goering's is in the Albert Hall*
> *Himmler has a bugger for a mother*
> *And Goebbels – his balls are – so small!*

When Willie and Jimmy calmed down from laughing, they decided they liked Isaac's version so much they adopted it as their own, and the three of them sang it together, walking up Benedict Street and back towards King's. Maybe it was the drink, or maybe it was the emotional release of having told his story, but for the first time Isaac felt not frustrated by his restricted English, but happy that it at least had this value, that he could unwittingly make these strange new friends – and they *were* his friends, he thought, even with all their differences – laugh. They were laughing and singing, all the way down King's Parade, and people were staring at them in the failing light, but they didn't notice, absorbed as they were in their song, right until the architectural confection of the college gate, underneath which Henry Fitch was waiting for them with a policeman.

'There he is, Officer,' he said, pointing directly at Isaac in the centre of their little group. 'That's your man.'

The policeman nodded and moved towards Isaac.

Jimmy Bailey stepped forward, blocking his way. 'Hold your horses, Mr Plod,' he said. 'What would be you be wanting with our mate? Has stupid old Fitch-face over there been spinning lies about the Prof?' Jimmy put his arm around Isaac; with his other, he waved a finger at Henry. ''E's one of us, you long streak of piss! 'E's not one of those fucking . . . *fifth-columnists* or whatever they're fucking called that you keep moaning on about!'

'Don't you talk to me like that, Bailey,' said Henry Fitch.

'Oh yeah? What you going to do about it?' said Jimmy, breaking away, fists raised.

Henry moved back sharply, towards the policeman. 'Officer – aren't you going to restrain this man?'

Wearily, the policeman stepped up to Jimmy. 'Sir,' he said. 'This is nothing to do with you. But if you carry on behaving in this way, I shall have to arrest you for obstructing the police in the course of their duty.'

'And for being drunk and disorderly!' said Henry.

Isaac looked round: Willie Gallagher, he noticed, had vanished. Jimmy's aggression turned suddenly soft and maudlin. He put his arm back round Isaac. 'But no . . . you don't understand . . . He's a Yid . . . aren't you, Prof?' Isaac, not sure what the best response to this was, nodded. 'So he can't be a spy for Hitler, can he? Stands to reason!'

'Sir . . .' said the policeman, to both Isaac and Jimmy, 'I am afraid we have instructions to arrest all persons of German nationality or descent presently living in the Cambridge area, following an emergency law issued this morning demanding their immediate internment.'

Jimmy looked confused. 'What, the government passed a law just for Germans living in the Cambridge area?'

'No, you drunken idiot,' said Henry Fitch. 'It affects all Germans in Britain. "Collar the lot!" Mr Churchill said, and, frankly, I agree with him. Better safe than sorry.'

'Internment?' said Isaac, as if he did not know what the word meant.

PART THREE

The Isle of Man, 1940

'It is probable that the Isle of Man in the summer of 1940 was the greatest Jewish cultural and religious centre in Europe.'

Moses Aberbach

The first letters Lulu received were written in Huyton, near Liverpool, from the unfinished housing development where Isaac was sent before being shipped over to the Isle of Man. They were written in Huyton, but not sent until he reached the Isle of Man, because, in the stark terror of May 1940, when a net of vapour trails was thrown across the cloudless blue of England's sky, thirty thousand Germans and Italians were not only interned, but also forbidden to correspond with their families until the end of July. So, for two months, Lulu had no knowledge of what was happening to Isaac, except for one official communication from the Home Office, which she ripped open like a starving woman might a food parcel, only to discover that her husband, internee no. H5/0031F2, was being held, indefinitely, while a state of emergency continued to obtain.

Lulu was not interned. This was contrary to the experience of most women, whom many in the British establishment considered to be the more suspect sex; Sir Neville Bland's pamphlet, 'The Fifth Column Menace', presently lying underneath memo INF 1/251 on June Murray's desk, stated baldly that 'The paltriest kitchen maid, with German connections, not only can be, but generally is, a menace to the safety of the country.' And indeed, a police officer charged with Lulu's arrest had been knocking on the door of Mrs Fricker's house in Hertford Street at virtually the same time that Isaac was being picked up outside the gates of King's College. But when she arrived, with Rebekka, at Castle Street Police Station, she asked a number of questions about the kind of provision that any of the proposed internment camps would have for a woman with such a small child, which caused Superintendent Grout so much confusion, and not a little male embarrassment, that he decided, what with her being Class C and all, to let her go, pending further instructions, after which she seemed to fall through the system. She was not able to talk to Isaac, because the men were being kept in a separate cell, although she saw him through the bars as she was escorted from the station. She tried to call, but his eyes were closed, and by the time he had looked up, confused, his wife and child had been ushered out.

When the first letter came – left for her on the hall table by Mrs Fricker – she had to read it quickly as Rebekka had been crying all morning, and she was already late for work. Isaac had clearly written it almost as quickly as Lulu read it, as it was in his most spidery hand, the words scrawled like veins across the page in imitation, as he had been taught at school, of Gothic script:

Dearest Lu,

I hope this gets to you. They have promised to send our letters, but it's so confusing here, and sometimes the men in charge of us seem to have less idea about what's meant to be happening than we do. I have been here four days and this is the first time I have been able to get hold of a pencil and paper. Assuming it does, I hope more than anything else that you and our darling Bekka are in good health and coping not too badly with this unfortunate new twist in our fortune.

We are being kept in some kind of barracks, in this place near Liverpool. There are around 5,000 of us. We sleep on either palliasses or sacks stuffed with straw, 500 men to each building. I got a palliasse, which is better than a sack of straw, because they are full of holes, so the straw falls out in the night, and by the morning you may as well be sleeping on the ground. I use my jacket for a pillow.

Every morning we line up in an enormous queue for a slice of bread and jam. It can take up to an hour to get your plate. Lunch is soup, and a plate of terrible English stew – I don't like to think what kind of meat it is. Supper is more bread and some cheese. We have all been given big metal cups, and they give us weak, soapy-tasting tea in those with each meal.

Between the meals there isn't much to do – we aren't

allowed out of the compound, although I wouldn't really want to go far as the weather has been terrible. But I have met some nice and interesting people – some writers, some academics, a couple of musicians. Virtually everyone is Jewish, although there is a group of about ten men who keep themselves to themselves whom I think may be Nazis, or at least sympathisers. There are also some Italians, who seem pretty nice too – one of them, Mauro, sings all day and most of the night, Puccini, Verdi, and then some songs he makes up about the camp.

Well, darling, I don't want to write too much in case this letter never reaches you. The word is that we are going to be taken to the Isle of Man, where they have set up more permanent camps. That's where the British held German prisoners of war in the last war, apparently. Once I'm there and I know the letters are getting through, I will write again.

All my love, always,

Izzy

She folded the letter four times and put it in the box by her bed in which she kept the few pieces of jewellery she had managed to bring with her from Germany. Its baldly informative tone seemed at first to her uncharacteristic of Isaac – the only letters she had ever received from him before had been love-letters, and those had been passionate outpourings from a man possessed by language – but then she looked again at the English words on the back of the envelope: 'OPENED AND READ BY HM CENSOR'. She knew immediately that Isaac would be too reserved to allow his soul to overflow in the presence of a stranger.

After the first letter, the next nine arrived in a batch the following day, evidence of the postmaster on the Isle of Man attempting to sort out the backlog. She took them with her to work, and opened them one by one in the outside toilet at Hamilton Road, speed-reading them as quickly as she could, partly because she was hungry for his words, and partly so that Mrs Lambert would not start shouting for her. At first, the language sounded the same, like a prison visit, lovers talking underneath the watchful eye of a government official, until letter number five, which started to show traces of real emotion:

Dearest Lu,

I hope as ever that this letter finds you and Bekka well. I hope it simply finds you, in fact, as we still have no evidence that our letters are getting through.

We have arrived on the Isle of Man. The journey over was terrible. The sea was raging and the crossing was very choppy – and you know I've never been much of a sea-dog! I was sick three times, which on the rations they were giving us at Huyton was a pity – even as I was leaning over the rail looking at the sea, I was thinking, What a waste! But the crossing was as nothing compared to getting onto the boat at the docks in Liverpool. About four hundred people had turned up, and they were shouting and screaming at us, calling us every foul name I ever heard Jimmy Bailey use and many I have never heard before. Some of us even got pushed and shoved while we were waiting to get on the walkway to the ship. Professor Renstein, who used to be Professor of Psychology at Heidelberg, was hit with a stone. I asked one of the guards, 'Why are they doing it?' and he said, 'Because you are Germans.' I couldn't believe it: yes, of course, we are Germans, but why don't they know that we are not Nazis? Why doesn't the British government explain our position? I wanted to stand on a platform in front of the crowd and shout that we are Jews, that we hate Hitler even more than they do, but it would have done no good. They would have heard my accent and shouted me down.

When we arrived at Douglas, which is the main town on the island, there were more crowds, although these were quieter: they just stood and watched, while the guards marched us to the camp. I was very surprised when we got here, as the camp is not a camp exactly – just a few streets by the sea, mainly made up of requisitioned boarding-houses. It is a strange sight indeed – an English seaside holiday town behind barbed wire. I am in quite a nice house really, with a view of the harbour. I am in a small room with three others. They are friendly: one is a writer and journalist, Irving Seligmann, a musician, Heinz Berg, and another a maths teacher, Herman Kaufmann. That's fairly representative of the kind of people here: most of them are educated, professional, academic or creative people, some of them quite distinguished. I have heard that Sigmund Freud's son, Martin, is here, but I don't know which house he is in. There is also a separate house for the rabbis, of which there are about twenty.

There is a canteen, where the food is rather better than it was at Huyton. There is even sometimes a choice at lunch. On the whole, life here looks as though it's not going to be <u>too</u> awful. But I miss you and Bekka so much, and I can't believe, after all we've been through, that we are going to be parted like this: that I should have to miss seeing the first years of my child's life due to no fault of my own. Not to know as well how long it will be until I shall see the two of you again, or to feel the sweet silk of your touch; that, too, is torture. Please stay well and kiss our little one for me, and have her kiss you back for me.

All love, for ever,

Izzy

Finally, she reached the ninth letter, which was shorter and more terse than the others:

Lu,

I don't know why I'm writing this, as I haven't heard from you, and for all I know, they just throw our letters straight into the sea. Unless of course they are getting through and you're not bothering to write back to me, which I can't believe. I can't believe it.

If you do get this, anything you can do to find out how long they're going to be keeping us here would be of value. I can feel my spirit falling into the mire, just at not knowing. I have spoken to the camp supervisor four times now, and I'm still none the wiser. He says a system will be set up in time, whereby internees can apply to leave, but not presently.

When I get a letter back from you, I will write again,
Isaac

Back in their room, she tried to put all these letters in the box, but there was not enough space: wanting still to keep them in some kind of special place, but not having any other receptacle, she laid them side-by-side underneath Rebekka's small mattress in her crib.

Then she set about writing to him. She considered staying up all night and writing ten letters, a reply to each of his, but realised that she would end up simply repeating herself. She wrote kindly, even though she was hurt by his last letter, and its implication of laxity; even though it reminded her that Isaac could sometimes show her a cold side, which she had seen for the first time only in the days immediately following their appearance at the Corn Exchange tribunal.

Dearest Izzy,

Thank you for all your letters. They arrived only yesterday and today. Before then, I didn't even know for sure where you were. Mrs Goldman said she thought that most of the men interned were going to the Isle of Man, but you know what she's like, certain about everything, whether she knows or not.

Bekka is doing very well. I read your letters out loud to her yesterday, instead of a bedtime story, and she loved them, even though she's been very insistent about having Goldilocks for the past three nights. She misses you terribly, though, I can tell: sometimes when I'm holding her up on my bed, she looks over to yours and sticks both her arms out towards it as if trying to hug the space where you were. Sometimes she says, 'Daddy,' as well, which is heartbreaking, it makes me want to cry. I am going to try to get some photographs taken of her at a place in town, opposite Joshua Taylor's. It is quite expensive, but apparently they can make more than one print, so I could send you one, and then you won't have to miss the sight of her growing after all, although obviously I know a thousand photographs would never replace that properly.

I'm sending a food parcel with this letter, not much I'm afraid, just two hard-boiled eggs, a tin of mince, and some cupcakes I made – they might be a bit dry as I had to make them without butter, but they should be sweet enough as Mr Henry at the shop on Alpha Road gave me some extra sugar this week. Maybe you can get some vegetables from the refectory you mentioned to go with the mince.

I am glad you have met some interesting people. Perhaps there will be some consolation to this experience in that.

I don't know what to tell you about the two months since you've been gone. Not very much has happened. Life goes on as usual – I work at the Lamberts' during the day and then look after Bekka in the evening. It is very hard here without you. The nights are long and dark, and once Bekka goes to sleep I have nothing to do except think about how much I'm missing you. She is sleeping very well at the moment – I put her down about eight o'clock and she doesn't stir until six the next morning. Sometimes I just stare at her in her crib; I am warmed inside most when I can see signs of you in her face, in her brown eyes and in the little lines on her forehead.

My English is improving, at least – perhaps because I don't have the excuse of talking German at home any more. I've even started reading *Hamlet*, by Shakespeare! I would have started with something easier but it's the only book Mrs Fricker was prepared to lend me from her shelves. Obviously, I hardly understand it, but I can still make out some of the beauty of the words.

Tomorrow, I am going to take an hour off work to go and see somebody at the Guildhall, to ask if they can tell us anything at all about when internment will be over. I'll try to explain our position as best I can. I still find it hard to believe that when someone is in possession of all the facts that they would not want to help us. The English are supposed to be all about fair play, aren't they?

Anyway, my love, I hope you get this soon and it sets your mind at rest about your letters. At least now we can speak to each other, if only in writing. I think of you every second of the day,

Stay well and try not to get too down-hearted – I know we will all be together again soon.

All my love,

Luxxx

She sent the letter at a post-box in the Market Square, on her way to the Guildhall. The late August sun was high in the sky; the air felt thick with summer. It was mid-morning and the market, despite the heat, was bustling with life. It always cheered Lulu up walking through the market, even though she rarely had enough money to buy much more than the most basic provisions: it was the traders, under their canvas awnings, with their endless hearty shouting of prices and weights – something about their *optimism*, their confidence that abundant produce was available in spite of rationing, made her feel uplifted. A delivery van, branded all over, on every door and every panel, with the legend *Baldry's Table Waters* blocked her way for a second at the far end of the square. Two of the burliest men Lulu had ever seen were lifting crates – marked *A Sparkling Bracing Healthful Beverage: Pepsi-Cola* – from the back of the van. Lulu had never drunk Pepsi-Cola but she had heard of it, and seen billboards advertising it. The sight of the bottles, racked up like liquid skittles, made her feel the dryness in her throat more keenly, a real thirst, as if her throat was clotted; before she knew it, she was staring, and then she noticed one of the men staring back at her, a loutish smile playing about his lips. Quickly, Lulu moved on, but she could feel his eyes travelling with her as she passed; a second later her face burned red from the sound of a wolf-whistle, a swooping, elongated and deeply sala-cious note such as, Lulu had come to learn, only the British labouring classes seemed to have the mouths to produce. Part of her wanted to turn round and fix the man with a cold stare, or maybe say something to him in German, to see what that would do to his desire, but she carried on walking, through the arched doors and into the Guildhall.

'Yes?' said the receptionist, an angry-faced woman whose buttoned-down regulation dress was making her sweat in the heat: her skin appeared to glare.

'I have an appointment to see the head of Civil Security.' Lulu produced a letter from her handbag, and handed it to her.

The receptionist glanced at it briefly, without taking it. 'Is it about a family member who's been interned?'

'My husband.'

'Room Twenty-four. Fourth floor, second door on the right-hand side. The lift's broken, I'm afraid, so you'll have to take the stairs.'

By the time she reached the fourth floor, Lulu was sweating too. In the corridor sat two other women, on a pair of splintery wooden chairs: there being no other chairs available, Lulu stood rather awkwardly against the opposite wall. The women were seated on either side of the door, like gatekeepers to some mystical portal. The one on the left was looking steadfastly at the floor, but the one on the right nodded in greeting at her. Lulu smiled and nodded back: the woman's face was open, prematurely lined, but in a pattern that she wore with an air of sophistication rather than exhaustion.

'Hello,' said the woman, in German, extending a hand. 'Lotte Gerard.'

'Lulu Fabian . . .' she replied. Lotte's hand felt cool in hers, making Lulu wonder if her own palms were sweaty. 'Have you been waiting long?'

'Half an hour . . .'

The door to the office opened, and a tall, thin woman in a black dress, a woman who had clearly thought that the appropriate style for this interview was funereal, was ushered out by Rear-Admiral Holloway.

'Well, thank you,' she said.

'That's all right, Frau Baerwald. I am sorry I couldn't be more help. All the very best,' he said, raising an arm for a goodbye wave slightly too early.

She nodded and moved off down the corridor, glancing briefly at each of the other women there in turn, her expression clearly conveying: *You're wasting your time.* Holloway consulted a card in his hand: 'Frau Grubach?'

The other woman looked up from the floor, slowly, as if the heaviness that Lulu immediately saw in her eyes were not metaphorical. *'Ja.* Yes.'

Holloway inclined his head politely, and she rose and followed him into the office. When the door closed, Lotte said: 'Husband on the Isle of Man?'

Lulu looked at her curiously: she seemed remarkably matter-of-fact. 'Yes. Yours?' she said, answering her in kind.

Lotte took a packet of cigarettes out of her handbag, and lit one, with a large silver lighter. She shook her head, making the smoke go this way and that. 'Father. I came here about seven years ago, met an Englishman, got married. Had two children. More or less *became* English – I learnt to love, with all my heart, the King, rain and bloody suet pudding.' Lulu laughed, but Lotte's face was deadpan. 'So my dad comes to visit last summer – he's only here two weeks and war breaks out. Well, between you and me, he's always hated Hitler and the stupid Nazi Party. So he decides not to go back.'

'What about your mother?'

'Yes, well, I think that was the other reason. He's always hated her, too. Certainly always wanted to leave her. Never quite had the courage to do it, though. Luckily for him, an international conflict provided him with the perfect excuse.'

Lulu laughed again.

Lotte's expression continued unchanged. 'So anyway, it's a bit of a strange decision for him. I mean, it's all right for me, I speak English. I mean, really, I speak *English.* Listen' – she extended a hand, and suddenly smiled, radiantly, her face remarkably transformed – 'How do you do?' she said, in sweet, musical tones, her voice tinkling, a deeply English sound, like tea poured into a china cup.

'God,' said Lulu. 'That's very impressive.'

'Isn't it?' said Lotte, her face returning to its impassive norm. She drew on her cigarette. 'I was meant to be an actress. Going to be

96

one. Before love screwed my life up.' She dropped the cigarette, and trod it into the floor with the toe of her shoe, a black patent-leather boot with an unusually high heel for this time of day. 'I can do other versions too: if Hitler invades and we have to run off to America or be shot, well' – she extended her hand again; again the flashing smile, although this time overlaid with something of a transatlantic smirk – 'Howdy you do, pardner.'

Lulu was taken aback; she had never really met a stranger whose personality was so immediate – who handed herself to you on a plate, with such a take-it-or-leave-it attitude.

'That must be . . . very useful,' she said.

'That's exactly what it is,' said Lotte, and Lulu felt relieved, because as soon as she had said it, she had felt she ought to have said something cleverer. '*Useful.* Stops all the terrible middle-aged Englishwomen looking at you on the bus like you're about to blow it up. You can buy the paper in the morning without the newsagent making a citizen's arrest. Anyway, what was I talking about? Oh yes, my dad. Well, of course, *he* can only just about say six words in English and when he does they tend to be "Where can I buy some bratwurst?"' Lulu laughed again at this, and this time Lotte smiled too. 'I mean, even when he's politely asking for two more sugars in his tea, he sounds like Dr Goebbels. What's more, he actually looks a bit like Goebbels. Same runty face.' Lotte sucked her cheeks in and drew her chin backwards in imitation of Hitler's propaganda mastermind. 'So you can imagine, it's been a bit of a difficult war for Pa. And then, wouldn't you know it, he gets interned on some godforsaken island in the Irish Sea with thirty thousand Jews! No disrespect . . .'

'None taken.'

'No, honestly . . .' For the first time, Lotte seemed to falter for a second in the flow of her speech. 'Stupid idiot I am. What I meant was . . . it must be – well, I know it is, he's written to me to tell me it is – difficult being on that island and *not* being Jewish. People just assume he's a Nazi. He's had death threats.'

'Oh . . . I'm sorry.'

'Don't be. I'm sure he's safe. But that's why I'm here, to see if there's any chance of getting him out . . .'

At this point, the door to the office opened, and Rear-Admiral Holloway ushered out the older woman, who had already gone back to looking at the floor.

'Well, there you are, Frau Grubach . . . I'll make sure your husband gets your letters this time. I can't understand why they were lost before.'

'Seventeen I already wrote.'

'Yes, you said . . . and as I said, I am sorry.'

Frau Grubach clicked her tongue and turned away. The action had an inappropriately German air, almost as if she'd clicked her heels and turned away.

Rear-Admiral Holloway, presumably expecting a polite exchange of goodbyes, flushed red, before collecting himself and looking to Lotte. 'Mrs Gerard?'

'That is me, sir, thank you,' said Lotte, meekly, and Lulu was surprised to hear in her voice more than a trace of her German accent. Holloway nodded and moved back into his office. Lotte followed him with her head down. Just before she crossed the threshold, she looked back, and, in answer to Lulu's quizzical expression, said to her, in German: 'Not a good place to sound *too* English . . . he'll think I'm a spy.'

Lulu nodded, and tried to look conspiratorial, although at heart she was simply overwhelmed by this woman's control: it brought home to her her own naivety, her own ignorance about how to manipulate this situation. It had not even occurred to her that the situation could *be* manipulated.

'We live in Trumpington Street, by the way. A flat above Fitzbillies, the cake shop. Do you know it?' asked Lotte.

'Yes . . . I think so.'

'Well, come by some time. I'm at home with my sons most evenings. *Dying* for some adult company.'

'Where's your husband?'

Lotte raised an eyebrow, easily, classically. 'Fighting our beloved countrymen, of course.'

'Mrs Gerard?' Holloway's voice came from within.

'Just coming, sir.' Again, Lotte added a splash of German accent to her English, just enough, presumably, to create the perfect linguistic cocktail for the persona she wished to adopt. With a knowing smile at Lulu, she turned and went into the office.

Ten minutes later, Lulu was herself sitting opposite Rear-Admiral Holloway as he rifled through a card-index on his desk. It was a tiny office, in desperate need of dusting, which had managed, in one of the most beautiful cities in Britain, to find a remarkably unpleasing view, of the rear of a textile factory, all pipes and chimneys and back windows on to bored workers.

'Eberhardt, Ehrlich, Eisenberg . . . I'm terribly sorry, Frau Fabian. I should of course have a secretary to do this, but the War Office in their wisdom don't appear to have allocated me one . . . Ah! Here we are. Fabian, Isaac. Category B. Presently interned in Camp Central on the Isle of Man.' He laid the card in front of him on the desk, pressing down the corners with his thumbs. 'How can I be of service to you?'

Lulu looked at him. His attitude reminded her of a salesman in Woolworth's keen to deal properly with a customer who was returning an oversize pair of trousers. She felt it best to state her position baldly. 'I would like to know when my husband will be released.'

Holloway looked at his lap; when he looked up again he was smiling the pained smile of the man who has been through this many times before. 'I'm afraid I can't possibly tell you that, Frau Fabian. The truth is, I – and virtually anyone else you may be able to speak to – have no idea when the government will sanction the release of internees. With the war in Europe going the way it is, I cannot imagine that the date will be soon. And, even if I did know, it would certainly be classified information, which I could not pass on to you.'

'But—'

'My guess is,' he continued, raising his palm to indicate that he had not finished, 'that the class of internees released initially will be C, anyway.' He leant back in his chair. 'So – without wishing to sound uncaring – if I were you, I . . . well . . .' he chanced a smirk, 'I wouldn't hold my breath.'

Lulu shook her head. 'I'm sorry, I do not understand.'

'What?'

'Hold my breath. Why should I hold my breath?'

Holloway knitted his corrugated brow. 'No . . . you *shouldn't* hold your b— Oh, it's just an expression. I probably oughtn't to have used it. What I mean is, we will inform you in good time when your husband is due for release.'

Having finished, the rear-admiral took a pipe out of his pocket and began tamping down the tobacco in the bowl. Lulu watched him grow absorbed in the task, almost as if he'd forgotten she was there.

'Well, can I visit him?'

Holloway dusted off his fingers and placed the pipe in his mouth. He seemed to take an age to light it, striking the match with great precision, and holding it to the tobacco fronds, puffing at carefully spaced intervals. Eventually, he removed it from his mouth. 'Not presently. You're in an unusual position, as the vast majority of wives of internees have themselves been interned on the island, at Erin and Port St Mary.'

'So they can see their husbands?'

'Well, no. Although it's possible that they will be able to, in time. But I can't see family visitors being allowed from the mainland. The security risks are simply too high.' He began to puff again at his pipe.

Lulu noticed a wedding ring on one of his elaborately gnarled fingers, which intensified the rush of outrage his complacency suddenly sparked in her. 'Oh, for God's sake,' she said, getting up from her seat, '*last* time Isaac was arrested, I was told no one could tell me when he would be released and there was nothing I could do about it.'

Holloway squinted at his card. 'Herr Fabian has been arrested? That's not on his record. We should know about that—'

'In *Germany*. For being a Jew.' Holloway made a noiseless *ah* . . . shape with his mouth. 'Aren't you fighting the Germans? Because this country is supposed to be different?'

'Please, Frau Fabian—'

'And stop calling me *Frau* Fabian. *Mrs* Fabian will do fine.'

Rear-Admiral Holloway coughed, causing his pipe to jog violently up and down in his mouth. He removed it. 'Mrs Fabian.

I am sorry I can't be more help. I do understand how difficult it must be for you . . .'

'Do you?' said Lulu, turning away from him. Outside, the sky still blazed imperviously blue. The sun's edges will not blur tonight, she thought, incongruously: it will set as a perfect circle, all the way down. 'Do you understand,' she said, not turning round, 'how frustrating all of it is . . . how frustrating not to be able to help the person you love at all?'

'If you wouldn't mind sitting down again . . .' he said, an element of pleading creeping into his voice.

She remained standing, silently staring out of the window, like they were lovers having a fight.

Eventually, he added: 'There is something you can do.'

She turned to him slowly, suspicion in her eyes. 'What?'

'Sit down, and I'll tell you.'

Reluctantly, she retook her seat.

'Thank you.' He picked up Isaac's card, and placed it back into his index. 'When internees' cases come up for review,' he said, speaking slowly, as if teaching, 'which they will do periodically once the government decides that the immediate threat to national security is over, the thing that will stand them in good stead – the thing, in other words, that will lead to their quickest release – is character recommendation from British citizens.'

Lulu shifted in her seat. 'Sorry? Character recommendation? What is that?'

'It's similar to when you go to court. Sometimes you have a character witness. To say that you're a decent chap, you know. Not likely to have committed whatever wrongdoing you're accused of.'

Lulu nodded. 'Yes, I see.'

Holloway rose from his chair and went over to a huge grey filing cabinet placed not quite flush against the wall. He pulled out the top drawer; it made the screeching sound of metal against metal. 'We're offering the same advice to all relatives of internees,' he said, pulling out a folder. 'This explains the kind of thing we're suggesting.' He handed an official-looking piece of paper to Lulu.

She scanned it quickly. 'What is this word?' she said, leaning over and pointing to it.

Holloway leant in to see. 'Affidavits,' he said, and looked up. For a second, when their faces were close, his eyes filled with sadness. She could not fathom the cause: she was too young and too self-effacing to know that it was the sadness of a man who knows he will never touch skin like hers again. He leant back in his chair, out of the immediate range of her beauty.

'It means a sworn declaration, in writing. A testimonial. Normally countersigned by a lawyer, you know? It's all made clear in the document, but, to cut a long story short, you need three of them, all from British citizens, resident in this country for at least twenty years, stating in clear and precise terms that they believe your husband is a good fellow, loyal to the Crown, not likely to be spying or doing anything detrimental to British interests at this time.'

Lulu looked at the piece of paper. It was difficult for her to read, and not just because of the language: the light was starting to fade from the window as the sun moved behind the higher wall of the textile factory.

'Where do I send them?'

'The finished affidavits? Send them here and we'll send them on to the Home Office.'

'Do they need to be written by – I don't know how to say this – separate people.'

'Of course.'

'No, I mean . . . does a husband and wife count?'

Holloway frowned. 'What? Twice, you mean?'

'Yes.'

Holloway's frown deepened. 'Um . . . do you know, I don't know. No one's asked in that detail before.' He ground his teeth, as if tasting the suggestion; his jawbone clicked in the corners. 'Well, if they are both British citizens resident for over twenty years, I can't see why not. Although each application will be processed on its own merits, and it'll probably stand you in better stead to have three completely distinct affidavits.'

Lulu looked back down at the paper. From where she stood, the task it outlined seemed gargantuan. Rear-Admiral Holloway looked at his watch, and got up from his chair; when Lulu raised her head, he was smiling but gesturing towards the door, his expression a strange mix of sympathy and officiousness. She gathered herself together and stood. Holloway held the door for her. As she passed his wide frame, she stopped, looking up at his overhanging face: his cheeks were starting to sprout a crop of grey stubble, less a shadow than a five o'clock shading. 'Yes?' he said.

'Er . . . I wondered . . . it is all right for the . . .'

'The affidavits?'

'Yes. It is all right for them to be signed by . . . Jews?'

He looked down at her; momentarily, she saw that sadness again.

'Anglo-Jews? Well, I think what I said before applies again. There's no reason why not. But I think . . . I think it may be better for you and your husband if all the signatories are' – he raised his chin thoughtfully, searching for the right word – '*straightforwardly* British.'

Lulu nodded. 'Thank you, sir.'

'Thank you, Frau . . .' He smiled at her apologetically. '*Mrs* Fabian.'

'Breathe in,' said Dr Mannstein, carefully adjusting the silver circle on Isaac's chest; his methodical precision with the stethoscope reminded Isaac of the safe-cracking motion that Henry Fitch used to use to pinpoint Lord Haw-Haw's speeches on the college kitchen radio. Isaac did as he was told; in doing so, he could feel his lungs fill with the salt air from the open window, blown in from the sea that glittered silver and blue across the wide sweep of Douglas Bay. Will this summer never end? he thought, noticing a calendar, hung, as if to make the point, close to the window frame, with half September's numbers already deleted. A heaviness hit his heart at the thought of yet another beautiful day spent behind barbed wire – another day in which the ever-present view of the sea would constitute not a pleasure, but a constant frustration, as if the British had put it there just to torture him, to remind him how he could not simply take off his clothes and leap into it. The onset of the heaviness felt so actual, so physical, he wondered if Dr Mannstein could hear it like a thud through his stethoscope.

'You seem fine to me,' said the doctor, taking the rubber tubes out of his ears and expertly folding the instrument into its long, thin black case. It was one of the few tools of his trade he had managed to salvage from his surgery in Vienna, along with his leather blood-pressure monitor and a set of thermometers.

'But I'm so tired all the time,' said Isaac.

'We're all tired, Isaac. Getting up for roll-call at six-thirty every morning will make you tired. Although, let me tell you, it will make you more tired when you're over sixty.'

'I don't think that's it. I've been getting up round about that time since Rebekka was born. I'm used to it.'

'Well, you're depressed. Depression will make you tired.'

'How do you know I'm depressed?'

Dr Mannstein's red-rimmed eyes peered at him over his half-moon glasses, the classically patronising look of the medical man. 'We're all depressed, Isaac.'

'You just said we're all tired.'

'Because we're *all* depressed!'

Isaac sighed, too weary to point out that Dr Mannstein had just put forward the early hour of daily roll-call as the reason for the communal exhaustion of Central Camp; weary, also, of his somewhat glib sagacity. He began buttoning up his shirt. 'Seligmann says . . .' he said and then hesitated; for some reason, the rumour he was about to voice felt covert, information that should be conveyed only in hushed tones.

'What does the all-seeing Seligmann say?' asked Dr Mannstein, settling back into the only chair in the room – Isaac was sitting opposite him on one of the three beds – and pushing his glasses back up his nose in an infuriating *let's-hear-it-then* manner.

'He says they put something in our food. Some chemical. What did he say it was . . . ?' Isaac's brow tightened with the effort of memory. The vocabulary of political science came to him easily, but real science falteringly.

'Bromide?' said Dr Mannstein, helpfully.

'That's it!' replied Isaac, pleased. Then his expression changed: 'What, you know?'

'I don't *know*, Isaac. I have tried my best to make of my little room here a surgery, but I do not have the facilities for blood tests, which are what I have to undertake to *know*.'

'But you think – from my symptoms . . .'

'How's your libido?'

'My what?'

Dr Mannstein tutted, and shook his head. 'Dear me, Isaac, I'm glad Martin Freud is in Onchan and not here, to witness that little piece of ignorance. The spirit of his father would turn within him. And you a philosopher as well . . .'

'A *political* philosopher, Dr Mannstein.'

'But everything is politics, isn't it, Isaac? Sex certainly is.'

Only Isaac's essential politeness stopped him from swearing at Dr Mannstein now: he had had enough of his epigrams. 'Is that what libido is? Something to do with sex?'

105

'It is the word my psychoanalytic colleagues back in Vienna would bandy about all day when talking about their patients' desires.'

Isaac took a deep breath. 'What are you saying, Dr Mannstein?'

'Potassium or sodium bromide, dissolved in tea, was administered to enlisted men, on both sides, during the Great War. It's principally a sedative, but one of its supposed side-effects is a quelling of – if I may use the phrase – the libido. Thus it was meant to limit the amount of forays soldiers would otherwise have made to brothels – and therefore in turn the acquisition of venereal disease.'

'I see.' Isaac put on his jacket – grey and woollen, it was too hot for the late-summer weather on the Isle of Man, but it was the one Lulu had forced him to take. He smiled a little, joining Dr Mannstein in the land of the gently amused. 'Well, I can't say really, Doctor. I would hope my –' he curled his tongue round the unfamiliar word – 'libido wouldn't be too alive in a male-only camp like this one.'

'Perhaps if you escaped and broke into Port St Mary we could test it out for sure.'

'Perhaps. Although, as you know, Doctor, I am married – as are virtually all the women in Port St Mary.'

Dr Mannstein raised his palms. 'I know. My beloved Irma is herself there. I'm not suggesting anything more than a hypothetical scenario . . .'

Outside, a gull flew over the sea, so low its wings hit the water with every beat; the plashing sound was loud and rhythmic, almost industrial. Isaac rose; when he reached the door, he turned. Dr Mannstein was scribbling on a notepad on his knees, for all the world like an ordinary doctor at home in his Viennese surgery.

'Seriously, though, Dr Mannstein. Do you think we've been sedated?'

Dr Mannstein put down his pen, and folded his arms. His expression became straightforward, for the first time. 'I think it's entirely possible that the British have been putting potassium or sodium bromide in our food and drink – quite possibly from before we got here, when they were holding us on the mainland. It's a fairly standard procedure in prisoner-of-war camps; helps to keep the inmates docile. I know they do it in Germany.'

'But we aren't prisoners of war. We're interned refugees.'

Dr Mannstein raised a pair of questioning eyebrows, and nodded towards the window, where the light above the water clung to the air so brightly it was like a fog. Between their requisitioned boarding-house and the sea, just beyond the barbed wire which cut them off from the other side of the street, stood a sentry, in full military uniform, at ease, his rifle and bayonet to one side. 'Do you think *he* recognises that distinction?' he said.

'Can I have your porridge?'

Isaac looked up. Even though he had been staring straight into his bowl, it was only this question that made him remember that, in fact, the grey, lumpy soup in front of him was indeed porridge. Breakfast options in Central Camp were limited. The kitchen would not make English breakfasts, which Isaac had rather taken to while working in the kitchens at King's, because so few of the Jewish refugees, even the non-kosher ones, would eat them. This left bread and cold meats with tea; or, the one other option, porridge. Milk being scarce, it was made with water. Sometimes, there was sugar available to put on it, which was why Isaac liked it – increasingly, he found himself craving sweet things, as sweet as possible, unbearably sweet, cakes and pastries and, if they weren't around, simple spoonfuls of sugar, because his depression could be lifted momentarily in the soul-burst sparked by overactivating his taste-buds. At the moment, however, camp rations were cut, and sugar was off the menu; so Isaac had just asked for porridge out of habit, leaving it to go cold in front of him.

'Certainly . . .' he replied, pushing the bowl over to the man opposite him, a man he had seen a few times before, balding at the front, with keen green eyes. This was not a great distance for the bowl to travel; the tables in the canteen, although very long, were cut very narrow, to accommodate the two hundred or so men eating along them. Isaac often felt the closeness of the opposite man's meal, its smells intermingling with his own.

'Going to any lectures today, Fabian?'

107

Isaac turned to his right: Herman Kaufmann, the maths teacher from Frankfurt who slept in the bed opposite him, asked this question every day.

'What's on?' said Isaac, wearily.

Kaufmann peered through his wire spectacles at the timetable laid out in front of him. He ran one of his small, dumpy fingers down one side of it. 'Tuesday. Tuesday, Tuesday, Tuesday. Ah! Professor Fiedler . . . late of the University of Bremen, continuing his series of lectures on political economy. Today: The Rise of the Industrialised Nations.'

Isaac leant back in his chair; he held on to the table to steady himself. 'I shouldn't think so.'

'Oh, but that's your subject – you'll find it fascinating, I'm sure.'

Isaac half nodded. He noticed that the man opposite had not eaten his porridge, but instead was spooning it methodically into a small, wooden box. Something about the way he was doing this was intriguing – his eyes seemed to be minutely calibrating the rising mound of oats, as if he knew exactly when the optimum amount would be reached. A chef? Isaac wondered.

'Have you ever thought, Kaufmann . . .' said Isaac, leaning across him, and picking up the timetable, 'have you ever wondered about *this*?'

'What?'

'All this teaching. And learning. Lectures, classes, seminars. Look what languages we can learn – not just English, no, why stop at something so useful? Look, we can learn French, and Spanish, and Italian, and Greek, and Russian, and classical Hebrew, of course. We can go to lectures on Byzantine art, and Renaissance architecture, and modern European theatre, and biochemistry, and Talmudic history, and applied mathematics, and medicine.'

'Everything except engineering,' said the man still spooning the porridge.

Isaac squinted at him. He was half smiling, not looking up. 'Yes, as the man says. Everything except engineering. Might involve some physical work, so we leave that to the goys.'

'What point are you making, Fabian?' asked Kaufmann, looking a little uncomfortable.

'The point I'm making, good Herman, is that any other racial group, put in this position – essentially made prisoners of war – *unjustly* made prisoners of war – would organise themselves along . . . what lines, do you think?'

Kaufmann took off his glasses and began to rub them with a black rag from his pocket. 'Military ones?' he said, hopefully, as if wanting to get the question right.

'Exactly!' said Isaac, slapping him on the back. 'They would organise themselves along military lines – they would try to replicate, as best they could, the conditions of their own army. But what do we do, we Jews?' He paused, for rhetorical effect; his voice was raised now, and some men along the row had stopped eating and were listening. It reminded Isaac of how he used to be, sometimes, holding court among the political science students of Königsberg. 'We organise ourselves along *academic* lines. We're here twenty seconds, and we've established a university. The University of the Interned Jew.'

'What's wrong with that, though?' asked Kaufmann, putting his glasses back on.

Isaac hesitated. There was a time when he would have thought there was nothing wrong with it; a time when nothing would have given him greater pleasure than to be confined on an island where all there was to do was learn. A shift had occurred in him since that time, but it was only now, in this moment of hanging fire, that he felt the force of it. 'What's wrong with it is what's wrong with us: the fact that we're so drawn to *inaction*. An injustice has been done to us. Just like it was in Germany. But, just like in Germany, do we organise, do we rally, do we fight? No. We bury ourselves in books. We talk. We turn away from the present to the past.'

'Some turn to academia,' said the porridge man, closing the lid on his box. 'Some to show business.'

'I'm sorry?' said Isaac, starting to get a little annoyed by this interloper.

The man looked up. Despite his weather-beaten skin, he had one of those faces that seemed to be smiling even when the mouth was not, as if possessed of a secret joke. 'Most of them, you're right: they make with the big university. But others, they do the other thing Jews do. Look.' He drew from his pocket a flyer, on which was printed a pencil drawing of a man, dancing and singing, in front of a fence of barbed wire. On the top of the flyer, in German, were the words: '*This Island Life. The Central Camp Hanukkah/Christmas Revue.*'

'Bit early for that, isn't it?' said Kaufmann.

'This isn't a poster for the show. It's their recruitment drive. They're looking for people to help mount the show.' He turned it round to read out loud. '*Anyone who can sing, dance, tell jokes, act, or in any way perform, please come to auditions in Room Twelve, Camp Building Five, The Promenade.*'

'Right . . .' said Isaac.

'You see? Academia or show business. I hear there's a string quartet started up at Hutchinson. And just down the road here, number thirty-two, a chef has started a small café that does Viennese pastries.'

'Yes, I know,' said Isaac. 'But that's neither academic nor show business.'

'No, it's food. The third option.'

Isaac smiled. He was starting to like this man. 'You've completely ruined my argument.'

'I haven't. You're right. Under pressure, everyone goes to what they know.'

There was a feeling that this aphorism ended the discussion. The man started to collect his things. Isaac continued to watch him, curiously.

'Which one are you? Food, academia or showbiz?'

The man smiled, revealing teeth speckled with brown tobacco spots. 'A bit of each,' he said.

'Can I have that flyer?' asked Kaufmann. 'I might—'

'Sorry.'

'You're going to the audition?' said Isaac.

'No, I'm going to cut it up and attach pieces of it to my porridge-creation.'

Isaac and Kaufmann looked at him, entirely confused.

'I'm a sculptor,' he said, putting the box under his arm and walking away.

*

That afternoon, Isaac was lying on his bed trying to sleep – he had never been one for sleeping during the day in Germany, but the type of exhaustion he was experiencing now would build to the point when staying awake all day was simply not an option – when there was a knock on the door.

'Come in.'

The door swung open, to reveal a man wearing a grey cap and some kind of boiler suit; to Isaac's eyes, he looked faintly like the driver of a steam train. He waited, glancing around in both directions before entering.

'Hello . . .' said Isaac, swinging his legs off the bed. 'Can I help you?'

The man looked round again, as if checking for something, before replying. He shut the door and removed his cap; in the light thrown on his face by the window, he was so thin and dark-skinned that he looked simultaneously young and wizened. 'Who else shares this room?'

His voice was low; from the accent, Isaac guessed, the man was Bavarian. Isaac wondered about whether he should tell him; then couldn't see why not – it was information easily discovered. 'Herman Kaufmann sleeps there; Irving Seligmann there.'

'And that fourth mattress?'

'A man called Berg was in here too, when we arrived. But then he got sick, and went to the infirmary. Either he's still there or they've sent him home.'

'Or something else has happened to him . . .' said the man, looking away.

Isaac stood up. 'No, I don't think so.'

'It's happening in Germany.'

'Excuse me. Would you mind telling me who you are?'

'The others – when will they be back?'

'Kaufmann's at a lecture. Seligmann, I don't know. Can you answer my question?'

The man resumed his glancing. 'My name is Waldstein. I heard what you said in the refectory today.'

'Oh . . . it wasn't intended to be as much of a public speech as it sounded. I was just talking to Kaufmann.'

111

The man came further into the room, moving in small, staccato steps, and sat down on the single chair, near the sink. He looked into it, intently, for some time. Isaac could not help but wonder if he had ever seen one before.

'You are wrong to think there were none of us fighting the Nazis,' he said eventually. 'Many of us tried. But you were right that it was not properly organised. It was all individuals. All men by themselves. Like Grynspan. I told him—'

'*Herschel* Grynspan?'

'Yes. I knew him.'

Isaac looked at Waldstein more closely. At some level, this mention of the man whose actions led to Kristallnacht felt like name-dropping. 'Is he dead?'

Waldstein paused for a moment. Isaac interpreted this as the hesitation of the man who does not know, but hates to be perceived as such.

'As far as we know.'

Isaac wondered who this 'we' might be. A silence fell upon the room. Through the window, he could hear the slow rushing of the sea. 'What did you tell him?'

'I told him that a lone assassination would achieve nothing. That resistance has to be widespread, international. Like revolution. As Trotsky says—'

'Trotsky's dead.'

Waldstein blinked, and his head jerked back, as if avoiding a slap. Isaac felt the pressure of his own stare, the edges of his eyes against his temples.

'His words live on, comrade.'

Isaac flicked his eyes away, avoiding the impulse to nod, the impulse to agree, to be involved. Although Waldstein scared him, a part of him couldn't help but feel pleased and excited at the incorporation implied by 'comrade'.

'Anyway: if you believe what you were saying at breakfast today, you will listen to me. I am not alone. There are a number of us here who are prepared to resist.'

'Resist what? The British have all but left us to our own devices.'

'So they would have us believe. But still, in some ways, they are scared of us; they are putting bromide in our tea.'

'Yes. So don't drink the tea.'

'I don't. But I am not talking about the British anyway. When we are more powerful, there will be organised resistance against the British, but for the moment . . . there are more obvious enemies.'

Isaac sighed. 'Who are you talking about?'

Waldstein's eyes narrowed, to slits, razor-cuts in his face. 'There are Nazis here.'

'I know.'

'We think there may be over four hundred on the island,' continued Waldstein, ignoring the interruption. 'Twenty or so here in Central. Most of them in Building Twenty-three.' He hesitated, as if expecting Isaac to react; Isaac didn't. 'You can hear them sometimes, singing their songs. We have reports that they have meetings, discussions. One of them has been seen with a copy of *Mein Kampf*.'

'I don't believe that,' said Isaac. 'The British would have confiscated it.'

'Smuggled in,' said Waldstein, with reflex certainty. 'Have you heard of Aaron Fleisch?' Isaac shook his head. 'He's a Jew, in Ramsay. Although presently in Douglas Hospital. He was found nearly battered to death three weeks ago, in his room.'

'It might have been an argument with another Jew.'

'He was found with swastikas painted all over his room.'

Isaac felt his stomach fall. 'What are you suggesting? That we go and challenge the Nazis to a fight?' he said, abruptly, suddenly irritated with this overly enigmatic intruder.

Waldstein rose from the chair, the thinness of his frame noticeably at odds with the power and potential implied by his words. 'I'm not suggesting anything here, now, to you. Nothing. I just want to know if you meant what you said.'

'I always mean what I say.'

'Good. Then we'll see each other again.'

Waldstein put on his cap. He seemed more confident under the shadow its brim threw over his eyes. For a second, he appeared to stick an arm out for a handshake, and then, perhaps thinking this was too bourgeois a gesture, withdrew it. As he darted sharply towards the door, Isaac felt the beginnings of dread, of having already enmeshed himself in something he might not be able to control. True though it was that he had moved from believing that political theorising was not enough – that Marx was right about philosophers explaining the world when the point was to change it – it was another move again to the point of action itself.

'Waldstein,' said Isaac, halting the man's hand on the doorknob. 'Grynspan. What was he like?'

Waldstein's dark and deliberately inscrutable face, just for a moment, opened like a window, revealing, Isaac could see, some kind of heart. 'Young,' he said. 'He was very young.' And then he was gone.

'**M**ichael?'

He looked round from his desk surprised, initially – it had been some time since their last meeting – but his features soon resumed their usual easy smirk. He moved his feet from their position on top of his drawing pad, and stubbed out his cigarette. 'Well, well. Long time, no see. Which is quite a feat on your part, considering your office is just down the hall.'

'Yes. I've had a lot of work on.' She stayed at the door, fidgeting with the letter in her hand. Against the back of it, the tips of her fingers could feel the indentations the heavy keys of her Underwood made on the creamy page.

'Well, it hasn't tired you out. You look fabulous.'

June Murray felt herself blush: she *had* put on more make-up than usual that morning, and worn what she considered to be her most fetching work outfit – the black Molyneux suit, described by the assistant at My Lady as 'impeccably tailored', whatever that meant, with a soft white blouse. She'd also had her hair cut, slightly longer than her usual high bob (she had been considering one of those finger waves that all the film stars had now, but had panicked at the last minute, thinking that it would be thought too attention-seeking for the Ministry). She felt, at once, obscurely resentful that she had to doll herself up to win over Michael, and, at the same time, flattered.

'Thank you . . .'

'Sorry!' He stood up and dragged over the chair from behind Jack Stevenson's desk for her to sit down.

June hung back, still unsure of whether to proceed.

'He won't be back for a while,' said Michael, misinterpreting her hesitation. 'You know how Jack likes to make his lunch-hour last . . .'

June smiled, and decided to take the seat. She glanced round the room, a workspace so obviously occupied by two men, its walls strewn with unfinished sketches, its wastepaper baskets overflowing, its air dense with stale cigarette smoke. She had an urge to open the one tiny window to let the brisk river wind clear the air.

'Are you all right?' asked Michael, after a short pause. 'You seem a bit . . . nervous.'

'No, I'm fine. Look, Michael, I may as well come out with it. I need your help.'

He nodded, doing his best to look serious. 'Anything I can do . . .' he said, opening his hands.

'Well, we'll see. Before I tell you what it is I want,' she looked round at the still-open door, 'I must be assured of your absolute discretion. Say no to my request by all means, but please don't go blabbing about it to everyone in the department afterwards.'

Michael nodded again, and got up to shut the door. As he came back to sit down, June could see that a slight air of levity had crept into his face already, the sort of expression an adult might adopt when a child is trying to tell them something they consider to be momentous. She wondered if that was because he couldn't take anything seriously, or if it was just that he couldn't take anything *she* said seriously.

'So . . . ?' said Michael, expectantly.

June had read somewhere about men who dived from high cliffs, in places like Mexico. She had read that the way they forced themselves to dive, to step over the crumbling edge into the sheer blue air, was to imagine another self, standing behind them and pushing. One hard push forward and you would fall. She handed him the letter.

'What's this?' said Michael.

'Just read it . . .'

He took it, amused. It looked like a regulation letter, on Ministry-headed notepaper:

Mr Nigel Henderson MP
Parliamentary Under-Secretary
Ministry of Information
House of Commons
London SW1

Lieutenant Colonel F. W. Rutter
General Commander, Isle of Man Internment Camps
Central Camp
Building 1
Douglas
Isle of Man

8/11/1940
Ref No: 345/x/00006

CONFIDENTIAL

Dear Lieutenant Colonel Rutter

Following our letter of 2 November, I am writing to confirm that we will be sending a Ministry of Information researcher to the Isle of Man in order to investigate more fully various claims presently coming out of Germany regarding the prevalence of Nazi 'crimes against humanity'. As discussed in our earlier letter, it is government policy that these and other 'atrocity stories' should not be allowed to be placed into mass circulation until their veracity is completely proven. I would suggest that our researcher be allowed some time with various internees – who may be selected by yourself – in order to put together a dossier of interviews that we may use for the purposes of divining the truth – or otherwise – of these claims.

Our researcher's name is June Murray. She will arrive on 1st December, bearing a copy of this letter.

Thank you for your co-operation in this matter.

Yours faithfully,

Nigel Henderson

pp. The Rt. Hon. Alfred Bassett, Minister of Information

Michael put down the letter, and looked up; for the first time, his composure had gone, as if drained from him. He looked at her, hard, for Michael, whose eyes were almost congenitally soft, and then back to the letter. 'I don't understand,' he said, eventually. 'Did Henderson write this?'

'No,' said June. 'I did.'

Michael leant back in his chair, and let out a long breath, something of a whistle. He was impressed. 'Well, well, well. You *are* a bold girl. Fooled me.'

'Thanks.'

'One question, before we proceed.' He flicked open a packet of cigarettes – Chesterfields, long tips – and offered it to June, who, unusually, took one. He took a gold Ronson pocket lighter from his jacket, slung across the back of his chair, bent forward and held the flame for June, his eyes on her at all times. As she inclined towards the flame, she felt how marked he was making this action, how sexual.

Leaning back again, Michael blew out an extended stream of smoke. 'Why?'

Internally, June tutted; she felt the build-up to this monosyllable had been unnecessarily dramatic. 'You remember that memo you showed me a few months ago?' Michael frowned. 'The one about Jews? About how Nazi atrocities against Jews should not be used in our propaganda?'

'Oh yes! I remember . . . you got quite worked up about it . . .'

'Yes . . . Anyway, as far as I can make out from the newspapers, this ties in with a general government policy that the atrocities should not be reported. At all.'

'Right . . .'

'And yet every day, I read reports about what they're doing. It's getting worse. It's awful. Torture and humiliation and random killings . . .'

'Oh, June . . .'

'What?'

'Look, I work in propaganda. I hear a lot of stuff about how appalling the Nazis are. How Hitler's the devil incarnate. That's more or less what I'm supposed to sum up in cartoon form. If I believed it all . . . well – I think I'd go mad.' His face melted back momentarily to his benchmark half smile. 'I shouldn't wonder if, in Germany, people are being told that over here we're busy wiping out the Irish or something.'

June shook her head. 'I can tell you exactly what the Germans say about us and it's not that. The point is, anyway – I believe what I've read. Or at least, I believe enough now to need to know if it's true. God, Michael, it's got to me. I can't sleep for thinking about it. The things I've read. That's why I want to go to the Isle of Man.'

'That's why? Just to satisfy your curiosity?'

She slammed her hand down on his desk. 'It's not curiosity, Michael! It's not . . . something *idle*. It's real. It's affecting me.' He pulled back, away from her; she became concerned that her reaction had alienated him. 'Sorry . . . but you see—'

'No, it's fine.'

'And . . . I also thought that if I find out some real, hard evidence – if I could present that to the Ministry – maybe they'll change their policy . . .'

Michael raised his right eyebrow, making his face clearly say, *Really?*

June looked down, embarrassed, feeling, for the first time in this dialogue, a little girlish. 'Well, I don't know. It might do something.'

He picked up the letter again, running his eyes down it. 'What's this about a previous letter . . . ?'

'Oh, that's a red herring. I just know the Ministry *would* have sent one.'

'So why didn't you?'

'Because then the people on the Isle of Man would have responded with an official reply direct to Henderson, and the whole thing would have fallen to pieces. So I thought I'd just turn up with this. The post being what it is at the moment, they'll just assume the other letter went astray.'

'God, June, that's a bit dangerous. What if they telephone here?'

June's thinking stopped in its tracks. 'Oh.' *Bugger*, she thought, and nearly said it. 'Yes, I hadn't considered that.' She looked at her feet, in their flat lace-up shoes; perhaps she should have worn heels; Michael probably would have liked that. She shrugged. 'I'll have to hope they don't, I suppose.'

Michael shook his head, slowly, unbelievingly. 'June. Do you know how dangerous this is? If it's discovered that you forged an official Ministry letter, you'll lose your job. For all I know, you'll be accused of spying or . . . prosecuted for *treason* or something!'

She looked back up at him. 'Yes, Michael, I know it's dangerous,' she replied, softly, but steadily. A silence fell between them: there seemed to be nothing left to say. June felt sorry and awkward that she had tried to involve this man, this office playboy. She reached for the ashtray on his desk and twisted out her half-smoked cigarette.

Michael checked his watch. 'Um . . . I don't want to hurry you . . . but Jack'll be back soon . . .'

'Yes . . . sorry,' said June, standing. Picking up the letter from his desk, she started to move towards the door. She was glad now that she had not worn heels, it meant she could leave faster, and besides, she noticed, looking out of the window, a hefty London shower had started; soon the streets would be scattered with puddles deep as wells.

'June?'

'Yes?'

'Excuse me, but . . . was that all you wanted? Just to show me the letter? And tell me what you intend to do with it?'

June blinked, recalling herself. Although that wasn't why she'd come to see him, a part of her had wanted to do just that: to tell someone about it. 'No . . . I . . . there was something else . . . but I assume . . . well, it doesn't matter.'

'I notice the letter is not signed.'

She halted. 'Yes.'

'Will Commander Rutter have received letters from Henderson before?'

'I've no idea. It's possible.'

'That's something of a problem, then, wouldn't you say?'

'Yes. Well.' She felt lost. 'Yes.'

He closed his eyes. 'I'm going to regret this . . .'

'Are you?' said June, adjusting her tone to playful, realising suddenly that that was the best way to draw Michael in. That was his arena – all the earnestness in the world wouldn't work. It would simply scare him away.

Michael opened his eyes and raised them to heaven. 'Have you got a copy of Henderson's signature?'

'It just so happens . . .' She came back to the chair and sat down, opening the clip on her handbag. From it, she took a copy of the final page of memorandum INF 1/251 – the very one that, as Michael put it, June was getting so worked up about. It was signed by Alfred Bassett, and underneath by Nigel Henderson. Michael focused his eyes on the lower signature for ten seconds, and then, with not a little theatricality – like a magician calling for a prop from his assistant – clicked his fingers. 'Your letter.'

'Don't you . . . maybe you should test it out on some scrap paper first?'

'Lose the moment,' he said, shaking his head. Uncertainly, she handed him her letter. Clearing a space, Michael placed it and the memo side-by-side on his desk, flattening them both carefully with his right hand. He dipped a pen in the bottle of ink lying open to one side. Then, lowering his head close to the pages, with his eyes flicking constantly back and forth, he wrote, quickly and confidently, on the bottom of June's letter. She was too nervous to watch over his shoulder. Lifting his pen, he looked at both letters on his desk. His mouth crept into its easy smile, as, pinching them between thumb and finger at the top, he held them up in a plane in front of her, like two photographs he had just developed.

To her eye, the signatures looked identical. It was indeed something of a magic trick. June clapped her hands together. 'Oh! Michael! That's wonderful!'

'Oh, I don't know,' he said, in his element now. 'That "N" isn't quite right . . . and I think the man himself dots his "i"s slightly higher . . . but maybe he was a little tired when he signed' – he held June's letter higher – '*this* one.'

Smiling, she took the letter. 'Really, Michael, thank you so much.'

'No trouble. Just don't let on that I ever helped you with this completely mad scheme.' He paused; his eyes lit up. 'By the way . . .

and I think this is probably above and beyond the call of duty . . . but I don't just do impressions of signatures. I can do voices as well.'

'Er . . . I know. I've heard you do Jack . . .'

'I think, if push came to shove, I could do Henderson. I've only heard him speak once, at the Ministry Christmas do, but it's' – his voice went up a few classes – 'basically Diplomatic Service posh, isn't it?'

'Um . . . well, yes. It's clipped.'

'Clipped, yes,' he said, in a clipped way.

'Sorry, Michael . . . it's a gift, I'm sure, but how does it help?'

He smiled at her and mimed dialling a telephone. Holding the imaginary receiver to his ear, he said, in a clipped, posh, Diplomatic Service voice: 'Hello? Is that Commander Rutter? Commander in charge of the internment camps on the Isle of Man? Oh good. Nigel Henderson here, from the Ministry of Information. Yes. Fine, thank you. Just calling to see if you got that letter, about our researcher coming to visit. You didn't? Oh blast. What the Blitz is doing to the Royal Mail, I don't know. Well, never mind. Another letter should be on the way. What? Oh yes. The researcher: her name is June Murray and she'll be coming on the first. Just a routine visit, to gather some research for us. She'll be carrying a copy of the letter from me explaining her brief. Just do the best you can for her if you would, old man. Thank you so much. The Minister sends his regards.' He replaced the imaginary receiver and looked up, beaming. 'What do you think?' he said in his own voice.

June was smiling herself, although her brow was knitted at the same time. 'I really don't know. Perhaps if you sounded a little less . . . like you were playing Nigel Henderson in a student revue . . .'

'I'll do my best.'

Time took a beat. They looked at each other, and then they both laughed, the hissing, wheezing laughter of two people trying to keep down the sound of their hysteria.

'Goodness me,' said June, eventually. 'Do you think it'll work?'

Michael shook his smiling head. 'Who knows? It can only smooth your passage. And in the very unlikely event Commander

Rutter gets the operator to trace the call, he'll get a Ministry of Information number. How's them apples, as our American cousins say?'

June looked at him in wonderment. This was what it took; for it to have become a game, and for the game to be driven by him. 'And you'll do it?'

Michael nodded. 'If you get me the camp number. They do have telephones on the Isle of Man, don't they? I've never been there, but I've heard the Manx are a little backward—'

To shut him up, June leant across and kissed him on the cheek. His skin felt smoother than any other man's she could remember. 'How can I thank you?' She knew the answer before he said it.

Michael arched his eyebrow. 'Well . . . you could say "yes" to that offer of a drink I made . . . oh, quite some time ago now . . .'

'Well I don't know, my dear,' said Mrs Fricker, eventually. 'I can't see anything wrong with the way it ends. It's perfectly understandable.'

Lulu sighed; she knew that Mrs Fricker was not an easy woman to shift at the best of times, and particularly not when she felt she was already going out of her way to help. That said, it didn't take much for Mrs Fricker to feel she was going out of her way, seeing as her way was always so impractically straight.

'I know it is understandable, Mrs Fricker. That is not my worry with it.' She hesitated. 'Well, it *is* my worry with it. People can understand it in only one way.'

Mrs Fricker sniffed, picked up her affidavit again, and replaced her glasses, which were tied with a string and had been resting for a while on her upholstered chest.

'*Mr Isaac Fabian, of forty-two Hertford Street, Cambridge,*' she read out loud, in a voice suddenly much louder and more booming than usual, '*poses, to my knowledge, no threat to our national security. I am not aware of any anti-British behaviour on his part while under my roof.*' She looked up suspiciously here, as if abruptly wondering if she might have missed some anti-British behaviour somewhere along the line. But Lulu only smiled innocently, so Mrs Fricker made a noise quite close to the classical *harrumph*, and continued: '*Had there been any, he would have been swiftly removed from residence under my roof. He is perfectly quiet and respectable, and seems to have been a good husband and father. In general, I would conclude that he is a fine, decent, upstanding fellow, for a German.*'

'Yes . . .'

'*I remain your most obedient etc., Mrs Randolph Fricker.*'

'Yes . . . you see, Mrs Fricker, that last part . . .'

'I always sign myself that way.'

'No, where you say, *for a German.*' At the edge of her hearing, she heard Rebekka's cry, muffled from upstairs. She was sleeping less during the day now. 'I don't think that that's . . .' Lulu chanced her arm, 'helpful.'

Mrs Fricker took off her glasses and stared at her. 'Do you not? Well, I'm terribly sorry, Mrs Fabian, but if you don't want my support . . .' She waved the paper in the air, as if about to throw it over her shoulder.

'No! Of course, I am very grateful, Mrs Fricker. I truly am.' Thank God Mrs Lambert had not been this difficult, she thought – Lulu had virtually been able to dictate that one. Mrs Fricker, however, had insisted on composing her own testimonial. Lulu rather suspected that, at least in terms of civic responsibility in wartime, Mrs Fricker saw it as her chance to shine.

'I mean, it's all very well, me helping you out, but I'm not so sure we should be letting all those people out of the Isle of Man. I think there's very good reason for some of them to be locked up. We are at war, you know.'

Are we really? crossed Lulu's mind, but luckily she repressed the desire to say it, as sarcasm would have killed any chance of Mrs Fricker lending her considerable weight to her cause, and probably led to eviction on top. Instead, she decided to try a different tactic. 'No, you are quite right, Mrs Fricker. But this will only help Isaac, I assure you. And do not misunderstand me, I think it is a fine letter. All I would say is that . . . the Council, they are very . . . how do you say . . .'

Mrs Fricker raised a warning finger. 'No German, now.'

But it was out before Lulu had a chance to stop: '. . . *bureaucratic.*' Luckily, for her, the word was the same in English. Mrs Fricker held fire; Rebekka's crying grew louder.

'Bossy, you mean? Pernickety?' said Mrs Fricker, raising a never-plucked eyebrow.

'Er . . . yes.'

Bossy and pernickety officialdom was something Mrs Fricker could understand, her late husband Randolph having been sacked from his clerical post with Cambridge City Council following a mix-up in the Guildhall mailing room in the spring of 1934. She had, despite his entreaty to let the matter lie, gone herself to see Randolph's superior – a Mr Wilkins, she had never forgotten – and argued for his reinstatement, only to have the insult compounded by the disdainful insinuation that the mix-up was not a mix-up at all, but a deliberate swapping around of employees' pay packets so as to benefit Mr Fricker and a so-called 'syndicate' of his friends.

In her heart, she had always blamed Cambridge City Council for Mr Fricker's subsequent demise – he lived only two more years, obsessed with plans for a garden shed that was never built – and thus now carried around with her a bitter antagonism to all things bureaucratic. She saw no contradiction between this position and her adherence to the letter of every minute new Civil Defence regulation that came through her door.

'Well, I know what that can be like, I assure you. I wouldn't want to give any of those sort of people the chance to play at being little Hitlers.'

Lulu nodded sagely, concealing a slight disorientation at her landlady's turn of phrase.

Mrs Fricker looked back at her affidavit. 'Right. Well, I'm loath to make changes now that I've written it out so neatly and all . . .'

'Yes, it looks lovely.' Lulu had tried to suggest that Mrs Fricker show her a rough draft first but had been waved away. 'But I was thinking I would go to get it typed up, anyway . . .'

'Were you?' Mrs Fricker looked down at her Basildon Bond, and wondered if this wasn't some kind of affront to her immaculate handwriting.

'Yes. Then I will bring it back for you to sign, of course.'

'I see. Well, all right then.' She handed over the letter.

Lulu smiled her best smile, in mute gratitude.

'If you insist, you can miss out that last part.' Mrs Fricker said it magnanimously, but slightly ruefully, as if knowing that this opportunity to demonstrate to the Council just what a patriotic citizen they had once snubbed would not come again.

In fact, Lulu had no idea how to get her two testimonials typed up, no more than she had an idea of who she could get to provide a third one. Time was passing, more time than she would have liked,

126

since her meeting at the Guildhall, but Mrs Fricker and Mrs Lambert were the only two – to use Rear-Admiral Holloway's term – *straightforwardly* British people she knew. She could have asked Mr Lambert as well, but remembered how Holloway had told her that that would not have been entirely appropriate. In her last letter to Isaac she had explained this, and he had written back to say that she should ignore Holloway's stricture – '*it's just that stupid capitalist thing of regarding a married couple as a single entity,*' he said – but Lulu, however, was convinced that the presentation of the testimonials had to be perfect.

She was thinking about what to do as she pushed Rebekka in her pram down Fitzwilliam Street, towards the museum. The sun was bright, and the sky an almost blinding blue, but virtually all the leaves, which up until recently had clung rusting to the trees, had fallen; every so often she had to bend down to remove large, wet clumps of them from the spokes of the pram's cumbersome wheels. She could feel winter in the air, which seemed almost thinner than in the autumn, as if the change of season was bringing with it an increase not only of cold, but also of altitude. Bekka was in a good mood, sitting up in the pram and pointing at everything in sight, and laughing – she was going through a stage when laughter was her primary response to the new and the exciting, which, for Bekka, included most of the world. Lulu found Bekka's laughter a source of wonder, from the breathy ha-ha-ha she would do virtually on cue, an oddly contrived sound, almost like a polite laugh, to her high-pitched version of an old man's cackle, when she would lose herself to hysteria, brought on by tickling or a piece of particularly appreciated play. As a girl, Lulu had grown up with animals, a cat and two dogs, and it was only when Bekka started to laugh, when she was about nine months old, that she realised with a start that the love she had felt for her daughter up to that point had not been too different from the love she used to have for her pets: that is, a deep, genuine affection motivated entirely by appearance and texture – by the fact that they looked and felt nice. Laughter signalled the beginning of something else – separateness, insight, the first sign that the being she held in her hands was capable of commenting on its universe, rather than simply existing within it – and with this realisation came the transformation of her love into something at once more complicated and more real. Now, Lulu loved hearing Bekka's laugh: remembering *Hamlet*, she thought it felt like the opposite of Claudius's poison, an elixir poured in her ear.

However, today, even the sound of Bekka laughing – and the fact that she was doing it while pointing at a distinguished-looking man with an overwaxed moustache – failed to distract her from her thoughts. She had found herself increasingly obsessed with the mission of obtaining these affidavits, possibly because, for the first time since arriving in Britain, it made her feel usefully employed: a sensation she never had from cleaning the Lamberts' house, nor even, in spite of all the love she felt towards her, from looking after Rebekka. Boredom, she had realised, is one of the less obvious, but no less difficult, symptoms of being a refugee.

Turning over in her head, for the hundredth time, her options, or rather lack of them, she failed at first to recognise the approaching woman, even though the confidence of her tread should have given her away.

'Lulu! Lulu Fabian, isn't it?'

Lulu looked up, confused to hear her name being said so loudly on the street in such a crisp English accent. The woman facing her was dark, and wearing a soft velvet hat, so soft it appeared to be just fronds of plush material piled up on her head, the kind of hat Lulu thought someone like Marlene Dietrich might wear. She looked familiar, but next to her was a tall, fair-haired man, with his overcoat collar raised up around his neck, whom Lulu couldn't place at all.

'Perhaps this will help,' said the woman. '*Lulu! Lulu Fabian, nicht wahr?* I might have said that before, but then I remembered what it says in my little refugee handbook about not shouting on the street in German. We wouldn't want to offend the delicate sensibilities of the English.'

Then she remembered: the woman outside Rear-Admiral Holloway's interview room.

'Hello . . .' said Lulu, in English, extending a hand.

'Lotte Gerard. We met . . .'

'Yes, yes, I remember. How are you?'

'Very well indeed. You must meet my friend, Douglas. Douglas, this is Lulu, a fellow refugee.'

He inclined his head politely. His face looked to her slightly Cubist, as if his features weren't quite arranged regularly on his face. Lulu was surprised that he was English: something about his manner had made her assume he was German.

'Is this your baby?' said Lotte. 'Good heavens, she's beautiful. Hello, beautiful!' Rebekka looked up, and instantly started to laugh. 'Yes, I know I'm *completely* ridiculous. And what would your name be?'

'She's called Rebekka.'

'Rebekka, how gorgeous!' She turned to Lulu with a mock-baleful eye. 'I don't remember you saying anything about a baby outside that dreadful man's office.'

'I'm not sure I did . . .'

'No, probably didn't get a chance with me blathering on as usual. Did I ask you a *single* thing about yourself?'

Lulu smiled at the memory. 'One or two things . . .'

'Well, that's not enough. We must remedy that. Why don't you come in for a cup of tea? We could raid my friends downstairs for some of their extraordinary chocolate gâteau.'

Lulu looked round, and saw a series of sugar and sponge creations spread like the landscape of a child's dream across the window of Fitzbillies, the cake shop above which, she now remembered, Lotte had said she lived.

'Tea and cakes,' said Lotte. 'I believe that's what the correct etiquette is, here in our treasured parent country?'

'Oh, I wouldn't want to put you to any—'

Lotte touched her arm. 'Now, now: let's not *overdo* the Englishness.'

The inside of Lotte's flat was a more welcoming space than Lulu would have imagined. It was warm, to begin with, because, as she noticed when they entered, the gas fire had been left on. On the mantelpiece stood a reassuring family photograph of a handsome man, in uniform, draping his arms around two beaming boys. Lulu wondered how long he had been away, and whether, when he came back, he would appreciate what his wife had done to their living-room. She couldn't believe that a man would want so many Persian rugs draped all over the floor, so many plants and flowers everywhere, and so much art on the walls – every space was claimed by a Picasso print, or a Degas, or some more obscure, modern artist whom she didn't know. It made the room a riot of colour, as if the icing of the cakes, yellow and blue and ice-white and brown, had burst through from the floor beneath. She wondered too if he would appreciate his wife enjoying the company of tall, blond men, but then felt slightly ashamed at the thought, because it implied a situation for which she had no evidence, and also because it was so old-fashioned.

Lotte had vanished into the kitchen, in order to make the tea, leaving Lulu alone with Douglas, who stood looking out of the window, his back operatically framed by the neo-Grecian pillars of the Fitzwilliam Museum. He reminded Lulu a little of her brother-in-law Gerhard; in a more general sense, of the type of man her parents had probably expected her to marry. He turned round, and she felt herself blush, the redness of her cheeks made more obvious by the light from the window as he moved away from it. She wanted to use his physical similarity to her brother-in-law as an explanation for why she had been looking at him, but felt that the proffering of that information to someone she had just met would be construed as overfamiliar, so just looked down, concentrating her attention on Bekka, dozing with her on the sofa.

'So . . . Mrs Fabian . . .' his voice surprised Lulu, not so much because it had an unusual depth, but because it made her realise with a start that he hadn't spoken a word up to this point, 'how old is your daughter?'

'She was two this summer.'

He came over and knelt down towards Rebekka, who had thrown her head back over Lulu's arm in the way of children suddenly drowned by sleep: together, mother and child had a touch of pietà. 'She's lovely. She looks very like you.'

Lulu looked up, wondering how to interpret this; but his eyes were neutral, unencumbered by implied significance.

'Thank you. She looks more like her father, I think.'

The intention of this reply was equally straightforward, but when Douglas stood upright, nodding, she felt that he had taken it with just a hint of rebuff – as if the mention of Isaac had been deliberate, the putting up of a sexual shield. She felt slightly surprised at herself for thinking these thoughts. Although physically little changed from the girl who had been much courted in Königsberg, for some time now she had ceased to imagine herself as attractive to men. Not because she was married; because she was a refugee with a baby.

'Where are you from?' he said, lowering himself in the armchair opposite.

'A place called Königsberg. In East Prussia. I do not think you will have heard of it . . .'

'Kant's home town, wasn't it?'

Lulu's face betrayed just a hint of gratitude. 'Yes! That is our . . . how do you say . . .'

'Claim to fame?'

Lulu laughed. 'Yes, I think so. That and the seven bridges.'

'The seven bridges?'

'The city is built on a river, the Pregel, and there are seven bridges that cross it.'

'Why are they famous?'

'Well, they are not really . . .'

'Oh, but they *are*,' said Lotte, returning from the kitchen with a tray, on which she'd arranged a selection of Fitzbillies' best around a beautiful Oriental teapot, reminiscent of Aladdin's lamp. 'I'm from Berlin, where, let me tell you, we really don't bother much with the provinces; and yet even *I've* heard of the seven bridges of Königsberg. Do the townspeople still come out every Sunday and walk them?'

'Yes! We would all do it, my whole family, every Sunday,' said Lulu.

'It's some sort of game, isn't it? Or riddle, or something?'

'That's right. We would be seeing if it is possible to walk round the bridges and . . . sorry . . . I . . .'

'Say it in German,' said Lotte, setting down the tray on a small table covered with a deep red tablecloth.

Lulu did so, feeling the flush come back to her cheeks as she spoke. German had come to seem to her like a forbidden language: she even spoke to Bekka now mainly in English. Something about the Englishman listening made her feel more self-conscious still, as if she were showing him a shameful part of herself.

'I see,' said Lotte, when she had finished. Turning to Douglas, she said: 'The Sunday walk involves trying to work out if they can find a route around the city, beginning and ending in the same place, where they would have to cross each bridge only once.'

'Really? How interesting,' he said, although Lulu found it hard to believe that he did find it so. His manner seemed underpinned by a polite boredom, in the same family tree but at the other end of the branches to Lotte's aristocratic enthusiasm. 'And is there?'

Lulu shook her head. 'We never found it. And a famous mathematician once worked out that it is not possible. But still we used to do it every Sunday, and so do – *did* – many others. When I was little, I used to spend hours with a map planning new . . .' She looked to Lotte.

'Routes.'

'Routes, yes. I always believed that there was a secret way.' She looked down, not sure why speaking these words was making her throat tighten. 'I probably still do.'

There was a pause. Lotte lifted the teapot into the air. 'Shall I be mother?' she said.

Douglas, his impassive face cracking for the first time, burst into laughter. 'How do you do it?' he said.

'What?'

'Sound so English!'

'I watch. I listen,' she said. An amber stream emerged from the spout of the Aladdin teapot into one of her white china cups.

After the tea had been handed round, and slices of Battenberg and chocolate gâteau dispensed on willow-pattern plates – the whole tea ceremony having been invested by its host with a patently ironic air – Lotte dusted cake crumbs off her fingers and said: 'Now, Lulu. How have you been getting on with your stupid testimonials, as demanded by the silly little man at the Guildhall?'

132

'Oh, quite well, thank you.' She put her Battenberg on her plate, holding back her instinct to stuff the lot into her mouth in one go, its sweetness was so rare. 'I have two already. What about you?'

'Well, that's the beauty of having lived in this country for years. I had friends practically knocking down my door to do it. So I could pick and choose which of them was liable to write the most favourable and elegant letter. Couldn't I, Douglas?' The Englishman did his polite inclination of the head again. 'So my little missives have gone off to the Council some time ago. In fact, I received a letter last month from one of their minions thanking me for them and promising that the matter of my father's custody will be reviewed shortly, bearing – how did he put it – yes, "bearing this new information in mind".' Lotte laughed, an unfeminine, throaty roar. 'Why these people have to use such absurdly pompous language is beyond me.'

Rebekka stirred in Lulu's arms; gingerly, she put her teacup and cake on the table, and laid her prone on the adjacent sofa cushion.

'I was wondering . . .' said Lulu, hesitantly, 'if you could help me, in fact.'

'Of course.'

'Well . . . do you have a typewriter? There is a notice in the shop near where we live advertising the services of a typist but she costs—'

Lotte shook her head. 'No, my dear, I don't. But I know someone who does.'

'Who?'

Lotte turned round, with a prompting smile.

'Me,' said Douglas. 'On which, not only did I write an affidavit for Lotte's father, I typed up the other two as well.'

'Some of your best work, I thought,' said Lotte.

'That's *too* kind of you.'

'Douglas is a playwright,' she expanded, in response to Lulu's confused expression.

'Failed . . .'

Lotte waved away his self-deprecation with an imperious wave. 'Nonsense. You just haven't quite written your masterpiece yet. He's a good typist as well, aren't you, Douglas? What's your speed now?'

'I'm afraid I wouldn't know about that.'

'At least fifty w.p.m., I shouldn't wonder. Why, if we got you a twin-set and a chiffon scarf, I imagine you could get yourself a good job as some businessman's secretary. Whether you'd be prepared to perform *all* the duties that come with the job would be up to you . . .'

Lulu blushed, again; she noticed that Douglas also looked a little embarrassed by Lotte's insinuation.

'I'd be happy to type up your letters for you, Mrs Fabian,' he said, in his rather stately way.

'Oh, thank you, that's so kind of you, Mr . . .' Lulu searched for his surname, then realised she hadn't been told it, 'Mr Douglas.'

He smiled; Lulu noticed that one side of his mouth appeared to go further up his face than the other, accentuating its asymmetry. 'My family name is Lean. But Douglas is fine, really.'

'Well, what shall I do? Shall I send them to you or . . . ?'

'Send them here, and I'll pass them on. Or better still, drop them round as soon as you can,' said Lotte. 'I don't want you staying out of my way for weeks this time round.'

Lulu smiled, externally and internally, at this invitation, this sense that she was being made a permanent member of Lotte's salon.

'And you are sure this is no trouble for you . . . ?'

'Absolutely: I'd be pleased to help in any way I can.'

Lulu felt herself inclining her head politely, in respectful mimicry of him.

'Actually, Douglas, if that's really the case . . .' said Lotte, after a short pause, mischief sparkling in her narrowed eyes, 'why don't you write Lulu's third testimonial for her?'

He turned to her, his face set in a quizzical expression. 'Pardon?'

'Why don't you write a glowing report of Mr Fabian?'

'Well, primarily, because I have never met Mr Fabian.'

'Tush, tush. You're a dramatist. Just imagine he's one of your "good" characters. The hero, in fact, of your next unwritten play!'

'Lotte,' said Lulu, 'really, I could never expect Mr Lean . . . Douglas . . . to do that.'

'Why not?'

'Well . . . because he would have to lie. And I am sure it is against the law.'

'Oh yes, it's probably high treason, and Douglas will go to the gallows. For goodness' sake, who's going to know?'

Lulu, although she could feel how much she wanted this third testimonial – felt it in her stomach like hunger pains – felt also a certain rage at Lotte: at being put in this awkward position, and also at how much, for Lotte, it was all just a game. It was all just aristocratic fun.

'No, Lotte. It is too much to ask.'

'Oh, Lulu, don't be so—'

'Lotte,' said Lulu, her face darkening. '*Es ist zu viel.*'

Lotte's face, on an arc towards its natural resting-place of naughty smile, halted. She shrugged her shoulders, disguising with a show of diffidence her shock at being chastened.

'I mean . . . I know you are only trying to help . . .' said Lulu, backpedalling. Somehow, telling her off in German, in front of the Englishman, had made the confrontation worse. She was starting to understand the full force of the English caricature, how to their ears every sentence in her language sounded like an order.

Lotte shrugged her shoulders again, and took a cigarette from her handbag.

'Well . . . it's a lovely idea, anyway,' said Douglas, breaking the momentary silence. 'If I *had* met your husband, I'm sure I would be only too pleased to write a testimonial. Assuming, of course, that he isn't actually a spy. He's not, is he?'

'Yes,' said Lulu, rather miserably, 'he is the only Jew in Germany in the pay of the Nazis.'

Douglas stared at her; Lotte even took her sulky gaze from the window for a second to look at her too. Then, catching a twist of a smile unfolding around the corners of Lulu's mouth, he began to laugh.

'God, you two! It's you lot who are supposed not to get our sense of humour, not the other way round. What's going on?'

Then they all laughed together, Lotte coming breezily out of her huff: her nature was too light to carry the weight of a grudge for long.

*

By the time Lulu left, darkness had begun to fall. In peacetime, the street would have been lit by now. Opening the door by the side of Fitzbillies, she could feel how the cold had become more radical; there was no wind, so the air did not bite, but rather gripped her face, sticking to her cheeks like fingers to frost. She gently drew a woollen blanket over a still-sleeping Rebekka, and took a breath, to steel herself to the task of stumbling the oversize pram down the steps to the street. She wrapped her palms round the wooden handle, first one gloved hand, then the other.

'Can I help?'

She turned round, to discover Douglas Lean, with his overcoat back on, the collar again worn up around his neck, standing behind her; in the half light of the hall corridor, he looked a foreboding presence, like a dark angel holding behind him his unspread black wings.

'Are you leaving too?'

'Yes. I remembered that I have a meeting at six. Please. Allow me.'

He moved past her, towards the pram; immediately, she gripped the handle tighter, but then, overcoming her instincts, let go. Douglas did not, as she expected, take the handle himself, but crouched down to one side, and then stood up, lifting the entire antique, the enormous baby bus, in his arms, as if the pram were the baby herself. He did it smoothly, with no weightlifting jerk, so as not to wake the child. Lulu held the door open, and he passed by. She watched, stifling a laugh as his back receded down the stairs, framed on either side by the pram's huge spoked wheels: it made him look, she thought, less frightening – less like a dark angel and more like a Model-T Ford. She noticed, as well, that he seemed to walk with a limp, although she could not perceive whether this was simply due to the weight he was carrying.

'Thank you,' she said, joining him at street level.

He was looking down into the pram and smiling. 'It was nothing. She's light as a feather.'

'I think the pram is not, though.'

He smiled again, revealing, this close, crinkled flesh around the eyes. 'No. But it does the heart good to see one like that still working. I think my mother must have pushed me around in something similar.'

'It brings back many memories?'

'Exactly.'

Lulu felt herself warming to him. After his initial distance, now, she felt, he was easy to talk to; specifically, easy to talk to in English – she felt almost as if she were using him to practise the language, to move up from the awkwardness of polite interchange to the ease of jokes and banter. She was using him, in other words, to learn how to *be* English; and this became so much her reading of the situation that it didn't occur to her that they were also flirting. 'Anyway . . .' she said. 'It was very nice to meet you.'

'You too.'

She swung the pram round in front of her. 'Goodbye.'

Lulu waited for him to respond in kind; instead, there was that inclination of the head again. For a second, she was unsure what to do: whether she was allowed to leave without him saying goodbye.

'Mrs Fabian . . .' he said, eventually, looking at her keenly. His eyes were grey as stone.

'Yes?'

'I feel quite shoddy about not agreeing to Lotte's suggestion. About writing a testimonial for your husband.'

'Shoddy?'

'Guilty. Not right in myself.'

'Really, Mr Lean' – she couldn't quite bring herself to call him Douglas; it felt contrived – 'you should not be troubled by it. It was only Lotte being silly. How can you write a testimonial of Isaac when you do not know Isaac?'

'But perhaps I *can* know him,' he said.

'How?'

'You can tell me about him.'

Lulu frowned. 'Now?'

Douglas laughed. 'No! I thought we could meet . . . perhaps for lunch, or, if you prefer, just for an hour at your house – and you could paint a little portrait of Mr Fabian in words for me. That should do the trick. As Lotte says, I am supposed to be a playwright. With your words, and a little bit of imagination on my part, I'm sure I could write as accurate a testimonial as one of his oldest friends.'

Lulu's first thought was, *Isaac's oldest friends?* Where are they? The intellectual gang he used to carouse and debate with at university had all managed swiftly to lose contact with him as soon as it was no longer a joke to be associated with a Jew; a testimonial from one of them now would be a fearful thing to read. And his friends from childhood, most of them she had never met; initially they had refused to meet her because she was not Jewish, and later most of them had vanished, because they were.

'I do not know, Mr Lean. It is very kind of you, I am sure, but I am very concerned that I should do the testimonials . . . how you say . . .'

'By the book?'

'Yes. If that means as correctly as possible, yes.'

'You think that if you take a short cut, and it's found out, they'll throw out the other two as well? And you'll have spoilt your husband's chances of release further?'

'A short cut . . . yes.'

He raised a hand to his face, scratching his temple. 'Hmm. Well . . . I think you should realise that you'll be about the only refugee in Britain compiling these testimonials who's *not* taking any short cuts. Lotte's the exception: most of them, like you, will not have had time to acquire several British friends, so I imagine the whole thing will be rife with fakes, aliases and semi-fictions.'

Lulu nodded, not entirely sure what he was saying – too much time with Lotte seemed to have led him to believe that, whatever they might pretend, all Germans could speak perfect English – but thought she had grasped the gist.

'So, fundamentally, what you're saying is,' he continued, in a new tone she had not heard before: definitive, brooking no contradiction, 'we need to do this thing properly. The imperative is on us to get our picture of Mr Fabian – and of course my long and informed acquaintance with him – right. My conclusion, therefore, is . . . lunch. An hour at your house simply won't be enough.'

Lulu peered at him in the failing light. She wished there was no blackout so that the streetlights would come on, allowing her to see his face properly. Without the help of their mercury wash, she could not read his expression, and therefore could not guess what his motives were: genuine, sexual or, worst of all, playful – that it was all to him a chance for some sport. But then a car passed, its shielded lights illuminating him for a few seconds, and his asymmetrical features seemed at least set, at least not further lopsided by a smirk. It was enough. Why not? she thought. Why not take a short cut for once? She had walked so many long roads only to reach this far.

Isaac felt that he could see something of his father in Rabbi Metzer. But then, he felt he could also see something of Isidor in Rabbi Nadel, Rabbi Schroeder, Rabbi Thalberg and Rabbi Hirsch, all of whom were presently shuffling about him like a swaying field of his fathers. The rabbinical look, he thought, is not one that allows for much variation.

'Eleven hundred and fifty-two,' said Rabbi Metzer, finally bending his frame up from a stooping position, 'not counting the black ones.'

'What's wrong with the black ones?' said Kaufmann, who had been lurking behind Isaac, more embarrassed than his friend by his lack of belief in the presence of priests.

'We explained that we were interested only in white beans.'

'Did you?' said Isaac. 'No one told me. Are the black ones not kosher?'

In response, the rabbi held up a black bean and bent his head towards it, closing his left eye; all he needed was a jeweller's eyeglass to appear as if he were examining one of the world's most valuable diamonds. 'By themselves, yes. But our Rabbinical Seminary here has decreed that eating the black ones *with* the white ones constitutes a version of Hilchos Basar B'chalav – the prohibition of the eating of milk and meat toge—'

'Yes, I know what it means.'

Rabbi Metzer raised an eyebrow, or at least appeared to – he had so much hair in so many places on his face that it was difficult to tell – but the abundance of grey fur above his right eye certainly slunk in a generally upwards direction, perhaps in doubt that this young man with no *yarmekel*, no *tzitzit*, whom he had never seen at any of his services, should possess any detailed scriptural knowledge. Isaac raised an eyebrow back, partly as a visual retort – he felt, in this overwhelmingly familiar situation, unable entirely to control his adolescent rebellious streak – but mainly because he was amazed at the ability of religious Jews always to make life as difficult for themselves as possible.

He had brought the beans because word had spread that the seventeen inhabitants of the rabbis' house – a white stuccoed building not on the Promenade, like most of the internees' houses in Central Camp, but set further up the cliff, on the road to Ramsay – would not eat the food provided in the refectory. Much of the food available in the refectory was theoretically kosher – much of it was vegetarian, in fact – but the rabbis had decided that, since the kitchens had not been ratified by the Beth Din, or any other Kashrut monitoring organisation, the only thing they were prepared to eat during their sojourn on the Isle of Man was beans – and now, it turned out, only white beans. They were willing to swap all their other rations for anyone bringing them white beans. Isaac, mainly out of curiosity, had volunteered for the task of methodically collecting his housemates' rations of beans, storing them in a metal bucket covered with greaseproof paper, and – with Kaufmann's help – carting them past a nodding sentry up the Ramsay road to the house, where Rabbi Metzer counted them out one by one in order to set them against whatever elaborately constructed bartering system the Rabbinical Seminary had decided was appropriate. Isaac and Kaufmann had already been standing in their living-room for over an hour.

'Reuben!' shouted Rabbi Metzer to Rabbi Nadel, who was seated next to him. 'Deaf as a post,' he said to Isaac by way of explanation. Then, louder: 'Reuben!' Rabbi Nadel looked round with a benevolent expression on what you could see of his face above his beard. 'Go fetch the most recent food box.'

'Eh?'

'The most recent food box, Reuben.'

'The shofar? Why? It's not Rosh Hashana. And besides, I don't think we have one. I've been worried about what we're going to use to trumpet in the New Year—'

Rabbi Metzer raised his eyes to heaven. '*The food box*, Reuben. What else are we doing here but working out the food? Even if you can't hear, you might guess, already.'

Rabbi Nadel continued to look rather confused, but got up and headed in the direction of the stark kitchen. Rabbis Thalberg and Hirsch, seeming to have lost interest, wandered out of the living-room, although not before Isaac noticed that their beards were almost exactly the same shape and length – together they looked like some sort of landscaped garden feature, a pair of identical small, dark hedges, an exquisite piece of Old Testament topiary.

'But, Rabbi,' said Isaac, more to fill the ensuing silence than because he was genuinely bothered, 'the Torah says simply that we must not bathe a kid in its mother's milk. I don't see how that can apply to black and white beans . . .'

Rabbi Metzer's expression sank easily into the half-sad smile that the religiously certain like to direct at the querying faithless. 'Kashrut, my boy, is not simply about not eating those foods which the ancients knew would contaminate. It is also about the pattern – the fish with scales, the cattle with cloven feet, these are the patterns – patterns which appeal to Hashem, and which it is our duty to try to replicate for Him. The black bean spoils the pattern.'

'I see. So it isn't simply a way of further restricting yourself – past the already immensely restrictive point of just eating beans – because restriction and self-deprivation is your way to feeling holy?'

'*Fabian* . . .' said Kaufmann, but not before Rabbi Metzer's face moved from complacency to disgust, as if there were suddenly a very bad smell in the room.

Even in the bullish mood the rabbis' house had brought out in him, this change of expression surprised Isaac, enough perhaps to tone down his views a little, until he realised that, no, in fact, there really *was* a very bad smell in the room.

'Shlomo!' said Rabbi Metzer to Rabbi Schroeder, who had been sitting quietly reading the Onchan Camp newspaper, the *Onchan Pioneer*, and only occasionally shifting a little in his seat. 'That's disgusting! How many times are you going to do that?'

Rabbi Schroeder, having looked up with an approximation of innocence on his face, saw from his colleague's conviction that there was no point.

'I'm sorry, Aaron, but it's all these *beans*.'

'Well, you don't see me breaking wind every five minutes.'

I'm not sure *see* is the right word, thought Isaac – there are other senses that spring quicker to mind. He tried not to look at Kaufmann, whose face belied a man struggling between awkwardness and hysteria.

'So that must just be your *particular* digestion,' said Rabbi Schroeder, beginning to sound a little plaintive. 'I know Reuben and Rabbi Thalberg both have a problem with it too. That's probably why they left the room!'

'Really. Well, I don't remember you raising this issue at the Seminary.'

'I didn't think about it then! I didn't know how bad it was going to be!'

Rabbi Metzer stroked his beard – which, given the size of it, involved opening his hand wide, as if gauging the weight of a bowling ball, and then scraping his hand forcefully through its matted grey length. He had an ability somehow to render this gesture aggressive, rather than simply ruminative. 'So you're saying, then, that the decision of the Seminary – voted for unanimously by all members of this house, yourself included, and since verified by Midrash Halakah, included in our prayers as part of our service to Hashem – you're saying now that this decision was wrong?'

Rabbi Schroeder looked down, back into his newspaper.

'I'm not saying it was *wrong*,' he muttered. 'Just that it's had this . . . unforeseen effect . . .'

By now, Rabbi Nadel had returned to the living-room, holding a large cardboard box. His head moved between the two arguing holy men, smiling obliviously at each in turn. Then, he himself farted, loudly and expressively, no obvious recognition of which action was betrayed in his still-smiling face. Kaufmann flung himself backwards, making the piglet snort of the man whose laughter now has to come out, if only through the nose; Isaac closed his eyes; Rabbi Schroeder looked up, and, raising both his eyebrows at Rabbi Metzer, conveyed clearly that he interpreted this as some sort of victory.

'For eleven hundred and fifty-two beans,' said Rabbi Metzer, choosing to ignore the whole incident, 'we can give you' – he peered into Rabbi Nadel's box – 'two tins of corned beef, two loaves of bread, a pound of cheese, three bottles of beer, four slices of smoked turkey, six apples and' – his brow puckered, as if working out an extremely complex calculation – '*three* oranges.'

'That's not going to go far in a house of thirty-four men,' said Isaac. He looked to Kaufmann for support, but he was still lost, breathing in gasps and staring at the carpet.

Rabbi Metzer, removing two bottles of wine from the box, shrugged his shoulders. 'Next time bring us more beans.'

'It takes a long time to collect this many. Over a week.'

'I can't help that, I'm afraid. We have the whole of Central and Onchan Camp coming here with beans every day. One house in Onchan brought us three buckets yesterday, over three thousand beans.'

'You count them all?' said Isaac, incredulously.

During this dialogue, four tins of corned beef, two boxes of eggs, a string of sausages, a loaf of bread and five bars of chocolate had left the box. Rabbi Metzer opened his palms. 'Ours is a religion of numbers.'

'Isaac . . .' said Kaufmann, placing a hand on his shoulder – one of the first times he had not called him by his surname – 'let's just take the box and go.'

Isaac looked at him, and realised from his complexion that he needed to be outside: whether this was so he might fully release his laughter or just so he could take in some breaths unpolluted by the scent of digested beans, Isaac wasn't sure.

'All right,' said Isaac, crouching down to pick up the box. 'Thank you, Rabbi. We'll come back next week with more beans.'

'Thank you, my boy. And you, my boy,' said Rabbi Metzer, reverting to the slightly unctuous tone that, as a pious man, he clearly preferred.

Isaac and Kaufmann bowed their heads together and left the room. Just as they left the house, they heard the distant quack of Rabbi Nadel's digestive system releasing itself once more.

'*Reuben!*'

Shutting the door, Isaac said, 'Come Rosh Hashana, I don't think they will have that much trouble finding something to replace the blowing of the shofar, after all.'

Kaufmann virtually fell with laughter down the steps into the fresh sea air.

Wolfgang Weber, sculptor, collagist, Dadaist, poet, composer and constructor of *The Basilica of Masturbatory Madness*, placed his hands around the half-formed head on the table in front of him; they sank satisfyingly into the temples. Porridge was not the perfect medium in which to sculpt a bust, but Weber's natural collage technique, which always involved augmenting his primary material with whatever else he could find – in this case toothpaste tubes, scraps of camp newspaper, cardboard, twigs, clothing rags, doodles, bottle tops and pages of print from various sources – created enough ballast to hold together the viscous oats, at least in the short term. Whether the sculpture could ever last like a clay piece, fired in the kiln, was doubtful, but the idea of longevity was alien to Weber's Dadaist outlook anyway. Art was not defined, for him, by its durability.

'Are you finished?' said Isaac, who was growing bored. This was the second time in three days he had been made to wait for ages while someone performed a peculiar microscopic action with their hands in front of him. His back was hurting from sitting on the one tiny wooden chair in the room.

'Don't be ridiculous,' said Weber, freeing one hand from his work in order to sprinkle flakes of tobacco from a leather pouch onto some cigarette papers: the flakes were dry and made an unpleasant crinkling sound when rolled. 'We've been going only two hours.'

'I don't know why I agreed to it in the first place.'

'Vanity, I would say,' said the artist, without looking up.

Isaac smiled. 'Possibly . . .' he said, although, having seen a selection of Weber's work – in which, should there be a human subject, he or she would rarely be rendered in any way recognisable – he doubted that that could indeed be his prime motivation. He chose not to say this, as to be so concerned with the figurative may have made him appear, to Weber, bourgeois.

He looked out of the window – where the view, as from all the internees' houses, was beautiful, even when, as presently, the sky was darkening over the sea – and tried to ward off a deepening of his boredom. The problem with boredom was not just that it was, well, boring – it also tended to exacerbate his depression. When there was nothing else to do but look out of the window, his thoughts would implode, leaving him with nothing else in his body except a dull, aching need to see Lulu and Rebekka. Weber was not helping. Isaac, who had come to know him better since the meeting in the refectory, generally thought of him as the least boring of men; but he had not known – until now – that his wild ideas, his habit of talking as fast as he could about anything and everything, his crazy stunts, all that manic energy became compressed into a quiet and intense focus when concentrating on his work.

His gaze returned to the room. Weber had covered it with sketches, most of them in blackout charcoal, which he had scraped off various windows of the house. The majority were his trademark abstract collages, although every so often there would be a more conventional figurative portrait. He had also grafted a number of three-dimensional structures to the walls – timber triangles, wastepaper pyramids, a nail stalactite hung from the ceiling, and around what would have been the fireplace there was a canvas awning decorated with litter and seaweed. The whole effect was to give the room the appearance of a cave, with distinct formations and areas, created not from stone but from trash: a garbage grotto.

'How do your roommates put up with all this?' he said.

Weber ran a piece of Isaac's nose between finger and thumb, extending the tip. 'They accept that I'm a great artist. It's very good of them.'

'But there's hardly room for their beds!'

'I can't agree.' He nodded his head in the direction of the corners, without taking his eyes off the bust. 'Ackermann sleeps there, and Herzog there.'

'What about you?'

'I sleep in the kennel.'

'Pardon?'

Weber tutted. 'Can you keep your head still?'

Isaac moved his head back round to where it had been prior to his double-take. 'What do you mean, you sleep in the kennel?'

'There's a kennel out the back – in the gardens between here and Hutchinson.'

'A big kennel?'

'Previous occupant was a Great Dane. I've converted it into my bedroom. There's a small bed in there, some blankets – all I need. I sleep there at night. Sometimes, when the German bombers fly over, I come out and bark.'

Isaac stared at him, wondering if he was joking, but Weber didn't look up. 'Are you mad?'

He shrugged, stubbing out his cigarette. 'Probably. As I said, I'm a great artist.'

A silence followed, except for the odd, squelching sound produced by fingers on porridge. To avoid sinking back into boredom, Isaac forced his thoughts to the political – a safe-house in his head. He began to wonder, as he had done before, about this art of Weber's, about its relationship to politics: specifically, about its *revolutionariness*. Weber's art, entirely representative of the important art of the moment, indeed of the important art of the first part of the century, was clearly revolutionary, in an artistic sense – it was undeniably overturning the conventions and expectations of its own genre. But was it genuinely revolutionary, which in Isaac's terms meant did it contribute in any way to the actual revolution, to the eventual overthrow of those who owned the means of production? This type of art was often described as being anti-bourgeois, but was it? The answer surely was no. It was only against the bourgeois in terms of taste (and even then, *which* bourgeois? Most art dealers, buyers and critics Isaac had ever heard of were intensely bourgeois), and taste was a frippery, a rootless thing – upsetting taste caused no deep, structural social quake. Modern art, Isaac decided, was perpetrating a purely formal revolution, or rather, a purely internal revolution, the after-effects of which extended no further than itself. Art – at least art that did not depict revolution itself, art that was not Delacroix's *Liberty Leading the People* – would always be at one remove from the actual. The only thing its modernisation could do was *symbolise* revolution, and Isaac had little time for symbols.

Which abstruse and tortuous thinking was essentially Isaac's way of becoming comfortable with the realisation that he actually preferred Weber's figurative portraits, a handful of which stood out on the weird wash of his walls like friends in an otherwise unfamiliar dream. As if reading his thoughts, Weber said: 'The portraits I do for cash.'

'Really?'

'Yes. Amazing how much some men in this camp have managed to smuggle out of the Fatherland. Unfortunately, they're not prepared to part with it for real art, hence the conservative pseudo-realist icons you see before you.'

'Real cash? Not camp coupons?'

'I'll take coupons if I have to. Which reminds me, what are you giving me for this?'

Isaac laughed incredulously. 'Hold on. This was *your* idea. You told me my face was perfect for an idea you had for a bust.'

'Never said it would be free.'

'Now you *are* joking, aren't you?'

Weber looked up from his work, dipping his fingers into a bowl of water next to the bust, for all the world like a fastidious diner pausing in the middle of eating a lobster. 'It's always best, I find, if there is some financial transaction at the wellspring of a work of art.'

'Do you?'

'Yes. I know that such an idea offends your Marxist sensibilities . . .'

'That's why you said it, wasn't it?'

'Partly. But also because I hear, on the grapevine, that you made a recent visit to the rabbis' house . . .'

'I can give you a tin of corned beef.'

Weber shook his head. 'The same grapevine told me that you picked up some fruit.' He moved closer in to the bust, smoothing down the top.

'What kind of grapevine is this that spreads secret information about rabbinical fruit?'

'Kaufmann.'

'Thought so.' Isaac smiled. He knew Kaufmann was always keen to impress Weber. 'You want fruit, rather than meat?'

'What did you get?'

'Six apples, and . . .' Isaac reached behind him and into the pocket of his coat, draped on the back of the wooden chair. 'Three oranges. Of which this' – he produced it and held it in the air, like a little sun – 'is the last one.'

'Done.'

'What is?'

'It's a deal. Your orange will do nicely.'

Isaac looked at his orange with some sense of loss: although food in general was more plentiful on the island than on the mainland, fruit, and especially fruit not indigenous to Britain, was still scarce. His mother, alive to the scourges of scurvy and rickets, had always done wonderful things with fruit. 'Fine,' he said, throwing it over, not sure what he was gaining from this.

Weber caught it. With his sculptor's hands, he peeled it quickly, tickling the flesh from the pith. 'Do you want this?' he said, holding up the peeled orange.

'What?'

He held it out on his palm. 'I don't really like them. I can taste their colour too much.'

Isaac leant over and cautiously took it back from him. 'What game are you playing now?'

'No game. This is what I'm after.' He opened his other palm: a pyramid of peel unfurled.

Isaac looked up at him. 'Do you know, for some time now, I've been wanting to know the recipe for your home-made marmalade.'

Weber laughed, taking out his tobacco pouch. 'Try again.'

Isaac racked his brains, halving the orange, and placing a segment into his mouth thoughtfully. The fruit tasted sweet, with just a hint of sourness, like one of this orange's distant ancestors had been cross-bred with a lemon. 'It's something artistic, I suppose,' he said, having swallowed. 'You'll be covering my face on that bust with bits of peel, like some kind of modernist acne.'

'Good try. But too terrible a waste. Some things are more important than art.' And with that, he dropped three segments of peel into his tobacco. 'Nothing else will keep it moist,' he said, shaking the pouch like a dice box, then tying the string on top into a tight knot. 'Want to come and look at yourself?'

Isaac blinked. 'What? It's finished?'

Weber nodded, picking up a towel to dry his palms.

'I thought you said we'd be here for at least another two hours?'

'Well, I changed my mind.'

Isaac's face became sardonic. 'Don't tell me. You're a great artist.'

'Exactly.'

Isaac levered himself out of the wooden chair, his back clicking and his feet tingling with pins and needles. He walked round the side of the porridge-head. Weber's post-Cubist technique ensured that Isaac was not greeted at the front by a sudden reveal of his own features, as would have been the case with a straightforward bust. Rather, looking at the sculpture side on, he could see sections of what he took to be his nose and eyes apparently protruding from his temples. It was in fact the best way to see it. From a static position in front, Isaac thought the bust a mess – he couldn't locate himself, or indeed anything resembling a face, within it at all – but he was prepared to admit that, taking his walk round it into account – adding, as it were, his 360-degree memory to the image – he could see how it was indeed a representation of him: like all modern art, it managed to exaggerate its subject while simultaneously obscuring it.

'It's beautiful,' said Isaac, because he felt he ought, and then coloured red as Weber burst out laughing.

'If you say so yourself!'

'Well, I didn't mean that I'm . . .'

'Oh, but Fabian, you *are*. You're a curly-haired Kafka: your hair, your eyes, your glasses. You're the living, breathing, physical archetype of the intellectual Jew.'

Isaac nodded, not entirely sure how to take this – not entirely sure either in what way it was beautiful; but Weber had already moved on.

'Do you like the glasses?'

'Where are the glasses?'

The artist tutted. 'Here,' he said, pointing to some kind of oblong, metal construction balanced off one ear, as if it was obvious, as if it was the most glasses-like object in the world.

'Oh. Yes. I see. Weber . . .' said Isaac, hesitantly – it had been something he had been wondering for a while, 'are you not Jewish?'

Weber looked up from the side of the bust, with something close to genuine surprise on his always ironic face. 'Me? No! What makes you think that?'

'Well, most of us are . . .'

'Joke, Fabian. I know why you thought it. But no . . .' He twisted his finger slowly into an elaborate theatrical point at himself. 'Look at my eyes. Are they not green? My hair? What's left of it. Is it not sandy? Blond almost? Oh no, I'd throw Hitler's scientists terribly off the scent. Aryan to the core.'

'So what are you doing here?'

He shook his head. 'Jews. Never pay a bit of attention to anyone else. Particularly when it comes to persecution.' He bent double, screwing up his face, and crooking a finger across his nose; his voice tightened into the nasal spit Isaac recognised – from his friends at university, from listening to German radio, from hearing people do it in England – as the goyish idea of how Jews speak. 'Oh Jahweh, everybody else gets off scot-free – *vy are ve ze only vuns viz all dis trouble?*' He unbent, and moved close to Isaac, mock-aggressively; Isaac smelt what a strange mix he was, tobacco and porridge and dried sweat. 'You're not the only ones Hitler had it in for, you know.'

Isaac looked away, mainly because he couldn't quite take Weber at this proximity; but what he saw cleared his confusion. 'The art . . .'

'Exactly. I believe, if you were to go to the vaults of' – the always sarcastic intonation of his voice doubled – 'the *Reich Chamber of Culture* – not a place where I especially recommend you to spend much time, in truth, Fabian – you'd find me classified under D, for *Degenerate*. Ah yes! I can still remember the day I read my first review denouncing me as a degenerate artist – one of the proudest days of my career.' He laughed, and turned back to the bust.

In the turn, Isaac could see Weber as he had just seen himself, in three dimensions, and was able to read the bitterness and the dismay beneath the constant smirking. He wondered what it must be like, living this decision, to *choose* persecution – for your status

151

as an enemy of the state to be something you could put away, but decide not to, for the sake of art.

'What's this bit of writing?' Isaac pointed at some print laid over the top left-hand side of the head.

The two of them peered at it like a pair of brain surgeons examining a patient.

'It's a torn-off piece of a page from *The Communist Manifesto*.'

'Really? In which language?'

'Norwegian.'

'Your own copy?'

'In a sense. It was given to me by a friend when I was living in Norway, the sort of fellow who can't accept that being an artist does not necessarily entail being a Marxist. It's come in useful in a few collages now . . .'

'Obviously not in any other way.'

'Obviously not.'

Isaac noticed a piece of newsprint joining the chin area to the neck: it was a section of the *Camp*, Central's own newspaper, some sort of advert or announcement, decorated with flowers and a cartoon of a couple dancing.

'I very much like it,' Weber was saying, about the bust in general. 'When I have my big post-war retrospective, you'll have pride of place . . . *The Eternal Jew*, I might call it . . .' but Isaac was ducking his head down to read.

'Do you know about this?' he said.

'What?'

'This.'

Weber looked. 'Well, yes. It's my little representation of the interned part of you.'

'But have you read it?'

He shook his head. 'My English could be better. Now, if it were in French . . . or even Norwegian . . .'

Isaac craned his neck round again. 'It's an announcement from the Camp Commandant.' He spoke from underneath the bust's chin, reading, in English: '*The Isle of Man Internment Camps Authority announces a special Christmas Event: a rendezvous of husbands and wives.*'

152

'A what?'

'A meeting-up of husbands and wives.'

Weber made a comic sound, an overdone intake of breath. 'Sounds fearful.'

'*All men presently interned in Camps Central, Rushen, Hutchinson and Onchan whose wives are interned in Camps Port Erin or Port St Mary are invited to Derby Castle on Sunday 14 December, for an evening with their loved ones, beginning at six o'clock. Refreshments will be* . . . That bit has been torn off. *Served*, it will be. *Refreshments will be served.*' He was pleased with himself for knowing the English phrase – generally pleased that his greater familiarity with the language awarded him suddenly the higher status. Weber carried with him a sense of having unlimited access to secret knowledge, which made him one of those men towards whom the power in any room seemed always to flow. At least in the small measure of language, however, Isaac now was the keeper of the gate to secret knowledge.

'Where's Derby Castle?'

'Up on the northern end of the bay, on the outskirts of town. I think I passed it on the way to the rabbis' house, up on the cliffside. It looks like an English seaside version of a Bavarian folly. But it's some sort of dance hall now, I think.'

'Hmm . . . interesting.' Weber took out his tobacco pouch once more. The clumps of burnished grass he laid across the paper, Isaac could see, were already fattened a little from the moisture of the orange peel. 'The British are doing their best to keep us happy. I might see if I can make it to this. Make a change from wanking like a chimpanzee.'

'Your wife's on the island?' asked Isaac, choosing to ignore Weber's lurid description, although assuming that therefore he must never drink the canteen tea.

'Louisa? No. She's in Hannover. But I should imagine it'll be an easy enough event to get into without a wife.'

Isaac frowned. 'Why would you want to do that?'

Weber laughed, phlegm gargling in the back of his throat. 'Oh Fabian, you're clever, but you're so innocent. Consider the possibilities. Consider how disappointed a wife may be whose husband, for whatever reason, doesn't turn up? Or a husband who, desperate for this one meeting to be right, says the wrong thing and whose wife storms off into the night? Consider how much those women will want the comforting shoulder of another man.' He looked back under the chin of the bust. 'Oh yes. *A rendezvous of husbands and wives*. Rich pickings. Rich, rich pickings.' He laughed again, the phlegm gradually flooding his throat and lungs, until the laughter became a cough, racking his ribs, making him place his cigarette-less hand on top of the bust for support: Isaac saw the tips of his fingers sink into the still-soft head.

June Murray looked out of the train window at the Wirral speeding by, and understood how its landscape deserved the adjective 'rolling': lit piercingly green by the late Indian summer sun, hill followed hill into the wide distance, making her eye feel like it was indeed on wheels, tracing the curves of the countryside. How England can look, she thought, what a feast for the gaze it can be – on days like these, when the long hedges make of the land a verdant grid, and light leaps up from its half-hidden brooks, and small timbered villages lie settled in the distance like promises of peace. It always had a calming effect on her, the countryside, although, at this moment, she knew that effect was a little negated by her need to feel it; her eyes were fixed on the moving picture-box framed by the train window in almost a hard stare, willing it to work its magic.

Across the compartment, an old woman lay asleep; her cheeks, which drooped in flesh-brackets on either side of her chin, vibrated with her snores. The compartment's only other occupant, a soldier on crutches, who had chanced the odd smile at June, had been gone for some time. Guessing that it was proving difficult for him to get in and out of the WC, June felt brave enough to open her handbag and look at the documents it was holding. The letter to Commander Rutter lay there, between a compact and her train tickets. She unfolded it with her finger and thumb, not taking it out of the bag, squinting at the words she knew by heart: *Isle of Man internment camps ... Nazi 'crimes against humanity' ... a dossier ... thank you for your cooperation ...* Now the words meant something, now that they acted as her passport, they rang hollow in her inner ear – she would have changed this word, that sentence, she would have made the whole thing less obviously a parody of Ministry correspondence. Her passport seemed suddenly false; she was carrying false papers.

Michael should have made the phone call to Commander Rutter

155

by now, at least, she thought, trying to reassure herself. June had taken off three weeks, ostensibly to visit her parents – which had raised a few eyebrows so close to Christmas – but in fact had spent only two days with them in their little cottage on the outskirts of Bewdley, in Worcestershire. Hugging her mother's tiny frame – when did she become smaller than her? – her usual sadness at leaving the cottage, with its wood fires and latticed windows over-looking the Severn, was edged this time by fear. She knew what the fear was about and yet, because she was hugging her mother, it felt like her anxiety was more primal, was related to her – to all our – deepest fears about the unknowability of what happens, about what we are going towards, when we leave a maternal embrace.

He should have made the phone call. He could have done it before she left, but they both decided that it would make more sense for him to telephone just before her arrival on the Isle of Man, as that would give Commander Rutter less time to check up on the details. It was difficult for her to trust him to help her, partly because Michael was too *twinkly* to be trustworthy at the best of times, but more because she knew he had become distant ever since the night she had gone out for a drink with him. It had been fine, they had gone straight from work, and shared a table at the Coach and Horses – she had been friendly and open, he had joked his way through most of the evening, eventually becoming more serious towards the end, revealing that he had been engaged to a girl two years before the war, but that it had fallen apart three weeks before the wedding for some reason he chose not to disclose – but then afterwards, as she was about to get into a cab on the Embankment, his attitude changed. Michael had held the door for her: smiling and saying goodbye, she had got in, at which point he had got in too, saying that he thought they could share it. She pointed out that he lived south and she lived north, but he demurred, saying that he was presently staying with a friend in Bloomsbury. June didn't believe it, and her suspicions were confirmed when the cab went sailing through Bloomsbury with not a word from him, and so she – literally – girded her loins for what she knew was coming. A part of her almost wanted to give in, because it was easier – she could never bear the tension that surrounded sexual expectation –

so when he placed a hand on her knee, she left it there for some time. But when it moved up her thigh, something about the way the line of her tweed skirt became ruffled and messy – the way the material on her lap became a series of annoying, misshapen rucks and ridges – made her feel defiant. *Enough*, she thought, enough going along with things that feel wrong.

Of course, he had gone into a sulk. Of course, when she had got out of the cab, he had been churlish enough to mention that now the whole journey was going to cost him three times more than if he'd just got a cab south in the first place (this despite her offer to pay half, rejected with an angry wave of the hand through a quickly wound-up window). Of course, next day at work he'd acted as if nothing had happened, but also as if they were not really friends any more, nor – more importantly – compatriots, fellow plotters. She didn't care all that much about Michael's wounded pride, but she cared about the withdrawal of his support. Finally, the day before leaving, she had passed him in the Ministry canteen, and said, 'I'll be in the Isle of Man on Monday afternoon. You are still going to make that telephone call, aren't you?' His response had been a bemused look, followed by a nonchalant 'Oh! That. Yes, of course.' It was all she had – they did not see each other again before she left work, before she stepped out of Electra House into the frozen air rising off the river, not knowing if she would ever be allowed back into the building.

She was broken from her reverie by the thump of the soldier's crutches sliding open the door, announcing his arrival back into the compartment. The old woman started a little from her sleep, even going so far as to emit a questioning 'Eh?' without actually regaining consciousness. Quickly – stupidly, she realised immediately, as he could not see what she was looking at, and even if he could, would not have thought anything amiss – she shut the clasps of her handbag. With some effort, he levered himself back into his seat, opposite her, to the left of the sleeping woman. The two of them exchanged awkward smiles.

'Going home for Christmas?' he said, eventually. His accent was lower middle class, underpinned by the guttural, almost Arabic, throatiness of the Scouse.

'Little early for that, I'm afraid.'

'Course, yes. Sorry. You lose track of time when you've been at the front.'

The use of the word 'front' startled June; it was not part of the modern phraseology of war, as used in the Ministry. 'Front' implied a stasis no longer relevant in present battle conditions – there was no front now, only the movement of German troops forwards and Allied troops backwards. It made the soldier seem like someone from another time, from the Great War.

'I *am* going home early for Christmas, myself, anyway,' he continued. 'Not much else to do with my leg as it is.'

'I'm sorry.'

'It'll be fine,' he said, shaking his head. 'There's a big piece of shrapnel still lodged in it, but the doctors think I'll be able to dig my garden all right when the war's over.'

June smiled politely, and looked out of the window. There were more houses now, as they approached the outskirts of Liverpool.

'So yourself?'

She looked back round. He had sharp blue eyes, which had stayed on her. 'I'm going to the Isle of Man.'

'Really?' His prematurely craggy features moved from interest to concern. 'You're not – Jerry, are you?'

'No.'

'Or married to one?'

June shook her head. 'I'm going on official business.'

'Oh, I see,' said the soldier, rather thrown by the idea of this attractive woman being involved in any way in 'official business'.

'Were you at Dunkirk?' she said, after a silence had set in.

'Yes. I was at the Miracle.' He laughed, mirthlessly. 'That's what they're calling it, aren't they? "The Miracle of Dunkirk". Because we managed to run away from the Germans so miraculously.'

'Well . . .' said June, the government official in her becoming defensive, 'it was a very successful retreat . . .'

His laugh became a snort. 'Sorry, miss, but . . . begging your pardon . . . but what in Christ's name do you know about it?'

'Well . . . I read the papers.'

'The papers. Right. The papers who would have us believe that

158

we got away scot-free. Nearly no casualties. Oh yes, the whole bloody British Expeditionary Force got out of there in one piece. Well, I must go and read some of those papers to the only other surviving member of my crew. When he comes out of his coma.'

June fell silent, taken aback by the change of gear in the soldier's attitude. He shut his eyes and rubbed his temples.

'Sorry, miss – didn't mean to raise my voice like that.'

'No, it's fine.'

He settled back into his seat, laying his crutches across his lap. The train began to adopt a slower, bumpier ride as it approached its terminal. 'So . . .' he said, his tone becoming brisk, as if remembering why he had begun speaking to June in the first place, 'what sort of official business are you in?'

'Oh,' said June, 'it's boring, really. I work for the civil service. Just compiling a government report about the internees.'

The soldier nodded, accepting what he saw as a brush-off. In fact, June did not want to tell him that she worked for the Ministry of Information – the primary censor of his side of the Dunkirk story, the very gag around its wider telling. Earlier, when he had asked 'What do you know about it?' she had thought, Quite a lot, actually, but the fierceness of his tone had made her wonder. She worked for the Ministry, she knew that its task was the treatment of information, the management, processing and refining of it, and yet still she had believed absolutely that the retreat from Dunkirk – the understanding of which in Britain had been controlled from start to finish by the Ministry of Information – had been a victory: she had believed it even though she was presently on her way to the Isle of Man because another story of this war was, she knew, not being completely told.

One of her first tasks on joining the Ministry, in fact, had been to translate the German press reports of Dunkirk, and it startled her, as the soldier began with difficulty to raise up his damaged body well before the train stopped, to realise how much she had simply assumed Berlin's version to be downright lies: *forty thousand English killed in battle; the same number drowned at sea.* The job had been routine, and on handing in her translation she thought her superiors would use the material purely to monitor the enemy.

Now, though, she wondered if they needed it because the only way through to the truth was to hear both sides' propaganda.

'And how was your journey?'

Lieutenant Colonel F. W. Rutter was doing his best to be polite to the lady from the Ministry of Information. Lieutenant Colonel Rutter had, in his normal dealings, very little to do with civil servants, and even less to do with women. But she seemed in earnest, and carried with her a letter from Alfred Bassett's private secretary, so he was really trying to overcome his natural distaste for both species.

'It was fine, thank you.'

'Sea not too choppy?'

'Well, I'm not much of a sailor. But I didn't get too sea-sick, no.' Not as sick as this coffee is making me feel, at least, thought June, who had made the mistake of asking for something other than tea following Rutter's offer of a hot beverage. It was almost definitely not the coffee, however, but her nerves that were making June feel sick. Lieutenant Colonel F. W. Rutter was a man whose combination of bug eyes and prominent moustache made for an almost permanently surprised expression – on first seeing him, June had thought he must be about to chase Laurel and Hardy around a kitchen with an enormous knife – but, without doubt, he *was* surprised by the entry into his office of this unannounced female bureaucrat. He had perused her copy of the letter to him from Nigel Henderson with his brows meeting in stark confusion, followed by a shake of the head and various muttered apologies. Michael – the bastard – had not made the call.

There was a knock on the door.

'Come!' said Rutter, with a sense of relief that at least something had broken the awkwardness in the room. The door opened and Corporal Arthur Penn entered, wearing the permanently grudging expression of a man who had enrolled on the first day of war expecting to win a large crop of medals in active service and ended up posted to the Isle of Man as Rutter's secretary. 'Well?' said Rutter, as Penn stood there holding various files and looking suspiciously at June. From the window to his side, a grey light, a light which denoted that the long-surviving Indian summer of this particular autumn had finally sputtered out, hardened the Corporal's already-granite features, making him look, literally, like a rock face, as if his features belonged to one of those big American president faces June had seen photographs of glaring from Mount Rushmore.

'No, sir. I can't find any record of any recent letters from the Ministry of Information. There are some bits and pieces relating to the opening of the camps and to the general treatment of internees, but they were all part of a bundle of papers that got sent out here back in the summer. Nothing about Miss . . .'

'Murray,' said June.

'Miss Murray's supposed visit.'

June caught his eye, trying to convey a blank confusion as to why he would have used the word 'supposed'.

'All right, Corporal,' said Rutter. 'That'll be all for the moment.'

'Thank you, sir.' With one more sideways glance at June, followed by a telling look back to his superior officer, Penn left.

Lieutenant Colonel Rutter sat forward, arms folded. 'Well, Miss Murray, as I say, I'm most dreadfully sorry.'

'Yes. I suppose it must be the post.'

'Yes, it must be. We've had quite a few problems with the postal service out here, especially with the volume of internees' correspondence still waiting to be gone through. We have to check every letter that comes and goes from the island.'

June nodded, wondering if that was for security reasons or, more likely, because they were trying to suppress any negative information about life in the camps reaching the mainland. 'Well, what shall we do?' she said, trying to remain breezy, dampening down the rising sense of dread in her bowels.

'Hmm. Well, obviously, we'll have to contact the Ministry and just check that everything's been rubber-stamped. Which may take a little while, I'm afraid. I know what ministers and their private secretaries are like to get hold of, especially in wartime. You are very welcome to stay in the meantime – we could put you up at one of the boarding-houses that aren't behind the wire. There's one on the far side of the bay I know of . . . very clean, with a wonderful view of the sea . . .'

June continued to look interested, but she wasn't listening. She was wondering how she could have been such an idiot as to expect Rutter – clearly a man with officialdom in his veins, clearly a man who didn't go to the bathroom without written authorisation – to wave her freely on into the camps without all the necessary correspondence in place. She was wondering how quickly she could get off the island. She was wondering what she might do for another job. She was wondering what it would be like in prison. She was wondering how soon the war would be over.

There was another knock on the door.

'Come!'

Corporal Penn bent his head into the room. 'Lieutenant Colonel, sir? There's a telephone call for you.' He turned to June: 'From the Ministry of Information.' He spoke each word as if he were loading it into a gun.

'Really? Well, splendid. Put them through, put them through.'

Penn exited. Lieutenant Colonel Rutter smiled benevolently at June, and she smiled back, hoping that he could not hear the sound of her heart thwacking against her rib-cage. Rutter's desk telephone rang.

'Hello, Lieutenant Colonel F. W. Rutter speaking? . . . Ah, Mr Henderson, sir, how good to speak to you . . . I'm very well, thank you . . . Well, thank you very much, sir, we try our best . . . Yes, everything's running pretty smoothly now – I think most of the people who are going to be interned have been, so we can get on with our work rather more easily now.'

June watched his eyes, trying to read them, but, even in the midst of her fear, became distracted by just how bug-eyed he was. She remembered a military expression she had once heard – 'Don't shoot until you see the whites of their eyes' – and thought that if Rutter was running at you, bayonet raised, that actually would be quite a long way away, possibly not in range at all.

He flicked his pupils, tiny brown yolks in rings of white, up towards her. 'Yes, that's right. Miss Murray. She's actually sitting in front of me right now . . . No, she just arrived, a little while ago . . . No, that's all right, Mr Henderson, I'm sure you're a busy man . . . Well, that's it, you see, I *didn't* receive a letter from you . . . Yes, I am sure . . . Yes, perfectly . . . Yes, that's true, I was just saying what

162

desperate straits our postal system is in . . . No . . . Yes, I am clear as to what you require . . . Well, I don't think it will be a problem. It will take a little organisation, and we will have to find accommodation for Miss Murray, all of which obviously would have been done in advance if we had been forewarned . . . I don't know, a day or so? . . . Yes. How long will she been staying?' He paused, frowning. 'Right. Fine. Hold on.' He looked to her, covering the mouthpiece. 'Mr Henderson seems slightly unclear as to how long you will be on the island . . .'

'Twelve days. A fortnight at the most.'

'I see.' He moved his hand away from the telephone. 'She will be here for about two weeks. I imagine we can have everything sorted out for her to start by the middle of the week . . . Fine. Good. No, it's no trouble . . . Well, thank you, Mr Henderson. And do send my regards to Chips, if you get a chance . . . Yes, we served in Belgium together, in the Great War . . . Well, no matter. Yes . . . Yes . . . Goodbye. Goodbye.' He replaced the receiver.

June smiled at him, expectantly.

'Would you excuse me a minute, Miss Murray,' he said, and left the room.

Through the prefabricated wall, June could hear that he was speaking to Corporal Penn, but could not make out the words. She felt relief flood over her like warm water. Michael had called, after all. He'd left it late – very late – but that was probably his way of punishing her, without destroying her completely: the action of an immature man, but not a cruel one.

Lieutenant Colonel Rutter returned, retaking his seat behind his desk. 'Do bear with us, Miss Murray, we just need to check something.'

June's heart began to beat faster again. They could be asking the telephone operator to find out where the call had originated, or they could be running a more vigorous check: perhaps Penn was actually going to try to get Alfred Bassett on the line? Or perhaps Rutter had not been fooled by any of it, and had sent his corporal out to round up some soldiers to escort her back to the ferry? Or perhaps—

'Come!'

She hadn't heard the knock. Corporal Penn stuck his head round the door once more. He was nodding his head. 'Everything seems to be in order, sir, as far as we can tell.'

'Good. Excellent. Thank you, Corporal.' Rutter looked back to June, whose bland smile had become something of a ghastly rictus, and who was beginning to wonder how many years had been taken off her life just since she had been in this room. 'So,' he said, raising a pencil over a pad, 'what kind of internees would be most suitable for your interviews?'

She went first to Port Erin, to the women. Port Erin lies at the far south of the island, separated by a narrow strip of land from its sister on the sea, Port St Mary. Coming down from the coast in one of the white carriages of the island's main public transport system, a single-track electric train, June could feel a childish excitement well up within her at seeing the white streets sloping unhurriedly up the gentle cliffs. For a second, she forgot what she was here for, and thought, despite the lowering December sky, that she was on holiday, a safe, comforting English type of holiday, in small towns where every house faces the sea.

This illusion was broken abruptly on meeting Dame Theresa Metcalfe, commander of the women's camp on the Isle of Man, and her assistant Miss Elizabeth Barrington. Dame Theresa was in her mid-sixties, and if her manner did not already suggest that she was intent on barring June's way to the female internees, her enormous frame certainly did.

Miss Barrington, a woman of indeterminate age, was as thin as Dame Theresa was wide, and talked faster than anyone June had ever heard. 'So we have had to make sure of course that the women who come forward are happy to speak to you don't assume that we commandeered anyone Dame Theresa and myself have insisted it should be volunteers some of these women have been through terrible things and may not want to confide in a stranger especially if what they are saying is to be written down and used for who-knows-what governmental purposes they are naturally suspicious a lot of the women hardly surprising considering what they have had to endure,' she said.

June nodded, listening in vain for any sign of a breath. 'So . . . *have* some women volunteered to be interviewed?'

'Yes,' said Miss Barrington, with a clear sense of disappointment.

'How did you explain to them what I want?'

'We simply said that you were a British government official doing research into their experience of life under the National Socialist regime that is what Lieutenant Colonel Rutter told us.'

'Yes,' said Dame Theresa. 'Although perhaps you could enlighten us a little further. What exactly do you intend to ask our internees about?'

'I just want them to tell me their story . . . why they left Germany. Especially those who have undergone, as Miss Barrington says, great difficulty . . .'

'Well, that's as maybe.' Dame Theresa took a deep breath. 'The fact is, Miss Murray, there are nearly four thousand women interned in Port St Erin and Port St Mary: it has been an enormous task organising and controlling such a large influx of people into such a small place, particularly as so many of them don't speak the language, or are wanted by the locals. However, we have, I would say, managed to achieve this task with some small modicum of success. We have managed, in other words, to keep virtually everybody, on all sides, reasonably happy. I would not want anyone coming into that situation and stirring up trouble.'

'I assure you, Dame Theresa—'

'I'm sure you will assure me of many things, Miss Murray, but the fact is, going round forcing people to relive their immediate past, if that past has not been particularly pleasant, is not necessarily conducive to the general peace.'

June looked out of the window of Dame Theresa's cramped office, a converted room which used to be the reception of the Royal Hotel. Some way out at sea, off the coast of Ireland, it had begun to rain, water falling onto water. 'As Miss Barrington points out,' she replied, looking back, 'due to your good offices, I shall not be *forcing* anybody to do anything. If these women have volunteered, I presume that they are keen to tell their stories.' *Desperate* to, most of them, June thought, but felt such strong language would not help her cause.

Dame Theresa sniffed, her triangular nostrils becoming even more so. 'You want mainly Jews, I assume?'

June blinked at her. 'Well . . . most of your inmates *are* Jewish, aren't they?'

'The majority are, yes.'

'Eighty-seven per cent.'

'Thank you, Miss Barrington. But a significant minority are not. Have you had much acquaintance with Jews?'

'Not especially.'

'Well. As I thought. As you have so kindly pointed out, we have not forced anyone to take part in these interviews, but I *have* strongly recommended that some of our Christian internees also come forward. Thankfully, some of them have agreed. I feel it is very important that you don't go back to the War Office with a picture of events that turns out to be . . .' Dame Theresa seemed to struggle for a second.

'Skew-whiff?' said Miss Barrington.

Dame Theresa shot her what looked to June like a sour glance. 'One-sided.'

'Thank you,' said June, deciding not to bother to correct Dame Theresa's assumption that she worked for the War Office. 'Of course, anything you have done, or can do, to provide me with a more complete picture of events is appreciated.'

Dame Theresa and Miss Barrington nodded in sequence, both of them managing to convey in their faces that nothing of what they had done was for June's benefit.

That evening, June sat in her small room at the Royal Hotel, looking out over Port Erin Bay. The sun was setting behind Bradda Head, which extended far out into the sea, a huge index finger of rock pointing to Ireland, to neutrality. The glowing orb of the sun was already soft enough to look at almost directly, bisected in the middle by some strange Celtic tower on the top of the cliff, that from this distance had the look of a giant key. The air had turned gold, and through her window came the sound of the waves. June could not help but be lulled by the sound, the way it came again and again and again, the endless whisper of the water. She wondered why there was no word in English for the sound of the waves on the shore. She knew of only one language that did have a word for it, Greek – not her speciality, but one of her best friends at university, studying classics, had taught her a smattering. The word was *flisvos*. We are an island, she thought; we should have such a word.

Sighing, she turned back from the window to her typewriter; the sound and the sight of the sea were distracting her. It was easy to be distracted, however, as translating and typing up the interviews was arduous: they were long – she hadn't cut anything out, not even exclamations and pauses – and they did not make for easy reading. Going to the women's camp first had turned out to be fortuitous, however, as her initial problem in conducting the interviews had been a secretarial one: June did not know shorthand, certainly not shorthand in German. As a result, her first two interviews – one woman, a marine biologist from Vienna, who was hoping to establish a research station at Port Erin, the other a nursery-school teacher from Frankfurt who had already set up a kindergarten in St Catherine's Church Hall – went by the board in a flurry of paper and apologies. The third woman she saw, however, had worked as a clerk in an insurance firm in Hamburg, and had, it turned out, invented her own form of shorthand. Her name was Irma; she was dark eyed and high cheekboned and she wrote down her own story, scribbling furiously on June's pad and hardly looking down as she spoke. Afterwards, June asked her if she would like to work with her on the rest of the interviews. Irma virtually bit her in her speed to say yes. Some women in the camp had found work of one sort or another, she said, but, for many, it was the time, the endless dry time, stretching out until God knew when, that was the problem. June worried that Dame Theresa would forbid it, but Irma just tutted, as if the opinions of her captors were entirely worthless, and told her not to tell them. She had sat in on the interviews since then.

As she pulled the last page of her ninth interview through the carriage of her typewriter, June was just starting to get the hang of Irma's shorthand. She no longer had to back-refer every five seconds to the little glossary her newly acquired secretary had laid out for her on the top page of her pad. Laying this page on the pile next to her, she decided to stop for the night: she was tired, and tomorrow was going to be another long day. One more day here, and then she would go to the men's camps. She shut the curtains on the sea view, and lay down on her single bed. A bit of light bedtime reading, she thought, as she switched on the bedside light, and arranged the pile as a manuscript on her lap.

3.12.1940

Interview 1:10 a.m.

Q: To begin with, could you just tell me your age, your name, and where you are from originally?

A: Irma Dreschler. Twenty-six. From Hamburg.

Q: Thank you. Now if you'd like to tell me, in your own words, why you left Germany to come to Britain.

A: Where should I start?

Q: Wherever you like.

(There is a pause.)

A: I had just begun work in Herling & Herling, a big insurance firm in Hamburg, in 1933, just as the Nazis came to power. I wasn't very interested in the Nazis - I wasn't very interested in politics, or religion for that matter. I remember - you have to excuse me, I was still very young then, just nineteen - saying to my mother that silly laws made by silly men in Berlin had nothing to do with me. I just wanted to do well at my job for a few years and then start a family. I was engaged at the time. Anyway, about a year later - this was before the Nuremberg Laws, before it was illegal to employ Jews - they sacked me. Of course, it was because I was Jewish, but they wouldn't say so. They sent me a letter saying that I had made a number of filing errors, which wasn't true. I went to work the next day anyway, and asked them to show me these mistakes, what they were exactly. Well, they couldn't, of course, but it made no difference, and eventually they threw me out.

Q: They actually physically threw you out of the building?

168

A: Well, I didn't land with a thump on the pavement.
But I was escorted out by two of the younger men, yes.

Q: Go on.

A: So that was that. I suppose I should be glad they
didn't just tell me the reason was that I was Jewish. A
year later and that would have been no problem – they'd
have been proud to announce that they had a policy of
not employing Jews. Anyway, so I've got no job. Who do I
turn to for support? My fiancé, of course. A lovely boy,
or so I thought. Klaus was his name, a trainee lawyer,
no less. Handsome, good prospects. My parents loved him.

Q: Even though he was not Jewish...?

A: Ach, my parents didn't care about that. My
father's an atheist, really. My mum might have
preferred I marry a Jew, but once she met Klaus she
didn't mind.

Q: You were saying ...

A: Yes. So I told Klaus that Herling & Herling had
sacked me, and he chooses that moment to tell me that
he'd like to break off our engagement! Well, not that
he'd like to, that he _has_ to. That _he_ will lose his job
if he continues to be seen with me. It was then I think
that I realised that what the silly men were doing in
Berlin _was_ going to have an effect on me.

Q: You were angry.

A: Furious. At first. I shouted and screamed and
called him a coward and I think I may even have hit
him. But I don't know. Perhaps it was true.

Q: I beg your pardon, what?

A: That he would have lost his job. Because he
started crying and saying he didn't know what else to
do, and even his friends were telling him he had to
leave me and ... well ... eventually, I ended up holding
him in my arms and telling him it was all right, it
wasn't his fault.

(There is a pause.)

A: Sorry. Anyway. My father, he was a manager of a

169

clothing store, he lost his job soon after this as well, so we had to move. We ended up in Altona, a much poorer district, because he had to sell our house for much less than it was worth. Altona, you probably know, used to be an autonomous Danish city within Hamburg, before the Greater Hamburg Decree.

Q: I'm sorry, I don't know ...

A: Hamburg is - <u>was</u> - a collection of cities, mainly Prussian, with this one Danish one. But the Nazis made all Hamburg one city. Altona's a working-class area, with many different nationalities. Anyway, by the time we moved there, a number of other Jewish families had moved there as well, because by then we were not allowed to own property, and houses there are cheap to rent. Because of this, and because the Nazis were putting up posters everywhere saying 'The Jew Is Our Misfortune', or whatever, a lot of our neighbours hated us. We had our windows broken, and once someone put a burning rag through our letter box. I found it hard to believe. This area, it's full of Danes, and Poles, and Russians - the Nazis hate all of them too, and yet they turn on us! So, life is not good. We have no money, no one will employ us - I managed to do the odd bit of cooking and cleaning work now and again, but no one would take me on permanently. My little brother, Fritz, he was still at school ...

Q: How old is he?

A: Now? Seventeen. At the time I'm talking about he was still a kid. He was a good student, but the teachers keep on finding reasons to mark him down. Fritz, he is good at writing, and his essays used to get read out in class, but then it stopped: a teacher said to him, 'Only a true German can be good at German.' Gradually, it gets worse: he starts getting bullied, other children calling him a Yid and kicking him and pulling his hair and throwing stones at him. They have lessons in classes teaching the other

170

children that Jews are evil and responsible for everything that's ever been wrong in Germany, so no wonder. He has to sit in class while these lessons are being taught! So one day he comes home from school at midday and his face is all cut and bruised and he says he never wants to go to school again. That's when my father stands up in the middle of the living-room and says it's time to go.

Q: To leave Germany?

A: Of course. But where are we going to go? He says the Netherlands. I say not on your life: America. If you're going to emigrate, do it in style. America, that's the place. But how do we leave without any money? And it wasn't easy to leave anyway; you had to get visas and I don't know what. So in the end, the Netherlands was easier; it's not that far from Hamburg. My father promised me that when everything was sorted out and we had more money we would move to America.

Q: Where did you go in the Netherlands?

A: Amsterdam. I got a job there quite easily, in a typing pool for some accountants. Dad got some part-time work tailoring. It wasn't too bad. We had a small flat, and we all had to sleep in one room, but no one was breaking the windows. I still dreamt of going to America, of course. Then the war starts and it seems like within seconds Hitler's at the Dutch border. So my father applies for visas for us all to come to Britain. He only got one.

Q: One?

A: Yes. I went with him to try to get visas for all of us. A centre was set up in the Town Hall in Amsterdam for people — Jews, mainly — wanting to emigrate because of the Nazis, but it was complete chaos: hundreds of people shouting, children running everywhere, no one knew who were the officials and who were the applicants. Somehow Dad managed to get one — just one, before someone else barged him out of the

way. He wanted to stay but it was no good, and time ...
well, time was running out in general. So he said that
we should go home and decide who was going to have this
one, and then he would try again tomorrow.

(There is a pause.)

Q: So how did you decide?

A: We sat around the table in our tiny kitchen with
the visa in the middle of the table. No one said
anything for what seemed like ages. I thought that
little piece of card was going to burn a hole in the
wood. Outside, we could hear luggage being loaded into
cars, doors slamming. Then my dad said: 'Irma. It has
to be you.' 'Why?' I said. 'Because I can't leave your
mother, she refuses to leave me, and Fritz is too
young.' 'I'm not!' says Fritz. 'You are,' says Dad.
'People under eighteen aren't allowed into Britain
without a guarantor and we don't have one.' Well, I
wanted to say no – I wanted to say then, 'I don't want
the visa, we either all go or none of us goes,' but I
looked at him and his eyes were pleading with me, Go.
Go. He wanted to know that at least one of us was safe.

(There is a pause.)

A: So I left the next day. I got the train to the
Hook of Holland, and then the ferry to Harwich. My
mother and brother came to see me on the train.

Q: Where was your father?

A: He said goodbye to me in the morning, at the
flat. He wanted to spend all day at the Town Hall,
trying to get visas for everybody else. He woke me up
with a cup of tea, to try to get me used to what life
would be like in Britain, he said. Tea with sugar. Are
you all right?

Q: I'm fine.

A: I drank it and then he hugged me and said that
everything would be fine, that he and Mum and Fritz
would come over just as soon as they got the visas. He
gave me an envelope with some money in it, some

172

guilders, some marks, and even five pounds - I don't
know where he got that from. Then he held my face in
his hands - he hadn't done that for years, not since I
was a child - and kissed me on the cheek ... and told me
to take care. It sounds so ordinary, doesn't it? 'Take
care.' But he said it with such ... force ... not loudly,
it was almost a whisper, but still ... I don't know how
to describe it. But I still hear it in my head every
night before I go to sleep.

    Q: Did they get visas?

    A: No. Can I stop now? Only I'm tired, and ... if I'm
going to be writing down all the other people's
stories ...

    Q: Yes, yes. That's fine. I'm sorry.

June put down the page. She flicked through some of the others.
Apart from Irma, the marine biologist, and the nursery-school
teacher, there was a Carmelite nun, a waitress at the Ritz, a fish-
monger's wife, a woman who claimed to have been Franz Kafka's
mistress, a diplomat's wife and a professional opera singer. The
realisation, which had been growing in June throughout the day,
suppressed only by the sheer mechanics of doing the interviews,
crashed in on her: they were not *bad* enough. Irma's story and all
the other similar stories she had heard that day were, in the context
of June's understanding of Nazi Germany, routine: routine economic injustice, routine domestic hardship, routine social exclusion.
It was terrible, but nothing that Irma had told her would have surprised the readers of the *Manchester Guardian* or the *Jewish
Chronicle*, both of which had been reporting on the wholesale dis-
enfranchisement of Jews in Nazi Germany for some years. In order
to go back to the Ministry with a document of any power, she
needed corroboration of far greater atrocities.

    With this realisation came another: *she knew more than they did.*
She had thought that a fair proportion of refugees would have at
least heard about, or knew people who had witnessed, the awful
scenes coming out of Central Europe which she had had to translate. But most of them had come to Britain in the mid-thirties, too

early for that. Some of them had relatives still in Germany, or German-occupied Europe, but when June tried to ask about them, she ran into one brick wall after another:

```
Q: Do you know what has happened to your parents?
A: No. I haven't heard from them for months.
(There is a pause.)
```

Or:

```
Q: Your brother, you say, is still in Vienna?
A: Well, I assume so. I haven't been able to get in
contact with him recently.
```

Once, with a woman who had come over later – who had been in Poland when the Germans invaded – she felt emboldened, initially:

```
Q: While you were in Poland, were you aware of any ...
rumours - or perhaps you've seen - things ... ?
A: I'm not quite with you.
Q: Sorry. I mean, you were not present at any ...
(There is a pause.)
```

But then June realised that *she* could not bring this information to *them*. She had no right to tell them of unproved things that would only provoke fear.

And then there was this one:

```
Interview 5:20 p.m.

Q: To begin with, could you just tell me your name,
your age, and where you come from?
A: Hannah Spitzy. Thirty-seven. Munich.
Q: Thank you.
(There is a pause.)
Q: Excuse me, but am I correct in assuming that you
are not Jewish?
```

174

A: That is correct.

Q: I see. Could you tell me why you are not presently living in Germany?

A: My husband, Reinhardt, is a diplomat. He had been here for some time prior to the war, attempting to resolve the conflict between our nations. I was with him. When war broke out, he was then arrested by the British government. I was offered the chance of returning to Germany myself, but preferred to stay in the same country as my husband.

Q: Your husband worked for Ribbentrop?

A: Yes.

(There is a pause.)

Q: What is your position regarding the policy of the current German government towards the Jews?

A: I agree with it.

(There is a pause.)

Q: Could you expand?

A: Well. There has been a policy, since the Führer came to power, of dealing – not before time, I would say – with the problems that have been caused in our society by the presence within it of a large number of Jews. This has involved correcting the basic imbalances that have existed for a long time, where Jews had simply too much power and influence. In order to pursue this policy, the government has promoted a situation where Jews have been encouraged to emigrate. I see this as right and proper, and a way back to creating a Germany more like the one in which most Germans want to live.

Q: What is your opinion of Jews?

A: As a nation?

Q: Yes ... if you like ...

A: You see, that is the problem. You are making the mistake that most people make about the Jews: they are not a nation. They are a race. Historically, they have never been able to create a nation for themselves, and

175

so have had to survive by attaching themselves to greater nations, and living off what that nation provides.

Q: Like a parasite?

A: Exactly. Now this is bound always to lead to disaster. Because the Jew, genetically, is virtually incapable of any kind of genuine physical work, and has an outlook on life opposed to the creation of anything besides wealth, eventually resentment will build up against them. They have no sense of civic responsibility. They care only for themselves, and the continuing propagation of their own racial imperatives.

Q: Sorry, I'm not sure what that means – 'their own racial imperatives'?

A: You did not understand the German?

Q: No, I understood it. I don't know what it means. What are the Jews' racial imperatives?

A: To overthrow their host nation. Eventually, to overthrow all Christian and Aryan cultures.

Q: Why?

A: Because they believe they are the chosen people.

(There is a pause.)

Q: Could I just move on a little? I wonder if you know anything about some of the reports we have been reading in this country about acts perpetrated by your government that go somewhat further than simply encouraging Jews to emigrate ...

A: I have no idea what you mean.

Q: Well, our newspapers have printed reports about Jews being attacked on the street, their property being damaged, even that some Jewish citizens have been killed, with the blessing of the authorities.

A: Well, that just proves how much the Jews are in control in your country, too.

Q: In what way?

A: It's just lies. Lies and atrocity propaganda. Lies and atrocity propaganda invented by Jews who are powerful enough to get it into your papers.

176

Q: Why should they want to invent lies of that scale?

A: To try to discredit Germany and the work of the Führer. Lying comes very naturally to the Jew.

Q: So you don't believe that any Jews in Germany have been maltreated?

A: No doubt some Jews have been surprised at the reaction of ordinary citizens to their behaviour now that those citizens have been allowed to voice their grievances. And I suppose it is possible that in righting some of the wrongs that the Jews have committed over many years against Germans, some Jews have been knocked about a bit. I wouldn't consider that to be maltreatment. I would consider it justice.

(There is a pause.)

Q: It must be difficult for you, here, to live among so many Jews.

A: Indeed. Luckily, I have been allotted a house in which most of the other inhabitants are Aryans. We are applying to Dame Theresa Metcalfe to be moved to Peel, which I believe is virtually Jew-free.

Q: But it's not a women's camp ...

A: I would much rather share my quarters with Aryan men than Jewish women.

June picked up her pen, poising it above the words 'Jewish women'. They weren't quite right. Frau Spitzy's exact sentence was '*Ich würde mein Quartier viel lieber mit arischen Männern als Jüdinnen teilen*'. *Jüdinnen*, not *Jüdische Frauen*, which, in June's linguistically correct heart, she knew was the German for 'Jewish women'. *Jüdinnen* was simply the feminine plural of *Jude*, Jew, female Jews . . . Jewesses? No, that didn't quite cut it in English – too biblical. And then there was Frau Spitzy's tone, effortlessly, reflexively contemptuous. Suddenly, she saw it. With her pen, June scrubbed out the three letters 'ish', so the sentence read: '*I would much rather share my quarters with Aryan men than Jew women.*'

That was it. A minuscule change – just one stroke of the pen –

but it made all the difference. Suddenly, June had successfully conveyed the insulting spirit of the Nazi woman's words. At first, she felt guiltily pleased with herself, but then realised with a start that this would always be the case with *Jew* as opposed to *Jewish*. A Jewish lawyer – a Jew lawyer. A Jewish banker – a Jew banker. A Jewish boy – a Jew boy. The words ran in her mind, changing from white to black as she said them. Racking her vocabulary-rich brain, June could not think of another word that you could do this with, where you could use the noun as an adjective in this manner. Why did dropping the suffix have such an effect? Maybe it implied that the speaker had so little time for Jews that he would not even spare them the consideration of grammar. Or perhaps saying a man is a Jewish banker implies that the man is a banker who happens to be a Jew, whereas saying that the same man is a Jew banker implies that he is primarily and always will be a Jew, irrespective of his job – the word itself will not change because he and all the others who share his race will never change. And beyond her intellectualisations and rationalisations, June realised, as she had not before, that the word itself, *Jew* – that is, not Jewish, or Judaic, but the word stripped bare, *Jude* – carried with it a streaming, virulent energy: that within its tiny syllable was contained all the time and all the fear and all the hate of its history. This is what makes the Gentile want to spit it out of his mouth.

After the interview, Hannah Spitzy, clearly pleased to have been given this chance to speak, had become friendly, gossipy, telling June about how she was certain Ribbentrop had been having an affair with Wallis Simpson. June remembered nodding and smiling. She turned her eyes back to the page. Only a few more words.

```
Q: Has it not changed your views at all, meeting so
many Jews, and living with them?
   A: No. Absolutely not.
```

June put the sheaf of papers down by the side of the bed and turned off the light. Unconsciousness came to her quickly, the whirl of the surf breathing sleep into her ear like the rhythmic repetition of a hypnotist's whisper.

'So tell me about your husband.'

Douglas and Lulu were lunching in Joshua Taylor's, a department store with its own café just off the market square. Joshua Taylor's was expensive by Lulu's standards – although so was virtually any eaterie beyond the fish-and-chip shop at the end of Chesterton Road – and at first she was unsure as to whether it was compromising to meet him there, but a combination of embarrassment and hunger made her quickly accede. Today, one of those English early winter days whose brightness somehow implies that soon it will rain, it was half full; most of the other customers were women, meeting one another, sharing news, hoping for more. Douglas had a slim notebook out on the table; his pen, silver and shining and expensive, was poised above it. Lulu smiled at the absurdity of his seriousness.

'I don't know where to start.'

'Perhaps telling me his name?'

Her face pulled a friendly grimace. 'His name is Isaac. He is twenty-seven years old. He has dark hair and wears glasses.'

A short scribble in his book and then Douglas, who also happened to be sporting glasses, took them off and folded them into the top pocket of his tweed jacket. Lulu wondered if he really needed them for reading and writing or whether he'd just decided to wear them to augment his seriousness.

'We're going to have to go a bit deeper.'

'Well, Mr Lean . . .'

'Douglas.'

'Douglas.' She opened the clasp of her handbag, and pulled out her two paper jewels, unfolding them carefully. 'The other testimonials I have already, they are quite simple . . .'

He put his hand on hers, pressing it and the testimonials to the table. His fingers were long, and cold, despite having been gloved. 'Mrs Fabian . . .'

'If I am to call you Douglas, you had better call me Lulu.'

He smiled, and nodded. 'Lulu. I think it's better if you don't get those out for everybody to see. After all' – he leant in, and lowered his voice – 'we are about to do something no doubt highly illegal.'

'Oh! Yes!' Lulu snatched the testimonials from under his hand, and replaced them in her bag. 'How stupid of me!'

Douglas pursed his lips and shook his head. 'Besides, I am not entirely certain that simplicity is what we're after. Don't get me wrong: I'm sure your landlady and whoever else wrote the other one have done a marvellous job. But did they really know your husband?'

'Well . . . no. Not really. But they had at least met him. Which is more than you have.'

'I know that. But I'm just a cipher.'

'A what?'

'A funnel, a vessel. The fact is that this is going to be *your* portrait in words of your husband. It's just going to go to the authorities under my name. But I'm no more than a ghost writer.'

'Douglas. We are not writing . . .' her mind searched for something appropriate, dismissing the first few titles that came to her mind, all German; then, she remembered, '*Hamlet* here.'

'No, of course. But I think – seriously – that a well-written testimonial that feels as if it has come from the heart – that really describes what is good and decent about your husband – will have more chance of convincing the people at the War Office or wherever to let him go.'

A waitress appeared with their food: a lamb casserole for him, a vegetable pie for her. Lulu had to stop herself from upending the plate into her mouth.

'Well . . .' she said, after the first few mouthfuls had assuaged her crying stomach, 'I am not sure you are right. But I can't see what harm it would do to send in one that was a little more . . .' Her fork wavered in the air.

'Detailed?'

'Detailed, yes.'

Douglas patted his lips with his napkin, and repoised his pen. 'I imagine what they'll be looking for – as well as a guarantee that the internee in question does not constitute a threat to national security – is some sense that his release will be of benefit to the community at large. Is there some sense of that?'

'I don't know.'

'Well, does he have any qualifications?'

'He has a degree from Königsberg University.'

'In what?'

Lulu took a sip of water. There was a slice of lemon in the glass. 'Political science.'

Douglas looked up from his pad and laughed. 'Political science? Hmm. I'm not sure that's going to be much help. The one thing the community at large probably doesn't need is more politicians.'

'Isaac is not a politician.'

'But he is political.'

'Yes.'

Douglas kept his eyes on her. She felt it, when he did that. 'There's something you're not telling me here.' Lulu remained silent. He pushed the pad to one side. 'Off the record.'

'I beg your pardon?'

'It's what journalists say when they want to know something that the other person doesn't want to tell them. It means it won't be written down. It won't be printed.'

'Does it? Usually they print it anyway, no?'

He smiled again, his lopsided crescent. 'Don't be so cynical.'

Lulu sighed. 'Isaac is a communist.'

'Ah.'

'Yes. I used to be proud of that, in a way. It made him different ... interesting. An intellectual, but not stuffy. Exciting. My background, it is ... how would Lotte put it? Rather bourgeois.'

'Presumably Isaac would have said that too.'

Lulu started: oddly, the idea had not occurred. Her thoughts had gone first to someone who was a physical presence in her life now. It made her realise how much she was talking about Isaac in the past tense. 'Yes, he would. Well, he did. He used to criticise, to tell me how the way my family lived, it was all wrong. But I am – I am painting the wrong picture. He is not a ... You imagine from

181

my words, I am sure, this kind of very serious man, the political man – but he is not really . . .'

'Certainly not. I myself, in my time, have had . . .' and here he paused, the creases by the sides of his eyes forming as his brow furrowed with the effort of finding the correct phrase, 'comparable leanings.'

Lulu's eyes widened with surprise: the richness of their blue, clearer in the wider oval, was not lost on Douglas Lean.

'Oh. I had not thought of you as someone interested in politics.'

From his jacket pocket, he took a gold cigarette case, and proffered it open. She shook her head. He lit one, drawing deeply as he leant back.

'I'm not any more. But once I was.' He seemed to hesitate, and, for a moment, became again the withdrawn, awkward figure he had appeared to be when they had first met. 'I was in Spain, during the Civil War. That's where I picked up this limp.'

'You went to fight?'

'Well, I went to report on my experiences. I do the odd bit of journalism now and again; a bit more than now and again these days, in fact, since the playwriting seems not actually to be providing food for my table. But I wasn't exactly a neutral. I was committed, then.'

'And now?'

'Now . . . I have echoes of it, in my head. I can sometimes feel it in my gut. When I hear about . . . you know . . .' he smiled, conveying with his eyes that the smile was nostalgic, 'injustices.' The smile faded. 'But I'm no longer moved to do anything about them. That's what happens with age.'

'Are you aged, then?' She said it as one syllable, *aged*, as of wine.

'Well, I'm in what people in this country call my "prime".'

'That is a good time, surely?'

He smiled again. Lulu noticed how straight and clean his teeth were, despite what she had heard about English men. 'I can only hope so. Anyway, we're getting off the point. We're not here to outline my character. We're here to try to put your husband on paper.' He turned over a new page on his pad, unnecessarily, as the first was blank. 'Is he still a communist?'

'As far as I know. There is nothing in his letters to make me think different. Except . . .' The waitress appeared again, and began collecting their plates. Lulu clicked her tongue. 'This is difficult to explain. You see – Isaac's communism, I always felt it was, at heart, simple. He is an intellectual, my husband, yes – he has read a lot of books, and when he talks politics, you know, it can be like physics or something – very . . . oh, I don't know the word. *Dunkel?*'

'Obscure?'

'Yes.' She halted. 'I thought you didn't speak German.'

Douglas raised his palms defensively. 'A smattering. Which I don't like to use when Lotte's around as she makes fun of me.'

Lulu nodded. Something about this information rang tiny alarm-bells in the back of her mind, but she dismissed it: perhaps, even though she was German, she had lived long enough in Britain to have absorbed a reflex suspicion of the language. 'Well, as I say, Isaac, his understanding of politics is very complicated, and his way of explaining political things, too, it is high, you know, difficult. But I always thought that he was a communist because of something quite, as I say, simple. Because he is a gentle man, my husband. He is a good man. Underneath all his politics – he just – he wants the best for us all. I don't mean just for me and for our daughter; for you, for everybody. And – although it may be that this is because I did not understand it all properly – I think that is why he is a communist. His politics are – they are an expression of him.'

'And now?'

Lulu knitted her brow. Her train of thought had got lost, somewhere between her attempts to explain and her own amazement at her ability to do so. 'Oh! Well. What I mean is, even though Isaac is . . . *ein Intellektueller, sehr raffiniert . . .*'

'Intellectually very sophisticated?'

'Yes . . . in his heart he is, how you say? . . . innocent. Naive, almost. But recently, in his letters, I don't see this so much. I see something else.' Her eyes fixed to a point. 'I see anger. I see hate.'

Douglas nodded, a slow, thoughtful movement. He stubbed out his cigarette, twisting it meticulously into the ashtray, well after its flame was extinguished. 'It's understandable.'

She shook her head. 'Not in Isaac. Not until now. He has had much sadness, of course, and regret, of course, but somehow, he never was angry.' She laughed. '*I* was. I am. But he seemed to carry it all with . . . I don't know – this hope he has. He has this belief in humanity, that is what I mean about him being a communist, which makes him think that in the end everything will be all right. And which makes him not angry.'

'*Made* him not angry.'

'Yes. That is right. It looks in some of his letters like that belief might have gone. Being interned might have finally broken it.' She looked down, suddenly aware that she was breaking a confidence here, sharing this information, this concern about her husband, with another man. Her tone became businesslike. 'But this is too much, of course. We cannot put these kind of things into the testimonial. And I do not think it is a good idea to put in anything about my husband's politics, in any case. It was his communism that made him get a B classification in the first place.'

Douglas, who had been jotting for a while, took his pen to the end of the sentence. 'You're right, of course. It's my own silly playwright's instinct, trying to know as much about a character as possible.'

'Yes. But Mr Lean, this is not a play. It is real life.'

As if to confirm this sentiment, a man in a brown overcoat entered Joshua Taylor's at exactly this point, carrying under his arm a newspaper bearing the headline 'SOUTHAMPTON BOMBED: OVER 70 FEARED DEAD'. Underneath was a photograph of what presumably had once been a street. Outside, Lulu noticed, the weather had been true to type: rain was falling in a bright shower.

'It is, yes.'

The bill arrived. Lulu picked up her bag, but with a tiny vibration of his hand, Douglas indicated that no contribution to lunch was necessary. Lulu felt sharply how much she would have liked to pay at least half of it – after all, it was he who was doing her the favour, and it would have helped to make her feel a little more in control of the situation – but there was no getting away from the reality of her relief.

'Well, thank you,' she said, taking her coat – her grey mackintosh, which was a little light for the season, but she preferred the shape of her body in it – from the back of her chair. 'Very much. You have been very kind. When do you think you might have written the testimonial?'

Douglas raised his fist to his mouth, in thought. 'Look, I think we should meet again.'

Lulu, standing now, looked down at him. 'But Mr . . . Douglas . . . I want to get on with it. I want to get the three of them written and hand them in to the Council. As soon as possible.' She stared out of the café's wide window. A church, St Benedict's, stood behind black railings on the other side of the street, its granite grey stone slowly darkening in rivulets of rain. For some reason, she felt an urge to go in and pray, even though she had not prayed in a church since meeting Isaac; even though St Benedict's was not Catholic. 'My daughter had just begun to call Isaac "Papa" in Germany. Then, when we came here, we taught her instead to say "Daddy". We know she could say "Papa" in England, but still it sounds foreign, we thought. So she learnt to call him "Daddy". And then when Isaac was first interned, every morning, at some point, she would say it, but now like a question: "Daddy? Daddy?" And I would say, "Daddy has gone away, my darling, for a little while, but soon he will come home."' Lulu moved her gaze from the church walls to Douglas Lean, whose eyes were charged with sympathy. 'And now – well, now – she has stopped saying it altogether. I show her his photograph and she just looks . . . she just . . . oh, what is the word?' Her voice cracked, the frustration of having a limited vocabulary almost breaking the back of her resolve not to cry.

'Confused.' His voice matched his eyes.

'Confused. Yes.' She stopped, and took a breath. 'So this is the point, Mr Lean. I want my husband back before my daughter has forgotten who he is. Before she is too frightened to go into his arms because she thinks he is a stranger.'

Douglas got up. 'Of course. I quite understand. I shall do as you wish. I shall go away, and by early next week I will have finished it. Just one request: I would like if possible to bring it to you, so you can check that everything is to your satisfaction.'

'Thank you . . . I'm sure that won't be necessary.'

185

'Please. I insist.' He took her arm, and looked her in the eye; once again, Lulu felt the force of his stare. 'I will not sleep easy otherwise.'

She nodded; she felt it difficult not to acquiesce in the face of his resolve. 'All right. We can meet again next week.'

He smiled graciously. 'Probably not in public, either; another of my mistakes.'

'Well . . . yes. If you think so.' She took a breath. 'And Douglas, thank you. When I spoke earlier, I did not mean – I mean – I know how much you are trying to help.'

He inclined his head, as he had done when they had first met. Lulu smiled, composed herself through the medium of thanking him again for lunch, and left. She had no umbrella, but the rain was sparse enough: she felt as if she could walk a path between the drops to dryness. As she moved away from the café, past the church, she made a conscious decision not to turn round; the extra moment of eye-contact, she knew, would be read as flirtation. Of course, he might not be watching her. True, she felt as if he was – indeed, as if his eyes were boring into her back – but then again, he could just as easily be reading his notes, or training his eyes on one of the other women in the café. She noticed, as she walked, that she was wondering more and more whether he was or he wasn't, and it made it hard, almost impossible, to keep facing forward.

The young man from Königsberg stopped talking, abruptly. June looked across at Irma, who returned her look with a mystified shake of the head. June was not entirely sure he was finished, but she had come across this before in the course of her interviews – a tendency for the interviewees suddenly to tire of telling their story, without warning, as if unexpectedly exhausted by their words. She waited a few minutes to see if he would start talking again, during which time Irma handed her the notes she'd taken so far. It was her last interview of the day; through the one window in the room, stars were beginning to shine in the darkening sky.

Reading over the notes made her heart sink a little. It had been difficult not to be disappointed since she had come to Central. She did not have enough time to visit all the men's camps, and it had seemed the most obvious, but now she wondered if Ramsay might have been better, or Hutchinson. It was the same problem as at Port St Mary – fundamentally, the experiences of the internees, awful though they were, simply did not tally with the level of horror contained in the Ministry of Information eyewitness reports. Almost farcically, she had found herself thinking during some of the interviews – as women talked of husbands held in prison for weeks without charge, and men of wives paraded through the streets with placards round their necks – *not atrocious enough* or *more horror, please*.

She flicked through the last section of interviews more quickly: a solicitor who'd been stripped of his right to practise; similarly a doctor; a tailor whose business had been relentlessly boycotted; a butcher whose shop window had been spray-painted with the words 'Rat Meat Sold Here'. Par for the course, came unfortunately into June's mind. There was only one, which she had conducted the previous day, which might have been fruitful, if she'd handled it a little differently:

187

Q: Would you mind telling me your name?

A: What for?

(There is a pause.)

Q: Well, I just need it for the record.

A: I don't see why. You're on a research job for the British government, correct? Finding out what we Jews have <u>suffered</u> ...

Q: Yes ... ?

A: So I don't see why you need to know my name. I can tell you what I've suffered. I can tell you what many more of my people are still suffering. Terrible things. The worst imaginable.

Q: What do you mean? What things? Can you describe them?

A: Not if I have to give you my name. Why should I trust you?

(There is a pause.)

Q: I have no intention of—

A: This information I could give you - where will it go?

Q: To the British Ministry of Information.

A: And what will they do with it?

(There is a pause.)

Q: It will become part of a dossier of material which I am going to present to my superiors at the Ministry. That dossier will then in turn become part of the Ministry's ongoing project to try to divine the reality of the present situation of the Jews in Europe.

A: You mean you don't believe us?

(There is a pause.)

Q: It's not a question of not believing; it's more just an issue of processing the enormous amount of information we are getting.

A: Bureaucratic nonsense ... You mean you - or your 'superiors' - think the Jews are liars. They think they always have been liars and that they're lying now.

Q: No. That is not it at all. We know that Jews are

being treated very badly by the Nazis. It's just—

A: And also, you British have blocked us from all information. We have no idea what is going on in the wider world. Germany may be about to invade, any minute; and then you come, asking us to tell you what the Germans have done to us, and you want to put it down in writing. What if they take over this country? What will happen to those of us who cooperated with you? I will tell you. There will be no chance of escape. We will be killed even quicker than we would have been.

Q: I can't answer for that. And I'm afraid I can't give you details about what's happening in the war. But ... look, I'm sorry. I'd be happy to explain what I'm trying to do here further, but I'm afraid I've got five more interviews to get through today and we're already running late. But I'm very interested in what you were saying earlier ... Please – it would be very helpful if you could expand ...

A: Do you still insist on needing to know my name on file?

(There is a pause.)

Q: Oh God. The problem is, if there is no name attached to this interview, I don't see how it will hold any credence with my—

A: My name is Waldstein. Rainer Waldstein. And now you know that, that is all I am prepared to tell you.

(The interviewee departs abruptly.)

June sighed internally: she wished now she'd agreed to keep Waldstein's identity a secret, if only to find out for herself what he had to say. Irma coughed, and asked if she could be excused; June gave her leave to go. The young man – she checked her notes: Fabian, Isaac; he, at least, had not been wary of giving his name – was still sitting hunched on the chair in the centre of the room, looking down. Her eyes scanned his story, just recently told. Again, the same problem: the business with his father on Kristallnacht

189

was, to be sure, deeply upsetting, and, to be sure, a gross contra-vention of human rights, but June, always pragmatic by nature and now pragmatised further by experience, knew it was another case of not quite enough. This was, without wishing to sound callous, a disappointment: as a Jew and a communist, one might have expected the worst possible treatment, beginning with deportation to a concentration camp, but he himself seemed to have been spared the worst as a result of his marriage to an Aryan.

She put the notes into her folder, and set them down on the table in front of her. She was wondering if Isaac might be her last inter-view of the entire trip, as well as of the day. She still had a few days left before she had to go back to the mainland, but the whole expe-rience was starting to depress her: the Ministry of Information might remain unmoved by the testimonies she had collated, but she was still the one having to sit and listen to the pain and the fear, all day. It had an effect. And going through her mind all the time, a critical undercurrent, critical of the pain and the fear, judging it, condemning it, as not good enough – not good enough because not bad enough – this conflict exhausted her, made her want it all to be over.

June was just thinking, in fact, about how quickly she could get back to London and her life, when Isaac said, in English: 'So how long will you be here for?'

She looked up, slightly startled. He had ceased his floor vigil and was looking at her; she felt he had probably been looking at her for some time. She made little of this – it was, she assumed, just tired eyes, resting where they lay – but she was surprised, as interviewees in general were not terribly keen to engage in small talk, especially after giving their testimonies.

'Oh, I have to be back in London by the middle of next week. I need to get on with submitting this report.'

He nodded. 'Do you think it will make a difference?'

She clicked her tongue. No interviewee had asked her this yet, and she hadn't thought about what her response should be. But there was a straightforwardness in the young man's eyes that made her feel there was no need for lies; no need for propaganda. 'I don't know. It's something of a sticking-point at the Ministry of

Information, the plight of the Jews. I'm trying to make them see how obviously something needs to be done, but . . .'

'What?'

'Well . . .' She paused, but she was too weary to self-censor, 'I'm not sure I should be telling you this, but I don't know if I've quite got to the heart of the matter.'

'The . . . ? I beg your pardon, I don't understand.'

'No. Well. It doesn't matter. I just think there must be more. I suppose what I mean is . . . perhaps I haven't really managed to get in touch with people here. Perhaps I haven't really got to know them properly.'

He nodded again, rubbing a hand on his stubbled chin, as if contemplating the best way to sort out her problem. June surveyed him, more seriously than before. His expression, she thought, was appealing; it gave out something, an openness, an accessibility, which was a welcome relief after some of the brick walls she'd faced. Also, he seemed to be lighter than earlier; perhaps something had been lifted by the telling of his story.

'Well . . .' he said, 'is this all you've been doing? These interviews?'

'Er . . . yes . . .'

He stood up and lifted his coat off the arm of the chair. 'Come with me,' he said.

The men passed by the outside of the café, carrying chairs.

'That's how you know they're on their way to something,' said Isaac.

June continued to look at the strange phalanx: so exotic, the Jews *en masse*, she thought – she'd missed that by interviewing them individually. All German, they must be, and yet they looked like men who drew their humanity not from that proscribed and impacted north, but from the widest net thrown across the southern and eastern seas, a dark rainbow of a race.

'Whatever it is,' Isaac continued, 'a lecture, a music recital, a piece of theatre – everyone who wants to go has to bring his own chair. Unless he's prepared to stand.'

They were speaking German, partly because June's German was

much better than Isaac's English, but also because it attracted less attention in the environs of Central Camp. Presently, they were being left to sit unmolested at a window table in Fritz Strang's café. Which is not to say that the sight of Isaac Fabian with a woman – a youngish English woman at that – did not attract attention among the other internees. But that attention was not, as it would have been with virtually any other imprisoned group, aggressive: it occasioned interest and comment rather than interruption. Besides, most of them had either been interviewed by June by now or else knew of her presence. She herself was more concerned about whether one of the British soldiers would take it upon himself to enquire what she thought she was doing fraternising so closely with the inmates, but her first surprise on venturing out of the interview room was how much the internees were left to their own devices. The British soldiers simply didn't come into the camp; from where she was sitting, she could see a sentry patrolling the Promenade beyond the barbed wire, but he couldn't have seen her. So, for the moment, she had no need of the story she'd concocted about having been given official leave to take her investigations a step further.

Strang brought them two Viennese coffees. June stared at hers: swirls of white from the topping were beginning to brown the black liquid underneath.

'It's whipped-up evaporated milk,' said Isaac, anticipating her question.

'You wouldn't know,' she said, reaching for a napkin, self-conscious about the *faux*-cream smudging her mouth. 'It's lovely.'

'It's not bad . . .' said Strang. 'It's not the way it used to taste when I made it in Vienna. But . . .' He shrugged – perhaps the most stereotypically Jewish gesture June had seen since she had arrived on the Isle of Man – and retreated, back to the kitchen. After he had gone, she noticed that a selection of cakes had somehow appeared on their table.

'Did you see him put those there?' she said.

Isaac smiled, for the first time since they'd met. It made quite a difference to his face, she noticed – it made his face into an invitation, although to what she didn't know.

'No. It's one of Strang's special skills: culinary sleight of hand . . .'

'How come you're able to eat like this?'

Isaac opened his hands. 'There's no rationing on the island, for some reason. Something to do with the abundance of its own produce . . .'

'No, I know that. But I had a cup of coffee when I arrived. In Lieutenant Colonel Rutter's office. It was astonishingly disgusting.' Isaac laughed, revealing, this close, a line of uneven bottom teeth. 'So, what I mean is – how is it with the same basic ingredients that the Jews manage to make a drink fit for a king while the British can't make one fit for my cat?'

Isaac's face eased into ironic. He considered her question for some time before answering. 'Because the British are the adults of the world and the Jews are the children.'

June nodded, in an understanding manner, an action which merged seamlessly into an uncomprehending shake of the head.

'What are the British good at?' he continued, by way of explanation. 'Book-keeping. Imperialism.' He counted with his fingers. 'Government. War. Engineering. Shipbuilding. Respectability. Inventing. Pensions. Driving.' Having reached ten, he put down his hands, but with a sense that he could have continued, if only he had more fingers. 'All the most grown-up – the most serious – projects in the world. Jews meanwhile are good at . . .' His fingers came up again. 'Food (including coffee). Music. Show business. Mordant wit.' *Sex*, his mind said. He felt an absurd urge to say it out loud, but resisted. 'Tailoring. Dancing. Talking. Money. Intellectualising. Narcissism. We're good, in other words, at pleasure. At playing. Like . . . children! Oh, and helplessness, of course. Something the Nazis knew. We're good at that, like children, too.' He paused, wondering whether he was talking too much, but he was enjoying himself now. 'Sigmund Freud's son is here, do you know that?'

'In Central?'

'No, he's in Onchan. I haven't read much of his father's work – I'm more of a Marx man myself, as I've told you – but he once said something about how growing up involves moving from the pleasure principle to the reality principle. That's why the Jews are the children of the world and the British the adults. The Jews just refuse to move away from the pleasure principle: the ones who run

Hollywood have gone so far as to make careers out of the pleasure principle. This country, on the other hand, is so relentlessly ruled by the reality principle one wonders if the British ever went through the pleasure principle.' He drained his coffee and set the cup back down again. 'And as for Freud, who else but a Jew would create an entire understanding of the adult psyche based on the self-pleasuring propensities of children?'

June sat back in her chair. Outside, the sea was calm, white waves forming long and easy on its surface like yarn on a loom. 'Well. That was quite a speech.'

'Yes. Sorry. I can become a bit fond of my own voice when I get going.' Isaac felt somewhat abashed. He had surprised himself, in fact. He was indeed given to speechifying, or at least to warming to his theme, but normally in a semi-public space like the refectory, among his peers; not while talking to a woman, a woman he had only just met. Was he trying to impress her? Or was there something about this woman that made him feel loosed, like a boat cut from its mooring?

'I'm not so sure that the British are quite as grown-up as you think,' said June. 'We're good at games, don't forget: cricket, rugby, football. And making jam. And I don't know how long you've been here, but a lot of what goes on in our attempts at government is extremely childish.'

Isaac laughed. He became aware that he was doing a lot of laughing in this conversation.

'And also, if you're a Marx man rather than a Freud man – how does *he* fit into this theory?'

'What do you mean?'

'I mean . . . if you're talking about being grown up . . . well – communism: that's about subjugating individual pleasure to the greater social good. That's the most grown-up idea ever invented. It's the Soviet Union, not Britain, that is ruled – iron-fist ruled – by the reality principle.'

Isaac nodded, more to himself than to her: she was clever, this woman, perhaps more than clever. She was an intellectual. Isaac had never met a genuinely intellectual woman before, even though, of course, as a Marxist, he had no doubt of their existence. 'It's a good point. Although I'm not sure the comrades presently suffering under Stalin think it's a regime too much concerned with reality.'

'I thought you were a communist?'

'I am a communist. I'm not a Stalinist.'

June smiled, and was aware, before she said them, that her next words were flirtatious. 'Well, you're not too grown up at least. For a communist, you're almost playful.'

Isaac returned her smile. He could feel his heart rising. 'I'm a *Jewish* communist, remember,' he said.

'So, what next? In half an hour there's a recital in one of the churches; or, a little later, there's a lecture on Goethe; or, if you really want to test yourself, we could go to a preview of the Christmas revue . . .'

'There's a Christmas revue?'

'Well, Hanukkah revue. *This Island Life*. I'm not sure I'd recommend it.'

They were standing on the steps outside Strang's café. Isaac was reading from the crumpled daily-event timetable. June was looking a little nervously out towards the sea, where a new sentry now stood beyond the wire, but with his back to the camp.

'Which one will tell me most about the people in here?' As she asked the question, her ear caught, from the house next door, the muffled sound of music. Not music in terms of pianos and violins, but the soft wail of prayer, a deeply Semitic sound, redolent somehow of flamenco and fado, a Sephardic song of hope and pain. June felt its foreignness, here on the shores of this Celtic sea. 'And that, presumably . . .'

Isaac continued to look at his timetable.

'We could go in there,' she continued, thinking perhaps he had not heard, or not understood. 'And join in the prayers.'

He looked up, although not towards the house of prayer. 'Not we . . .'

June frowned, then moved down the steps in order to squint at an angle through the dimly lit window. Inside, thirty or more men, in various shades of black, eyes shut, were swaying backwards and

195

forwards as if entranced, possessed by the pulse of their prayers. June's sense of another culture, uprooted and transferred, of the foreign transplanted, intensified. 'No women, of course . . .'

'No.'

'Do you not need to pray? I don't want to be keeping you from—'

'I don't pray.'

She stared at him. He was looking down again, although the timetable had been compressed into a ball inside the fist of his right hand.

'Sorry, I didn't mean . . . It's just I remember you told me your father was a rabbi . . .'

'He is a rabbi.' He looked at the makeshift temple for the first time. June spotted the change of tense, and cursed herself. 'But it was his religion that forced us apart.'

June, wanting to know more, not wanting to force herself too much into his world, waited to see if he would expand. He did not.

'What about *This Island Life?*' she said.

A little later, they were sitting in St George's Church, waiting to hear Schubert's String Quartet in A Minor, Opus 29: the *Rosamunde Quartet*, the first of the late, great string quartets to be written after Schubert had heard that he was terminally ill, as explained by a short man with thick glasses and a severe side-parting who was introducing the concert.

'Who's that?' whispered June.

'Hans Gal,' said Isaac. 'He's a composer himself. And a musicologist. He used to be head of the Vienna Bach Choir. And someone told me he's editor of *The Complete Brahms*, as well.'

This Island Life had been full; from outside they had heard much laughter and what sounded like a satirical song about the intense danger posed to Britain by its enemy aliens.

June shook her head. 'Where are the plumbers?'

'Pardon?'

'Here. Where are the plumbers? And the gasmen? And the welders? How can *everyone* here be an eminent musicologist, or a distinguished academic, or a Nobel Prize-winning writer? I've seen all of these here – *and* a host of leading architects and physicists and doctors and lawyers, but not a single plumber.'

The string quartet began. Isaac, though unmusical, found himself easily carried away by music. Like many intellectuals, he craved at times the direct effect of the abstract. Also, he liked to think of his ability with words as a kind of musicality, a way of singing the song of his soul without instrumentation.

'Is it because there are no Jewish plumbers?' June was continuing, *sotto voce*.

'Not many. But there are some, yes. Unfortunately, your best bet for getting out of Germany was being, in some way, a notable.'

'Because then another country would be interested in taking you . . .'

'Yes. And in a capitalist society, even the greatest plumber would not be considered a notable.'

June looked at him. Just as within the sprightly first movement of the quartet one could hear, if one listened carefully, Schubert's sadness, camouflaged within his overriding instinct for melody, she could see within Isaac's mask of friendliness something serious, something unswerving. She turned to look at the musicians, transported elsewhere, back to Vienna or even further, by their playing, and it occurred to her that her voyage of discovery beyond the interview room was turning into a date of sorts, and that it was the strangest date she had ever been on.

As they left the church, without speaking, they turned left, to walk round the back of the building towards the communal gardens. June, since arriving at Central, was staying at the Douglas Arms, an inn with rooms just on the other side of the wire, and it would have been easier to walk parallel to the Promenade. However, this way, they were more likely to continue to avoid the gaze of the sentry; and also perhaps because it would have felt too romantic walking along by the sea, the sweet pain of Schubert still resounding in their ears. The temperature had dropped, and it was dark, although half an hour remained before the ten o'clock curfew.

'So . . .' said June, slightly self-consciously, as if the cold air had returned her to her professional purpose, 'what do most people feel about being interned here?'

Isaac dug his hands into the pockets of his jacket. 'They accept it. Unfortunately. Most of them. It's an unusual kind of imprisonment – in holiday homes by the sea, with lectures and recitals and cabarets . . .'

'Birds in gilded cages,' said June, in English.

'Pardon?'

She approximated the expression in German.

'Well, yes, I suppose so,' said Isaac. 'And they know how much worse it would be for them in Germany.'

June sighed, and stopped walking.

'What?'

'Oh . . . I don't know.' She hesitated, not certain again why there should be a need for secrecy, but her years of working in the Ministry of Information had instilled in her a base sense that the giving of information must always remain proscribed. 'Well . . . this is my point. This is where I feel frustrated. There's this general sense that everybody's escaped something – something terrible. But no one seems to be able to say exactly what it is.'

Isaac frowned. In this air, he could feel the lines on his forehead forming. 'But what about all the things you've heard? What about the Nuremberg Laws? What about what *I* told you about being arrested, about my father?'

June screwed up her face; this was so difficult to explain. 'No, of course. I know how awful the Nazi state is. The problem is, so do my bosses. So does everybody.' She paused. When she began speaking again, she had reverted to English, and spoke slowly, as much for her own sake as for Isaac's. 'Well, no, that's wrong. That's not what I mean. What I mean is . . . everybody *thinks* they know how awful the regime is. They think they know and they've accepted it: it's bad, and we're at war with it, fine, we're doing what we can. But I think . . . I don't think, I *know*: the regime is more awful than everybody thinks. Much more awful.' She stopped and looked away from him. Rain was starting to fall. There was no shelter in the garden; the trees lining its outskirts were huge and leafless. 'That's what I came here hoping to prove. Or, at least, to corroborate.' She shook her head; water fell from her hair. 'And I've failed.'

Isaac looked at her face in profile, lit dimly by the weak rays from the church windows. There was something about June's face, he realised, that looked painted, not as in made-up, but as in a work of portraiture – even in movement there was about it a still-ness, a held shimmering, made more acute now by the rain, shining on her skin in droplets, as if her face were a work of art in progress, as if the paint had slightly run.

When he spoke, his voice was couched in the tones of someone who was trying to help. 'I spoke to Waldstein. You remember him? Slight man, wears a cap . . .' She nodded, turning to face him. He wondered if there were tears mixed in with the rain, but something about her steadiness of manner told him otherwise. 'I talked to him about you. I bumped into him outside my house just before I came to do my interview.'

'What did he say?'

'He said that he hadn't told you things that might help you . . .'

She blinked, in acquiescence. 'Why not?'

'Because he doesn't trust you. He doesn't trust the British. He thinks, Why should we trust them when they put us in here? Actually, of course, he doesn't trust anyone. That's part of who he is.'

June pulled a lock of wet hair away from her forehead, sharply, almost with irritation. 'Well, why should he? Why should anyone here trust me?' She wrapped her arms around herself, so tightly that water bled from her coat sleeves. Her eyes fixed his. 'Do you?'

He looked down. One voice of the many inside him was crying desperately, *Yes*. 'I don't know yet.'

She nodded, as if she knew this would be the answer; but no sense of resignation could stop her asking the next question. 'Are there things *you* haven't told me?'

Isaac's eyes stayed on the earth: his shoes, one of only two pairs he owned, were scuffed, but at least the rainwater had the effect of polishing the tips, even if he could feel it trickling into the myriad gaps between the leather and the wooden sole. He removed his glasses, and rubbed them against the outside of his jacket, beads of water having collected on the lenses like condensation on a cold bottle of beer. 'I have a suggestion,' he said, replacing them, look-ing up. Her face went into soft focus through the smears. 'You

199

must be in touch with the camp authorities. Perhaps if you speak to them on our behalf about something – about getting us something – then people here would trust you more, I think.'

'Yes . . . all right. But what? I thought you said life here was basically fine.'

'It's comfortable enough, in terms of food and furniture. But we're completely deprived of information. We're not allowed to listen to the radio, or even read newspapers. Half of the fear and anxiety in camp is due to that; to men thinking that, for all we know, Hitler has already occupied mainland Britain.'

June smiled. Isaac noticed how unperturbed she seemed by the rain and what it might be doing to her face and hair. 'He hasn't. I promise you. I'm not a double-agent, working for the Nazis.' She thought for a second. 'Well, to be honest, I was about to give up. But I will – I'll speak to Rutter about it. It can't make things worse. And, if nothing else, it'll make me feel that it hasn't just been a completely wasted trip – that I've achieved something for the people here.'

The sense of social responsibility contained in these words seemed to draw their dialogue towards a formal end. Isaac said something about how he really thought she should get out of the rain, and she replied with something equally polite about how he must get back before the curfew. There was a moment of hesitation, a beat just before their parting, when neither of them knew what gesture to use to mark it; and then Isaac put out his arm, and, as befits a meeting of minds designed to promote and consider the general good, they shook hands.

'What do you think? Is he . . . ?'
    'Kosher?'
Lulu laughed. 'Kosher?'

Lotte, deadpan, turned back to a print of Blake's *Urizen Creating the Heaven and the Earth*: God in all His cosmic insubstantiality. 'It's a phrase some of the London plebeians use to mean legitimate. Shows how deeply your husband's people have penetrated this culture.'

The two of them, with their children in tow, were walking through the English Painters section at the Fitzwilliam Museum. After an initial closure, at the start of the war, the museum was now open again for business, with Cambridge increasingly looking like it was not going to be a prime target for the Luftwaffe. Hitler had made a promise to Churchill, Lotte said, in return for the RAF not bombing Heidelberg.

'Well, my curiosity has always been aroused by Douglas,' continued Lotte. 'He can appear a bit of a cold fish at first, undoubtedly, but then again, he is English. Quite a lot going on beneath that unruffled exterior.'

Has he ever . . . ? Lulu wanted to ask. *Have you and he ever . . . ?*

'I think he'll do a good job on the testimonial, though. He's actually not a bad writer. He's had a couple of pieces published in the *Daily Mail*.'

'Mummy! Mummy! Ice-cream! I want!'

'Shush, Bekka.'

'Where has she had ice-cream?'

'They gave her some at the nursery, for their Christmas lunch. She hasn't stopped asking for it since.'

'Can we have some ice-cream, Mum?'

'Don't be ridiculous, James. We're in a museum.'

James and Steven, Lotte's very English – to Lulu's eyes – sons, had been hanging ten yards behind them for most of the trip, exaggerating their yawns and rolling their eyes. Lulu had noticed that Lotte's way of dealing with them was at once to talk to them as if they were adults and yet still somehow to patronise them.

'Painting, Mama,' said Bekka, pointing to another Blake, *The Whirlwind of Lovers*. 'It's a painting.'

'Yes, darling,' said Lulu absently. It was a thing her daughter did all the time now, identifying the world, exhibiting her understanding of it through nomenclature. Lulu hoped she would not repeat the word, as she often did, in German. 'Have you ever read any of Douglas's plays?'

Lotte laughed. A grey-haired man who was sitting at an easel sketching a copy of Turner's *A Beech Wood with Gypsies around a Fire* looked up and tutted, then tutted again when he realised that the noisy party included children.

'Yes, funnily enough. He gave me his last one to read. *The Forbidden Man*, I think it was called. It was fine. Not Shakespeare, but not Harley Granville-Barker either, thank God. All about his experiences in Spain . . .'

'Oh yes, he told me about that . . .'

'Did he? I'm rather surprised . . .'

'Bekka! Leave that alone!' She was unfastening the hose of a fire extinguisher, right under the not very watchful – in fact, closed – eye of a sleeping attendant. 'Bekka!' By this time, she was holding the nozzle in front of her gently enquiring face. '*Lasse das!*'

The sound of a German raised voice stirred the attendant from his slumber considerably quicker than the possibility of a little girl covering herself in foaming anti-flammable liquid. He looked up, eyebrows raised, sharp as a sentry.

'Oh dear,' said Lotte. 'Not in a public place, remember.'

'Oh, I'm sorry,' said Lulu, reddening. She wasn't entirely sure whether to apologise to Lotte or to the attendant. 'But when I'm worried – when I have to say things quickly to her – I forget.'

'Just don't let it happen again,' said the attendant, adjusting the peak of his museum hat to give himself more of a military air.

Bekka dropped the hose and began to cry.

'I think maybe we should head for the exit,' said Lotte.

*

Outside, it was colder than before. A few flakes of snow were falling, much to the joy of James and Steven, who began rolling and falling on the ground around the museum gates as if it already lay inches thick. Rebekka watched their movements, hypnotised.

'When are you meeting him?' said Lotte, apparently unconcerned by the danger level of her sons' play. She spoke in German, quietly.

'Tomorrow. At our rooms.'

Lotte raised an eyebrow, an action at which she was immensely skilled. 'At yours?'

Lulu tried to affect boredom. 'Yes. It was awkward trying to write the thing in a public place. And I didn't fancy going to his.'

'You thought it was overfamiliar?'

'If you like.'

Lotte sniffed. Lulu wondered if her amazement at the idea of Douglas visiting her at home was more to do with Lotte's imagination of what her home must be like than any other impropriety.

'Probably all for the best. You're safer on your own turf. Assuming safety is your object . . .'

'Lotte . . .'

Lotte held up her hands in innocence, but said nothing. A silence fell between them. The snow seemed to ease off, although the bite in the air suggested it would be back. Rebekka ran her unsteady run between the two boys, trying to join in, causing them to shout demands for her removal towards the two mothers. *Has he ever . . . ? Have you and he ever . . . ?*

'Well . . .' said Lotte, preparing to gather in her children, 'best of British luck, anyway. Or German. Whichever is luckier.'

'How did you meet him?'

Lotte looked round, surprised by the non sequitur, and by the intensity of Lulu's tone. 'He's an old schoolfriend of my husband's,' she replied. 'I had to meet them all when we first got engaged. Richard threw an enormous dinner party for them and all their peculiar little wives. Worse than meeting his family in some respects. The English gentleman tends to be closer to – certainly, he takes more account of the opinions of – his old public-school chums than his mother and father. Ghastly, most of them. Douglas, however,

I rather took to, partly because he was quiet and reserved but mainly because he didn't have a peculiar little wife.'

'So you saw him before the war?'

'Well, now and again. He'd come and visit. I rather looked forward to his visits.' She smiled, the left edge of her mouth rising further into her face than the right. It was a smile Lulu was learning to recognise. 'Did you know that in Eskimo culture, it's the done thing, when a man visits a friend of his, for the host to offer the visitor the pleasure of sleeping with his wife?'

Lulu looked at her, refusing to be shocked. 'Really? I never knew.'

'Yes. I think it's rather a super idea. Although I'm not sure I'd be prepared to support it in an igloo.'

'So . . . ?' said Lulu, suppressing her own smile. 'What are you saying, Mrs Gerard? Was Douglas offered you over dinner?'

Lotte's face was a mask of mock-horror. 'Good Lord, no. Heavens. You've seen our house. We're hardly Eskimos. James! Steven! Time to go!' The boys turned as one, and, without demur, ran in her direction. 'Besides, as far as I know, Douglas prefers blondes . . .'

Lulu, on her way to prevent Bekka, confused by the boys' sudden disappearance, from heading towards the street, turned sharply, but Lotte was already walking away, one hand trailing in the air behind her, signalling goodbye.

Looking at it now, June began to wonder again if Lieutenant Colonel Rutter's face had actually been designed for indignant surprise. In repose it looked wrong, his watery eyes and grey moustache providing for the viewer no focus, presenting no pattern, a face that looked as if it must be on its way to somewhere else. But now, with those watery eyes widening, and the moustache twitching, and the creases at every facial edge filled out, he looked . . . right.

'Well, Miss Murray, I must say I'm surprised.'

June nodded, finding it hard not to reply, *You don't say?*

'I was taken aback by your appearance on this island – at this camp indeed.' June continued nodding, not entirely sure what 'indeed' could mean in that context, but understanding that the Lieutenant Colonel was flustered. 'You arrived without warning—'

'That wasn't my fault, sir.'

'Well. The point is, we did our best to accommodate you under the circumstances – you've had unlimited access to the prisoners—'

'Internees,' corrected Corporal Penn, who was minuting the meeting, a recent innovation by his superior.

'Internees, yes. Thank you, Corporal.' Lieutenant Colonel Rutter's tone did not entirely match the sense of gratitude conveyed by his words. 'And I had assumed this meeting to be something in the way of a wrapping-up job. Thanks very much and goodbye and all that. But now it seems as if you want more from us . . .'

June stifled a sigh. 'It's just a suggestion, sir. Obviously, I wouldn't want to presume . . . I wouldn't in any way want to . . .' she hesitated over the choice of words, and then couldn't be bothered to worry about it, 'tell you how to do your job.' Rutter's face returned sharply to its home look. 'But I have spent the last ten days talking extensively to the men and women on this island, and I know that what many of them would like above all is to know what's going on in the world. One radio per house would do it. And newspapers.'

'Supplied free, I suppose?'

'No, they could buy them with camp currency, like they do everything else.'

'What's wrong with the camp periodicals? The *Onchan Pioneer* I particularly like . . .'

'Yes, it's very good . . . if you want to know about the camp laundry arrangements, or about an upcoming poetry reading, or to admire a cartoon of someone Germanic gazing at the sea. But not so good if you want to know the progress of the war in North Africa, or whether your home town may have recently been bombed.'

Rutter and Penn exchanged glances. The phrase 'women, they've got an answer for everything' hung between them almost as palpably as if they had spoken it simultaneously.

'What you have to understand, Miss Murray, is that these people are being kept here on suspicion. There is a reason for their internment: which is, at this time, we have no way of knowing who is an innocent and who is a guilty German. Who is just a common-or-garden citizen and who is a Nazi.'

Ask them what religion they are, perhaps? June felt herself suppressing.

'So our government has deemed it best for our national security to take no chances, and intern the lot. Now, assuming that therefore, among the innocent, there no doubt does exist a number of Nazi spies, what's the last thing you want to dish out to Nazi spies? Hmm?' June remained silent. Rutter's teeth, tiny in his mouth, came into view, as a small smirk fluttered under his moustache. 'Come now, Miss Murray, coming from the Ministry that you do, I would have thought it's a word that wouldn't take much finding?'

Drawing on reserves of calm she didn't know she possessed, June said flatly, 'Information?'

'Exactly! *Confuse* the enemy – one of the first principles I was ever taught. Keep him in the dark at all times.'

He sat back, his face now set in a new mask of self-satisfaction.

It didn't suit him as much as indignant surprise, June felt, but it was settling in nicely. She composed herself by looking out of the window. The snow had been falling now for over three hours. It was a pity there were no mountains on the island, she thought, to become snow-capped.

'Well, thank you, Lieutenant Colonel. I appreciate everything you've said. There are just a couple of points I would like to make, if I may.' Saying this, she infused her voice with vulnerability, as if knowing that his authority on the subject was far greater than hers: the tactic worked, as he granted her a condescending nod that she might proceed. 'First, the vast majority of people here are not "the enemy". They are refugees from the enemy. Secondly, I am not suggesting we provide them with classified documents procured from the War Office or Military High Command, simply with the BBC and a few copies of the *Daily Telegraph*. Not exactly prime sources of information, and not ones Berlin couldn't get hold of if it wanted to. And lastly, assuming that somewhere among all these frightened, Hitler-hating people, there does exist someone sympathetic to the Nazi state, and that somehow he or she does find out something in the newspapers or on the radio that might be of security value, how on earth is he or she going to relay that information to the enemy? You're not going to tell me that any of the camps are run so slackly that a potential spy could possibly have access to that kind of communication?'

Rutter shifted uncomfortably in his chair; out of the corner of his eye, he thought he could see Penn smirking, but could not be sure of it. He felt the urge to reprimand him, if only because it would reassert for a moment his sense of how things should be, his sense of structure. He was used to the strict geometry of military interaction, where you knew who was superior and who was inferior, and you adjusted your speech accordingly. Not to this type of talk, where someone appeared to be paying you respect but clearly was not. It was all so civilian, and so bloody feminine.

'The thing is, Lieutenant Colonel, sir,' said June, genuinely imploring, 'information is incredibly important to the people here. More important than it is to us, in a way. Because, truly, *we* are not the target of Hitler's bullets. *They* are. If the Nazis win the war, we may be unhappy living under a German flag. We may be angry, humiliated, frustrated and disenfranchised. They, however, will be dead. So . . . why not at least keep them up to date with how the war is going?'

Rutter's self-satisfaction seemed to have drained away as June talked. Even indignation was gone; instead, he let his features go flat, and his face fall, until it was just empty and tired. 'Well, I'm impressed with your conviction, Miss Murray, although I don't think any of us can say exactly what might or might not happen in the event of a German victory – let's hope we never have to find out. But the fact is, my hands are tied: official policy is that internees are not to receive radio broadcasts or read any news-papers save the camp periodicals.'

'Er . . . I'm not sure that's entirely correct, sir,' said Penn, looking up from his notes.

'I beg your pardon, Corporal?'

'Well, sir, I process all the correspondence from Whitehall, and, as far as I remember, the barring of radio and newspapers from internees was only a recommendation and could be lifted at your discretion.'

Rutter glared at his secretary, unbelievingly: not disbelieving what he was being told, but disbelieving that he had the imperti-nence to tell him now. And yet he knew that, officially, Penn could not be punished simply for relaying information contained in his correspondence. 'Are you sure?'

'Pretty sure. But if you hold on a second, I'll just go and check the files.'

A surge of panic went through Rutter at the thought of the awk-wardness of being left alone in the room with June at this point. 'No, no doubt you're right.'

'And, of course, sir, you'll remember memo G34/HP4.'

Rutter looked at his secretary with some suspicion. 'Ye-es . . .'

'The one we received from the Home Office last week?'

'Yes . . . just refresh my memory, would you?'

'Well, I can't recall the exact words, but in the main it was a letter recommending that, following questions being asked in

Parliament and some press attention about the situation here, all camp controllers should take measures to demonstrate their commitment to maintaining a high quality of life for the internees.'

Rutter's forehead creased. He did remember Penn mentioning that a letter from the Home Office had arrived last week, but he'd been characteristically vague about it, as if it wasn't of much importance. 'Right.'

'Well,' said June, 'I don't wish to poke my nose in any further, but it sounds to me as if giving them newspapers and radios fulfils the prescription of the memo perfectly.'

'Hmm,' said Rutter, who could see that it did, but didn't want it to look as if he'd been boxed into a corner. 'Well, all right. Leave it with me. I'll think about it.'

'Thank you, sir.'

Rutter nodded. His face made a not very successful stab at magnanimity. June lifted her coat from the back of her chair. A glance passed between her and Corporal Penn, but he looked away, unsmiling. There was an awkward pause, which Rutter instantly felt a rush to avoid.

'How much longer do we have the pleasure of your company, Miss Murray?'

'Not much longer; don't worry. There's a dance next week, isn't there? For husbands and wives who have been living in separate camps?'

'Yes, at Derby Castle.'

'I thought I might stay for that. I'm trying to get more of an insight into what the internees are really like as people. I thought that would be a good event to go to for that reason.'

Rutter nodded again, but absent-mindedly. He was not a bad man, but he found all this need to see the prisoners – the internees – as human beings exhausting. 'Well, well. Very good. Show Miss Murray out, Corporal.'

Penn rose with her. They walked in single file to the door.

'Just one thing, Miss Murray.' She turned. 'You mentioned the *Telegraph*. I can assure you that if – and it remains an if – *if* a newspaper is provided for the internees, it shall be the *Daily Mail*. It's the only truly respectable newspaper, as far as I'm concerned.'

June smiled graciously. 'And of course the one most virulently behind internment . . .' she said.

Once more, with a vengeance, Rutter's face became an archetype of indignant surprise. He wanted to shout *'Dismissed!'*, but instead waved his hand vaguely and mumbled, 'Yes, that's as maybe.'

In the ante-room to Lieutenant Colonel Rutter's office, Corporal Penn walked straight over to his desk and began arranging paper-work on it. June, a little uncertainly, tarried at the door long enough to catch his eye for a second and say, 'Thanks.'

'For what?'

She was taken aback by his frostiness. 'For helping me in there.'

Penn looked up briefly. His eyes were as cold as his tone. 'I wasn't helping you out. Minute the meetings, my arse. I'm a soldier, not a fucking clerk.' And, with that, he returned to his paperwork.

Isaac lay on his bed, watching the snow fall. It was mesmerising, the lilting dance of the flakes down through the black air. It was like looking at a flat section of the sky, on a night when it was peppered with slowly shooting stars.

Isaac was not a man much given to long introspection, to gazing out of windows. Brought up in Talmudic study, and then in Marxist exegesis, his inner ear had been trained to hear the fugal counter-point of argument and analysis, not the long, linear monotone of absorption. But depression, he had discovered, did not just slow down his thought process, forcing his mind to drag its wheels through the marshlands of self-pity and regret; it also twisted and fragmented the path of reason itself, rendering through lines hard to trace, thesis and antithesis tricky to balance, rational progress impossible to pursue. Yet, for the first time in a long time, he wasn't certain that he was depressed. In fact, he hadn't been certain that he was depressed since he'd finished telling his story in the interview room two days before. At first, he thought it might be something to do simply with the telling – perhaps it was true what Freud and his friends contended, that there was something psychically curative simply in talking, that it thawed out the frozen elements of the mind. But he had told it before, to Willie and Jimmy in the pub, and here to Kaufmann and others, and the effect had not been the same.

He knew what it was, of course. But still he had to find his way there by thinking, by turning over all the other possibilities in his mind: it still had to be a *conclusion*. He couldn't just admit to himself what his heart already knew: that his depression had been lifted by June. Whatever words he scatter-gunned around his head, the sight of her in the rain, her face wet and her eyes alive, would return, and every time it did, something in his spirit would shift upwards. He remembered how easily he'd talked about himself to her – how she'd said he was playful! Playful? Perhaps he was – perhaps that was what made him not a Stalinist. He felt the shallow amazement, as young men and women do, of thinking he had met someone able, so quickly, to read him, to see straight and sure into his soul.

On his chest lay a letter from Lulu. He had put off reading it, because its arrival had made him feel guilty. At this stage, he wasn't entirely sure why he should feel guilty, but he knew the sensation well enough – he knew it, paradoxically, from when he had first fallen in love with Lulu. He knew then the source of his guilt – his father – which at first seemed irrelevant to his present situation, but then he began to wonder. He loved his father. Whatever had happened between them since, this was incontrovertible. And he had known that, by falling in love with Lulu, he was going to be causing this other person whom he loved pain: mortal pain. A new conclusion, Aristotelian in form, was becoming inescapable. He felt something for June, which was in danger of causing Lulu a similar degree of pain. Therefore: he was falling in love with June.

He could not, would not, believe it. Isaac knew very little about love. Before Lulu, there had been talk of an arranged marriage with a girl from the synagogue – Esther, her name was – a tiny girl with a squishy nose and hair so black it looked dyed, and the young Isaac had been content with that, until he had gone to university. That was when the problem started, with the decision to go to university. His father had always wanted him to go to a *yeshiva*, of which there were three in Königsberg, to train to be a rabbi, but something, felt but not articulated, had propelled him to the

211

enormous classical building where Kant had taught. In one respect, it was his father's fault, for being a man for whom religion was a matter of intellect rather than faith. There is always that dichotomy in Judaism, with its emphasis on learning, and study, and commentary. Despite the odd element of mysticism, it does not promote the quality perhaps most central to all other religions – the emotional leap, the blind moment of belief. Not that they do not have faith; but Jews are always thinking, wrongly, that faith is something you can intellectually break down. This is where Isaac had inherited his need to find out.

But a university is not just a place where what you find out is all in books. And Isaac quickly picked up a lot of non-bookish news: that most people were not Jews; that the gaining of respect from your peers had little to do with how hard you studied; and, principally, that women had power. This was something he had not quite felt before, not even at puberty, because Isaac came at puberty via religion: his becoming a man physically, coincided with his becoming a man spiritually, with his bar mitzvah. Literally: he woke on the morning of his bar mitzvah to find his sheets sticky and stained for the first time, and thought for a second with horror that perhaps this was part of God's ritual, that members of the congregation would come and hold the linen aloft in celebration as he sang his way through Maftir and Haftorah. But just as the physical onset of adolescence was retarded in him, so too was the psychology; far from being rebellious at thirteen, as he stood upon the altar, singing out verse upon verse from the sacred text, he felt as if suddenly he understood – that these arcane words, and hundreds of others which previously he'd parroted, day in, day out, since he first learnt to speak, *meant* something. And so all the restless energy of puberty, all the raging desire, became channelled into God. Isaac's teenage years were spent in a state of virtually permanent spiritual ecstasy – he was a Jewish St Theresa, so preoccupied by prayer even his father was at one stage concerned.

Once he came out of the trance-state there was communism to fill the fervour, but, however intellectually fixated he became with the teachings of Marx, politics failed to match up to religion in one crucial sense: it didn't transport him. It excited him, it stimulated him, it exercised his mind, it concentrated his attention, but he wasn't lost in it. Nothing in his studies emptied him of words and made his soul liquid. Nothing in his studies – but something at the university did.

Lulu's face wasn't actually the first. Upon arrival, walking through the concourse of the university's Great Hall, Isaac thought he might faint from the faces. Everywhere he looked, there seemed to be a more beautiful confluence of female features. His life had been so closed up to that point, and had involved contact with so few women outside his family, that, in that instant, and at the age of nineteen, he discovered something about himself that most men know much earlier: he was in thrall to skin – soft, light-reflecting women's skin, their beautiful buffer against death. There were bodies everywhere too, of course, and Isaac's eyes would in time be drawn to them; but principally he was what you might call a face man. He couldn't believe the force of it, the way that some of the women's faces would draw his gaze towards them like their skin was steel and his eyes were magnets. It wasn't a sexual thing; or, at least, not exclusively. It was to do with rapture. Sex was part of it, but not central; nor did it figure straightforwardly as lust. Some of the faces would create in him the oddest mixture of feelings: at once a great sense of potential calm, that if he could look at this face for ever, then eternity would be sorted out, he would have for ever a feeling of well-being, and with that a terrible panic, that if he could not look at this face for ever, then he would be for ever outside, excluded, that peace would be eternally barred to him. All this from an instant's view, without any knowledge of the workings of the brain behind the face.

It was uncontrolled, his looking at that stage – his gaze would flit from face to face, like a crazed bee searching for its flower – but then, when his eyes came to rest, as they did, on Lulu's face, the day after she had seen him in the refectory, they stayed. Hers were the first eyes to return his gaze, and the effect of that was locking. Here was the face he could drown in. Here was the face that would let him look at it for ever.

Now, with the letter from his wife boring a hole in his chest, he realised he had never before stopped to consider whether the feeling

213

of for ever, instilled by that first moment of looking at Lulu, actually was lasting for ever. He had just assumed that it would. Isaac was a man of commitment; his instincts were fiercely defensive, under the assumption that whatever he loved – Judaism, communism, his family – would be attacked, and he would fight to protect it. But he had never contemplated the possibility that the attack might be launched from within. Lulu had been right, when she'd told Douglas that Isaac was, in a sense, naive, at some level, an innocent. It was as if no one had ever told him that the thing about love – that kind of love, the rapture – is that it doesn't last. He knew the rapture had gone, because he could feel it returning, only this time propelled by a different face – darker, more complicated in feature, but somehow familiar: more like the face prescribed for him, the one he would have expected to see resting on the pillow opposite his every night when he was still under his father's sway. He could feel the rapture coming back, and its return was terrifying because it rendered all else empty in comparison; it made him feel the lack at the centre of life without it.

His thoughts were going nowhere. They made no sense to him – why all this focus on June's face when what had seemed to hook his interest in the first place was her obvious intelligence? The heart was such a maze: it made him yearn for the straight lines of politics. He took the letter off his chest and folded open the thin blue paper. The OPENED AND READ BY HM CENSOR stamp tore in half.

Dearest Isaac,

Hello my love. How are you? I hope everything is as good as it can be. Thank you so much for your last letter, which I read out loud to Bekka, as usual. Did you go to that Schubert recital you mentioned? Perhaps you thought of me during the slow movement; you remember how much I always liked Schubert when he's sad. I'm glad you enjoyed the food parcel I sent. I'll try to get another sausage for the next one.

Things are fine here. Mrs L thinks she might be able to get me some more cleaning work for a friend of hers who lives in Cherry Hinton. It's a bus ride, but it will really help with money. Maybe if it works out I'll be able to send a string of sausages next time!

Bekka is very well – she's growing into such a lovely, pretty girl. Some people have said that she looks like me, but I see much more of you in her. Her hair is starting to curl. Lotte thinks I should get it cut, but I like it messy. I think children look much older once they have their hair cut. It's probably selfish of me, but I want her to stay looking as young as possible for as long as possible.

The mention of Bekka – and particularly this rendering of her, the sense that Lulu was attempting in some way to freeze her, to preserve her, subconsciously, as Isaac interpreted it, for him – forced him to put down the letter for a second. His daughter was always in his thoughts. Always: the point which he had not articulated to Jimmy and Willie that time in the Eagle, about the stability of a man's love for his child, held true even in her absence. His thoughts of Lulu could oscillate, one day stronger than ever, another day weak, like the signal of a radio station, but the image of Bekka held fast in his mind, steady as breathing, an unquestioned constant. An image came to him now, a day in the spring when, because Lulu had had to clean very early in the morning, Isaac had for the first time taken Bekka out in the pram by himself. He remembered that the sky was classically blue, that the trees were holding out buds of white like gifts to pedestrians, and that the pram had to be held fast so as not to drag him like the owner of a mad dog down Hertford Street; but most of all he remembered the thrill of responsibility, the strange excitement that came with being utterly liable for the welfare of another human being, engendered every time he looked down and saw his daughter's pleadingly blank face.

Yet here was something, obvious but still unconsidered: she would be changing. This image around which his love clustered was out of date; by the time he was released perhaps unrecognisably so.

This thought made his insides give. His love for Bekka might be constant, but she was not; nor indeed, he realised, thinking back over his previous ruminations, was his relationship to her. It was, like everything else – and he felt a stab of self-distaste, unprecedented but intense, for always having this vocabulary to hand – a *dialectic*, which could change as her life did, or – as he had been contemplating, incredible though it felt – as his did. He felt suddenly angered, suddenly furious that desire was turning out to be yet another force – like Nazism, like internment – pushing him towards places he did not necessarily want to go, causing terrible damage to him and everything he loved. He resolved again to put any more thoughts of June out of his mind, and continued reading.

Talking of Lotte, you remember her friend Douglas Lean, whom you became so close to last year? Well, I've got great news. He's agreed to do your third testimonial for me. He's a playwright, and a journalist, as you know, of course, so at least his one should be extremely well written! He should have done it by next week, so I'll send all three of them in as soon as I get it, and – I want to say God willing, but I know that'll annoy you, so I'll just say with a bit of luck – we should have you back with us early next year.

Are you going to any more concerts? Do you remember seeing Ottilie Metzger-Lattermann singing that Clara Schumann song-cycle in Bayreuth? I held your hand during that beautiful song, the one that went . . .

Why will you question others, who are not faithful to
*   you?*
Believe nothing but what both these eyes say!
Believe not strange people, believe not peculiar fancies;
Even my actions you shouldn't interpret, but look in
*   these eyes!*
Will lips silence your questions, or turn them against
*   me?*
Whatever my lips may say, see my eyes: I love you!

If only you could see my eyes! They would be saying the same thing. Anyway, my darling, I can hear our little girl crying now so I'd better go and see what she wants. Keep yourself well, please, especially as it's getting so cold – it

snowed here yesterday, and it must surely be colder still, living so near the sea. You are in our thoughts always,
All our love,
Luluxxx

The last part of the letter threw Isaac further out of his reverie than he had expected. Now that the postal system on the island was working properly, he and Lulu corresponded at least once and sometimes twice a week. Originally, their letters had been laced with suppressed emotion, or at least as much emotion as could be suppressed and still contained within lines that the sender knows are to be read by HM Censor. Recently, however, Isaac realised, their correspondence had settled somewhat. Although the letters still regularly contained proclamations of affection and yearning, the intensity of these proclamations had become becalmed in the humdrum swapping of information, food, money, clothes and all the other business of everyday life. Mundanity was winning over pain and passion, as it does all battles in the end, being the only truly permanent state.

Isaac had taken it for granted that the letter would provide simply the usual information; he had been avoiding it, in fact, for precisely that reason, fearing, correctly, that nothing would exacerbate his guilt more than the humdrum, the innocent and cosy detailing of his wife's life in Cambridge with Bekka. And then suddenly there was this – 'Douglas Lean'. At first, Isaac wondered if separation and perhaps food deprivation had driven his wife a little mad – he had never met Lotte, aware of her only as someone whom Lulu had mentioned once or twice before in her letters, let alone any of her gentleman friends. Then, the song: he remembered going to a Clara Schumann recital in Bayreuth early on in their courtship, and, yes, he remembered it as a romantic evening, but this particular song? He racked his memory, but the words stayed unfamiliar. It was so out of character for Lulu to write it all down as well. Her handwriting in the letters was a small, bunched version of her normal hand, because, he knew, she was always trying to save space, and get in as many words as possible; and yet this song took up virtually a quarter of a page.

And then, as it were, the pfennig dropped. For all his tendency to deep thinking, Isaac was essentially gullible: he took things at face value, like a good materialist should – only the religious see the hidden everywhere. So it was only on a second reading that it occurred to him that Lulu might be trying to tell him something – something that she did not want HM Censor to know. She was telling him that she'd found someone to write the third testimonial, someone he'd never met. That must be what was behind all that business about how close he and Douglas Lean had become; it was all a ploy to disguise the (no doubt illegal) truth from the Censor. But what sort of character reference could someone who didn't know him write anyway? And – more to the point – how on earth had Lulu persuaded him to do it?

This was presumably where the song came in. She was telling him to trust her. She was saying that if she could see him – or, rather, if he could see her – he would understand that whatever she was doing, she was doing it for love.

Outside, on the street, he could hear Kaufmann and Seligmann on their way into the house, arguing loudly about the lecture they had just attended: 'Greek Tragedy'. He felt no wish to talk to them. He put the letter away in the tiny drawer by the side of his narrow bed, and, undressing quickly, clenched himself like a fist under the blankets, trying to feel all parts of him covered against the cold, although the sheet on first touch felt icy as the snow still falling outside his window. Swinging slowly into sleep, he felt strangely proud – of himself, initially, for having deciphered the letter's code – and then of his wife, for doing such a thing on his behalf, and – almost more so – for managing to convey the information to him. He held on to these feelings, quite until the moment of unconsciousness, when images began melting, one into another, Lulu into snow into strange men into his father into June, her face, her face.

Lulu busied herself trying to make their room look respectable. She had found that while she was reasonably competent at cleaning other people's houses, she was unable to devote the same energy to laundering their own living-quarters. Partly, she was simply too tired when she returned from work to pick up a duster; partly there was always Bekka to feed and bathe; and most importantly, recently, she had surrendered, come to the conclusion that it was always going to be a grim little room, however spotless the surfaces.

Today, though, she was going at it; she had even surreptitiously brought back a tin of furniture polish from Mrs Lambert's, most of which had gone on Bekka's crib, because it was the only piece of furniture in the room that was worth polishing. On another day, the irony of spending so much time buffing and preening something which she didn't use any more – Bekka was too big for it now, and slept with Lulu, in her bed – would have perhaps sapped her will to continue the job, but she wanted Douglas Lean to think well of them.

And it allowed her to channel her anxiety about his impending visit into work, the perpetual rubbing expending her nervous energy at least slightly. Lulu was not by nature anxious, but this last week she had woken up with butterflies already fluttering in her stomach, before she even had time to work out what she was nervous about. It would not dissipate much during the day, either; it was as if the thermostat of her body had been reset a touch higher. She told herself it was just another symptom of living without Isaac, but a part of her knew that was not the whole truth.

She was alone in the house. Mrs Fricker was away, visiting her sister in Kings Langley – there would have been no possibility of Lulu receiving visitors otherwise, certainly not male ones – and she had managed to beg a favour from one of the women at the church nursery, to look after Bekka for an extra couple of hours. She wasn't entirely sure of her own motives for asking that last favour, but told herself that if they were going to get this testimonial finished, the last thing they needed was a two-year-old demanding her tea the whole time.

She checked the face of her bedside clock, ten minutes fast as ever beneath its pair of rusty bells: five o'clock. He would be here any minute. On the mantelpiece, next to the photograph of her and Isaac in Danzig, stood a new purchase: a small, stand-alone face mirror. A hairline crack spidering across its left-hand corner had reduced it to under a shilling at a junk shop in town. She looked at herself. Lulu knew she was an attractive woman, and this basic confidence in her appearance – plus, until recently, the sheer lack of a mirror – meant that she was not usually given to lengthy or microscopic self-scrutiny. Perhaps, as well, she had been married for long enough now to take her husband's attraction to her for granted, or, as couples do once each other's face becomes as the wallpaper, not to consider it at all. However, today, and without wishing to think too hard about why, she looked at herself.

Her eye had been caught by how old she had looked. At first, she thought it was just a trick of the light, but when she looked closer it was true: time had smeared itself in shadows underneath each eye, in pin-pricks across her cheeks, in a spider's web on her brow. She wondered if this was what happened if you made do without a proper mirror for a long time. Prevented from looking at yourself every day, you lose the imperceptibility of ageing; then, when you finally are confronted with your own face, it's a shock, the same shock that normally one experiences only when meeting a long-lost friend, or at a school reunion.

Quickly, she found her handbag. Rummaging inside it, she picked out her one tube of lipstick. It was worn down virtually to the end; she could feel the cold of the metal circle on her lips, scraping against the red wax, but at least she hadn't been driven to using beetroot, like the women in the newspapers were always telling you to. There was a gentle knock on the door. She checked her image in the mirror; her lips looked fuller and more colourful, but for a second, and with a stab of fear, she thought she had made it worse – she looked older still – before realising that she was look-ing at the crack in the mirror, lying across her face.

Immediately after letting him in, she wished she had gone to his flat for this meeting. There was something about having to lead him directly upstairs, as soon as he'd come through the door, that didn't feel at all right. And once they were upstairs, although they sat round the table by the bay window, drinking tea and discussing how long the snow might last for all the world as if they were in a living-room, the heavy presence of the two beds immediately behind his chair hung over them like a smell, like something she could breathe. She could tell, as well, that he was taken aback by the sparseness of their living arrangements – in the pit of her, she did not know herself whether the cause of her self-consciousness was sexual or economic; whether she felt more awkward because they were near the beds, or because it was clear that she and Isaac did not have any other rooms. She considered transferring the meeting down to the house living-room, but was too frightened, knowing that if Mrs Fricker came back to find a cushion set at the wrong angle, questions would be asked, questions to which the only answer would be eviction.

'So . . .' said Lulu, almost as soon as he'd set down his tea from the first sip, 'shall we get on?'

Douglas looked so surprised at this sudden curtailment of small talk that Lulu wondered if she'd got it all wrong, if only she had felt the self-consciousness in the room, and that her briskness was therefore misjudged. She was a little ashamed, and her mood soft-ened with it.

'Certainly. Yes. Why not?' he said. He leant over and brought to the table a small, hard case. He clicked it open, to reveal a deeply black Remington typewriter, which squatted on the table with such a sense of weight that Lulu could not imagine how it could be con-ceived of as portable. Having fed the carriage with paper, he produced his notebook from the top pocket of his jacket. His glasses, Lulu noticed, were not in evidence this time. 'Well,' he said, flicking over a couple of pages, 'I've done a rough draft. I thought we'd go through it bit by bit – and once you give me the nod, I'll type it up.'

'Immediately?'

'Yes. I've got nearly forty words per minute, you know. I could make virtually any typing pool in the country.' His eyes went to the pad; then he looked up at her. 'Shall I . . . ?'

Lulu wanted to laugh now. It was strange how half of her was frightened of this man, and half of her found him endearing. 'Please do.'

He smiled. 'I feel I should clear my throat theatrically . . .'

'If that feels right, Mr Lean.'

'Douglas. Ahem.' She laughed. He looked pleased, and then glanced down to his notes. '*Mr Isaac Fabian, of 42 Hertford Street, Cambridge, became known to me* . . . I wasn't sure when we should say this was, actually . . .'

'Well, we arrived in the country only in August of last year.'

'Right. So when did you meet Lotte?'

'Lotte? About seven months ago . . .'

'But you could have met her earlier . . . You may even have known her in Germany . . .'

Lulu laughed a different laugh. 'I don't think so. Well. I might have known her before I got married. But afterwards, I did not really mix in Lotte's circles.'

Douglas put his finger and thumb to his forehead in classical 'thinking' mode. 'Hmm . . . I think that's good enough. They won't investigate in that sort of detail.'

'I am not quite with you . . .'

'Well, I can always say I met Lotte in Germany, some time ago. I've been to Germany a number of times. If I can say I met you and Isaac there, as friends of Lotte, we can increase the time I've known him – therefore making me a better referee.'

Lulu bit gently on her lower lip. Instinctively, she didn't want to tell Douglas that she had already written to Isaac, trying to tell him if he should ever be questioned about it, that of course he knew Douglas Lean, had become a close friend of his last year. 'I don't know, Douglas. It seems to me we should try to keep the lies . . .'

'To a minimum.'

'Yes. I think it would be better if you just say that you met here.'

He stroked the palm of his right hand with the thumb of his left.

Something about his manner suggested a reluctance to change his proposal: whether this was because he was convinced it was the right way to proceed or just because it was his idea, Lulu was not sure. 'Fine,' he said, resuming his smile, and striking some lines boldly through the pad. 'So what if it just says ... *Mr Isaac Fabian, of blah, blah ... became known to me on my being introduced to him by my friend Lotte Gerard in the summer of last year.* Actually, that's convoluted. *I was first introduced to Mr Isaac Fabian, of blah, blah, by my friend Lotte Gerard in the summer of 1939.* All right?' Lulu nodded. Douglas's fingers went to the keys, typing in quick, firm strokes. He finished and continued reading from the pad: '*Straight away, I was impressed by what a friendly, open man he was ...*' He stopped, raising a finger in the air. 'Actually, I tell you what works well with meeting here: ... *especially considering what he and his family had recently been through in Germany.*' He looked up, enquiringly, with an air of having incorporated her wishes, and although Lulu nodded again, she felt oddly excluded from the process. Douglas typed it in. '*From there, we met several times over the next few months, and it was in the course of that time that we became ...*'

'Close ... friends.'

Douglas looked up. 'I was going to say "good friends". But I think you're right. "Close" is better. *We became*', he typed as he spoke, '*close friends, up to the time of his internment.* Right, that's the introductory details out of the way, now we can get on with praising your husband to the skies! Stop me if I've gone too far ...' He rechecked his pad. '*I can honestly say that Isaac Fabian is one of the most gentle ...* That was the word you used when we met last time, wasn't it?'

'Yes.' She felt the truth of it. She wondered how gentle Douglas was. Outside the window, the snow had started to fall again, in flakes fat and white enough to be visible without the hazy auras of the blacked-out streetlights.

'*One of most gentle men I have ever met. Any kind of violence, or subversion, is totally antithetical to his nature.*'

'Antithetical?'

'Opposed to. I was going to say "alien" but I think that's

probably an unfortunate word. *He has spoken to me with great forcefulness of his delight and gratitude at being granted refuge in this country. He has also communicated, on other occasions, his support of the British role in the present conflict, although always with a sense that all he would wish is for the war to be over, and for both our nations to live again in peace.'*

'That is excellent, Douglas,' she said. 'Thank you so much.'

He smiled, with some attempt at bashfulness, typing as he did so.

'Is there more?' asked Lulu.

'Not much.' He coughed. *'Isaac Fabian, despite the difficult circumstances associated with his coming to and staying in this country, has always been as kind and generous to those around him as possible. I remember going for a walk with him along King's Parade, and seeing him surreptitiously slip considerably more change than he could afford into the hat of a poor unfortunate who was sitting there.'*

'I am not sure about that part,' said Lulu.

'No, neither am I. "Poor unfortunate" is a bit Dickensian. "Beggar" sounds too harsh, though.'

'No, I do not mean the words. I mean the thing you are saying he is doing. Isaac does not believe in giving money to beggars. He says it is the job of the state to provide for them.'

'Oh. Right. Of course.' He clicked his tongue. 'It's just that I thought it was a good thing, because of – you know – the way Jews are' – he hesitated – 'the way they are *supposed* to be. Certainly how the man from the Home Office will suppose Jews to be. I thought it would be good to contradict that, as it were – to suggest that Isaac is not like that.'

'He is not like that,' said Lulu, defensively.

'No. But it might not be a bad thing to say, anyway.'

She raised a hand to her mouth, trying to formulate what she was going to say next without making it sound too aggressive. 'But Douglas . . . I thought the whole idea of this was to try to create a real picture of my husband. If you just wanted to say whatever you like about him, why are you talking to me?'

For a second, the Englishman looked young, like a boy, with his

224

secret shames on show. He flushed, and opened his mouth to answer, but before he could begin, into the room came the cry, like a creature in chronic pain, of the air-raid siren. It grew quickly to its high, strident note, wailing across the Fens and through the ancient cloisters of Cambridge.

Lulu stood immediately, her first thought coming to her faster than sound. 'Bekka!'

'Where is she?'

'At the nursery! They are looking after her until six . . .'

'Do they have an air-raid shelter there?'

'They go in the church crypt. It has happened once before, when I was there.'

Douglas got up. 'Well, she'll be fine then.' But Lulu was frantically opening their one cupboard, searching for her coat. 'Lulu, what are you doing?'

'I must go to her. She'll be frightened.'

'But you can't go out during the air raid! What if you get killed? What will happen to Bekka then?'

Lulu stopped, holding her coat limply in her hand. The noise of the siren was swamping her thoughts. She felt the tears welling, urgently. 'What am I going to do? What should I do?'

He came over, his tread steady, and put his hand on her shoulder. 'Is there an air-raid shelter here?'

'There is an Anderson shelter. In the garden.'

'Right. Well, you and I – before we both get killed – are going to get ourselves in there. Most likely the all-clear siren will sound in ten minutes anyway – it's probably just some bombers passing through on their way to Ipswich.'

Hitler has made a pact not to bomb Cambridge, because of Heidelberg, ran breathlessly through Lulu's mind.

'If not, if it goes on for longer, we'll brave the streets together. I'll come with you to the nursery shelter.'

Lulu looked at him. His stone-grey eyes radiated certainty; he had become a man of action, a man who immediately knows what is best in a crisis, a man who had fought in Spain. She had lived a long time now without a man, and it felt good, it felt right, to relinquish the decision to him. And anyway, before she had time to agree, he was pushing her out of the room and down the brown-carpeted stairs towards the back door.

The Anderson shelter, named after its inventor, Churchill's Home Secretary, Sir John Anderson, and issued free during the war to all households earning under £250 a year (including Mrs Fricker's, therefore, particularly if one didn't take into account – and usually she didn't – the rent paid to her in cash by the Fabians), was not, in general, a salubrious space: six sheets of corrugated iron, bolted together and covered with soil, they tended to be, at best, cold, damp, draughty and cramped. For Mrs Fricker, however, the arrival of the Shelter Construction Kit at her house had occasioned not drab thoughts of toolkits and long nights in hiding from circling Junkers, but something of an epiphany: with these materials, she realised that she could, in a sense, fulfil her late husband's dearest wish to build a garden shed. So Mrs Fricker's Anderson shelter was not just another one of the rudimentary metal huts you could see leaning against back walls in gardens all down Hertford Street. Indeed, it was much more than a substitute shed. Using the money left to her by Randolph, she set about making her Anderson shelter a place her late husband would have been proud to sit in for hours on end, smoking his over-stuffed pipe and wondering where the faint smell of gas was coming from. The floor, left bare in most shelters, was covered in the finest black linoleum; a high-quality second-hand rug lay on top of it; on the curved walls hung, at a slightly uncomfortable angle, a series of paintings of flowers; there was a felt covering on the roof, which protected the shelter from moisture seeping through the covering of earth; tucked against the far wall, a camp bed, covered with blankets; in one corner, a bookcase, containing an anthology of Dickens, and a copy of the Ministry of Home Security booklet, 'Air Raids: What You Must KNOW, What You Must DO'; and, in another, beautifully arranged on a four-foot wooden trellis, stood a series of flowerpots, in each of which Mrs Fricker had placed candles, which served as sources of both light and warmth. Isaac, on first going in there, had remarked how preferable it was to his and Lulu's room.

226

Douglas Lean struck a match. Lulu heard the sharp sandpaper rasp, and then saw his face, more Cubist than ever in matchlight, all hard-angled planes of light and shade, as he brought the flame up to a cigarette.

'Would you like one?'

'No. Thank you. But could I have a match, please?'

He lit another.

She took it, her hand trembling, or at least appearing to tremble in comparison to the almost inhuman steadiness of his. She lit each flowerpot in turn, until the whole terracotta altar was alight. Then, one by one, she covered each pot with another. She glanced back over her shoulder to see Douglas looking at her intently. 'If you cover them with other pots, they heat up quicker. And, you see, the light still shines through the hole in the bottom of the pot on top.'

'I see,' he said.

She drew back onto one of the two armchairs set on the Persian rug. He sat opposite her. The light from the candles took a while to settle, each individual flame shivering into life, before they seemed to merge into a general illumination.

'Perhaps this will help while we're waiting . . .' From his jacket pocket, Douglas drew what at first sight to Lulu appeared to be a shining shield, a circle of light, but which, once her eyes grew accustomed to its reflection of the candles, turned out to be a concave hip flask. 'Brandy . . .'

Lulu hesitated; she was not a great drinker, but the air in the shelter was biting. Her breath was so visible in the half light, it seemed as if she had accepted the offer of a cigarette. She remembered, as a precocious child, pretending on winter days that she was smoking, lifting two fingers away from her mouth and breathing out long, luxurious breaths.

'Thank you,' she said, reaching for the flask. The metal was warm, from his body. The liquid was oily, and warmer still; it tasted of the colour she could not see it was, amber. Inside her, it worked its heating magic.

'Shall we continue?' said Douglas.

'Pardon?'

'With the testimonial . . .'

Lulu laughed. She noticed he had brought the typewriter with him; it was resting on his lap. 'In here?'

'Why not? The light's not too bad. And I'll bet there's a torch in here somewhere too . . .'

'Yes, there is.' Lulu picked it up from under her chair. Turning it on, the beam was trained on his face, briefly clear, washed out in white light. He looked startled, caught out, as people picked out in spotlight do.

'Thank you,' he said, taking it from her. He took his pad from his pocket and placed it on the tiny metal table between them. Holding the torch in his cigarette hand – the two lights were like a little display, the white sweep and the crumbling orange glow – he directed it towards the writing. 'There's not much more anyway. We'll just forget the bit about giving money to the beggar, then, and cut straight to . . . *I am of the opinion, moreover, that should Mr Fabian, who possesses an eminent degree from Königsberg University* – I thought it best not to say in what – *be released back into society, he would become a useful and prized member of the community. I pledge my wholehearted and freely given support for that release, as soon as it may become possible.*' He looked up at her. 'And then I sign it. That's it. Should I type?'

'Please.'

Using his free hand, he one-finger-typed the final words of the testimonial, agonisingly slowly for Lulu. She realised, as he did so, how much it meant to her to have got this done; the thwack of each key was like a dent in her brain. She took another sip of brandy. Outside, she could hear the bombers, impossible to tell from their distant thrum whether they were circling or just passing overhead.

'Done,' he said, lifting the paper free from the carriage. He laid the testimonial on the table between them. 'Now I just have to put my name to it . . .' He took his pen from his jacket. About to sign, he poised it above the bottom of the page for a second. 'Is there anything else you'd like? Or don't like? Now's the time to tell me.'

'No,' she said, and worried she had said it too quickly, thinking she had sounded greedy for it. 'It is perfect.'

He wrote. Her senses seemed inflamed: she could hear the nib, the scratch of gold on paper. She saw the sweep of his name,

Gothic, florid and underscored, and thought, in an almost giggly way, how typically adult it was of him to possess a proper, fancy signature.

'There you are.' He pushed it across the table towards her, like a contract, as if she were to sign it too.

She picked it up, holding it up to the light like a piece of parchment, as if searching for something, a watermark, a hidden inscription in the margin. 'Thank you,' she said eventually.

Douglas leant back into his chair and took a long drag at his cigarette. 'Do you recognise your husband in my description?' he said.

'Perhaps. A little. It is difficult, because I know you do not know him. So I . . . I hear the lie more than the truth. I mean . . .' she added, quickly, looking over the page to him, 'please do not mistake me, I am so grateful. And it is very good. I think it is exactly what I need to send to the Council. It is very nice about him.'

Douglas nodded. 'Does it make you feel proud?'

'Proud?' Lulu laughed. 'Yes, in a way. I suppose I should be proud for being married to such a . . . what did you say? . . . *useful and prized member of the community*!'

Douglas laughed too. 'Perhaps I should put in some of his bad points just to make it sound a bit more realistic. Has he got any?'

'Well, yes.'

There was a pause. Then they both laughed together. Lulu felt her mind slipping on the brandy.

'Are you going to tell me?' said Douglas.

Lulu looked at him mock-reproachfully. 'Hmm. He snores quite badly, sometimes. And he has a habit . . . it is, if he has an itch, on his arm, say, he will scratch it and scratch it, until you think it must not be itching now any more, but still he will be scratching away. That does . . .'

'Get on your nerves?'

'Yes.' She was not sure she should be telling him these things, but he had an ability to steer her towards play. She raised the brandy to her mouth once more, then wiped her lips, thinking of other things. 'Oh! And even though he is supposed to be more a communist than a Jew now, still he always wants to eat the most terrible Jewish food. These things he always wants me to cook, these potato pancakes. Can you imagine trying to cook potato pancakes on that stove in our room? I hate them!'

They laughed again. Lulu felt herself relaxing with relief, and with relief came a desire to celebrate the gaining of the third testimonial. She drank some more brandy, noticing she was starting to enjoy the taste, rather than the taste being an obstacle she had to overcome to get the warming fuel into her stomach. Playfully, she grabbed his notepad. 'Did you write some more?'

He lurched forward, swinging his arm to take it from her, but it was a move made clumsy by the cramped space, and she easily dodged his hand, holding the pad above her head.

'Yes. Some. I made some notes. But I don't think you need concern yourself—'

She flipped a page. On it were not, as she expected, notes, rough doodlings towards what she had already heard, but a whole neat paragraph of new words, written in his elegant scrawl.

'*Isaac Fabian is also a caring father and loving husband, much missed by his two-year-old daughter Rebekka and wife Lulu. She herself is also a valuable member of the community, who has made a wonderful job of bringing up Rebekka virtually on her own.*' She looked up, smiling, quizzical. 'Well, thank you, Douglas. I had not thought – but now you mention it . . . yes. Perhaps we should have included that.'

'Lulu. Please. Give me the notepad.'

She shook her head, laughing. '*Moreover . . .*' and now her look shifted as she caught sight of the words in advance of reading them aloud, '*she is a beautiful, beautiful woman – she has an outer beauty which makes me stop breathing . . . but which I know is just the reflection of her inner truth.*'

Her voice had slowed as she had read, the fall of each word in the air measuring the change taking place between them. Distantly, somewhere out over the Fens, she thought she could hear the bombs falling. She put the pad down on the table. There was a moment of nothing, and then he picked it up.

'Douglas . . .'

'*I did not realise this at first.*' He read steadfastly, unswervingly, as if the words themselves would carry him home. His eyes did not leave the page. '*I did not write this testimonial because of her. At least, not consciously. But through continued contact with her, while trying to help her out of her present difficulty, I have realised what she is – some sort of angel – and I . . .*'

She stood. 'Douglas, you must not go on. You must not.'

He looked up from his pad, finally. His voice seemed to break in two: '*. . . have fallen in love with her.*'

For some reason, in the stillness that followed this statement, Lulu had a vision of the shelter seen from outside, the earth on top of it, the snow on top of the earth, like icing on fruitcake, the grass and flowers tickling its walls, the raised voices inside it breaking the blackout hush. She looked at Douglas and the first thought that came into her head was: *why does he not stand? Surely such passion should bring a man to his feet?* And then she realised that if he did, he would hit his head on the roof. She wondered if perhaps her thoughts would continue for ever in this way, one surreal observation after another, until he spoke; if that was where her mind would always go, at such a time as this, when she had no idea what to say or how to act.

Slowly, with some self-conscious gravitas, Douglas Lean put the pad down. He moved forward, and Lulu thought that perhaps he was about to throw himself at her feet, but his hands just went to his knees. When he spoke, his voice was the most direct she had ever heard it, stripped, for the first time, of all enigma.

'I'm sorry,' he said. 'These were just words I was writing, for myself . . . A fantasy; a day-dream. Notes towards a poem, perhaps. I had not intended for it to come out now, like this.' He paused. 'I don't know how I had intended for it to come out, to tell the truth. If at all.'

She looked away; she wished, mainly, that they were not in this place. She wished for a window.

'Say something, Lulu. Please. You must want to say something.'

'I don't know, Douglas. I do not know what to say.'

'Well,' he said, something of his old manner returning, some slight ironic lilt, 'I'm sorry to be clichéd, but . . . I can't believe you haven't felt something too.'

Lulu turned, and tried to look him in the eye, but as often

seemed to be the case at crucial times with this man, it was too dark. She was aware that he was looking at her, but the light was not strong enough for their eyes to be sharing a thread of vision. It made it all the more difficult to know. Did she feel something? *Something* was perhaps right. She had felt something. Not love, not attraction, straightforwardly, but she had felt drawn towards him, yes – had possibly even accepted the idea that he should come here today knowing that it could lead to this – because – it was clarifying slowly in her mind – he represented something for her, some opportunity. She saw it now, even in the half light, in the shadows, that Douglas, with his asymmetric masculinity, his rugged confidence, his semi-aristocratic bearing, his blondness, his – her mind forced the word on to her, even though she did not want to hear it, shouted it into her consciousness like a heckler – *Aryanness*: he represented Lulu's lost future, the kind of man she might have shared her life with, and therefore the kind of life she might have had, if she had not chosen to marry Fabian the Jew.

The weight of this realisation pushed Lulu down through the air, back into her seat, as forcefully as if paternal hands had been placed on her shoulders, and Douglas took it as his chance. He shuffled his body forward and leant into her, his face close enough for her to smell that he had not drunk any of the brandy, and wonder if that decision had been calculated. There was a moment, no longer than the beat of the pulse in her wrist, a moment during which she did not turn her face away, but neither did she proffer anything in the way of permission, and he had fixed his lips on hers. His lips were firm and poised, and perhaps it was just the way her mind was running, but she felt she could taste in them safety, infinite safety. He put his hands on her hair, and her hands went to his chest: from his point of view, a gesture that could have been an erotic response or could have been a push away; but, for her, she was touching not his body, but his body type, a body type which in this hemisphere would always be regarded as the human mean. She felt as if she could wrap her arms around him and hold freedom from persecution.

His kiss intensified its strength; his lips began to manoeuvre hers apart. Behind her back, his hands were pulling her body to his. She could feel herself resigning to it, to his will, to her own desire, to the

232

intense pull of the security he offered, and his tongue was in her mouth, tasting of tobacco, touching her own at last – and then the all-clear siren sounded, a keening scream, a call to prayer, piercing Lulu's consciousness like a shard of glass in which she could see the reflection of what she was doing. She pulled her face away, and stood up.

'Where are you going?' said Douglas, with an edge of panic.

'To get Bekka. That was the all-clear.'

'But . . . hold on. We can't just leave it there.'

She smoothed her mackintosh down. 'We can. We should. We must.'

'But . . . why?'

She carried on smoothing, not wanting to look at him. 'Because I am a married woman. What am I doing here? I am supposed to be helping my husband, not betraying him.'

Now he stood up too, crouching to avoid the ceiling, making him look slightly simian. His cigarette, which had been balanced on the edge of the table, fell with the movement. He twisted it out with his foot, making Lulu wince at the thought of Mrs Fricker's lino; she would come back and do her best to clean it up later.

'Don't be so . . .' he grasped her arms, searching for the word, 'self-deceiving.'

She almost laughed. 'What?'

'You know you love me too. I could tell. I wasn't sure myself, until now. I wouldn't' – he looked down, demurely – 'have presumed. But once I felt you in my arms, once I felt your lips on mine . . . I could feel your spirit responding.'

Lulu shivered, possibly with the cold, but with an overlay of disgust, partly at him – the arrogance, the presumptuousness of his lover's language – but also at herself, and the extent to which his words were true. 'I cannot talk like this now. I need to go and fetch Bekka.'

'Please, wait.' His grip on her arms tightened.

Her elbows began to hurt. She felt, with a certain weariness, with a certain awareness of how many women must have felt something similar before, how much stronger than her he was. She did what he wanted: she waited for him to speak.

'I . . . *we* must take this opportunity. It doesn't come round twice. I know it's not easy, I know our situation is not perfect, but we have to get over all that. We have to. In the name of . . .'

'What?'

Even in the dark, she could tell the directness of her question had made him blush. 'Love,' he said. 'In the name of love.'

Not God, then, she thought. He has invoked love rather than God. 'Take your hands off my arms, please,' she said.

He did so, stepping back, holding his head up as best he could under the roof. He looked like a boy again, doing that thing boys do to avoid looking ashamed.

'The thing is, Douglas, love is not so simple for me as it is for you. Maybe I . . . maybe I do feel something for you. But that does not mean I suddenly do not feel anything for my husband. Nor that what I feel for you is more important, or better, just because it is . . . new. And besides, there is also the small matter of what is right and what is wrong.'

He looked away, an element of distaste on his lips. 'Please, Lulu, no bourgeois morality . . .'

That made her want to slap him. These men and their politics, she thought. 'You think we are above that?'

'Success is the sole earthly judge of right and wrong.'

'What?'

'Nothing. Just something I remember reading once. But the point is – we can't be hidebound by all that. It might feel wrong now, but . . . you have to live the thing you want. Only then can you judge what is right and what is wrong. And I know that if we live it, it will be right.'

'Yes. Well. I have had enough of living my life according to what is written in books. And I do not have time, now, for philosophy. I must fetch my daughter.'

And with that, she made to go past him. He blocked her way at first, not violently, but just by not moving; it was easy for him to do, his greater size seeming to be magnified in the shelter. She stared at him. They were close again now, the position of their stand-off replicating that of their kiss.

'Please, Douglas. She will be frightened.'

He sighed, forcefully, and shifted his weight away, giving her enough room to squeeze past. She looked down as she went, not wanting to catch his eye, constricting her body to minimise the touch of his torso on hers.

'Lulu,' he said, just as she reached the door.

She turned her face back to his; she had expected – or perhaps hoped, her mind was too tired to examine her own heart – that he would speak one more time.

'Can we see each other again? We need to talk about this.'

She closed her eyes. It was blacker behind the lids than she had anticipated, having thought that the contrast with the dim light would be minimal. Lulu had little experience of love beyond marriage to Isaac, and although that had proved to be complex and difficult, its complexity and difficulty had been all to do with the rest of the world, not with the thing itself. She was used to the path of love being long and twisting, but her tread steady. Now, she had a vision of a different kind of love, much more fractured, much more friable, a love that was all about choice, about parleying possibilities, about the constant calibration of hurt and healing. Instinctively, instantly, she rejected it: she had no wish to spend the rest of her life juggling the spinning plates of loss.

'No,' she said. 'I don't think so.'

He nodded, a slow, almost painful movement, like a man with a migraine. He exhaled, a long and steady lungful, the steam from his breath hitting a ray of candlelight and twirling there like dust motes in the sun. Some shift happened within him, some decision. Then he bent down and picked up the testimonial, which, in her haste, Lulu had left on the table. His thumbs and index fingers met in the centre of the page, at the top.

'Are you sure about that?' he said, beginning, gently, to tear.

'Verbs,' said Professor Inkelmann, 'are described as either active or passive.' He turned, and wrote the words *active* and *passive* on the blackboard behind him. Isaac watched the men on either side of him write the same words down in their notebooks. 'In the active voice, the subject and verb relationship is straightforward: the subject is a be-er or a doer and the verb moves the sentence along.' He took up his chalk again, and wrote, speaking the words as he said them: '*The Committee approved the resolution.*' He turned back. 'In the passive voice, the subject of the sentence is neither a doer nor a be-er, but is acted upon by some other agent or by something unnamed: *The resolution was approved by the Committee.*'

It had been Isaac's intention, from first arriving on the Isle of Man, to go to English classes. He had failed to do so up to this point, mainly out of listlessness, with just an element of his old adolescent rebellion against the whole concept of the University of the Interned Jew. In his mind, there was no particular reason for getting over these objections now. He felt less listless since meeting June, it was true, but he could not equate that with a desire to speak his host language better. Had he chased it further, he might have equated it with a desire to speak *her* language better: with a desire for him, a man of words, not to feel disabled when, or if, the time came to articulate what was in his heart.

'The presence of the passive voice,' continued Professor Inkelmann, a bald man who, demonstrating his command of one of the more obscure phrases in his chosen language of study, liked to describe himself to friends as 'tending to fat', 'can indicate, in some cases, a sense that an absolution of responsibility is taking place. In a military report, for example, *The order to fire was given* gives no sense of who gave the order. It is very different from the active *The sergeant gave the order to fire* or *I gave the order to fire.*'

The professor spoke in English, with no let-up: his process was to immerse his pupils in the language, rather than help them into it through the crutches of German. Isaac wondered if he should not have gone to a beginners' class. He found it difficult to accept, seeing as he could, after all, speak English, had been speaking it to Englishmen for nearly a year and a half, but the fact remained that much of what the professor was saying was going over his head. He looked out of the window of the classroom – more specifically, he looked out of the window of the saloon bar of the Claremont Hotel, which had been converted into a classroom – and saw that the snow, falling now for over two days, had settled thick and white for the first time on the Promenade. Still agitated by the confusion that June had created in him, it made him feel momentarily relieved, as settled snow always did, that while it lay clotted on the ground, all bets were off, all decisions were postponed – everything was cancelled for the time being. It always made him remember what it felt like to be a child and know that, today, there was no way of getting to school.

He was just thinking of slipping out, in fact, to walk up to the barbed wire and look out over the headland – he'd already started to imagine the wide white yonder – when a voice behind him hissed, in German: 'What about you, Fabian? Are you active or passive? What about *your* responsibility?'

Isaac peered round to see a pair of narrow brown eyes blazing furiously at him: Waldstein. He had leant forward to whisper, close enough for his breath to have been warm in Isaac's ear. 'How long have you been there?'

Waldstein ignored the question, although permitted himself a half smile at the idea that Isaac had not seen him, that he was someone with the power to enter and leave rooms invisibly. 'Well?'

'Well what?'

'Active or passive?'

Isaac rolled his eyes. 'It's a grammar lesson, Waldstein. Not a rally.'

Waldstein looked away. 'We need to talk.'

'I don't think this is quite the right place.'

'Meet me afterwards. Your room?'

'I have a feeling Kaufmann may be sleeping in it . . .'

Waldstein tutted. He pulled one of his fingers backwards, making a painful click. 'Not in one of the cafés. Outside.'

'You've seen it's snowing, I take it.'

'The snow's settled. It'll be good for you to get a breath of fresh air.'

'Where?'

'At the wire. Opposite the second tram stop on the Promenade.'

'Of course, there are some situations, such as scientific experiments,' Professor Inkelmann was saying, 'where the passive voice is practically mandatory. *Twenty-five cc of acid was poured in the test-tube* is much more likely to be used than *I poured twenty-five cc of acid into the test-tube*, because here, it is the principle rather than the agent that takes centre stage. Which is not to say, if there are any scientists among us, that I am suggesting that your role in the experimental process is redundant . . .'

A ripple of laughter went around the room, more because some of the students had managed to understand the professor's joke than because any of them thought it was funny. Isaac turned back to Waldstein, ready to continue the discussion, but he was gone.

Standing at the camp perimeter, his feet slowly sinking into snow-prints, Isaac looked out towards England, his vista criss-crossed by the barbed wire. The sea looked calm, virtually crystalline in the cold. The air was clear, so clear he could taste its purity in his nostrils. A troop of Manx gulls were swarming round a fishing boat making its way into the harbour, the white sweeps of their wings a series of sculptures flown in to match the background hills. Along each rung of the wire, snow had settled in crumbling lines: he ran his finger between two knots of metal, letting the powder build to a point and then fall. Beyond, citizens of the Isle of Man went about their business, buttoned up against the frost, braving the cold to buy Christmas presents. Isaac remembered how, when he had first arrived, so many of them used to dawdle on the Promenade, watching the internees from what they perceived to be a safe distance, like spectators at a human zoo. Now, they went past with barely a glance: Isaac felt almost a little resentful that his moment of colour and novelty and exoticism – his moment of glamour – was gone.

'Wondering what it's like to be on the other side?'

Isaac didn't bother to turn round. 'Not really, Waldstein. I've got a fair idea of what life is like on the Isle of Man from looking out of the window of my room. I'm not sure it's any more interesting than in here.' Then he did turn. Waldstein was wearing his train-driver's cap, and had acquired a tartan scarf, with which he was covering most of his face. Isaac considered how much he must enjoy the fact that the cold gave him the excuse to do that. 'And if, by that, what you're planning to talk to me about is some sort of escape plan, forget it. I'm not interested. My wife is doing well getting my testimonials together and—'

'It's not an escape plan. Cigarette?' He held out a packet of Gîtanes, taken from the inside pocket of his black workman's jacket.

Isaac thought for a moment, and then accepted. He had never smoked much, but even though he was right that the Jews on this island had redefined the experience of imprisonment, they followed the stereotype in this one respect: tobacco had currency. Waldstein held out a lighter for him, a fat metal block that may once have been silver in colour but was now blackened with oil deposits. The smell of the flame in the cold air was like a hurricane lamp; it suddenly brought back to Isaac memories of holidays under canvas with his sisters, safety and adventure all mixed up in the one smell. It was cancelled by the pull of the smoke in his lungs, the donkey kick of the Gîtane.

'What is it, then?' he said, trying not to sound too throat-constricted.

Waldstein did a 180-degree search of the area with his check-point eyes. The only conceivable danger was a sentry, about a hundred yards away, standing sullenly in the snow. The two Jews seemed to hold little interest for him. 'You remember me telling you that there were Nazis here?'

'Of course. I remember me telling you that I knew that already.'

'Well, all of them – twenty-five or so – are now in the Red House.'

'The Red House?'

Waldstein smiled, pleased, Isaac thought, that he possessed information which Isaac did not. 'It's a house between here and Ramsay. It's where the British have relocated a number of' – he stuck out his lower lip; it was pink, and had the quality of sausage meat – 'undesirables.'

'I see.'

'By which they mean the small number of violent criminals kept here, and the Nazis. You should go and have a look at it, next time they take you out for some exercise.'

Isaac nodded. It was undoubtedly true that the occasional confrontations and bursts of anti-Semitic song that had peppered his first days on the island were no more. He had hardly noticed the absence, so inured was he to it, so expectant of its eventual return.

'But typically, the British have not been entirely equal in this re-accommodation,' Waldstein was continuing. His sharp little beak of a nose was reddening violently at its tip.

'What do you mean?'

'Well, most of the criminals are being kept in the house itself, virtually under lock and key. But the Nazis live in a converted stables round the back, like a barracks. Where they are more or less free to come and go as they please. Some of them – the highest-ranking ones – regularly have dinner with Rutter and some of the other camp commandants.'

'You've seen that yourself, I presume.'

Waldstein's eyes narrowed, with some disgust. 'I know what I need to know, Fabian. I know enough to know what is true and what is not.'

Isaac blinked, not wanting to challenge him further. 'So . . . what are you telling me? That you're furious about this?'

'No. Quite the opposite. I'm overjoyed about it.'

Isaac took a drag on his cigarette. The smoke tasted metallic against the crackling air. 'Why?'

'Because it makes them easier to get to.'

Isaac coughed, his lungs expelling the smoke in one quick jolt. He held his hand to his mouth, and looked round himself now to check the position of the sentry. He had not moved. 'What are you saying?' He spoke quietly.

'I'll spell it out for you. We're planning an attack on the Nazis in the Red House.' Waldstein's face and voice went deadpan, allowing the power of the words to speak for themselves.

Isaac held his gaze, trying to mirror him, to prevent his features from registering shock and fear, but then began to wonder why he bothered playing these power games with Waldstein: the information was shocking and fearful, why not therefore let him know that he was shocked and afraid? A relaxation occurred between them, now that the secret was out. In Isaac's ears, he heard the screams of the gulls rising as the fish from the nets were unloaded. An image came into his mind: the trinacria, the three legs of Man symbol, imprinted all along the harbour wall. He remembered seeing it running above the waves as the ferry from Liverpool had entered Douglas, and the stomach-collapsing second when he'd mistaken it for a swastika.

'We?' he said, eventually.

'Myself and some friends.' The closed set of Waldstein's face made it clear that no more information would be forthcoming on this.

'When you say an attack . . . you mean you plan to kill them? All of them?'

'We have a specific target.' He looked over Isaac's shoulder and his dark brow furrowed: the sentry was moving, not especially hurriedly, in their direction. 'I'm not prepared to tell you anything further at this stage.'

'Why have you told me anything at all?'

'Because we need one more man.'

'And that's me, is it?'

Waldstein shrugged. 'Philosophers have argued about the world. The point is to change it.'

'Interpreted,' said Isaac.

'What?'

'It's "interpreted". Not "argued about".'

Waldstein raised his eyes to the overcast Manx heaven. 'Exactly the sort of pedantic distinction that a philosopher would make.'

241

Isaac looked down, but tried not to look abashed. It seemed not entirely pedantic to him that if Waldstein was trying to win him over by quoting sections of his own bible, then they should be right; also that he had given the cerebral, sedate act of interpretation a characteristically aggressive spin by misremembering it as argument. Then, immediately, he wondered if Waldstein was right, if he was indeed just like all the other useless thinkers, that these thoughts themselves were a form of hesitation, designed to interpose something between himself and action.

'I'm not sure I'd be much use to you, to be honest, Waldstein. Violence doesn't really come naturally to me. You're right, I do the theory, not the practice.'

'Well,' he replied, the brown leather lines of his face softening a little, for the first time, 'don't get me wrong. Thinking is all very well. There's just a point where it has to stop.'

'I agree. But I still don't think I can help. I'd be no good. If it came to it, I've no idea if I could kill someone.'

'We don't need a killer. We just need a lookout. Someone to warn us if the British are coming.'

'Surely there will be British soldiers on duty at the Red House anyway?'

'Look. We have worked it out. We know when and how to get to the Nazis. But I'm not going to tell you any of the details unless I know you're on board.'

Isaac's cigarette fizzed as he threw the stub of it into the snow. He sighed, letting the last swirls of French smoke leave his lungs. 'What would be the point, Waldstein? What would it achieve?'

'Very much what Jews in Germany said when others like me spoke before of retaliation.'

Isaac looked away. A tram drew up by the stop opposite, its hydraulic brakes heaving, snow brushing off its roof. The sentry was only ten yards away, hoisting his boots up through the snow with every step. They were normally so unsuspicious, the sentries – only Waldstein's showy mysteriousness could have drawn him over. Despite clearly seeing himself as a sort of secret agent, he would have been terrible at espionage, Isaac thought – you could smell his subterfuge at fifty paces. But that simply meant, effectively, that he was

242

bad at hiding. What he was like when he came out of hiding – what he was like at fighting, in other words – Isaac could only guess.

'Where can I find you?'

'Building Eighteen, Room Seven.' He nodded, a minute gesture, to one side.

Isaac took the point, and they moved away from the wire, leaving the soldier, who had just opened his mouth to speak, looking a little crestfallen. He stood in the snow and watched the two Germans walk back to different parts of the camp, before spitting into the white ground, and turning back solidly, purposefully, as if patrolling up and down the wire were something he always did while on sentry duty.

June Murray was collating her material. This involved deciding the order of interviews; whether to include Hannah Spitzy's interview for balance, or Rainer Waldstein's despite its abrupt foreclosure; and whether to cut some interviews purely to make the whole dossier more readable. A woman, normally, of considerable decisiveness – she would not have been here otherwise – she had been obsessing over this collation, shifting piles of paper about like a croupier cutting and recutting a deck of cards, for the last five hours.

Dropping to the side of the main document one fat section – a pharmacist from Leipzig who had spent so long railing against his previous employers that June felt inclined to believe they may have been within their rights to sack him – she blew on her hands for warmth. Her room at the Douglas Arms was less comfortable than the one at Port St Mary; any joy the sea view may have given her was undermined by the three-inch gap between the window and its frame, a gap that no amount of pushing down on the splintering white wood would reduce. Each morning so far she had been awoken at dawn by a rousing combination of the unmuffled screams of the gulls and gusts of snow blown in through the gap onto her sleeping profile. She was beginning again to wonder about the wisdom of extending her trip.

There were, however, two areas of hope. First, the newspapers. Rutter had written to her to say that, indeed, each house, in each camp, was to receive one copy of the *Daily Mail* from the start of next week. He had managed to convey in the letter a sense that this decision was wholly his idea, albeit sparked by a directive from the Home Office, but that bothered her not at all. She knew it would get around, via Isaac, that she was responsible, and if the problem with her relationship with the internees was indeed one of trust, it could only help. Moreover, the sheer presence of the newspapers – the sheer fact of information – would, she knew, get the internees talking, specifically about the ongoing situation in Europe. Second, the Derby Castle husbands and wives event. Assuming by then an ability to walk among the internees virtually unnoticed, she was planning simply to attend, and listen. It was an occasion when she could assume an outpouring of emotion – and if there was anything left worth hearing from these people, she would surely hear it then. She had not as yet worked out how to process this listening – what form its presentation should take in her eventual dossier – but she felt sure she could incorporate it somehow in her introduction, which, knowing the higher echelons of the Ministry as she did, may well be the only part that would be read.

And perhaps, forgetting all her tactics, she thought that it was where she herself – dossier or no dossier – would find out the truth. She hoped that, in the darkness of the dance hall, their minds unbuttoned by love, the internees would speak of fears and dreams and facts that they would never reveal under the naked bulb of the interview room. Derby Castle would be her Tabernacle, in which she would find the Ark of her Covenant.

June felt uncomfortable suddenly, thinking like this. A coldness came over her that was nothing to do with the draught. She did not know when she had become this mercenary – so dedicated to knowledge that people's emotions became relegated only to what they could reveal. She got up and crouched down by the narrow gas fire, and held her palms towards its weakly flickering flame; the warmth was so minimal that it scarcely registered on her bare skin. She glanced over at the window, and noticed two internees walking back towards the buildings of Central from the wire. They were some distance away, but one of them, the one with the cap, the one who radiated trouble, she recognised straight away as Waldstein. The other took her a little longer, and it was only with a start, and a move over to the cold plane of the window, that she realised it was Isaac.

They were moving in different directions, leaving a V-shaped track in the snow. June wondered what they had to talk about together. She remembered that Isaac had mentioned knowing Waldstein before, which had meant little to her at the time, but now confused her, as he seemed so gentle, and the other man so abrasive. A part of her hoped that Isaac had been doing the job she had already assumed he would: talking about June's involvement in the bringing of newspapers and radio to the camp. Another part, she realised, just hoped that he had been discussing her.

Because June was not as confused by her emotions as Isaac was about his. He was the silent reason, underpinning the others, why she was staying on the island. She had known while she was walking away from him in the rain three nights ago that the key had been turned, that something inexorable had been started. She had felt it only once before, and that was with a married man, too: it made her worry that she might be one of those women who had a penchant for them. He had been a lecturer at Goldsmiths', twice her age, but from the moment he stepped off his podium and addressed her directly, asking her to stay behind on some diversionary academic trifle, she marked the feeling: *so this is what it is like.* The falling of the soul, down through the sweet and the dark, this is how it begins. When it came, she felt like she had been waiting for it all her life. And now here it was again, a decade later, directed towards this refugee, three years younger than her; and, once again, she went along with it, without understanding its origin, without knowing what prime motor was driving her. Something to do with the way he held his pain, like he knew it was here to stay; something to do with his melancholy calm; something to do with his skin, made rich through race, that shade of olive that seems to have been spun from olive oil, a skin which time will never truly crack; something to do with his eyes, brown and burning, like molten chocolate. Something to do, in essence, with his being a Jew: although that made no sense, she'd interviewed nearly a hundred Jews and felt only pity, not – her mind hesitated before the word, then gulped it down – not love, or at least not this mix of affection and hope and desire she understood to be the embryonic form of love. Yet it was true – obscurely, she knew it, and wondered if she had somehow allowed her convictions

245

to become mixed up with her emotions; if it was all about some need to prove, at the deepest level, her allegiance to this race.

'June!'

The voice startled her, not so much because of the pure surprise, but because its timbre was so in tune with her thoughts; for a second she thought it had only happened in her imagination. But then, the part of her that had surrendered, that had put her faith in the long slide, concluded it was all part of the plan, that even the gap in the window which had allowed her to hear his voice so quickly and so clearly had been preordained. She looked out, to see Isaac standing ankle-deep in the snow, his hands holding the wire. She felt her heart clutch a little at the sight.

'June! Are you there?'

She discovered that although the window did not go down, it went up without difficulty. 'Hello!' she said. They were close enough for her hardly to have to raise her voice. In German, she continued: 'What on earth are you doing? Aren't you cold? Haven't you got any gloves?'

He withdrew his hands, and looked at them; the metal had left imprints in red strips on his palms. 'Somewhere.' He smiled, rather aimlessly, as if whatever it was he'd planned to say was now evading him. 'I came out before to speak to someone, and I saw the Douglas Arms, and it made me wonder . . . if you were still here . . .'

'I am. I wasn't planning on leaving just yet. What about you?'

Isaac laughed. 'I thought I might just stay for Christmas. Seems a shame to spoil such a nice holiday at this stage.'

'You're absolutely right,' she said, laughing in response. There was an awkward pause, the sort of pause that often inserts itself in this kind of light banter between men and women, although intensified in this case by the couple being separated by twenty feet of barbed wire.

'Shall I come down?' said June.

'No,' he replied, pleased, though, that she had offered. 'I have to go back for supper. And the sentry . . .' His words trailed away.

June looked over the camp, to see the sentry staring in their direction, as yet uncertain whether to make the long trek over again. 'I'm staying for the event at Derby Castle on Sunday,' she said. 'Are you going to that?'

Isaac raised his hand to his face, the tips of his fingers grazing his stubbled skin. 'Oh. I – well, I wasn't going to. It's for husbands and wives.' As soon as he'd said it, he regretted it, wished he had not referred to that particular coupling.

'Does that mean you can't go?'

He contemplated, scratching his head. 'I don't know. Probably I can. I don't think they're checking.' And I *am* married, he thought to himself, with a lurch in his stomach.

'Well, I'll be there,' said June. And then, lightly, it coming to her how much power was sometimes contained in politeness: 'It would be lovely to see you.'

Isaac's features opened, not unlike the way they had when he'd first raised his face from the floor of the interview room, into a smile. 'The pleasure would be all mine,' he said.

Fitzbillies was as busy as Lulu had ever seen it. Perhaps it was something to do with recent increases in sugar rationing, but the shop was as crammed as a public air-raid shelter, and their cakes were selling – the expression came into her head, having heard a few of her English neighbours say it from time to time – like hot cakes. She wondered if that made sense in English, saying that cakes were selling like hot cakes – perhaps the only thing that could not be described as selling like hot cakes were cakes, especially cold ones – and then Lotte opened the door. Following her up the stairs, where the bustle in the shop could still be heard muffled through the side wall, Lulu marvelled again at her brain's ability, at times of difficulty, to distract itself with trivia.

Lotte was dressed down, by her standards: she was wearing an ordinary striped cotton dress and her hair was loose, something Lulu had not seen before. It made her face look drawn, or perhaps it just *was* drawn, this was how it looked without the addition of the flashing smiles and the eyebrow-raisings and the camp expression-pulling that normally played across it. Her manner was not just subdued, but rather switched off. The actress, for the afternoon at least, had been rested.

'Would you like some tea?' she said, as Lulu entered the living-room, having settled Bekka onto James's bed, fast asleep. Since the night of the air attack, she had been unhappy about leaving her with anyone else for any length of time.

'No, thank you.' Lulu tried not to sound cold. She was finding it difficult to know how to pitch her mood. What had happened with Douglas was not, of course, Lotte's fault, but none the less, it was hard for Lulu not in some way to blame her for having introduced them in the first place.

'Well, please sit down, at any rate,' said Lotte, with an edge of her old archness. 'We've got at least an hour before the boys come back from school.'

Lulu considered saying, *No thank you, I prefer to stand*, and then sat, realising that would be too much.

'So look,' said Lotte, 'you know I hate any kind of awkwardness, especially between friends, so let's get straight to the point. I understand from your telephone call that it didn't go too well with Douglas the other night?'

Lulu had braved her natural fear of being caught, and telephoned Lotte from Mrs Lambert's house. They had exchanged only enough words for Lotte to deduce that there was a problem, and that it was best not to discuss it over the phone.

'You could say that, yes.'

'I had some idea.'

'You have seen him?'

'Yes.'

Lulu felt herself blush, embarrassed at herself for the rush with which the next words came out. 'What did he say?'

Lotte shook her head. 'Virtually nothing. I tried some playful questions – oh, I was my usual sparkling self – but he remained tight-lipped. Which is why I knew it hadn't gone according to plan.'

'What plan?'

Lotte's palms went up. 'Calm down, Lulu. It's just an expression. Perhaps it would be easier to discuss the matter in German.'

Lulu looked to the ground, where her feet, held primly together, were framed by the blue horns of some abstract motif on one of the floor's Persian rugs. She felt suddenly sorry for her little feet, in their flat black shoes, and sorry for herself, out of her depth with these people and their many meanings. She felt her throat constrict, and then tightened it further, to hold back the tears.

'So what happened?' Lotte was continuing, in a more kindly voice.

'He tore up the testimonial.'

'He what?'

'He tore up the testimonial.' The saying of it again reinforced the blank horror of it in her mind, made her realise it was true.

Lotte was open-mouthed. 'He did write it, then?'

'Yes. He came round with some notes and then he typed it up, in front of me.' Then she made an uncharacteristic noise, a noise that sounded as if it was new to her mouth: a bitter laugh. 'And then he *tore* it up in front of me.'

'Why?'

The bitterness, like a taste, remained. It seemed to impel her to take up the other woman's suggestion, and speak in German. 'Why do you think?'

Lotte looked uncomprehending for a moment, and then her face became knowing. 'Ah. Well, well, well. Douglas, who would have thought it?'

'Well . . . you, surely?'

'How do you mean?'

'Oh, come on, Lotte! You knew what he was after! You as good as said it that day we went to the museum!'

'I was just having fun with you! And besides, if you knew what I meant, then you knew, too. You were warned . . .'

Lulu raised her head, ready for an angry riposte, and then let it sink back down, realising that it was, in a sense, true. The problem was that, until it happened, until everything became real, Lotte's insinuations, Douglas's flirtations – even her own instincts – felt like a form of play, warnings in a way, yes, but warnings emptied of danger. She wished it were simpler, she wished she could just scream that she had been tricked, that she was an innocent whom an evil man had tried to seduce with bribery, but, although that was true, it wasn't all there was to the truth. The truth, Lulu was coming to realise, was always complex.

'He tore up the testimonial, though,' said Lotte. 'That's brutal. God, you must have really got to him . . .'

'Please don't excuse him, Lotte.'

'I'm not. Really, I'm not. I just know him well enough to know – it won't just have been a passing fancy. Oh no, far too grubby. He'll have thought of it as a high and noble thing. He'll have scripted the whole thing in his head, as some great drama. That's probably why he reacted so badly when you didn't – you know – play your part. Even so' – she pinched her brow between two fingers, as if trying to picture it – 'I wouldn't have thought him capable of something so . . . violent. I like him . . . excuse me, I've liked him in the past . . . but still, he always struck me as a cold fish. Grand, in his own way, but cold.' She paused. 'He didn't – he wasn't violent with – I mean, he didn't try to force himself . . . ?'

Lulu shook her head. 'It wasn't quite . . . like that.'

'It wasn't?'

'Lotte, I'd rather not go into it. He tore it up because I made it clear that I was not interested in him, in that way. But you're right, he is cold. Even tearing up the testimonial – yes, it's a violent act, but it's . . . it's a coldly violent act.' She remembered how he did it, painstakingly, fastidiously, with an edge of regret, like a teacher telling a pupil that a caning hurts him more than it hurts the pupil. It was true, his anger was cold, as cold as the snow that had cocooned the air-raid shelter around them. 'Some men, when they are angry, they lose control, they hit, they punch. Others, they think about how to hurt. And they are worse.'

'Like Hitler,' said Lotte.

'Sorry?'

'Hitler. He always struck me as *such* an angry little man. But not strong enough to hit anyone, to win a fight. So he writes his anger down, or shouts it in one of his stupid speeches.'

Despite herself, Lulu laughed. Lotte had a way of making the easiest banality sound like sophisticated metropolitan insight.

'I don't think they're entirely comparable, Lotte. Especially not given Douglas's politics.'

'I beg your pardon?'

'Douglas's politics. Which is another thing I don't understand. If he shares the same beliefs as Isaac, how could he have—'

'What are you talking about? I thought your husband was a communist.'

Lulu pulled up short. 'He is. But Douglas told me he was as well . . .'

Lotte's face seemed to start backwards in surprise. 'Are you sure? I suppose he might have said anything if you'd turned his head, but – really, he is *not* a communist.'

Lulu's memory whirred. *Had* he told her he was a communist?

251

What had he actually said? 'But . . . he went to fight in Spain . . . he said . . .'

'Oh yes, he went to fight in Spain, all right. For *Franco*.'

The information was like a slap. '*Franco?*'

'Yes. Well, I don't know how much actual fighting he did. I think he was planning just to write some reports in support of the Nationalists, you know, a kind of riposte to Orwell and Isherwood and all the other lefties who went off flying the flag of the Republic. But he ended up getting shot in the leg somewhere in Andalucia.'

Lulu shook her head, unable to process this. 'How could I have been so wrong about him?'

Lotte's head shook in mirror-image. 'I suppose he doesn't give too much away. But I've always thought Douglas had a touch of the crypto-fascist about him, to be honest. I've heard him make the odd anti-Semitic remark in his time.'

'Have you?'

'Oh yes. Just the sort of reflex nonsense about bankers and financiers I've come to expect to hear in the drawing-rooms of this country. And his German's rather too good as well. Actually, it did occur to me that that might have something to do with his interest in you.'

'His German?'

Lotte laughed. 'No, his anti-Semitism. Rescuing the lovely Aryan girl from the clutches of the filthy Jew and all that. Not that he would have needed a political motive to be attracted to you, don't get me wrong . . . But, as I say, it may all have formed part of what I imagine he thought of as his higher purpose . . .'

The wet sound of sleet beginning to hit the window made them turn away from each other. Over the last few days, the snow in Cambridge had begun to melt, sliding off the turrets and towers of the colleges in heaps of grey slush.

'Why didn't you tell me all this?' said Lulu, turning back.

'Well, I'm sorry, Lulu, but I thought you were old enough to look after yourself. And I thought you knew about his politics. I remember last time we met you said something about how he'd told you of his experiences in Spain . . .'

'But I *didn't* know!'

Lotte's face implied a shrug. 'I'm not sure that's my fault.'

Lulu felt a desperate frustration come upon her, driven by a childlike despair at the unfairness of it all. 'But why are you even *friends* with him?'

Lotte laughed, and in it Lulu could hear her usual self, the sort of laugh she imagined you might hear rising above the tinkle of glasses at cocktail parties.

'My dear, if I refused to be friends with all the people I met in this country who made offhand anti-Semitic remarks, I'd be a hermit. I've heard more thoughtless anti-Jew comments here than I ever did in Germany. The only difference is that, here, they come wrapped in a gentlemanly distaste for ever actually doing anything about it.'

A silence set in. The two women had reached a stand-off, but it didn't last: Lulu cracked.

'Oh Lotte,' she said, the tears coming out all at once, running fast into the hollows of her cheeks, 'what am I going to do?'

Lulu's crying had a chemical effect on Lotte. Her front came down in an instant, and she was out of her seat and crouching by Lulu's chair, stroking her neck. 'Oh, you poor thing,' she said. 'I'm so sorry. Of course, I should have told you. Of course. I'm so stupid . . .'

'I've written to Isaac telling him that Douglas is going to write his third testimonial now!' Lulu gasped, in between sobs. She wished she hadn't said 'now'; it made her sound so infantile.

'Someone else will do it, I'm sure. I've got some other English friends . . .' Lulu looked at her; her eyes were sharp, though moist. 'Women friends, I mean.'

Lulu laughed, through the tears, having reached that particular extremity where the body can do both poles of emotion at once.

'It is my fault,' said Lotte.

'No . . .'

'It is. A part of me wanted to get the two of you together.' Lotte sighed, a deep, internal cadence, her face turning to the weeping window. 'I'm bored, Lulu. I'm not a bad person, but I'm bored. And it was a little drama for me, you and Douglas. A woman can do a lot of damage just in the name of maintaining a bit of interest in this life.' She looked back to Lulu. 'Before this war, my life was really rather glittering, you know. Oh, my marriage had grown a tad stale, but then they do, don't they? But at least there was our social life, and if we didn't mix in quite the highest of high society, I still managed to enjoy myself. Now, I may as well be any other lower-middle-class housewife struggling to cope with hubby away at the war. God, if only Hitler and Churchill and all the rest of them had thought for a minute about what they were about to do to *society*.'

Lulu nodded. She knew about boredom. Her life may not have fallen from the same height as Lotte's, but her mind was acute enough to feel the atrophy of the times.

'So again, my dear,' Lotte was continuing, reaching out to hold Lulu's hand, 'I apologise. I had no right to play with your life. Although I must confess I had no idea I was playing with, in Douglas's case, such fire. Such cold fire, if you are to be believed.' A breath was taken, as if by both of them simultaneously; they had reached a point of rest, come round to each other once more. Then, Lotte added: 'Tell me, though, as one woman to another: were you really not interested in him at all?'

Lulu felt that an explanation of the way in which she had considered Douglas's proposition seriously was impossible – or perhaps she did not want to explain, was more comfortable with occupying in Lotte's mind the position of victim. Despite her lack of response, though, the question had made her blush, which was reflexively read by Lotte as something of a silent 'maybe'.

'All I know,' said Lulu, 'is that I never want to see or hear from him again.' She spoke firmly, a response to seeing the beginnings of a smile creeping onto Lotte's face, and wanting it not to be there.

Lotte did not stop her smile from coming, however, but rather changed the shape of it, from one that was about to be smirking to one that was protective. She remained a woman who could be whoever she wanted, whenever she wanted. 'I'm sure you won't have to,' she said, patting Lulu's hand.

Babel, Dr Mannstein thought, has toppled and come to earth. The array of voices – German and English and Yiddish, with smatterings of Dutch, Polish, French and Russian – rose in his ears until he could bear it no longer and brought his fist crashing down upon the table like Hashem striking the accursed Tower itself.

'I call this meeting of the Central Camp House Representatives Committee to order!' he said. A solid variety of Jews, all with that slightly dumbfounded expression that Jews have when they have just been told to be quiet, looked round. Each house in each camp had a leader, a representative, and these representatives gathered together at the end of each month, to discuss and argue and vote and resolve, but mainly to create among the internees the illusion of power. Presently sitting on wooden chairs carried from their rooms were, among others: Kurt Joos, ballet master and Germany's leading choreographer; Rudolf Older, editor of the *Berliner Tageblatt*, the last newspaper in Germany to resist Nazi influence; Dr Ludwig Munz, art historian and specialist in educating blind children; Dr G. V. Lachman, one of the world's leading aerodynamicists; Peter Stadlen, the concert pianist; Professor E. Pringsheim, an authority on Roman law, arrested for internment while teaching at Oxford; and Helmut Herzfelde, the pioneer of photo-montage. From Dr Mannstein's point of view – Dr Mannstein having recently been voted chairman of the Representatives Committee – it felt like addressing a reunion of Nobel Prize-winners.

'Point of order, Dr Mannstein,' said Hermann Gottlieb, the representative of House 14 and one of the few men in the room with no particular accomplishments, except perhaps his moustache, of which a walrus would have been proud, 'but the previous chairman, Herr Dankberger, always conducted the meetings in German.'

'Yes, I'm aware of that, Mr Gottlieb,' said Dr Mannstein, pointedly answering in English despite the question having been put in

255

German, 'but Mr Dankberger has now been released to live back in Hampstead Garden Suburb, where it will be interesting indeed to see how he and his barely submerged conviction that, despite all the evidence to the contrary, German culture is superior to English, get on. From now on these meetings will be conducted in the language of our host country, unless anyone here literally cannot understand what is going on, in which case I would venture to suggest that you should not have been voted your house representative.'

'But Dr Mannstein . . .'

'That was a pause for breath, Mr Gottlieb, not objections. So. Item One on today's agenda: the provision of a camp library. This has been proposed by Mr Artraub, the representative of House Six, and, if passed, would in fact be the second attempt by this committee to urge Lieutenant Colonel Rutter to find funds for the creation of a library . . .'

'Point of information, Dr Mannstein. Douglas Camp has had a library virtually since it was opened.'

'Yes, now you see, Mr Gottlieb, if you want that point to be minuted, you are going to have to say it again in English . . .'

Isaac stifled a yawn. Dr Mannstein's promotion to the chair had left a vacancy for House 18, and since no one especially wanted the job, the inhabitants of House 18 were rotating the duty. Today was Isaac's day, but he found it hard to be interested in the minutiae of the Representatives Committee. In the past, he might have enjoyed it, if only because it would have provided him with a good example of how, even in the most extreme of situations, the bourgeoisie will still persist with their shallow idea of democracy. But presently, too many other issues were snapping at the heels of his consciousness. This morning, he had done what Waldstein had suggested: he had gone to take a look at the Red House. He had signed up with a group going on a short walking tour entitled 'The Surrounds of Douglas', and they had been escorted, by British soldiers of course, along the cliffs about halfway to Ramsay. Isaac had been fairly bored – if surprised, as he often was, by the sanguine beauty of the island – until they passed by Onchan Head, and the group leader asked them to direct their gaze rightwards, where in the distance they could make out the

Groudie Glen Railway; at that point, Isaac directed his gaze leftwards, and saw, on the far side of the coast road, a solitary house near the cliff. It was not exactly red, more simply redbrick, although that was fairly unusual on the island, most houses being painted white; and the woodwork, he noticed – all the window frames and, most prominently, the door – was indeed coated in a deep shade of traffic-light red. The house looked peculiar, alone in that landscape, but Isaac presumed the British chose it for its isolation. He wandered to the edge of the group, and tried to peer inside, but he was still too far away, and the day too bright, to make out anything behind its windows. He could see the converted stable area to the side of the house, and while he was watching, two men emerged from it, talking animatedly, putting on their coats. Instinctively, Isaac moved backwards with a start: something about these men, the heft of their bodies, the way they held themselves, touched the nerve of Nazi recognition within him, and his first reaction was to cower. They disappeared round the back, and he could feel himself relax, letting out a long breath he had not realised he was holding. The group moved on, back towards Douglas, and Isaac turned away, although he turned back a number of times to look at the house, trying to feel if it resonated evil; if you would know just from looking at it.

A laugh from the room, at some jibe of Dr Mannstein's, brought him back to the meeting of the Representatives Committee. He wondered what Waldstein would have made of it. Presumably, he would have scowled darkly all through the meeting before declaiming that the point was violently to reject our incarceration, not to ameliorate the conditions within it. Thinking this made Isaac realise that, despite his early reference to Trotsky, he had never actually discovered Waldstein's political affiliation, and the thought made him blush, it coming to him that the man was much more of a revolutionary than he would ever be, an instinctive revolutionary, someone who would kick over the statues of whatever system he felt oppressed by, without waiting around to work out what might be put in its place. He had no need of an intellectual superstructure to impose on that instinct. It made Isaac wonder if he himself had only ever used communism as a critique, as a descriptive tool, a

257

device to take apart – but with no intention of actually *taking apart* – the status quo.

'Goethe?'

'Of course. *The Complete Works.*'

'And Schiller. And Hesse.'

'Well, obviously . . .'

The various representatives were continuing the discussion, making suggestions for the primary texts that needed to be stocked by the prospective library. Dr Mannstein was writing them down, all the while painstakingly ignoring Hermann Gottlieb's demonstrative smirk. Isaac wondered whether to join in by shouting out Marx's name, and then could not be bothered. His eyes strayed to the window, where he could see a white strip leading to the far edge of the camp, the place where he had last seen June.

He had gone back to his room after seeing her, and sat and looked out of the window for an hour, at the end of which he had written two letters, one to Lulu and one to June. The one to Lulu had been the easier:

Dear Lulu,

Thank you so much for your letter. Yes, I did enjoy the sausage, very much. If you can send me another one that would be marvellous, although not if it's going to take too much out of your purse. On that note, I'm glad to hear about the other job, every little helps. I worry so much about you and our little darling, all alone there in that tiny room. If you're reading this out to her now, please give her a special kiss from me. I miss her so much. And when I write that, it comes to me, the truth of it. I am missing seeing her grow, missing hearing her speak new words for the first time, missing seeing her face separate out from that of all babies and become her own; things I now shall never see.

Thank you especially for all the effort you've put into getting the three testimonials together to ensure my release. Yes, of course, I remember Douglas. How is he? How nice of him to offer to write the last testimonial. I'm sure I don't deserve as good a writer as him, although maybe we need someone as clever as him to find my good points, wherever they may be.

And another thing I remember. I remember that night in Bayreuth. I remember, and will always remember, Clara Schumann's song, and what it means to both of us. I am looking into your eyes now as I write this, and I know what they say.

Soon, my love – I want to write God willing, my love, how much must that prove I want it to happen?! – soon we will be together. All this will be over, and we will be able to live the life together we were meant to have.

Yours for ever,

Izzyx

He had not been entirely happy with it. Only the sentences about Bekka truly matched his feelings. Before beginning to write, he had thought the letter would spill over with passion, charged as it was with secret guilts and rekindled loyalty, but, reading it back, it felt flat, full of the things lovers always say, the words they always use. Perhaps that language could only be tired, he thought, or perhaps he could not express himself in that way any more with HM Censor looking over his shoulder, but as he went to post it, he felt oddly hollow, as if the line he had attempted to draw under his life were not as thick and black and defined as he had hoped; so much so, that it was with a certain relief that he discovered that the Camp Post Office, which operated out of the dining-room of the All Seasons Bed and Breakfast, was temporarily shut, for security reasons.

He made the decision there and then not to send June's letter, either; in some obscure way the two letters constituted, as it were, a pair, making him feel he should not send one without the other. The closure of the Post Office gave him little choice in the matter anyway – the Douglas Arms may have been only a hundred yards away on the other side of the wire, but he could not trust a sentry to take it there without asking questions, or demanding to see what the note said. Not that it said anything too incriminating, at least to the untutored eye:

Dear Miss Murray,

    I am afraid that, after all, I will not be attending the event at Derby Castle on Sunday. I hope, however, that you enjoy it and also that your research here proves to be valuable.

    Yours sincerely,

    Isaac Fabian

He had stood for a while outside the Post Office, looking out at the sea and sky merging into grey, and feeling intensely – if it is possible for such a thing to be felt intensely – at a loose end. The intensity was perhaps motivated by a sense of momentousness missed, of having expected to come out of the All Seasons with the cleansed sensation of a chapter closed, of moving on sadder but wiser and so forth, and, instead, feeling that his life had been put – even in the context of being an internee, a prisoner of interim measures – more firmly on hold than ever. With nothing else to do, he had come to the Representatives Committee meeting, the two letters still in the inner pocket of his jacket.

'What about Thomas Mann?'

'Well, let's move on,' Dr Mannstein was saying. 'Item Two—'

He was interrupted by the slam of the door. 'Extra! Extra! Read all about it!'

The assembled group turned as one at the sound of this absurd Germanic parody of an English cockney voice. 'Extra, extra, read all about it! First Nazi defeat of the war!' It was Wolfgang Weber, standing at the entrance of the room, holding aloft, like Liberty her torch, a copy of the *Daily Mail*. In vast black headlines, the front page said: BRITISH ARMY COUNTER-OFFENSIVE BEGINS IN NORTH AFRICA; AXIS POWERS IN RETREAT FROM SIDI BARANI.

If Dr Mannstein had felt overwhelmed by the mélange of voices before the meeting started, it was as nothing to the response this received. Suddenly, it sounded as if there were many more people in the room than there were, all much keener to make themselves heard than before.

'Hold on! Calm down!' shouted Weber, fending off a number of hands trying to grab at his paper, like they were lepers and it was Jesus.

'Herr Weber,' said Hermann Gottlieb, utilising the hysteria of the moment to revert to his native tongue, 'are you a house representative?'

Weber looked at him, his green eyes neutral, amused. 'Unfortunately not. I've tried, but I just can't convince my housemates . . .'

'Well, may I ask you to leave? This is a meeting of the Central Camp House Representatives Committee.'

'Oh, don't be ridiculous, Gottlieb,' said Dr Mannstein, standing up. 'He's got a newspaper. A *newspaper*. Do you honestly think we should continue to sit around discussing whether' – he checked his notes – 'roll-call can be made fifteen minutes later? Or whether the canteen is serving enough sausages?'

'That was my motion!'

'I know.'

'It's not just any old newspaper, my friends,' continued Weber. 'It's an *uncensored* newspaper. Most of the houses are getting ones with sections cut out – whatever the British have decided we're not allowed to see. But *this* one' – he held it up again – 'I managed to intercept before it got to our cherished commandant's office.'

'How?'

'One of the benefits of sleeping outside. All sorts of things end up blowing into your kennel . . .'

'Well, Mr Weber,' said Dr Mannstein, ignoring the confused expressions of the men surrounding the artist, 'that *is* resourceful of you. Now, would you be so kind as to read out the article for us?'

Weber shook his head. 'I'm not sure my English is up to it, Dr Mannstein.'

'Then would you please pass it here?'

With a certain ironic reluctance, as if not wanting to relinquish the power of his possession of it, Weber handed his copy of the *Daily Mail* to the house representative immediately in front of him. Gradually, with some solemnity, it was passed from hand to hand along the length of the room, not unlike, Isaac thought – the notion coming to him before he could stop it – a Sefar Torah among a congregation. Eventually, it reached Dr Mannstein, who, still standing, held it in front of himself, his hands looking as if they would like to rest on a lectern.

'*The North African town of Sidi Barani was last night in the hands of General O'Connor and the Seventh Armoured Division of the British army,*' he read, in a measured, if somewhat stentorian, voice. '*Following a heavy bombardment, the Italian Tenth Army Corps, who had previously been in control of the city, have retreated to the neighbouring areas of Sollum and Sidi Omar.*' He looked up.

A couple of men cheered, but mainly there was a silence, as the listeners took in these facts, and the feeling of fact itself, coming into the room and dissolving in a second all the rumours, myths and half truths that had defined their understanding of outside events up to this point.

'That's excellent!' said a voice, eventually. 'Perhaps the tide has turned!'

'It's only the Italians,' said another. 'Who cares about them?'

Dr Mannstein coughed, theatrically. 'Gentlemen. Perhaps if you allow me to read on? Then we can talk afterwards . . .'

The noise and opinions died down, and Dr Mannstein did indeed read on: he read and read, his voice hardly faltering, letting someone else stand up to switch on the lights when the sky outside began to turn black, translating words he felt most of them would not understand, filling them in on all that they thirsted to know, about how the world was – not just North Africa, but also Gibraltar and Somaliland and Vichy France and Crete; Churchill and Hitler and Mussolini and Roosevelt; yellow stars and U-boats and the Blitz and the Desert Rats. At the end of it, there hung within the room almost an exhaustion, as when guests at a large dining-table have eaten too much: the men sat back replete, over-stuffed, with knowledge.

'Does it say anything about us?' said a lone voice, breaking the silence eventually. He spoke in German, the rules established by Dr Mannstein at the start of the meeting seeming to have been suspended by exceptional circumstances.

'Us?' said Doctor Mannstein.

'Yes, us. Internees.'

'That's true, Doctor. Is there nothing about how long we're going to be kept here?'

'Yes, doesn't it say anything about government policy on refugees?'

'Gentlemen, it is just a newspaper. It's not an oracle.' He flicked through the pages again. 'No, nothing I'm afraid.'

'Are you quite sure of that, Dr Mannstein?' Everybody looked round. The voice had been Weber's. He was leaning against the door-frame, lighting a roll-up. He waved out the match, his face deadpan, but there was a challenge in the shake of his wrist.

'What do you mean?' asked Dr Mannstein, raising his grey eyebrows above the rim of his spectacles.

'Well, as I say, my English isn't that great – it's certainly nowhere near as good as yours – but I was pretty sure there was a whole page more or less devoted to . . . "us". Page thirteen, if I remember correctly.'

The attention of the room converged back on Dr Mannstein. He thought about making a show of reopening the paper and pretending to spot the section Weber was referring to, but he was a man whom time and weariness had stripped of the power to pretend.

'You're right, of course, Mr Weber,' he sighed. 'I had deliberately chosen not to read out the contents of page thirteen.'

'Why?' came the cry from a number of quarters.

Dr Mannstein opened the paper, and turned it round to face the room. The main headline on the page, in monoliths of bold print, said: THE SCANDAL OF INTERNMENT: A SPECIAL REPORT. Underneath it, across the page, ran a series of smaller headlines: NO RATIONING FOR REFUGEES; AN ISLAND PARADISE?; FREE ROOMS IN SEA-SIDE HOTELS, TAXPAYER'S EXPENSE; CAMPS 'HOT-BEDS OF INTRIGUE'; MANX CITIZENS' COMPLAINTS; RELEASE PROCEDURES ABUSED. He held the paper at the men for some time; they looked into it blankly, as if staring into some form of print mirror.

'What does it all mean?' asked Hermann Gottlieb, the first to speak, his voice subdued.

'You don't understand the words?'

'No, I understand them – most of them – I just don't understand *it*. Why are they writing it? They put us here. We don't want to be here.'

Dr Mannstein shrugged. 'Who knows? Perhaps life here *is* better for us than for some people on the mainland. Perhaps they need a scapegoat. Either way, it is just words in a newspaper. It doesn't mean it's true, or that everyone believes it.'

Isaac, who had been silent up to this point, said, 'That report you just read out about North Africa was just words in a newspaper, too. Do you think that's not true, either? Or that people don't believe it?'

Dr Mannstein seemed to half sigh and half smile at the same time. 'Well, I think if we had been reading about the same events in a German newspaper, it would be a different truth, wouldn't it?'

'Good Doctor. Fabian. I'm sure everybody here would love to hear the two of you debate the nature of truth all evening,' said Weber, 'but I, for one, would very much like the reading of the newspaper to continue. I, for one, would like to hear exactly what the *Daily Mail* is busy telling our fine host nation about how we are abusing their hospitality.'

Mannstein shook his head. 'Not from me, I'm afraid, Mr Weber. I chose not to read it out for a reason; the reason being that as chairman of this committee, I don't particularly think it would improve morale in the camp.'

Weber looked at him; the brown spots on his teeth came into view as his smile became mocking. 'Well, Doctor, I'm sure I speak for the entire room' – he opened his arms, taking them in – 'when I say how much we appreciate your concern for our psychological welfare, but I would prefer to know what's being said about us.'

'So would I!' came from somewhere in the room.

'And me!'

Mannstein shrugged. 'Well, you'll have to find another reader.' To make the point, he tossed the newspaper down on the table, got up, folded his glasses rather ceremoniously into the top pocket of his jacket, and, picking a zigzag route through the erratically seated representatives, left the room. This took not a little time, and created on his exit an odd 'what shall we do now?' feeling in the air, like when a teacher unexpectedly leaves a classroom.

Weber, a man who clearly lived for such moments, took the stage, striding up to the table and holding the paper aloft once more. 'Well, we *are* a bunch of renegades! Who wants to be our voice?' The representatives looked at one another, unsure how their small stab at officialdom had taken this messy turn. 'Artraub? Gottlieb? English not up to it?' His eyes scanned the room; men were looking down and fidgeting, as when a magician asks for volunteers. 'Ah! Fabian! Of course. You've demonstrated your command of the native tongue to me in the past. Fancy the job?'

'Not really . . .'

'Come now, my friend.' He put on a whingeing voice. '"*Not really*." Do you think that's what Lenin said when the International asked him to be their leader? Do you think that's what Trotsky said when—'

'Yes, all right, Weber,' he said, coming forward. 'I get it.'

Isaac approached the table, where Weber was waiting, smiling and holding the newspaper out like a relay baton. Isaac grasped it, and shook it open. The other man leant back onto the table.

'Go on, Fabian. Let us know the worst.'

'Page thirteen?'

'Page thirteen.'

He flicked it open; the English newspaper had a crêpe-like quality to its pages, grimy against his fingers. Page thirteen fell open to his view. This close, the armada of negativity coming out of it made him feel slightly afraid. 'I don't know where to start,' he said.

'Wherever you like,' said Weber.

His eyes scanned the page, speed-reading. AN ISLAND PARADISE? Reports of the internees enjoying swimming in the sun and country walks. HOT-BEDS OF INTRIGUE. Suggestions that spying and anti-British activity were rife. MANX CITIZENS' COMPLAINTS. A series of local people quoted protesting about being moved, and about the 'arrogant' behaviour of the internees. RELEASE PROCEDURES ABUSED. Perhaps this was a good point to begin; after all, release was the issue always uppermost in the internees' minds.

'Right. Well.' He looked up; forty or so pairs of dark eyes were staring at him, expectantly. '*Release procedures abused* is the headline.'

'Abused?' came a voice.

'I'm not sure . . .'

'*Missbraucht*,' said someone.

'Yes, that sounds right. Underneath is a smaller headline that says, *A personal investigation.* And then it says: *Already, over two thousand of the aliens who were interned on the Isle of Man in June of this year have been released.*' As he read, he heard the murmur, like a whispered echo, of translation. '*The government insists that those released have been subjected to the most string . . . stringent?*' He pronounced it with a hard 'g'. He looked around for suggestions as to what this word might mean, but none was forthcoming. '*The most stringent . . . checks possible. But your correspondent has discovered evidence to the contrary.* Then there is a sub-headline which says: *Faked testimonials.*'

'Faked what?'

'Testimonials. You know . . .'

'Shh. Let him read.'

'*The Home Office has encouraged the release of internees through a scheme involving the production of written testimonials. These testimonials are affidavits, written and signed by British citizens, which . . . attest?*'

'*Bezeugen.*'

'*Attest to the fact that the internee is a decent, honest and responsible person who does not consti . . . constitute a threat to our national security. The submission of three testimonials to the Home Office will enormously speed up the process of an internee's release.*'

'I didn't know that!'

'Shh!'

'*No doubt the majority of these testimonials are written and signed by British citizens in good faith, and refer mainly to those aliens who do indeed deserve to be released. But very little is being done to check that the testimonials being presented to the Home Office are genuine. Signatures are not analysed for forgeries, and, more importantly, the consideration of whether inducements have been offered is not even taken into account. Stories abound of money – which some of the refugees, despite their apparent circumstances, are not short of – being offered to British citizens for the writing of testimonials. Worse still, there have been instances, which this newspaper can confirm, where alien women have not been beyond offering "favours" in exchange for them. This is despite the fact that most of these women are seeking testimonials on behalf of their husbands!'*

'Favours?'

'You know what he means . . .'

'Which of our wives are doing this?'

'Be quiet!'

Isaac waited for the reaction to die down. 'Then there's one more sub-headline: *Favours offered. Only three days ago, a woman whom your correspondent had met as part of these investigations, married to an alien interned on the Isle of Man, came forward with an offer: write a testimonial on behalf of her husband, and together we could repair to her bedroom.'*

This provoked uproar in the room.

'I don't believe it!'

'Who would do it?'

'It's your wife, Hermann. I'm sure of it.'

'Shut your mouth!'

'Let him finish!'

'*This was extraordinary, especially given that, until this point, all she had talked about was her love for her husband. Proof, perhaps, that the morality of the alien is very different to our own; certainly, the morality of the alien woman would seem to be. With some embarrassment, her attentions were refused, at which point she became more insistent, and more directly physical, which is when your correspondent deemed it best to leave. But how many men would not have left, and would have gone on to write a false testimonial, for a husband about whom they knew nothing? How many men, in fact, have already . . .'*

Here, Isaac, who had gone into something of a reading trance, concerned mainly with getting the words right, and interested to discover that his English seemed to be improving as he went on, petered out. Around him, the men were shouting, urging him to continue, a welter of faces, some outraged, some laughing, contortions which seemed to him suddenly similar to those undergone by faces in dreams, all bulging eyes, and cramped brows, and distorted, oversized mouths. He got up and walked through this living

267

cartoon, unhearing as they bayed at him, unfeeling as his coat was pulled back. When he reached the door, he noticed that Weber had followed him, with what appeared to be the nearest thing he had so far seen on his face to an expression of concern. This shook him from his stupor for a moment, long enough for him to open the paper again, and check the name at the bottom of the article he had just read out. Yes, it was still there, underneath the rectangle of words, in small capitals: DOUGLAS LEAN. As he read it, he thought he could feel the inner lining of his jacket, where the same name was written in his letter to Lulu, vibrate in response. He tried to move on, out through the door, but Weber put up his arm, blocking Isaac's way.

'What?' said Isaac.

'Give me back the paper.'

'Why?'

The concerned expression intensified. 'I want to incorporate it in a sculpture.'

The room Isaac was standing outside would, he knew, be much like any other, and yet he felt there was something indefinably powerful and mysterious about the door. Raising his hand to knock, the dark grain of the wood seemed to swirl, in a series of sea-horse-shaped waves, to a central point, inviting his knuckles to place themselves just there, as if preordained, as if pointed to that particular target by Nature.

He was aware, of course, that this nightmarish overfocusing on details was just another symptom of his present state of mind, but one of his discoveries – since being in this state of mind – was that being aware that one was in the grip of mental disorder did not especially help to bring one out of it. It made him want to go straight round to Martin Freud's room and bawl him out about his father's stupid insistence on insight, his absurd idea that displaying the map of the mind's fractures to itself was curative, that all you needed was knowledge, self-knowledge, and you would be better. Isaac knew why he had gone slightly mad – it was because the name Douglas Lean had been written at the bottom of that *Daily Mail* article – and it made no difference.

Since leaving the meeting of the Representatives Committee so abruptly yesterday evening, he had tried his best to bring his mind under control, by combating the mad thoughts with sensible ones. There was nothing in the article that mentioned Lulu by name, for a start. It could easily have been referring to another woman, another wife of another refugee. That he told himself continually. *The piece was deliberately inflammatory* came next, *almost certainly an exaggeration, if not downright lies.* The homely *there are two sides to every story*, easier to say as an internal mantra, appeared often. But whatever portions of rationality these thoughts meted out in his mind, he still *felt* crazy. His skin itched, his armpits tingled, his solar plexus was bricked up with tension;

despite the snow, which, in contrast with that on the mainland, remained crunchy and thick on the island's roads, he found himself continually sweating – a strange, clotted sweat, which felt like it rose from further beneath the skin than the cooling droplets of healthy athletic perspiration. And when the wall of sensible thinking crumbled, which it did almost as soon as the enormous effort of willpower required to keep it propped up was relaxed for a second, behind it lay a fatal part of the mind, where his thoughts – or rather just thoughts; in this place they no longer seemed *his* – would feel as if set on fire, like people set on fire, running madly and uncontrollably around in helplessly repeating circles. They had no structure, these thoughts, no logic, and the key thing about them was their repetitiveness, like a terrible song whose banging melody the mind insists on playing and replaying: *she wanted to fuck him, she did fuck him, she has fucked other men while I've been gone, she is a whore, she would have fucked him, he fucked her, I am an idiot, she fucked him.* No amount of saying them would burn them out.

He was exhausted, as well. For two days now, he had refused tea at breakfast, in order to avoid the potential bromide, but the first night this created in him a rabid insomnia, and the second – last night – he was plagued throughout until roll-call with his distorted song of songs. It was made even more tiring because, alongside all the dread and anger and jealousy and paranoid fantasy, the article in the *Daily Mail* had also provoked a desperate *worry* about his wife – out there, over the sea, on her own, frantically searching among the bad men for the means to save him from internment. It was contradictory, but consciousness, especially at four o'clock in the morning, is powered by contradiction. He needed to *know* – not knowing was, in a way, worse than knowing the worst – but the only remedy, some kind of direct communication with Lulu, was barred to him. Eventually, unable to bear the conflicting voices any longer, Isaac had come here, to this door. It seemed the only way of shutting his mind down. Taking his cue from the arrows of the grain, he knocked, his overwrought senses feeling each rap as small bursts of pain in his fingers.

'Who is it?' said a voice inside.

'Isaac Fabian.'

There was a short pause, during which Isaac thought seriously about turning around to flee, and then the door opened.

'I knew you'd come.'

Waldstein's demeanour in saying it was only partially smug – in another way, he sounded relieved, like a lover. Isaac wondered if these would have been the words that June would have used, had he somehow made his way to her door. But the one other thought which he could offer up as a defence against madness, the one that went *I am in no position to judge her, given what I've started to feel for June* – this was a thought which didn't know what side it was on, which seemed to create in him as much anxiety as the terrible thoughts, until eventually he decided that the only way out was not to think of either June or Lulu, or love at all, but head in the opposite direction, towards men and war and death.

Isaac walked into the room, which Waldstein had somehow contrived to be darker than any other room he had ever seen in Central Camp, even given the mandatory blackout charcoal on all windows. Virtually everyone else had scratched some kind of view of the sea into their windows (some rather beautifully, as whatever scratched-out abstract shape or ship had sea-water swimming through its lines: Isaac had seen a sea-filled Star of David, and in Wolfgang Weber's room there was, etched into the window, a portrait of Adolf Hitler as a dog). But Waldstein had left his as blankets of black, and the room was consequently so dim it took Isaac some time to recognise the presence of four other men in it, skulking around a small central table, half hidden again by cigarette smoke, like Americans playing poker in an illegal drinking den.

'Your timing is impeccable, Fabian,' said Waldstein. 'Let me introduce you to some new friends.' He raised his hand to begin, and then froze. 'You are here, I assume, because you want to join us?'

Isaac looked at Waldstein's outstretched hand. His eyes, gradually becoming accustomed to the dark, focused on minute details again, seeing the lines on Waldstein's palm intricately, a series of trenches dug into his skin, like an aerial photograph of some erratically carved-up land. He wished he had some mystical power –

271

even any idea of which line was the 'life' one – so he could get some sense of whether 'yes' or 'no' was the right answer. Such choices, thought Isaac: how was a man supposed to make them? No wonder he had renounced God, when He gave you so little clue.

'Yes,' he said. Isaac did not know if it was the right answer. But he knew – or, rather, he might have found out were he ever to submit to the Freudian couch he so abjured – that he was a man who responded to emotional turmoil politically; that he craved the surrender, the internal laying down of arms that comes with the external taking up of them.

Waldstein smiled, the dark yellow sections of his teeth matching the sepia light, making it seem as if they were missing, and consequently giving him a quizzically urchin-like look. 'Good,' he said, with a 'to-business' air. 'So this is,' he continued, indicating the nearest member of the seated group, a bearded man with an incongruously polite demeanour, 'Johann Hirsch, a comrade I've known for many years, and who worked with me in Munich before the war.' Isaac shook his hand. His grip was light, his skin sandy. 'This is Nikolas Tort, who controls our operations in Onchan; and this Jacob Krauss, who does so in Hutchinson.'

Isaac shook hands with them in turn, both slight men who, like Hirsch, did not look as if they had it in them to be terrorists. Tort was older, perhaps nearly fifty, bald with a doughy, friendly face, and Krauss olive-skinned and obscurely handsome. He wondered what Waldstein meant by their 'operations' in Onchan and Hutchinson. He wondered, too, how men from other camps could so easily come into Central, but this was answered immediately by Waldstein saying, 'And lastly, this is Siegfried Steinhoffer, our treasurer, who does his best to make sure that most of what we need from the British comes our way . . .'

'Including the turning of blind eyes,' said Steinhoffer, a burlier man than the others, with a healthy shock of grey hair, and a broad grin set between broader jowls. He was the only one who stood to shake hands, covering Isaac's with both of his.

The men round the table laughed at his remark; Isaac smiled as best he could, not comfortable with hearty male laughter, even when being employed in its supposed capacity to defuse tension.

Waldstein dragged another chair for him from the side of the room. Isaac noticed that the walls where scattered with anti-Nazi iconography, posters and pamphlets, some of which he recognised from the time in Germany when people were still unafraid enough to stick them furtively on fences and lamp-posts, others which looked like Waldstein must have drawn them himself.

Isaac sat, and slid the chair awkwardly close to the table's edge, feeling himself becoming part of their circle. 'So . . .' he said, his voice a little cracked – he realised as he said it that it was only the second syllable he had uttered since entering the room – 'that's it? I mean . . .' he corrected himself, embarrassed, 'no one else is involved?'

'We have other supporters, of course – but this is all we need for our present purposes. Can I get you a drink?' asked Waldstein. Since Isaac had been recruited, Waldstein's manner towards him had become avuncular, almost paternal.

'No, thank you.'

Waldstein took his seat at the table. 'Well, now that we have a new addition, perhaps we'd better start from the beginning again. Comrades?'

There was a general murmur of assent. Isaac found himself thrilled once more by the inclusiveness of being addressed as a comrade, although he realised now that no real political context lay behind Waldstein's use of the term.

'All right,' Waldstein was continuing, 'I'll just outline it – we can go into any details later.' From the table, he picked up a grey cardboard folder, from which he produced a series of tatty-looking documents, hand-drawn maps, out-of-focus photographs, scribbled lists. On the back of his hand, the veins were nearly as visible as the lines on the palm. 'This is the target,' he said, holding up one of the photographs.

Through the gloom, Isaac could make out a soft shot of a tall, balding man, thin, with deepset eyes, and a nose long enough to make him wonder if they'd definitely got the right man. The *target*? he thought.

'His name is Klaus Bauermann. Before the war, a high-ranking member of the Nazi Party in Hannover. Virulent anti-Semite; close friend of Julius Streicher. He was in London on the invitation of Mosley, trying to forge links between British fascists and the Nazis, when war broke out. He was arrested in Dover trying to smuggle himself back to Germany. Since he's been on the island, we've observed him leading a number of Nazi singalongs, and shouting abuse at Jewish camp members. There is some evidence that he may have been the brains behind the attack on Aaron Fleisch.'

Around Isaac, heads that had clearly heard all this many times before were nodding. Isaac concentrated hard on what Waldstein was saying, trying not to let the words slip under the bursts of broken song still echoing in the caves of his mind: *she would have fucked him, she wanted to fuck him, they were about to fuck in our bed.* He damped it down as best he could by focusing on the photograph of Bauermann. Squinting at it, he came to the conclusion that it was one of the men he had seen coming out of the Red House a few days before.

'He lives in Room Nine in the Red House. He is unmarried.'

'That's good,' said Isaac.

'I'm not adding that information out of sympathy, Fabian. The Nazi fuck could have a wife and a brood of twenty Aryan brats for all I care. The point is: therefore, he will not be going to the rendezvous of husbands and wives on Sunday night.'

Isaac started. 'That's when the attack is planned for?'

'Yes. It's a perfect night for it. The British will be mainly concerned with making sure the event runs smoothly, so there'll be fewer sentries out and about. All the other Nazis are married, so Bauermann should be in on his own. Everything about it works in our favour.'

Isaac looked around him, at the dark faces, placid, unsurprised by the information. 'This *Sunday*?'

'You've come on board late, Fabian. If you'd come earlier, you'd have had more time to get used to the idea.'

'What if I hadn't come on board at all?'

Waldstein smiled, a knowing uncle to a naive nephew. 'I had faith in you.'

Isaac suppressed the impulse to pull a childish face at him. 'Fine. But how can you be sure that Bauermann isn't going?'

For the first time, Waldstein looked confused. 'Did you not hear me? I said he isn't married.'

'Well, I was thinking of going, and I'm not married.'

All five men looked to him as one; the power in the room swung like a searchlight his way. His reaction, however, was not too different from theirs; he was shocked and confounded, still reeling from the unprecedented experience of hearing words come out of his mouth before they had formed properly in his brain. Perhaps there were too many words in there at the moment, he thought, what with Waldstein's plan, and the uncontrollable repetition of the Lulu and Douglas Lean litany, giving this sentence no room to gestate.

'Sorry,' he said. 'That isn't right. I *am* married. But my wife isn't on the island.'

'Well, either way, Bauermann definitely won't be going to the Derby Castle event,' said Steinhoffer, lighting a new cigarette. 'None of the Nazis are. They're going to a separate event in Port Erin, where their wives are. The British didn't want to risk any trouble at Derby Castle.'

'So, how do you know he isn't going to Port Erin?' said Isaac.

Steinhoffer shook his head, smoke coming out of either side of his mouth. 'We don't, for certain. But there are only about twenty Nazi couples on the island, and thousands of Jewish ones. It'll be much easier for the British to police who's going to the Port Erin event than the Derby Castle one. A single man there will be much easier to spot. Besides, they always monitor them more carefully than us.'

'Fabian,' said Waldstein, 'you said you were *thinking* of going to Derby Castle?'

'Yes. I was. But if I'm needed . . . I suppose . . .'

'No, bear with me. I think – anyone who disagrees feel free to say so – I think it might be a good idea for you to go. Derby Castle is just a few hundred yards past the Red House on the Ramsay road. If you can slip out of it at the right time, I think you'll attract less attention than coming from here. And we won't have to bribe another sentry to get you through the gates.' He addressed the table. 'How are most men getting there?'

'They're setting off in groups, one every ten minutes, from four o'clock.' Steinhoffer appeared to have all the information at his fingertips. 'Two British soldiers will march each group there.'

Waldstein jotted this down, then turned back to Isaac. 'You think it will be easy enough for you to get into one of these groups?'

Isaac opened his palms. 'Who knows? It's on my files that I'm married. And if you're right, they probably won't be checking the groups too carefully.'

Waldstein consulted his notes. 'Right. Well, as long as you're out of Derby Castle and in place by the right time, I think you – *we* – will be better served by that plan. Are we all in agreement?' A small nod, like a bouncing ball, went round the table.

It flashed into Isaac's mind to wonder whether this was a good idea for other reasons, but in fact the knowledge that now he was definitely going to see June again created in him a nugget of comfort, which he was happy to cling to for the moment. 'In place where?' he said.

Waldstein took an audible breath through his nose. 'The operation will begin at ten p.m.' He lifted up a pencil drawing, which on closer inspection turned out to be a rudimentary map: in the centre of it a house, with a road in front, and a rectangular area marked STABLES behind. On the far right of the page, Isaac thought he could make out the squiggly waves of a heartbreakingly hand-drawn sea. 'Can you see this all right?' Isaac nodded. Waldstein pointed to the road. 'Krauss will be creating a diversion here, on the far side of the road, at ten o'clock, in order to get the attention of the Red House sentry. Once he's gone to investigate, myself, Tort and Hirsch will enter the stables, via the back door.'

'How do you know it will be open?' said Isaac.

'It won't. But the British used internee labour to convert the stables, and one of our friends who worked there has provided us with' – and here, for dramatic effect, he produced them from within the grey folder, tinkling like wind chimes – 'a copy of the keys.'

'I see. Then what?'

'The operation should be over by ten past ten. We can't expect Krauss to distract the sentry for any longer than that. We will exit by the same door. All we need you to do—'

'Hold on.' Isaac held up a hand. 'What do you mean, the operation should be over by ten past ten?' A silence hung over the gathering, a silence that dared him to fill in the gap left by Waldstein's ten-minute elision. 'You mean Bauermann will be dead by then?'

The men all seemed to glance at one another.

'Yes,' said Waldstein, shiftily, like a man who has just had a euphemism for some particularly graphic act needlessly explained.

'How?'

'*How?*'

'Yes, how? How will you kill him?'

Waldstein tutted, a dry, insect's click. 'Those details need not concern you, Fabian.'

'I can't agree, Waldstein. I think they—'

'I shall have garrotted him.'

Isaac and Waldstein turned from their duel. It had been Johann Hirsch speaking. His attitude was calm, almost urbane. Isaac's eyes went instinctively to Hirsch's hands, resting together on the table. They looked small and ungnarled, even a touch feminine: the hands of an accountant, not an executioner.

'I have already cut the necessary section of barbed wire from the camp perimeter.'

'Johann,' said Waldstein, touching the other man on the forearm, 'there is no need for you to tell him that.'

Hirsch shrugged. 'I am proud of it,' he said.

Isaac still could not equate the demeanour with the act; he wondered how many other people Johann Hirsch had killed, in Munich, working with Waldstein. An image came into his mind: Bauermann's neck, and how the veins in it would stiffen against the knots in the barbed wire, the small spots of blood that would appear before they broke.

'So,' said Waldstein, after a suitable pause had elapsed, 'to continue. All we need you to do is be in place here at nine fifty-five. We'll be approaching from the back of the house – it'll be too dangerous for us to call out or cross the road in case it alerts any of the Nazis, so if you say you're going to be there, mean it.' He held Isaac's gaze for a short time. Isaac nodded, acknowledging the responsibility. Waldstein pointed to a cross, marked on the map. 'There is a small hillock by the side of the road, on the seaward side. If you lie on top of that, you should be fairly invisible in the dark, but it gives you a good view up and down the Ramsay road, in case any British soldiers should be wandering around. Obviously, with Derby Castle being so close, some of them may come up from there.'

'What do I do if one appears?'

Waldstein nodded silently towards Nikolas Tort, who reached down towards a briefcase by his feet.

'You blow on this, twice,' said Tort, laying on the table what looked like a miniature flute.

There was a silence. Tort gestured for Isaac to pick it up. Isaac did so, stifling a desire to laugh. The instrument was wooden, and on closer inspection was more like a recorder, except, instead of numerous holes along the length of it, there was a single one near the mouthpiece.

'I'm not especially musical,' said Isaac.

'It doesn't matter. All you need to do is blow, and flutter your hand on the hole. Try it.'

Aware of being watched in deep seriousness by five pairs of eyes – which only intensified in him the need to laugh – Isaac picked up the wooden tube, and did what he was told. The bodily pressure to recognise the absurdity of it all seemed unbearable, the release of shaking hysterics seconds away, when out came the sound. It was an owl hoot. Had it been in any way cartoonish, had it been at all a broad approximation of an owl hoot, Isaac would have collapsed, would have laughed so much that his involvement in the operation would almost certainly have ended there and then. But it wasn't: it was a perfect replica of the owl's call, and, because of its perfection, there came upon Isaac instead a chill, felt not just in his soul, but on his skin, the creep of the flesh, an ancient and instinctive response to this sound of the night, this desolate song of the shadows.

'It was made by Mikael Fingelstein, an inmate of my camp,' said Tort, as Isaac stared at the innocuous piece of wood in his hands. 'The best maker of musical instruments in Austria, in my opinion.'

'It's extraordinary,' said Isaac, turning the instrument in his fingers. 'It's so realistic I worry that if a real owl hoots twice, you'll think it's me.'

Most of them laughed at this, although Waldstein, who seemed entirely dispossessed of a sense of humour – apart from his regular 'the man of mystery laughs at another's naivety' put-downs – became concerned, and spent some time trying to demonstrate how Isaac could achieve the same effect, only with not absolutely the same level of verisimilitude, by cupping his hands and blowing into them. He was voted down, however, making it clear to Isaac that Waldstein was not quite as much the leader of this particular underground organisation as he liked to appear.

'So, that's all I have to do?' said Isaac, bringing the attention back to the matter in hand. 'Lie on this hill and watch for British sentries for fifteen minutes? And make like an owl if I see them?'

'Yes,' said Waldstein, a touch sulkily, taking a while to get over losing the vote. 'If we get your signal before we've gone into the house, we'll wait, then you can blow it again when the coast is clear. If we get it while we're in the house, similarly, we'll wait before coming out.'

'Right. Well, that seems simple enough.'

'Good.'

'Rainer,' said Hirsch, 'I need to be getting back . . .'

'Fine, fine. We can finish the meeting there.' The men began to rise, coughing, lifting coats from the back of chairs. Then, he added, with a sense of moment: 'Next time we meet will be Sunday night.'

The other men seemed to take this information in their stride. Isaac, who had remained in his seat, said, 'Not before? We're not going through it again? We're not going to' – he searched for the right word – 'rehearse at all?'

'*Rehearse?*' said Waldstein.

'You know . . . go through it. Have a dry run.'

Steinhoffer laughed. 'Yes, of course. I'm sure the British would take no interest in the six of us going up to where the Nazis live and practising our assault tactics. Perhaps Saturday afternoon, to make sure they don't miss us?'

His laughter was so booming and friendly – it gave him the aspect, somewhat, of a Semitic Santa – that Isaac could not find it in him to mind the sarcasm, and simply smiled apologetically, accepting that his question was foolish. None the less, now that the talking was over, and his involvement in a murder – a *murder!* – had been so quickly sealed, he was unable to suppress a rising panic. 'Wait,' he said.

Krauss, Tort and Hirsch had already shaken hands with Waldstein – definitive, meaningful handshakes, packed with destiny – and were on their way to the door, when Isaac's word turned them around. All eyes were on him. Once again, he felt the pressure of the moment, of being pushed into the centre of this strange stage.

'Are we all . . .' he hesitated, knowing that the words he was speaking were obvious, and that the people he was speaking them to must be well past the stage they outlined, but then continued, feeling that they still had to be said, 'sure about this? I mean . . .' he carried on, in the face of Waldstein sighing heavily, and the others looking disappointed, 'are we all absolutely certain that this man *deserves* to die?'

'We don't have time for this,' said Hirsch, immediately, to Waldstein. 'I thought you said he was committed.'

'I *am* committed,' said Isaac, although the words sounded not entirely convincing in his mouth. 'It's just happening so much faster for me than it is for all of you. That's all.'

'If you don't want to be a part of it, don't be,' said Tort. 'We can find someone else.'

'Before Sunday?' asked Steinhoffer.

Tort looked away. A sickly silence filled the air.

Steinhoffer considered Isaac with the closest to a conciliatory expression among the men. 'Do you think that the Nazi would give any of us the same consideration, given the chance?' he said, in an even tone. 'Do you think, if he had a gun and we were lined up in front of him, that he would stop and ask the same questions?'

Isaac shook his head. 'Of course not. But we're better than them.' He looked at each of the men in turn. He wondered why he was saying this, questioning, holding things up, when only a little while earlier he had so desperately craved the unconditional rush of righteous action; but, for the moment, his own madness had been cowed by the sudden reality of a potentially greater one. 'Aren't we?'

'Tush, tush, Fabian,' said Waldstein. 'What is this liberal, humanist claptrap? Are you or are you not a communist?'

'Yes,' said Isaac, a little weakly.

'Well then, you know – you know from history – that political action – *real* political action – always costs blood.'

'Oh, fuck off, Waldstein.' Waldstein looked shocked. 'Stop using my beliefs – about which you know *nothing* – against me. What I believe has to do with the evolution of history – about great seismic shifts of social order. In those terms, I'm not even certain what we're planning here *is* a political act.' He felt his sure grasp of this vocabulary pump up his confidence. 'Bauermann is a prisoner, too. We are all prisoners. The ruling class here is the British.'

'Oh, so you think we should be killing one of the British,' sneered Waldstein.

'No! Don't deliberately misinterpret me. I—'

'Fabian,' said Jacob Krauss. It was the first time he had spoken in the entire meeting. His voice was Prussian-accented and quiet. He went back to the table and sat down opposite Isaac, the slightly Red-Indian beauty of his features coming out more strongly in that light. 'Your problem, I assume, is that we appear to have chosen Bauermann more or less randomly – to represent Nazism. And that therefore the act of killing him is simply some sort of symbolic gesture.'

'Yes, said Isaac, taken aback by how succinctly Krauss had summed up his concern.

'Well, you should remember that they have chosen us – more or less randomly – to represent vermin. So really, we have no need to know for certain that one Nazi is any worse than another. Wearing the swastika is enough. But, as it happens, I do know Klaus Bauermann. I am from Hannover. Two years ago he was an official at the Jewish Immigration Office there. To get an exit visa, you had to – essentially – pay him as much money as you had.' He took from his pocket a grimy-looking handkerchief and wiped his nose; despite his outwardly fine appearance, Krauss seemed as if he may be ill. 'So that was what my parents did. They sold our house – for

281

much less than it was worth, of course – and virtually all our possessions, and gave the money to Bauermann. Then, when they went to collect their visas, he said they weren't ready. My father got angry – just for a second, he reacted, he didn't just sit there and take it – and so Bauermann produced the visas, after all, but then tore them up, in front of my father and mother. My father told me it was the first time since I was born that he'd seen my mother cry.' Krauss paused.

How dull is evil, thought Isaac, as his mental image of this story took shape, his mind colouring in the crestfallen old couple, the bits of card falling in front of them in a perversion of confetti, the Nazi laughing like a pantomime villain, his subordinates turning to point and join in, the laughter rising as the tears fall; how crushingly familiar its power-plays, its humiliations, its destructions of hope.

'Soon after, I was smuggled across the border to France, and then, when that fell, the Resistance got me onto a boat here. To Britain.' Krauss sat back in his chair. 'Last I heard, my parents had been "resettled", somewhere on the Polish border. My last five letters to them have not been answered.'

The implication of this epilogue to his story hung in the air with the stale cigarette smoke. The men shuffled and coughed, like an audience between movements of a symphony. Isaac felt his complexity shrinking. That was the other thing about evil: it provokes only the simple response. In love, in politics, in the thousand pernickety dilemmas of the everyday, he could be complex, he could be individual, his choices could be oblique and distinctive and idiosyncratic. But not here: here, there was no spectrum of choice.

'Well, then. I'll be on that hill on Sunday night,' he said.

Private Thomas Fisher was amazed, as ever, by how compliant the internees were. 'Fall in!' he shouted, and they did, even though some of them didn't know what the words meant. His father had been a guard at Knockaloe, one of the camps they had set up on the island during the last war, and he'd told him that the Germans there were always acting up, refusing to do the camp work, trying to escape and all sorts. But this lot – well, they were like lambs, and he was the sheepdog. Private Fisher couldn't quite understand this, although he knew that most of his bunch were Jewish whereas most of those guarded by his dad probably hadn't been, but, then again, he wasn't entirely sure what difference that made, not being entirely clear what a Jew was. There hadn't been any in Ramsay while he was growing up; he wasn't even certain there had been any on the island. 'Fall in!' he said again, just because he knew that any corporal shouting it at him would have to say it twice; and he liked shouting it – it made him feel as if he'd gone up a rank.

This was the third lot he'd been assigned to take up to Derby Castle, this Sunday afternoon. It was all fairly typical of his work here. Private Fisher had not expected to remain on the Isle of Man when he'd enrolled in the forces, but once internment started, the British military had encouraged Manxmen in the army to stay, partly because it meant they had to divert fewer soldiers from the mainland, and partly because they thought it would help to ease tensions with the locals. He was, not very secretly, pleased. Thomas Fisher had never been much of a traveller; his only time away to date had been a shopping trip to Liverpool in 1934, and he hadn't been that impressed – it didn't smell as fresh as the island, and there was too much traffic.

Nice evening for it, at least, he thought, looking out over the bay, where the still-bright air of the fading winter day was reflected on the sea in a liquid patchwork of light. It threw a golden hue over most of the internees presently standing in front of him, who, he noticed, much like the last two groups, had made quite an effort, finding jackets and clean shirts and ties to wear, and shaving for the occasion. This moved Fisher, a soft-hearted man who hoped one day to be able to find a wife himself whom he might dress up for to dance with. He checked his watch: four-thirty; time to get weaving.

'Are they all in, Private Saunders?'

Saunders poked his face round from the back of the group, his face set as usual in the deepest boredom, although crossed also by a smidgen of surprise, as if he had gone so far into this particular vacant trance that he'd forgotten, for a moment, who he was and what he was doing here.

'Surnames F to J, Saunders.'

'I know.'

'Well, have you checked them?'

'Course I have.'

This was not true. What Private Saunders, who was twenty, from Plymouth, and concerned mainly with the fact that his crotch had not stopped itching since he'd seen that prozzer down the docks on his last period of leave, *had* done was call out the letters 'F' and 'J' and idly glance at a checklist of names as various internees had formed into lines. He could have called out each name in turn, and had them respond, but seeing as he had never actually had a conversation with an internee, let alone been able to match any of their faces to their names, that would have been a fairly redundant exercise.

'Well, good. Let's get going.'

'How do we get there?'

Fisher sighed: for Saunders to have spent three months here and still not to know the location of one of their main attractions pained the Manxman in him. 'Up to the end of the Promenade, then follow the path of the railway. But I'll lead, anyway. Rows of four, if you please.'

Private Saunders nodded, and then, with intense apathy, broken only by the odd scratch of his groin, made a quarter-hearted attempt to arrange the two hundred Central Camp internees into marching rows of four, before his older colleague tutted, raised his eyes to heaven, and set off.

It was only walking up the hill leading out of Douglas, with the cliffs rising in front of him, that Isaac really began to feel his lack of sleep. It was now four days, and four nights, since he'd stopped drinking the tea, and his body had still not adjusted. He wished he'd had a cup yesterday morning, but he'd been too concerned about clouding his mind with bromide this close to the event; and besides, he'd been convinced that he would sleep during the night to come anyway, having not done so for the previous three. In fact, he did get some sleep, but it was not the refreshing brain-wipe of an uninterrupted eight-hour coma, such as one might expect after such a long period of insomnia; rather, it was a jagged journey into a semi-altered consciousness, broken by many startled sitting-ups and unprovoked eye-openings, which, once his heart had ceased to rabbit-punch his ribs, revealed only the doubled darkness of the blacked-out room. Into that darkness, on the rack of insomnia, he cursed Waldstein and Lulu and June and Bauermann and everything else that was racing round the carousel of his mind, stopping him from sleeping; only, being Isaac, he cursed in whispers, so as not to wake the slumbering shadows of his roommates.

Today, however, the thought of the job ahead – and, underlying that, the thought of seeing June – had overridden his tiredness, although adrenalin had produced in him not a normal wakefulness, but rather a migrainous brightness, as if his head had been sharpened to a point. The feeling had remained until they reached this hill, when suddenly his heart started to race and his breath falter. Though it was December, his feet dragged as if the road had melted and he was wading through tar. Beside him, to make it worse, rose the carriages of one of the electric trains, on their way to the Derby Castle terminus, its passengers watching him and his fellow marchers with mild interest, as if they were part of the view, along with the sea and the Manx birdlife. He would have stopped, to avoid becoming dizzy, but somehow the slow march of the others kept him going, like a sleeping man being held standing by his friends. He felt inside his jacket pocket, the jacket that Lulu had insisted he take against the cold, and let his fingers brush against the wood – cool, despite its closeness to his body – of the owl-flute. He hoped this would reassure him, and initially it did, insofar as it was still there, he had not forgotten it; but almost instantly afterwards, it just reminded him, in that insistent, compulsive way the brain will, of the dread he felt about his involvement in Waldstein's plot. He took some deep breaths: the air today was milder than it had been, and the snow had begun to melt on the grassy verges by the side of the road, if not on some of the more distant clifftops. In the waning light, he tried to focus on something ahead, as his mother had once told him to do in order to avoid sea-sickness, but could find no still point, only the three fleshy lines, speckled with a fringe of grey, which defined the border of neck and skull on the bald man in front. Isaac reached out and touched the man's shoulder.

'Isaac,' said Dr Mannstein, without turning round. 'I thought you weren't speaking to me.'

'Not at all, Doctor. I'm just very tired. I haven't been sleeping well.'

Mannstein craned his head round, with some difficulty. 'Are you trying to have a consultation with me now?'

'No . . .' said Isaac, smiling, although, like all Jews, he wouldn't particularly want to pass up the opportunity of a quick diagnosis. 'It might be the bromide . . .'

'Ah, the bromide . . .'

'Yes . . . I stopped drinking it four days ago and it's played havoc with my sleep.'

Mannstein's face remained firmly frontward. They marched further up the hill, the road following the curve of the cliff.

'Mannstein . . .' said Isaac, quietly, after he realised that the doctor was not going to proffer any medical advice, 'this group is F to J.'

'I know.'

'And your surname begins with M.'

Sighing, Dr Mannstein slowed his step to allow him to fall back into Isaac's line.

'Yes, Isaac Fabian, you're right. But if you must know, I wanted to get to Derby Castle early, and I didn't think the British would really be bothering to check who went in which group. Which turns out to be right . . .'

'Why do you want to get there early?'

'To make sure I'm ready for my wife,' said Dr Mannstein, as though that were obvious.

'I think the women are arriving later, though. Once all the men are there.'

Mannstein shrugged. 'I just wanted to be certain I was there, waiting for her, when she gets there.'

Isaac nodded, feeling, as he often did when talking to Dr Mannstein, chastened, although this time, for some reason, he absorbed what he was saying, rather than reacting against it. 'You're looking forward to the dance, I take it,' he said, trying to sound sage.

'Very much.'

'Where is your wife coming from?'

'Port St Mary.'

'Oh yes, I think you've told me. And how long since you last saw her?'

Mannstein blinked; he rubbed his finger and thumb on the edge of his white beard, which, Isaac noticed, had been neatly clipped, presumably by Freidkin the barber in House 3. It made him wonder if he should perhaps have dressed more smartly – most of the men had, he noticed – but then most of them were not going to spend the latter half of the night lying face down on a hillock.

'We arrived together on the twelfth of June. I was taken to Central, Irma to Port St Mary. So that's nearly six months.'

'It's a long time . . .'

Mannstein smiled. 'We've been married for thirty-two years. You would not think six months would seem so long. Six months, it's a drop in the thirty-two-year ocean! But then we have never been apart for even one night, before. And so, it turns out, these six months have felt longer, to me, than all the rest of my time with her. Longer still: six months have felt like two hundred years.' He smiled again, a little apologetically this time, the smile containing a plea to excuse an old man his sentimentality.

There was no need: Isaac felt the hard lump forming in his throat at the words, the simplicity of them, their underlying assumption that of course this was what marriage was. What else should it be? He wished he could find his way back to such green, disingenuous love. As if to compound Isaac's malaise, Mannstein took his wallet out of the inner lining of his coat and thrust into the younger man's hands a small photograph.

'That's my wife,' he said, proudly. 'That's Irma.'

Isaac saw a head and shoulders quartered by white folds. Irma's face, smiling the awkward smile of the rarely photographed, was expansively chinned, and, to Isaac's eyes, overrun with lines. How does love get *here?* he thought, feeling more adrift than ever. 'She looks lovely,' he said, handing it back to Mannstein.

'She is.' He put it tenderly back into his wallet.

The troop had gone past the summit of the hill, and was descending into a small valley between the cliffs, at the end of which, just before the road rose again, sat Derby Castle, its fairy-tale turrets and tower just visible above the huge structure of the dance hall in front. The sight of it provoked an audible intake of breath from the men; their eyes raced to it like the wheels of another electric train passing them on their left, but Isaac was looking beyond and above it, to where a patch of red lay among the white, a drop of blood in the snow.

'Look at that,' said Dr Mannstein, breaking his concentration.

'What?' said Isaac.

'There,' he said, pointing to the side of the road. He slowed down, forcing the rows of men behind to slow, too.

There were anxious tuts from those who wanted to reach the castle quickly, now that it was in sight. Isaac squinted in the direction of the doctor's finger.

'Can't you see? Winter jasmine. Crocus. Coming through where the snow has melted.'

'Flowers?'

'Yes . . .'

'How can they be growing under the snow?'

Mannstein laughed. 'They're winter flowers. A lot of flowers grow here in the winter. The island's got what I believe is called a micro-climate . . .'

Isaac looked again, and, now knowing what he was looking for, was able to make out some rings of violet, some shards of blue, some sprigs of white. Next thing he knew, Dr Mannstein's hand was among them, pulling them from the earth.

'Dr Mannstein . . . what are you doing?'

'What do you think?' he shouted. 'Getting flowers for Irma!'

Within seconds, three other pairs of hands had joined his, trying to find anything that was blooming amid the mud and the snow.

'Oi!' Private Saunders was approaching from the back of the group, his face petulant. 'What are you blokes doing? You're breaking up the whole bloody march . . .'

'Hold on, Saunders,' said Private Fisher, joining him from the front. More and more of the men were copying Dr Mannstein; some had gone to the other bank, nearer the sea, where different flowers were visible. Bouquets began to appear in the men's hands, small sparse arrangements, decorated as best they could with sprigs of grass and dusted with snow. One man was meticulously picking holly from a bush. 'Can't you see what they're doing?'

'What?'

'Oh, never mind.' He raised his voice. 'All right, lads, you've got another two minutes exactly to pick flowers for your better halves – after that, we're off!'

This information caused a rush, as all the rest of the internees – some of whom had been bemused, and others who had been too unsure of breaking ranks – burst, like a sea parting, towards either side of the road. The only internee left standing in the middle was Isaac, who felt at a loss, and not a little exposed, as if his deception in going to the event had been suddenly unmasked by his failure to react like all the others. Eventually, he wandered over to the bank on the right, and looked down, his eyes searching for remaining flora amid the scrabbling hands and bent backs. Flowers had never been his strong point. Occasionally, in the past, he had bought Lulu roses – the obvious choice, but also the only flower in the shop he could name – and she had seemed more pleased than he could understand; he did not know how so much joy could come from the possession of something that would soon die. He stood there for a while, looking out to sea.

'Wondering what to pick?' Isaac looked round. It was Private Fisher, standing by him with his hands affably in his pockets and an air of wanting to help, like that of a local man seeing a tourist holding a map upside-down.

'Yes,' said Isaac.

'Right,' he said, pointing to some green shoots, surrounded by a corolla of white flowers, sprouting against the bricks of the sea-wall. 'That is sea campion. Grows only on the coastal roads, but all year round. Very nice for the ladies. Next to it is scurvy grass, which you'll always see with it. There's a touch of sea-pink around it, too. That's one of our national flowers.' His voice was thickly coated in pride.

'Are there any roses?' said Isaac, trying to sound polite but wishing to avoid a botany lecture.

'Roses?' Fisher laughed, a wheezy, wispy sound. 'Well not like your Valentine's rose from the florist, no. Further back I saw some burnet's rose, but, truth be told, that's a white flower. Smells a bit doggy.'

'What about this?' said Isaac, touching what looked to him like a little red bush. It felt stringy, and rough enough to graze the skin.

'That's heather. Red bell heather.'

Isaac pulled at it. It took more vigour than he expected to remove it from the earth, despite the thinness of its roots. He held it up in front of him, close to his eyes, trying to see how red its leaves were, a difficult job against the purple and orange light of the setting sun. He wanted it to be red, the colour of love but also of blood, appropriate because at some level he didn't know for whom he was picking it, June or Klaus Bauermann.

'Tom . . .' said a voice behind them. It was Private Saunders. 'They've had about three and a half minutes. I'm not bothered, but if we're not careful, we'll still be 'ere when the next lot go by.'

'Thank you, Private Saunders,' said Fisher. 'All right, you men!' he shouted. 'Let's have you all back, ready to march, or we'll never get to the big event!'

Slowly, the internees turned away from the banks and shuffled – some, who had collected only the odd bit of gorse, disconsolately; others, their hands garlanded and wreathed, with a happier step – back to the centre of the road. Isaac stuffed the heather into the pocket of his jacket. He felt a hand, its hearty weight unmistakably British, pat him on the back.

'Hope it's lucky for you,' said Private Fisher, out of the side of his mouth, in an exaggerated stage whisper.

June stood on the balcony above the ballroom at Derby Castle, holding on to the balustrade, and watched the last of the men file in. She had been granted permission to come to the event, but had been advised by the British to remain on the upper floor until the women arrived, because, as Lieutenant Colonel Rutter had put it, 'some of the men from the other camps won't have seen a woman for months'. June had smiled internally at his words, betraying as they did the fact that, since their last meeting, he seemed to have developed, if not a soft spot for her, at least a desire to prove that he was not quite the stuffy old colonel she might have thought he was. She had wondered what he imagined these fair-sex-starved Jews might do – ravish her limb from limb just before their wives arrived? Implode with lust? – but had taken the advice, because she did not want to draw attention to herself, and also because she had no wish to detract from the main event of the evening, the entrance of the wives.

Derby Castle was a peculiar architectural miscellany, having been built, as June read in a framed history by the entrance, in 1845, to be the private Gothic folly of a wealthy Manxman; then, in 1886, the dance hall was added, presaging the addition of a theatre, a pleasure gardens, and the wholesale takeover of the establishment by the Isle of Man Tourist Board. From the outside, therefore, there was just too much going on, too many different styles competing for the eye, and dwarfing what may originally have been powerful about the original villa, a little Camelot on the sea. But the dance hall itself, and especially the ballroom, was mightily impressive: a vast room – able to hold over two thousand dancers, the history said – shaped like a cross, and bordered at each end by porthole-like

French windows, it was dominated by an enormous curved ceiling, held together by arching struts of white wrought iron, great rainbows of white looking down on the tiny twirling shapes underneath. The mixture of glass and iron reminded June of the Crystal Palace, in London, which she had visited as a child, and remembered as a place more magical even than its name. Looking around, she realised that this white wrought iron was everywhere, in fact, elaborately filigreed and decorated, on the balustrade, the cornices, the pillars and even the long line of ceiling rosettes, from which hung a cascading vista of chandeliers, producing a series of lights so bright that the eyes of the men coming in from the dark had to readjust before they could take in the whole place.

She had been watching for nearly two hours, as the soldiers delivered the male internees in shambling groups through the gates of the castle; watching as they came through the entrance to the ballroom itself; watching as each group stopped, blinked, and gazed up at the ceiling, dwarfed and humbled by the scale of the great dance cathedral. It was a larger group of internees than she had seen so far, including three camps – Onchan, Rushen and Hutchinson – she had not visited, as well as those arriving from Central. She had seen Isaac early on, but had withdrawn into the shadows of the balcony, not wanting him to call out to her and demonstrate her presence to the room or perhaps simply not wanting him to see her just yet. She watched the men, smoking, talking, sitting, pacing, laughing in staccato bursts, nervousness rising off them like mist from the sea; she felt privileged to be able secretly to observe, at such close quarters, the mass character of men waiting for women. It felt exciting, knowing she was the only woman in the place. Despite which, she could detect no aggression in the air, no hormonal charge such as you might expect with men crowded so tensely together. Only anticipation and, shot through it, patience: a sense that this group of men, nervous or not, were prepared to wait, for as long as it took.

At one end of the ballroom stood a large Christmas tree, festooned with fairy-lights; June had looked around hopelessly for any sign, elsewhere in the hall, of 'Happy Hanukkah' bunting. At the other end, a stage had been built, on which had been set a series of chairs, a lectern and a cumbersome radio microphone, and when all the men were in, around half-past six, a small orchestra appeared. It was made up, June noticed, entirely of internees, some of whom she had already seen playing in St Nicholas's Church a week earlier. Fabulously, they were wearing dinner suits, or at least approximations of dinner suits – two of the violinists were actually in coats, she spotted, and one of the trumpet players appeared to have on a work jacket – but every musician was wearing black, with white shirts and bow ties. The emergence of the conductor, a man with an expanse of forehead topped by a mad shock of white hair – wearing tails, no less! – was greeted by a ripple of applause that went round the room, and the air of expectancy rose, with the possibility that this presaged the entry of the women. Men seated all along the sides of the ballroom looked up or stood, angling their hopeful eyes towards the windows and the entrance.

Then, she saw Lieutenant Colonel Rutter emerge from the shadows of the opposite balcony – she wondered how long he had been there, and whether he had been watching her – and give a tight, controlled, military nod to the conductor, who nodded back, then turned, and tapped twice with his baton on the lectern in the middle of the stage. The orchestra began to play – beautifully, brilliantly, because, of course, they were all professionals, all among the best in Europe.

She could not recognise the music at first. Somehow, the setting, the Germanness and the proximity – always, with the internees – of high culture had led her to expect Beethoven, or Schubert, or Brahms; but then, after the first few chords had reverberated richly around the cavernous acoustics of the room, she realised that they were playing 'The Night was Made for Love', a song she remembered well from an evening at the movies a few years back – at home, she had the gramophone record. Goosebumps rose on her arms, as nostalgia, and, for some reason, hope, flooded through her. A singer appeared from the wings, a man she half recognised, in fact thought might perhaps be the celebrated tenor Richard Tauber – she was aware that he was on the island, and he was wearing a monocle, something she knew Tauber always did on stage. But just before he reached the microphone her attention, and everyone else's, was knocked sideways by the banging of the entrance doors against the ballroom wall. Forgetting the risk of discovery, she leant over the edge of the balcony and looked down, to see an extraordinary sight: hundreds of women, maybe even over a thousand, a rushing river of women, flooding into the Derby Castle ballroom. A cry went up, louder than the music, an indecipherable mix of a thousand names, a burst of language, and then the men ran from the walls to meet them: like two armies charging each other, thought June. Her heart went soft for a moment towards Lieutenant Colonel Rutter, watching silently from the other balcony, because he'd organised all this so carefully, stage-managed it, in fact, getting the men in first, and then letting all the women arrive at once, the band, the singer, everything, proving that he had at last understood that the people he was in charge of deserved something; something more than soup and sentries and barbed wire.

She watched, as husband found wife, and wife found husband; she felt the squeeze of each embrace, and the amazement of each kiss; she saw the unbelieving, joyous recognition, the mutual, infinite smiling, the outstretched arms, the restraint of some and the passion of others; the flower-giving and the flower-taking; and then she heard, above the talk and the tears:

> *This night was made for love*
> *It's in the air*
> *In the fall of your hair*
> *This night was made for love.*
>
> *I pray to the heavens above*
> *Come out the moon*
> *It can't happen too soon*
> *This night was made for love . . .*

Richard Tauber had stepped up to the microphone and begun to sing. His voice was a little Teutonic and grand for the lyrics, but he was smiling, and the half closure of his right eye necessitated by the monocle in his left made it appear that he was winking, which may not have been the case, but somehow suited the great tenor lowering himself to sing this popular song. There was a ripple of awareness, as his audience turned to acknowledge him, but it lasted only a few seconds, as they turned back to their pairs, to talk more. This seemed not to bother Tauber, who continued:

> *Don't fret about the weather*
> *Or what dress to wear*
> *Just as long as we're together*
> *We shan't have a care.*

The talk in the room grew louder, and gradually, one by one, the married couples began hand-in-hand to leave the dance floor, heading towards the booths and tables around the side of the ballroom. The conductor started to look a little panicked – the intention had clearly been that the women should arrive, meet the men on the floor and dance – but the British, who had choreographed the whole evening well up to this point, had not bargained for the fact that, although Jews do like to dance, the primary thing they like to do is talk.

> *Stars as white as doves*
> *Shining in the sky*
> *Your eyes, they tell me why*
> *This night was made for love.*

By now, large holes had appeared in the once-crowded dance floor. A spectator unaware of the context would think it the worst reception Tauber had ever received. He seemed blasé, however, continuing to smile, despite beads of sweat beginning profusely to speckle the conductor's forehead. June wanted to laugh, but realised the time had come for her to descend to the lower floor, as her primary purpose tonight was to listen, and she could see that, around the room, the most intense talking – talking where you could hear in every word the knowledge that time was limited – was taking place.

*

By the end of the third song – 'It's Only a Paper Moon' – every single married couple had retreated to the relative privacy of the sides of the room. Which left, standing in the centre of the dance floor, two men: Isaac Fabian and Wolfgang Weber. Isaac felt, for the second time this evening, stripped, revealed in all his deceit. He looked at Weber, who, for the first time since Isaac had known him, was also looking a little uncomfortable.

'Shall we dance?' said Isaac.

'Very funny, Fabian. We might have to in a minute.' He nodded to the side, where a couple of British soldiers, given orders to remain discreet tonight, were none the less watching the two of them with some curiosity.

'No love-sick stragglers for you to pick off after all, then?' said Isaac.

'Turns out not. You bloody Jews, so conventional. So *settled*. You don't even rock the boat of *marriage*.'

'Cheer up. There's always wanking like a chimpanzee.'

Weber shot him an 'I'm not going to dignify that with a response' look, and then glanced back towards the soldiers. 'Right, I'm going to storm out in tears as if my beloved wife of thirty years has failed to show. And if I were you, I'd give it two minutes and then do the same.' And with that, he screwed up his face, began to howl, and, shaking his fists in the air, ran for the exit.

To Isaac's eyes, it looked absurdly theatrical, like a hammy King Lear storming onto the rain-lashed heath, but it got Weber easily enough past the bemused expressions of the watching soldiers. One of them turned to follow, but another took his arm and muttered something, which led to the first relaxing back into his previous position, slumped against the massive door-frame, looking in at the room.

The conductor, meanwhile, was consulting Richard Tauber. He had turned away from the audience, but none the less, it was apparent he was frantic. His whole frame was shaking, and his arms were gesturing so much Isaac wondered if some wag from the orchestra was about to remind him that they had stopped playing. Clearly, the impact of having had his moment playing with the great tenor so ruined, so unwatched, had affected him deeply.

Tauber himself, though, continued to look detached and amused, facing the floor with its now sole spectator.

Perhaps detached and amused is all you can look when you are sporting a monocle, thought Isaac, staring at him; perhaps if you start to look worried, or cry, it just falls out. This was his last thought, however, before his flippancy deserted him. As the single male alone on the dance floor, the British soldiers were viewing him more aggressively now; he also noticed another group to his left, one of whom was pointing at him while speaking to his superior officer. He felt panic start to come upon him, like someone emptying a bucket in his gut, and swung his face, cartoon-like, from one side to the other. His head movement turned out to be bizarrely in time with the orchestra, who just at that point started playing again, their conductor having made a desperate, last-minute revision to the programme.

The soldier who had been leaning against the entrance shifted his weight forward and began to walk, with a loping, rolling gait, towards Isaac.

'*There may be trouble ahead,*' sang Richard Tauber. '*But while there's moonlight and music and love and romance . . .*'

Shit, thought Isaac, looking down. Shit, shit, shit. I can't believe I've fucked up the operation before I've even started. What am I going to tell him? What am I even doing here—

At which point his thoughts were interrupted by the sensation of a pair of hands being strung through his, and his body forcibly being turned, marionette-like, from left to right, in time with the music.

'*Let's face the music and dance,*' went the song, as the conductor turned round to face the room, his expression saying very clearly, *Please, this is a clue as to what your role in this evening is supposed to be.* His face visibly brightened, though, on seeing, finally, a young couple dancing, although he was surprised at just how much the woman appeared to be leading.

'I wonder,' said June, forcing Isaac's body back into line with hers, 'if I could have this dance?'

'Certainly,' said Isaac, doing his best to join in with her mock-suavity, although finding it difficult between trying not to cry out in pain from being tossed about and trying to look nonchalant in order to ward off the interest of the still-watching soldier. His hand searched for her waist, and his palm felt something raised, something jewelled. Stealing a glance down at her, he saw she was wearing a black beaded dress; pricks of light spun off it as she moved.

'Have you done much dancing before?' she said, smiling, and skilfully swerving to avoid his feet trapping hers. She spoke in German.

'Quite a lot, actually.'

'Really?'

'Yes.' Her eyebrow raised, and her smile became enquiring. 'Just not . . . this sort of dancing. More like . . . crouching down, kicking my legs out, in a circle of men with their arms around one another. That sort of dancing.'

She laughed. 'Do you want us to try to do one of those now?'

'No, it won't go with the music.'

As if in agreement, she raised her arm, and twirled her body underneath it, gracefully coming back between his arms. Isaac could not believe himself, how easily he was flirting, suddenly a roué, suddenly a charmer. Perhaps it was his knowledge of the job ahead, later that night, which made him so at ease with her, as if the prospect of real danger easily eclipsed any nervousness associated with social danger; or perhaps it was just June, and the way she instantly made him feel.

Soon, we'll be without the moon
Humming a diff'rent tune – and then . . .

He remembered that, in truth, he had danced like this once before, with Lulu, at a May ball at Königsberg University, before it was illegal for Aryans and Jews to dance together. He remembered that the dance was slow, and she had put her head on his chest, the first physical contact they had had beyond holding hands. He put it out of his mind.

'Relax . . .' said June, wheeling them round towards the stage. 'It's easier if you're not so stiff.'

He felt his blood rushing at this focus on his body. 'I *am* relaxed. I just don't know where to put my feet.'

'You don't have to put them anywhere. There's no map. Just move them in time with the music.'

At this point, the soldier who had been observing them throughout shrugged and turned away. With that, Isaac did indeed relax; his muscles loosened, and he let himself be folded more easily into June's patterns, her sways, her loops, her twists and turns. He wondered how she could be an intellectual and yet dance like this. To his eye, she seemed to have all the grace and ease of movement of a ribbon of flame.

'Thank you . . .' he said, in a semi-whisper, wanting to say it quietly but not sure of his licence to speak too closely to her ear.

'For what?' Her eyes widened, making her look genuinely innocent, a beguiling mix with her intelligent features.

'Coming to my rescue.'

She smiled, her face lifting with it, looking up at him. 'That's all right. I'm on your side.'

He felt the warmth of her left hand in his, and the grasp of her right on his waist. He tried, as he had done sometimes before in moments of intensity, to encase these feelings in memory, to remember them as they were happening. Even though he knew he had the dance to thank for the experience, at some level he wanted the dancing to stop so that he could feel them in stasis: only when still may one truly savour.

She gasped a little, as he swung her body in a semicircle, taking the lead for a beat. 'That's more like it,' she said. 'You see, you *can* dance.'

The orchestra rounded back on the melody, towards the coda.

There may be trouble ahead
But while there's moonlight and music and love and
*   romance,*
Let's face the music and dance,
Let's face the music and dance,
Let's face the music . . .

Tauber stepped back, and the conductor, whose confidence seemed to have increased with Isaac's dancing capabilities, swung his baton-less hand vertically across his chest, causing the music to come to a dead stop. June and Isaac hung fire in the middle of the floor, turning towards the stage. Without looking around, both of them became aware, through the silence, that the room had stopped talking and was looking at them, as if they were competitors in an ice-skating contest. Then, Richard Tauber did something extraordinary: he took out his monocle – an action he had never been known to perform on stage before – and did in fact wink, more towards Isaac than June, with his uncovered eye. Isaac, not knowing what else to do, reflexively winked back. Tauber nodded in paternal recognition, and then, with just a quick rearrangement of his features, not unlike that which normally precedes a sneeze, expertly replaced the glass circle, puffed his mighty chest out to the point that the buttons on his dress shirt looked like they might burst, and sang: '*And daaaaaaaaa . . .*' Holding the last note, holding it and holding it, to the point where some of the watching couples turned to each other in amazement, at just how much breath this man could hold in his body. June, seizing the moment, pulled Isaac's hand sharply and wheeled on the ball of her right foot, making the two of them pirouette, round and round and round, dizzier and dizzier, until finally, with an absurdly foppish flourish of his right arm, Tauber declaimed: '*. . . aaaaance!*'

And the conductor, who had been watching him like a hawk, with a mighty sweep of his arms, brought the orchestra back precisely one beat after the singer's final note, rounding off the song with a double-time repetition of the main melody, a terrific glissando and a booming, climactic end chord. June put a brake on hers and Isaac's carousel, and they stopped, as, at last, the conductor's wish was granted: around the room, men and women broke from their secret-swapping just long enough to stand and cheer and applaud. Isaac heard them and saw them, but his vision was still swimming with the effects of so much rotation, so he fixed on a point immediately in front of him, as his mother had always told him to when he felt dizzy: June's face, her skin glazed by the lights above, laughing, her head back and her mouth opening wide enough for him to feel he may fall

300

into it, like his daughter's when she was trying to fit his heart in there.

Abruptly, the clapping stopped, and the tide of talk rose again around the room.

'Let's go and join them,' said June, taking Isaac's hand and leading him off the dance floor.

They sat in a booth, on benches, near the side of the stage. If the course of the evening had run as planned, the ebb and flow of couples to the dance floor would have created more space, but with everybody trying to find a place to talk at the same time, all the booths were crammed. In theirs sat two other couples: a pair who were little more than teenagers, only recently married; and a man and a woman in their late fifties, but looking almost as young. Love – or at least meeting their beloved in a dance hall after separation – had remade them strangers, had renewed their youth. Both couples were sitting together, facing each other on the same side of the table, creating a private space out of the air between their eyes, or in the touch of their hands. For Isaac and June, who took their places on opposite sides of the table, this made being together at once easier, because the other men and women were so closed-off they could feel unobtrusive, and stranger, because their more formal seating reflected their lack of everything the others shared: history, familiarity, intimacy, legitimacy. Momentarily, sitting down, the spell of her face broke, and all he was aware of was that they were outlaws in this palace of marriage.

'Are you all right?' said June, seeing the shadow fall across his face.

'Yes,' he said.

'Are you sure? Would you like a drink?' She gestured towards the far end of the room, where a British soldier stood disconsolately behind a table laid with bottles of stout and pale ale: one glass per person had been the stipulation from Lieutenant Colonel Rutter. So far, the table had remained virtually unapproached.

'No, thanks. I don't really like English beer.'

'Neither do I. I don't like any beer, as far as I'm aware. But maybe they've got something else stashed away somewhere,' said June, getting up from her seat, and pulling her dress down where it had rucked up. 'See you in a minute.'

301

He watched her leave, noticing for the first time that she was wearing high heels. It made him yet more impressed with her dancing. He wondered, too, whether she had brought this outfit with her, or had bought it somewhere on the island on deciding to come tonight.

'Excuse me,' said the older man along the bench, craning his neck away from his wife – from his accent, a Berliner originally, Isaac guessed – 'but do you have the time?' He had white hair, which started a long way back on his head.

'Yes,' said Isaac, glancing at his wrist. 'It's half-past six.'

'Thank you. I wouldn't normally ask, but when I arrived at Rushen, the British confiscated all my things. They returned them, of course, but not my watch, for some reason.'

Isaac nodded sympathetically, but his eyes stayed on his watch. Like everyone else in the room, he was calculating the time he had left in this place, but in his case for different reasons. The thought of his work later in the evening, underlying his consciousness in spreading and twisting roots of fear, had left him for the duration of the dance, but with the mention of the time, it came back to him with menaces. Anxiety crept over him, and seemed to infect everything: acutely, he felt the reality of what might be happening between him and June, the seriousness and consequence of it, and that too made his stomach turn over. He felt beset by multiple dreads, the twin terrors of sex and death in a pincer movement on his soul.

A bottle of red wine and two glasses appeared in front of his face.

'Well, order's completely broken down, it seems,' said June, retaking her seat. 'The soldier manning the bar is so bored – and so pleased that someone had at last come up to ask for a drink – that he's given us one of the bottles of wine they were keeping in reserve for the more refined ladies. I brought you a glass just in case . . .'

'Thank you,' he said, and poured himself a large amount. He raised it quickly to his lips and downed it in one gulp. The liquid was warm; he shivered at its sourness.

'. . . you change your mind about wanting a drink.'

'Sorry. Yes,' he said, wiping his mouth with the back of his hand. 'While you were gone, I did.'

'So I see.'

She smiled at him, a smile of mock-admonishment, and poured herself a more measured glass. Above the rim of it, she took him in with her eyes, which were steadfast and dark enough to make Isaac turn away. She felt calm with her interest in him, but at another level bemused by it. In the odd evening out with other women who worked at the Ministry – not a regular occurrence for June: she was not one for group socialising, especially the slightly manic quality that the Ministry females possessed when out *en masse*, feverish with innuendo and gossip – it had been decided for her that she had a *type*, and that this type was tall, smart, confident, posh and athletic, something of a cross between Stewart Granger and Denis Compton. How far Isaac was from her type, then, or at least how far from it he seemed now, this shady-faced urchin, sweating a little and tapping his fingers ten to the dozen on the table. She felt that strange pity which women sometimes feel for men they know desire them.

'So . . .' said Isaac, 'how's your research going?' Although reasonable, it felt a stupid question, once out of his mouth, and, like their seating, distinctly formal in this setting: the opening question of someone who does not know the person sitting opposite them very well.

'All right, I suppose. To be honest, I'm banking quite a lot on tonight.'

'Really?'

'Yes.' She switched to English. 'It's bad of me, I know, but my main objective tonight was eavesdropping.'

'Eavesdropping?'

'*Belauschung*,' she whispered.

'Oh, I see.' He shook his head. 'No, in fact, I don't.'

She took a sip of wine. 'God. Hideous.' She put down the glass and pressed her fingertips to the table, making tents of her hands. 'I thought that here would be the perfect place to hear people tell the truth.'

'The truth?'

'Their truth. I thought that in the moment, with all the' – she felt her articulation rise, as it had once before in Alfred Bassett's office, and she almost stopped herself again, not knowing if he would understand; but then continued, in English, feeling he would get the point, if not the exact words – 'intensity in this room, all the emotions flying about, that everybody's mouth – everybody's soul – would be loosened. And that I could just drift about and hear things people would never have told me otherwise.'

Isaac nodded, and poured himself a second glass of wine, the first mouthful of which tasted not as bad as he remembered; but then, he had not eaten since lunchtime, and was too innocent of drink to know that drunkenness feeds upon itself by adjusting the taste buds accordingly.

'And has it worked?'

She pursed her lips. 'Not quite as I would have wished, so far.' She looked out into the great hall, where couples were locked like diplomats in endless talks. The orchestra had stopped playing for the moment, and all one could hear was a massive murmur, two thousand whispers, like she was sitting on the edge of an enormous but only gently bubbling spring. 'People are talking quietly, apart from anything. And it's not exactly the place for me to poke my head between them and say, "Pardon? I didn't quite catch that . . ."'

Isaac laughed: he could feel his tension start to disperse with the warmth of the wine spreading across his stomach.

'Besides, what I can catch – as I might have guessed – is not hard facts about mistreatment at the hands of the Nazis, but just . . .' and here she coloured, even her self-possession trembling a little, 'you know . . . words of love.'

'From everybody? Everybody is saying, "I love you"?'

She looked around. She had heard *darling* and *my love* and *I'm so happy to see you* and *you look lovely*; she had heard all these, and the trickle-down to *So, how have you been keeping? Have you been eating? Where did you get your hair cut? Have you heard from the family?* 'More or less.'

'So the whole thing has been a waste of time?'

'I wouldn't say that. It's been inspiring. And not a complete washout for my purposes. I overheard a man in that corner telling his wife he's heard news from Germany that their whole community has been resettled somewhere in Poland. And a man three booths down was saying how much nicer life's been here than it was in the camp he was in in Germany, where the guards used to beat them every day. It's all grist to my mill.' Isaac's eyes held hers for a second, looking for the truth. It took about three seconds to come out, her shoulders falling a little as her resolve crumbled. 'All right, yes, I suppose I'm a bit disappointed. I don't know what I expected, really. Just that someone would say something in my earshot that was news to me, or would let something slip that I could maybe chase up later.'

'And . . . ?'

She shook her head. There was a pause, during which she drained the dregs of her glass of wine.

'June?' said Isaac, refilling her glass. The bottle was already half empty. 'What is it you want to hear? What exactly?'

She shut her eyes. She was tired – exhausted – and starting to feel drunk, and the question cut to the core of her; but somewhere in the blackness behind her lids she thought she could see the answer. 'Evil,' she said, without opening her eyes. 'I want to hear about evil.' Her eyelids parted, revealing pupils black in this light, coal just waiting for the match. 'I want to hear about torture; starvation; random executions; men and women and children killed on a whim. And I want to hear about it happening not to the odd person, but to many. I want to hear about it happening *en masse*. You flinch . . .'

Isaac started: he was not aware he had.

'. . . but – and I hate the expression, my bloody geography teacher used to use it when she was caning me – but I have to be cruel to be kind.'

'What do you mean?'

'Cruel to be kind. It means . . . do you want me to say it in German?'

'No, I . . . I prefer it when we speak English.' *Did he?* So many things he was saying these days came out of his mouth before he knew them to be true. But perhaps he did: he liked the easy rolls of English, the pitch of it, a language that occupied the centre ground, neither too florid nor too harsh, and he liked its smallness in the mouth, the way it used only a restricted area of the tongue, whereas

German, because of all of its clacks and spits, required you to use everything, from the back of the throat to the tip of the palate. And he liked the fact that he was beginning to speak it well: it made him feel like he was becoming someone else.

'Well, it means that I somehow have to . . . I have to get people to talk about things they may not want to talk about – to face things they may not want to face – in order to help them. Because, unless I get some eyewitness reports of . . . well . . . I don't want to overuse the word, but, as I say, evil' – she shook her head – 'if I don't get that, I don't know if this report's going to get any attention at all, really.' She upended the bottle, forcing the last drops into each of their glasses.

Isaac laughed.

'What?'

'Sorry. It is just you doing that. With the wine.'

She squinted at him, demanding more explanation.

'Like we are both people who like to . . . Sorry, I think I may be drunk.'

'Yes, so might I. Is that so bad?'

'I don't know.'

'You don't know?'

'I am not sure I have ever been this drunk before.'

Now it was her turn to laugh. 'What, on half a bottle of plonk? I thought Germans like a drink.'

'Yes, but Jews don't.' It was odd, he thought, how sometimes the British simply could not make the distinction. It was endearing, on one level, because it was so in contrast to the Nazis' frantic insistence on the distinction. 'Even on Pesach . . .'

'Pesach?'

'Passover. Even on Passover, when we are commanded by God to drink, we drink only four glasses, and then it is kosher wine, which I think is not so alcoholic.'

'I thought you'd given all that up?'

Isaac smiled, his uneven bottom teeth making him look vulnerable, young, she thought. But then she remembered, he *was* young: he'd just been through more things than a man of his age should.

'I have. But that does not mean I have forgotten all about it.'

'Don't you miss it? I always thought that believing in God would be such a comfort.'

'Yes, well. That is what it is: comfortable. It gives you hope, reassurance, safety. But it is all false. At least the hope that communism gives you is not that.'

'Isn't it?' As yet, June had not pushed him on this, his politics. It was something she liked about him, but only in essence, not especially in content: that is, she liked the fact that he believed in *something*. It removed him from most of the men she knew at the Ministry, who prided themselves on their cynicism, on their lack of belief – but she was not sure about communism, which secretly she thought a little vulgar, a little the preserve of the immature mind. 'They seem very similar to me. Both of them promise a better world. I'm not convinced either of them delivers it in reality.'

Isaac finished his glass. 'I think, if we are going to have a political argument, you are going to have to get another bottle.' He was pleased with this remark; it made him feel again like a roué. The drink was making him forget himself, and the tasks ahead.

'Hmm. I think we might be a bit late.' She gestured for him to look over.

Isaac felt how even this small movement of the head seemed interesting to him, the way the bob of her hair moved like a bell swinging across his field of vision. He glanced over his shoulder, to see two of the British soldiers pouring themselves liberal measures from what appeared to be the last bottle. Various other soldiers were standing by with open bottles of beer.

'How can they . . . ?'

'Rutter left about twenty minutes ago. Clearly, he thought the evening was under control. We'll see.'

Isaac looked around: everywhere, the couples seemed still oblivious of everything except each other, although one or two had stopped talking and were chancing a kiss, not least the youngsters immediately to June's right. When he looked back, she had lifted her glass and was rotating it in front of her face thoughtfully. It was still three-quarters full; the redness of the wine moving across her cheeks made him aware that she was looking a little flushed. The fix of her eyes on him spoke directly of how discreetly she was ignoring the kissing of the couple next to her, the irruption of their sexuality into that teetering between her and Isaac.

'I'm not sure I want to go and interrupt a group of squaddies carousing, to be honest. It might be interesting to let them get on with it.'

'What am I going to do?' he said, raising his own empty glass.

June shrugged her shoulders, and then, changing her face to a more determined expression, took it out of his hands. Gently, deliberately, she poured half of her wine into his glass; he watched the liquid fall, like blood from a wound, a small wave on Homer's wine-dark sea. She passed it to him, her fingers holding it by the rim. Their eyes met as he took it, and it was what it was, a tiny thing, but still a moment of transaction, a moment of shared awareness: they both knew that in offering to mix her cells swimming in this wine with his, she was moving things on, she was pushing whatever consequence they were going to share to its conclusion.

'*Prost?* Cheers? What shall we say?' she said, raising her depleted glass up to forehead height, and leaning across the table.

'*L'chaim*,' said Isaac.

'*L'chaim?*'

'It's Hebrew. It means "to life".' He took joy in telling her, this woman who knew what all words meant. He saw her memorise it, saw it go into her language bank.

'*L'chaim*,' she said, smiling.

'*L'chaim*,' he replied, and touched his glass to hers.

'It's beautiful, the island. Don't you think?' said Isaac, some time later.

An uninformed observer might have thought that such a polite observation indicated that conversation was starting to dry up between this particular husband and wife, that all it had taken was an hour and a half for the dead air that cuts great swaths through all marital discourse to re-establish itself; but they would be mistaken. In fact, as some dialogues around the room were indeed beginning to falter, with the novelty of reacquaintance starting to wear off, Isaac and June, in contrast, began to talk 'ten to the dozen' – which was just one of the many idioms he learnt during the process; finding, as well, that the urge he might have had in the past, to question how it was that ten could possibly constitute a dozen, was diminished. Like everyone else, they were talking against the clock, but, unlike everyone else, who had had much time to do so in the past, they felt the sheer space of the ground they had yet to cover, to make up for lost time. They talked of things large and things small: of parents and pre-life, his in Königsberg, hers in Bewdley; of the war, of England and Germany; of favourites, food (him, sausages; her, chicken), animals (both cats), music (him, classical, Bach, Mendelssohn; her, jazz, Louis Armstrong, Glenn Miller), reading (him, politics, history, philosophy; her, fiction, mainly modern – she liked Virginia Woolf, and Camus, and a new English writer Isaac did not know called Graham Greene, whom she described as 'a great poet of disgust'); she told him about the men at the Ministry, and he pointed out some of the characters around the room representative of the internment community; and lastly, they were talking of here and now, this island, at this time.

'Yes, it is,' she answered. They were speaking a little louder than before, the orchestra having started playing again. Richard Tauber was singing *'Bei Mir Bist Du Schön'*, brazenly defying British orders not to perform German songs. None of the soldiers seemed particularly bothered, and the strategy had, to some extent, worked: a smattering of the talked-out couples had risen and were dancing languorously around the floor. 'It's not somewhere you ever think of going much, actually – the Isle of Man. As a British person, I mean. None of these places, the Isle of Wight, the Channel Islands . . . Islands off Britain, when you're on the mainland, they don't feel like the Canaries must do from Spain, or the Cyclades from Greece. You just imagine it'll be exactly the same, only rainier.' Isaac smiled, at how even she, who was so distinctive in many ways, shared the British obsession with rain. 'But it's not. I mean, obviously Douglas has got that thing that all British coastal resorts have, where they've managed to make the seaside depressing – why is it that only this country thinks that the things that go best with the sea – the *sea*! – are chip shops and amusement arcades? – but elsewhere . . . God! It's lovely. Have you been to the Calf of Man?'

Isaac laughed. 'No. You forget, I think: I am not a tourist here. They don't let us out for trips for the day.'

She blushed. 'Sorry. How stupid of me.'

'Please, do not apologise. It was me who began to talk of the island and the beauty it has, and so you may have thought I have seen more than I have. But I just meant – to be in prison, as we are, and have . . .'

'A sea view.'

'Yes. I never knew how long one can look at such a view. Even at night it can be beautiful.'

'At night?'

'Yes. From my window, at night, it is so black that I cannot see any water, but I can still hear it. Sense it. And there is something beautiful about that. *Gefühl des Vorhandenseins des Meeres in der Dunkelheit.*'

She nodded, appreciating his need to revert to German in order to express this: *Feeling the presence of the sea in the dark.*

'Something so big, when it is there but you cannot see it, you feel it. As if it is waiting.'

'I understand,' she said. 'I know what you mean.' She glanced over his shoulder, towards the porthole-shaped window, her incisive eyes searching for something.

'What?'

'It's meant to be a full moon tonight.'

'Yes, I know.'

Her gaze came back to his, quizzically. 'I'm surprised.'

'Why?'

'I don't know. The cycles of the moon, it's just one of those things – like knowing what day you were born on – that men never know.'

He looked down; both her hands were cupping her now-empty glass as if it contained a hot drink, radiating warmth. 'A fair amount of the men here would know. Our . . .' He made a small grimace, then continued, 'The Jewish calendar. It's set by the moon. All the holy days, the festivals, are marked by the new moon. Religious Jews count all time, in fact, by the moon.' He pointed across the dance floor, to a narrow-shouldered, bearded man, nodding so fast at his wife's words that he may well have been praying.

'According to that fellow, we are now in the year 5700.'

'5700?'

'In lunar years, since the creation of the world. Or since the creation of Judaism, whichever you prefer.'

June sat back, her spine straight against the hard wood of the booth. 'Is a lunar year longer or shorter than a solar one?'

'Longer. We've just been around a ridiculously long time.' Isaac smiled, he hoped self-effacingly, trying to disguise the truth that, although his upbringing had indeed given him a greater awareness than most men of the waxing and waning of the moon, his particular knowledge of tonight's lunar apex was primarily a function of his later mission, his upcoming night watch. 'But why did you mention the moon, anyway . . . ?'

'Oh.' June blinked, a rapid fluttering, as if water were in her eyes. 'I just thought the sea would be visible. If there is a full moon.'

Suddenly, there was a loud crash, followed by two or three incomprehensible shouts, the violence of which was much amplified by its interruptive effect. The orchestra ceased to play, winding down in a sad spiral of honks and plucks, and the hum of talk stopped dead like a bee crushed underfoot. The room looked round, to see that a fight had broken out between two of the British soldiers. Private Saunders was involved: he had drunk the best part of two bottles of wine, and had been enjoying the slower, more mild intoxication than he – already, at home, a nine-pints-a-night man – was used to, when on a sixpence it all turned, his head started to rage, the itch sparked like electricity in his groin, and then that cunt from Hutchinson – whatsisname? – Bryant, was making jokes about West Country folk being thick, doing that stupid voice that people do. As his fists piled in to Private Bryant's face, feeling even in the quickest contact how fragile the small bones of the skull are, the young man did have a vague memory that only a short while earlier, he had been laughing with his colleague, possibly at exactly the same things that had now so angered him, but he put the contradiction out of his mind in order to get on with the fight. It was hard enough to do, with suddenly lots of other squaddies holding him back and telling him to calm down.

311

Immediately after the initial impact, most of the couples in the room chose to ignore the fight. Those who had turned looked back to their partners again, their faces studies in indifference. June, however, stood up, wondering whether to intervene: vaguely, she remembered that she was a member of the civil service, and therefore somehow should assume responsibility. This moment of social conscience soon crumbled, however, in the face of the horror of getting hit by a drunken flying fist, but in the time it took to fade, the kissing couple on their table had wordlessly shuffled along the gap she had left on the bench, stood up, glanced furtively at each other, and stolen away.

'Where are they going?' asked Isaac, standing as well.

'Outside, I think.' She smiled at him. 'They saw their chance and they took it.'

Her smile held; and, for a second, her unconventional beauty, which was veiled from some angles, seemed luminous. He saw that it was linked, in some mystical way, to her intelligence, and that the idea, prevalent among most men, that you could divide what was attractive about a woman into categories, physical and psychological, was nonsense. Once love took hold, everything became mixed, like one of Weber's busts: the physical seemed suddenly to speak of the psychological, and vice versa. In that second, Isaac felt the real power of what he had thought to be his secondary fear, the potent fear of his desire for her, and what it meant – what acting on it would destabilise, not just in terms of his life with Lulu and Rebekka (*Bekka; oh, Bekka!*) but also in terms of his idea of self. The fear, in other words, was motivated by the sudden onrush of choice, the terrible fact of decision.

'Perhaps we should too,' he said, swallowing his fear: this felt like a literal sensation, as though he were pushing it down from his chest into his stomach. He knew as soon as he said it that he had made his choice, because the fear subsided. Fear may be about the possibility of making the wrong choice, but it still disappears once that choice – right or wrong – is made.

'Pardon?' she said. Her face affected innocence, but some widening of the pupils denoted that she knew this was the first move, the first shift away from double-talk and into direct statement.

312

A part of him knew she knew too, because he did not repeat himself, but just put his hand in hers; her fingers wrapped around his palm more tightly than he had expected. The trouble with choice is the scales are never even. Except when shopping, one choice is always likely to be absent, and the power will always be, therefore, with whatever is present. Without speaking, without either of them leading, they made their way towards the exit.

Leaving Derby Castle was not difficult: the only soldier who had not got involved in the brawl was asleep, curled up like a house-less snail on the entrance steps. Outside, the air was milder than either of them had expected, the snow having continued to melt even into the night. This suited June, who had not picked up her coat from the cloakroom, partly because to do so would have broken their wordless momentum out of the hall, and partly because she did not want to assume that they would not be coming back. Isaac checked his watch by the light spilling out of the ballroom: eight-forty. Time enough, he thought, although for what exactly he was not prepared as yet to contemplate. They halted at the bottom of the steps, and faced each other. Her face was half obscured by shadow.

'So, as I was saying,' she said, 'what chance should we take?'

For some reason, the answer came to him quickly. 'To see if the moon has lit up the sea.'

She smiled and their hands touched again. They walked down the drive of the dance hall, through the outer gates, across the road and towards the cliff's edge, towards the ocean. Approaching, they could hear its calm roar rising.

'I don't know if we should go any closer,' she said, moving her hand to his chest. 'Perhaps I should have told you I'm scared of heights. Or at least of falling to my death on rocks.'

'Just a bit further.'

They made their steps smaller. A yard or two from the water June looked down, but with her eyes only, avoiding the full head-tilt, as if her body might tumble with it.

'I can't see much,' she said.

'That's because the moon's in hiding.'

313

Her eyes came up again, to see Isaac in a posture somewhat reminiscent of the Soviet iconography she assumed he loved, his chin raised, staring at the sky. He was right: a bank of clouds, only just visible themselves, had formed since the blue day closed, allowing only the most diffuse light through.

'Oh . . .' she said, looking out. 'Well, maybe that'll work in our favour. Maybe we can see a city on the mainland. Liverpool, perhaps . . .'

Isaac laughed, shaking his head. 'During the blackout?'

She laughed too, knowing that it had been a foolish thought, said because she had wanted to continue the game, to continue the sense for just a bit longer that this *was* a game.

'All right, that was stupid,' she admitted. 'I just said it because I like the idea. I like seeing towns and cities from a distance at night.' She paused, realising with a pang how long it was since she had seen such a sight, how comforting city lights were, the sense they gave that people were alive and up and doing things even in the dead of the night, how they spoke now of peace. 'Well, I used to; before the war.'

Isaac turned to look at her; she was in profile, staring out intently, as if she *could* see the lights of Liverpool, a cluster of pearls at the end of the sea. 'So do I,' he said, his jibing tone gone. 'Sometimes, I think it's better not to know anything more about a place. When I see a city, from a distance, and it looks . . . it looks . . .'

'Sparkling. Enticing.'

'Yes . . . then I just want to be there. As I imagine it.' *I imagine somehow*, he wanted to say, *that the streets are made of light*. 'I don't need to know how it really is.'

June nodded, without turning round. She was wondering what it was that caused light to twinkle; why seen from a distance it is not static, why it seems to pulse. She was also beginning to feel a little cold, and thinking that perhaps she should have picked up her coat after all. The cold brought her back to herself, brought her back, in a practical, almost pragmatic, way, to the business in hand: how she was going to make him take the next step, even if it was the one off the cliff.

And then, a sliver of white shimmered in the sea, like a surrender flag unfurled. Together, they looked up; in between two clouds the night sky was proffering the full moon like a communion wafer. When June looked down again, at the suddenly visible spray, she felt as if her gaze were gliding, skimming like a stone across the water.

It was Isaac who spoke first. 'Friday . . .' he said.

She looked at him, questioningly, wondering for a second if he was in fact a spy and this was code.

'I was born on a Friday.'

Lieutenant Colonel Rutter could hardly believe his eyes. He had had to get used to the somewhat relaxed, by his standards, atmosphere of the internment camps; had, in fact, made a conscious decision to accept that he was not running a prisoner-of-war operation here, and that therefore the usual forms of military observance would not always be appropriate. But this was too much.

He had not intended to return to Derby Castle tonight, but once he arrived at his office in Central, he found he could not stop worrying about how the event was going. The Rendezvous of Husbands and Wives had been his great concession to implementing a more humane regime; and he was, even though he was unlikely to admit it, proud of himself. The event, in other words, was his baby, and he wanted to keep an eye on it. He had also seen Miss Murray on the balcony, and felt he would not have minded asking her for her opinion of the evening. He knew, somewhere in his ordered, rectangular heart, that the turnaround of his thoughts was linked to her; that, despite his unswerving commitment to the two loves of his life – Mrs Rutter and the British army – the continued presence of Miss Murray was exerting some effect on him; that, having initially just found her an awkward annoyance, now, when he thought of her, something trickled behind his eyes, something foundered within him.

And so, instead of making his way upstairs to his quarters, he rebuttoned his uniform, and went out again into the night, up the Ramsay road towards Derby Castle. The air was cold but clean, and he felt his step spring against the pitch-black tarmac. 'What do you think, then, Miss Murray? Not a bad do, is it? Shame so few fancied a dance, but—' These were the words he was not exactly rehearsing in his head, more just enjoying the idea of saying, when his train of thought was interrupted by tripping over a body on the entrance steps. His stomach lurched, as his first thought was that it was one of the internees, dead; that somehow one of the Nazis had got in and had either killed one of the Jews or been killed himself. He had already started to compose his letter of resignation in his head, when he realised that the body was in uniform. Crouching down, he poked the soldier gently in the ribs; a mumbled 'fuck off' made it clear to him that this particular body was both very alive and very drunk. Making a mental note of the number on the man's epaulette, Lieutenant Colonel Rutter got up, straightened his jacket, and, as a soldier does, prepared to face the worst.

Within seconds of entering the ballroom, however, it was clear to him that what had happened was not the worst. What had happened, rather obviously, was that he had made the mistake of leaving a group of soldiers alone with an enormous cache of drink, which the people for whom it was intended were not drinking. One soldier – he knew this one, the youngster from Plymouth – was being simultaneously tended to – he was bleeding from above his right eye – and restrained, while another seemed to be unconscious in the middle of the dance floor. A third was leaning against a pillar, swigging from a bottle of red wine like a man in the desert would water, while dangling another bottle in his other hand. At least the dance floor was finally seeing some action, although only from a pair of soldiers, stumbling through a mock-waltz while singing a filthy version of 'Rule Britannia'. Rutter mentally kicked himself: he was fully aware that there is only a certain amount of time that a British soldier – it might be true to say a British *man* – can stand by while alcohol is allowed to go to waste. He should have ordered the bottles removed.

He watched for some small time, wondering whether at least one of them would notice his entrance. When that did not happen, he drew a fulsome breath into his lungs, and then shouted, with the deafening decibels he could still draw on from his days on the parade-ground: 'FALL IN!' Instantly, the dreamy, cushioned mood of group intoxication broke; and, within twenty seconds, following a collage of startled expressions, despair, fear and scurrying, every British soldier was lined up and standing to attention (some more successfully than others) in the middle of the dance floor.

317

It was only at this point, as he made his way furiously towards the uneasily shifting line, that Lieutenant Colonel Rutter noticed that none of the couples at the event seemed to have taken any notice of the antics of his men. They were all behaving much as he had left them, sitting around the dance floor, talking in whispers, focused on each other, enclosed in a bubble of love and race. Well, that's as may be, he thought: the fact that the behaviour of his soldiers had not affected the internees overmuch was irrelevant. Things had gone too far. He would make the men sober up, and then make them check every booth and every table to ensure that no one had left the building; and, if any had, search the surrounding area. When he stopped in front of the line, face to face with his cowering colleagues, it crossed his mind that he could not see Miss Murray, and, for a second, the thought of her made him pause, knowing that she would prefer him to let it lie, and not disturb the evening further. He looked up to the balcony, and across to the other side of the room, but could see no sign of her. She must have gone back to her hotel, he thought, and, glad of her absence, glad to be free of dilemma, took in another large breath, ready to bark out his orders.

There is a moment, when waking from untroubled sleep, which is the closest in this life that human beings can approach to paradise. It is that moment, unknowable in length, between the end of dreaming and the opening up of full consciousness, during which the soul still swims in the balm of sleep, but the mind has started to wake, stretching and yawning in the foothills of perception. For those of us who are not shamans or maharishis, it is the only gateway to the sublime, or at least to the conscious experience of peace. Isaac Fabian was in this state now, lying entwined among the grass and heather of the Isle of Man, and the limbs of June Murray.

For some reason, which is the key to its sublimity, always absent from awareness during this time is any sense of consequence: the self is able to contemplate its actions, however twisted and troublesome, without dread. And so, for this moment, in this half-life of the mind, Isaac luxuriated, weightlessly, in his immediate memory. He dwelt on specifics: the two of them falling together to the ground, like a continuation of their dance; the feel of the grass, moist with melted snow, on more and more of his body; the interplay of their mouths, her taste mixed with wine, making him think uncontrollably of the Song of Songs – '*O daughter of Jerusalem, honey and milk are under thy tongue, and the smell of thy garments is as the smell of Lebanon*'; her on her knees, undoing her underclothes – that moment of pause, of interruption, a greater and more erotic revelation in its own way, to display to him this domestic secret, the meticulous way she takes off her brassiere; his intense wish for light, for the moon to become the sun, or larger, like it sometimes did, at harvest-time, so he could see as well as touch; the gorgeous run of his hands, once his fingers felt confident enough that total licence had been granted, sculpting her, a straightforwardly representational movement, from life, not one of Weber's distorted figures; her touch on him, more probing, more searching than he was used to, as if she were looking for something on his body that she had lost; the folding of her waist as they moved; a sound she made later, a sigh, with something of death in it, as though she had been softly, reverently, stabbed; then falling apart exhausted, desire, like his father's sins, washed from him, somewhere out to sea; and lastly, he remembered, even in this semi-sleep, falling asleep, the touch of her hand on his eyelids, brushing the lashes in a gentle rhythm, until he fell into the deep.

This memory – essentially, this realisation: that he had been asleep – was the one that woke him up properly. He felt the up-and-down surge: up to full consciousness, and then down, as consequence came with it, down at speed, as if his stomach were a well, and his fear a stone dropped into it. The first word in his brain, before all the others, was *Lulu*. Then, before he even had time for all the other words banging on the door of his conscience to pile in, like the most unwelcome gatecrashers at what had been a heavenly party, he instinctively – without even remembering why as yet, the echo of sleep still muffling his understanding – checked his watch. Just past quarter to ten, it said, and as his heart started to beat even faster, it came to him what was bad about this; very, very bad. His fingers scurrying, he did himself up, trousers and shirt, and stood, knowing only one thing – that he should run – but a mixture of hangover and anxiety made it difficult to work out in which direction.

Something came to him, a memory of Waldstein saying, 'The sentries may come up from Derby Castle,' and that was enough. He could see the castle, still shining across the road, and knew which way to turn. He made to run, and then realised he did not have his jacket on, the jacket with the flute inside it: panicked, he looked around madly, his head shaking like a man overstressing *no*, and then he saw it, covering June, a makeshift blanket for her makeshift sleep. Despite the pressing seconds, he bent down and lifted it off her with care. She shifted in her sleep, screwing up her face and then relaxing it again like a child. It occurred to Isaac that it might be more caring to wake her up, but he knew he did not have the time to deal with the conversation – the reassurances, the qualifications, the half promises – that that would entail, and besides, the tropes already set out in the mind made more sense of the idea that it was better to let her sleep. He took out the flute, and replaced the jacket on top of her.

He wished he had time to write a note, a word, something in English, something to explain that he had not just run away, and then realised what he could do; putting his hand in the pocket, he felt the scratchy stems, and pulled out the sprig of heather. No longer deep red, against the night, it looked like a grapeless vine – he felt a little like a man visiting a hospitalised relative whose failure to wake has led him to eat all the fruit himself. But beggars, he thought – his mind threw up the English idiom, unexpectedly – cannot be choosers. He placed it very gingerly on her chest, in some way hoping to compensate for the fact of his absence when she awoke with the reverence of the action. And then he turned to run.

It was, in fact, a distance of only about two thousand yards from Derby Castle to the Red House, but, to Isaac, it felt as if he were traversing a meridian. Running was not a natural activity for him at the best of times – on the few occasions he had been forced into cross-country activities at school, he had been amazed by how quickly his whole body would go into revolt, and how untrue it was that, after a little while, 'the pain begins to recede'. He remembered one teacher who had told him how good it was for the mind, how many different things one would think of while running. Isaac could remember thinking of only one thing, running, and how much he wanted to stop doing it. Now, feeling each foot hit the ground, he had begun well, amazed initially by the power of the mind to propel the body. He could not believe his speed, he was like a toy that had been wound up for years and finally set down, until suddenly, about halfway there, it all gave way, and he had to slow down in a fit of coughing, choking and stabbing pains in his chest. He did not actually stop, but realised that he had adopted a pace that was in truth hardly more than a brisk walk. He tried to go faster, but his chest and legs were adamant.

Part of his problem was that his mind was split: when he set off, all he could think about was trying to get to his hillock in time; but, as tiredness hit him, he found himself reliving what had just happened. It was a testament, in some sense, to the power of love, or at least to love in all its contortions, that despite the extremity of the moment, his thoughts were drawn not to the present, but round and round a different spiral. The quality of these thoughts, however, was quite distinct from those of a few minutes previously. Should he tell Lulu? Was he going to stay with Lulu? Perhaps he should be with June? Would she want that? And then the image of Rebekka came to him, still in his mind a baby, and his heart, clanking against his ribs, cracked apart: he could feel the cold lines down his face where the wind was touching his tears. He tried to harden himself, thinking: *she fucked him, she was going to fuck him, she deserves it,* all that, but it had no clout any more, the phrases repeated emptily to the rhythm of his feet, as if they were just a chant, one of those mindless chants that training soldiers march to. Self-pity flooded over him, mixed with the running pains, and, despite being too breathless even to sob, he wanted to cry, racked with the unfairness of it all, the sense that he had planned none of this: not the Nazis, not England, not internment, not Waldstein, not June, not this run on this ever-steepening road on this dark night.

With about fifty yards to go, the sight of some lights on in the Red House brought Isaac Fabian back to himself: he remembered he was a man, the responsibility of whom it is to deal with whatever context life places you in, as best you can. He forced his chest to swallow air, pushed his focus away from the widening stitch in his side, and pumped his legs forward. He may not have increased his speed a great deal, but the effort still felt gargantuan, the road a dirt track up a mountain. As he drew closer, he could see figures moving inside the house, pelting by the windows; adrenalin flooded his veins and pulled him over the last few yards. Finally, holding out his flute like a baton – and, in truth, wishing there was someone here he could pass it to – he saw the hillock, rising at the side of the road about ten yards from the house itself. He fell upon it as if it were the softest of beds, face forward, and then rolled over, his mouth open like a screaming baby bird, breathing harder than a man rescued from drowning. His first thought was whether he had enough air in his lungs to blow on the flute if the time came, but then he began to calm down and assess the situation. He checked his watch: two minutes past. Only seven minutes late. He would have had to be very unlucky for any British soldiers to have passed in the last seven minutes. And he had seen no sign of anything in the distance while running, although it had been too dark really to tell.

For a few seconds, coming down from the run, Isaac saw the events of the night in a different light. He had committed adultery; he had sneaked illegally into a British army-controlled event, and then out of it again, in order to make love to a woman who was not his wife; and now he was a lookout on behalf of the Resistance. He basked for a short time in the sheer *adultness* of it all: Look at me, he thought, living. Me, the rabbi's boy, destined for prayer and piety. This is life, he thought, however complex; this is adventure. He leant back against the grass, and raised the flute to his lips between two fingers, like it was a big cigar. He wondered whether to chance a short blow, just to check. No: it might create a false alarm. For some reason – perhaps because it just felt like the kind of thing lookouts do – he wet his thumb and held it up to the air: the wind, gentler than it had seemed when he was running, was blowing off the sea, west onto the cliff. Apart from the distant crash of the waves, the night seemed intensely quiet, a blanket over the sleeping island.

Then, he heard behind him the muffled sounds of murder – footsteps, a distant crash, a shout, the sound of a door slamming. It's happening! he thought, and, unable to contain his excitement, turned round on the grass, crawled like a bug the short way up the hillock and peered over: to see Hirsch and Tort coming out in single file with their hands on their heads. Their faces, in the light from the Red House's windows, were impassive, resigned. But Waldstein, who came out last, followed by a British soldier poking a rifle against his back like a cattle prod – his face, moving sharply from side to side in search of their failed lookout, was contorted with fury; his face buzzed. Even in the semi-darkness, Isaac could feel its febrile energy. Waldstein's face was like a dragonfly's wings.

His heart sank, but not just in the way that usually implies, a momentary loss of hope, a flip reaction to one of the world's daily traumas. He felt as if the centre of him had turned to quicksand. It reminded him of how he had felt on seeing his father's face when he'd first told him about his marriage to Lulu: how all his puffed-up resolve had crumbled, and all he was aware of was the sense of having let him, the family, everyone down. But then at least he had a whole series of justifications to fall back on, all the demands of love and politics and youth, and he had gathered them together in his gut, holding them up like a shield against the overwhelming instinct to fall into his father's arms, crying and apologising and promising to divorce Lulu immediately. Now he had nothing: just a pathetic failure to be at his post when he was needed, because he was drunk and because he was committing adultery, neither of which looked or sounded glamorous any more. Of course, it was more complicated than that, said a weak voice in his head, but then it always is; and when the time comes to give your excuses for your life, you should know they will always sound hollow, that the final judgements of good and bad brook no complexity.

'Halt!' said the soldier behind Waldstein, and the three conspirators stopped in their tracks. His voice, northern in accent, as Isaac had come to recognise, shattered the silence of the night like a glass breaking. 'Stay there. I don't want any trouble from any of you.' He looked around. 'Banks! Anyone else?'

'Yes, Sergeant, sir,' came a voice near by. Out of the darkness, followed by another British soldier, appeared Krauss, looking bizarrely more handsome than ever, his face sad and composed and dappled with shadows. Isaac thought with a pang of Krauss's lost and now unavenged parents. 'I found this one hiding in the bushes up the road.'

The four of them were lined up in front of the Red House. For a moment, in his fear and self-loathing, Isaac forgot which country he was in and thought they were going to be shot, there and then. Instead, they were made to wait, while the sergeant lit a cigarette, and coughed violently, all the time narrowing his eyes and looking into the night, as if wondering whether others may yet be abroad. At one point, he took a length of something out of his pocket and stared at it for a while. Isaac could not tell what it was at first, and then, as the sergeant replaced it, he caught a glint of light reflected from the house and knew it must be the murder weapon, the twine of barbed wire. A figure emerged from the front door of the house; even at this distance, in the dark, Isaac could tell it was Bauermann. Including his close study of the photograph in Waldstein's room, this was the third time he had seen him. He was wearing a dressing-gown, not, as Isaac vaguely imagined a Nazi might have, a black silk, kimono-style affair, but something made out of grey flannel, with a hood, very similar to one Isaac himself used to have as a child: his family used to call it a *Badermunkel*, based on Isaac's childish mispronunciation of *Bademantel*. Bauermann's seemed slightly too small for him – he had to hold the two halves of it together over his chest, and his white legs were exposed to the night air from the calves down. He looked, with small tufts of thin-ning hair sticking up on his head, not smug, or triumphant, but vulnerable, and in a state of some shock. In all the noise of his thoughts, it came to Isaac how quickly a man may revert to normal once taken out of an abnormal environment; how Bauermann, a prisoner in Britain now for well over a year, having been through the decompression chamber of its tolerance, would not necessarily any longer live and breathe violence and extremity and distortion. Which is perhaps why Isaac could see in his face, not just shock, but a certain bewilderment, a certain *why me?* As if he had already for-gotten his own history.

The sergeant nodded in Bauermann's direction – a nod that was the dictionary definition of 'cursory' and carried with it a sense that this particular soldier would have been perfectly happy to see the

Nazi dead; or possibly, taking into account Isaac's now more detailed understanding of the British attitude, happy for the Nazis and Jews to fight it out between themselves. 'We'd be better off without any of 'em: Nazis, Jews, they're all Krauts,' he remembered overhearing Henry Fitch say one day in the King's College kitchens, and then he could not understand how someone could possibly not be prepared to make the distinction, but now he knew that the fundamental building-block of this country and its centuries of revolution-free democracy was *laziness*. That was the key to its tolerance, that was why fascism was never going to happen in Britain, because the optimum state the British working-man wishes to reach, at all times, on all occasions, is *unbothered*.

'Right, you lot,' said the sergeant, turning his attention back to his captives. 'I think it's time for a brisk walk back to town.' He pointed his rifle at them, and then swung it to the left, indicating the direction they should march. The other soldier, who was younger and seemed keen to impress his superior, rather pointlessly copied this action, and then fell in behind the line.

Isaac lowered his head under the rim of the hillock, and turned round to face the sea, pressing his back into the grass, as if this would somehow help him to elude capture; he could feel the blades flattening, and his mind presented him with a cartoon image of a man outlined on the hillock in crushed grass. For the second time in this part of the island, although this time fully aware of it, Isaac found himself holding his breath. He listened to the footsteps as they went past. It occurred to him that one of them could easily decide to tell the British soldier to go and look behind that hillock; they would feel justified in so doing. But that did not happen. Instead, as they began walking down the hill towards the lights of Douglas, Rainer Waldstein threw a single word out into the night, pronouncing each syllable slowly, methodically: '*Verräter*.' He repeated it again and again, allowing the others to join in – '*Verräter, Verräter, Verräter, Verräter*' – until it became the rhythm to their surrender march. Isaac, who had been speaking English all evening, wished to high heaven that the language had so suffused his system that he could no longer understand his own, but that was not the case. He knew what it meant: *Traitor*.

He almost wanted to laugh; how ridiculous that such a word, with all its connotations of deliberate, planned betrayal, should be applied to him and his impulsive, accident-prone, blind stumbling tonight. A traitor is in control, he knows everything; Isaac thought of himself at this moment as entirely lacking control, knowing nothing, least of all the way all this was going to end; entirely at the mercy of fate. But still he heard it: *Verräter, Verräter*. It did not seem to fade as they walked away – he could still hear it, over the wash of the sea and twitter of the night birds. He could still hear it when they should have been well out of earshot; still, in fact, after the sergeant had ordered the four men to be quiet. And he could still hear it when he returned to where June had been sleeping, and saw only his jacket and a sprig of heather, planted lopsided in the ground where she had lain.

Dearest Isaac,

My love, my dearest: I hope you are well. Unfortunately, I can't spend long on pleasantries in this letter. It is a hard one to write, especially knowing that it will be read by someone else.

You may remember that, in my last letter, I mentioned Douglas Lean, a man who I thought was a friend of ours. I explained how he was going to write a testimonial on your behalf to help with your release. Well, he turns out not to be the man I thought he was. His interest was not in fact in you. It was in me. It makes me blush to think of it, but, for whatever reason, perhaps just because I am here on my own, he thought he had some kind of opportunity – by which I mean romantic – with me. When he made his feelings plain, I was of course amazed, having obviously given him no reason whatsoever to think so. As you know, I don't have much experience with men, but it still astounds me the way their minds work. Some of them, anyway.

Please don't worry about it, my darling. Nothing bad happened – at least not in that way – but the upshot of it all is that he shan't now be writing that testimonial. I don't in this letter want to go into the ins and outs of exactly why this is, but I think you'll understand that, either way, it would no longer have been appropriate for him to do so.

I would not have wanted to bother you about this, except for two reasons. Firstly, I have to tell you, because I know you are waiting on news of your testimonials, and secondly, because we are husband and wife, and I think we should have no secrets between us. I would not want you to find out about this somehow, even in years to come, and feel that I was keeping it from you. I want to tell you the truth. Not much talking goes on, I know, in some marriages, but you have always been the person I first want to tell about <u>everything</u> that happens to me. It's one of the things that has been most difficult about our enforced separation. The only person I can talk to about this here is Lotte, and, while she does provide a friendly ear, it's not of course like talking to you.

Anyway, my love, I don't want to burden you with all this. I know you must be disappointed enough to hear about the setback with the testimonial. Maybe someone else will write one: I will keep looking. Perhaps someone who knew you at the kitchens in King's College? I know I never met any of them, but if you write to me with their name, I will make enquiries.

Bekka is really well. Her new words (in English!) this week are 'dark', 'hat', 'time' and 'strawberry' (which she saw in a cartoon book – God knows when she'll ever actually get to eat one!). I'm teaching her to say, 'Welcome home, Daddy!' ready for when you come back!

So, please, Isaac, keep well, don't fret about what's in this letter, and I'm sure whatever happens we will soon be together again, as a family.

We love you,
Luluxxx Bekkaxx

P.S. Excuse the tear-stains at the bottom of this letter. At first I wasn't going to add this p.s., because I didn't want to worry you more than I already have, but I have to, I don't know what else to do. I was just about to seal the envelope when I saw a copy of the *Daily Mail* here on the table at Mrs Lambert's, open at a page about refugees. I know you don't get the newspapers, but it includes a piece written by Douglas Lean, which I think refers to me. It does not mention my name, thank God, but he has written an article which suggests that the wives of some internees will behave improperly in order to get men to produce testimonials for them. My English is better now than when you were first

interned and I understood every word. I am so upset, I don't
know what to do. I'm glad someone from the Home Office
is reading this letter now because you should know it's not
true, it's not true, it's not true.

Even though the notice was written in both languages, Dr
Mannstein, true to his ideals, chose to read the English version,
even to himself. And besides, Kaufmann's head was one of a
number crowded in the way of the German translation underneath.

```
To all internees of Camps Central, Hutchinson, Onchan,
Rushen and Peel. Due to the increasing uncertainty of
the situation in Europe, and because of overcrowding
on the island, the British government has taken
the decision that a number of internees shall be
transported to new camps in the colonies, specifically
Canada and Australia. The camps will be well run,
comfortable, and will provide more than adequate
protection for any internees who undertake the journey.
A random selection procedure will operate.
```

Dr Mannstein had to read this sentence twice, not because he did
not understand it, but because he could not believe it; he could not
believe it was in English. 'However,' the notice continued, as if it
were a man talking, 'if any internee particularly wishes to go, he
should give his name to his house representative before 20/12/1940.
The first transport, on the luxury cruise liner, the SS *Apollo Rising*,
will sail on 6 January. God bless the King.'

It was signed 'Lieutenant Colonel F. W. Rutter' and stamped
with the official seal of the British army.

'When did this go up?' asked Dr Mannstein, turning away from
the wall.

'This morning,' replied Fritz Strang. 'Two soldiers came into the
café and told me it had to go there. Right there. I said, "That's
where I put up the specials," and they said, "The specials will have
to go somewhere else." What do they know? I've got regulars.

They look up, they see no specials . . .' he shrugged and grimaced at the same time – 'no one orders my *Gerstnertorte*!'

Mannstein nodded distractedly, not listening. He went and took a seat at one of the many empty tables in the café, all customers being crowded round the notice.

'Doctor?' said a voice behind him. It was Kaufmann, having fought his way back through the throng.

'Yes?'

'Have you ever been to Canada? Or Australia?'

Mannstein smiled. 'I'm afraid not. I've heard they're both very pleasant countries.'

Kaufmann gestured sheepishly to the opposite chair at the table; with a neat nod, Dr Mannstein granted permission for him to sit.

'Nice weather, I believe.'

'Well, Canada can be cold in the winter. Are you thinking of going?'

'I don't know. You know, me and my wife, we always intended to go to America. And Canada – well, it's more or less America, isn't it?'

'Kaufmann,' said Wolfgang Weber, who appeared by his shoulder and had clearly been listening for some time, 'it's not a free holiday they're offering here.' He sat down next to Mannstein, without ceremony.

'I'm not an idiot, Weber,' said Kaufmann, looking into the table.

'I know. It's just you do such a good impression of one.'

'Weber, behave yourself,' said Mannstein. 'Herman . . .'

Kaufmann looked confused, before his face cleared, suggesting that it had been a long time since someone had addressed him by his first name.

'I'm not sure that you'll be able to take your wife.'

Kaufmann's face, always low anyway, dropped. 'What?'

'Well, there's no mention of that on the notice.'

'Which you'll have spotted is addressed only to internees at male camps . . .' Weber added, beginning to roll a cigarette paper between his fingers.

'Yes,' said Mannstein. 'And I'd be surprised if either the ships or the camps are set up with separate quarters for married couples.'

Kaufmann's expression was that of a man slapped. 'You mean . . . you think they will split up families?'

Mannstein shrugged. 'Well, they have already. Our wives are on the other side of this island.'

'Yes, but not on the other side of the world.'

A silence fell over them.

'Are they *resettling* us, Doctor?' said Weber, eventually, the sardonic stress heavy on the word, a word whose meaning echoed jaggedly around all their histories.

'Of course not,' said Mannstein, quickly, although his faith in the British – specifically his faith in their *difference*, their difference from the Nazis – had been shaken. 'I'm sure it is only a practical measure. It puts anyone who leaves further away from Hitler, anyway.'

'Yes, I'm sure they've got simply our best interests at heart.'

'How many will they send? How will they choose who goes?' said Kaufmann.

'I don't know, Herman. I didn't write the notice.'

'Troublemakers will go first,' said Weber. 'So that lot who tried to do in the Nazi the other night – they'll be on the first boat out. Then, Kaufmann, I imagine, you'll be next.'

'I'm not a troublemaker!'

'*You* say. I hear you haven't made your bed in weeks.' He put the roll-up to his lips, and closed the bag of tobacco with care.

More men came into the café, drawn from outside by the sight of the crowd around the notice. Fritz Strang glided by their table, invisibly placing a cup of Viennese coffee in front of each of them. They nodded their appreciation in his direction.

'That may be something to do with this,' said Mannstein.

'What?'

'That assassination attempt. It might be that this transportation business is a reaction to it. The British probably felt they were getting too lenient with the Derby Castle event.'

'So, what – we're all being punished because of the actions of a few?'

Dr Mannstein, uncomfortable with this interpretation – it smacked too much of the stories one heard of concentration camps, of twenty men being shot for every escapee – none the less said: 'Yes.'

'What's happened to those men?' asked Kaufmann, towards Weber, but sullenly, like a bullied boy who still wants to talk to his persecutor.

'I hear they're being held at Peel,' said Weber. 'With all the other criminals.'

'It was that Bavarian, wasn't it?' said Mannstein. 'The little dark fellow. Wears a cap. It was his gang.'

'Yes, I've never much liked the cut of his jib. Always seemed to me like he was looking for trouble.'

'That's rich, coming from someone who collects rubbish, and sleeps in a kennel!'

Weber took a deep drag of his roll-up, causing the thin paper to burn from its end to his mouth in virtually one go. 'What I'm creating there, Kaufmann,' he said, blowing the smoke deliberately in the smaller man's direction, 'is a quite different kind of trouble.'

'He's a friend of Fabian, isn't he?' asked Dr Mannstein, dabbing evaporated cream from his lip with a napkin fashioned from toilet paper – Strang's latest improvisation.

'Who?'

'The Bavarian. I've seen Fabian with him.' The doctor frowned, the lines on his expansive forehead contracting. 'Who, now I come to mention him, I haven't seen for days. Where is he, Herman?'

Kaufmann coloured a little at this question, the acne craters on his face going purple at their centres. 'I don't know.'

Weber looked at him with suspicion. 'That's not true, is it?'

'Why on earth would you say that?'

'Well, firstly, because you're blushing, and, secondly, because you share a room with him.'

'Perhaps he's gone to sleep in a kennel.'

'Your feeble attempts at sarcasm are not distracting me, Kaufmann. Go on – tell us where he is.'

Kaufmann looked to Dr Mannstein to tell him what to do. Mannstein nodded, the base of his mouth jutting out a little in encouragement.

'Oh, I don't know,' said Kaufmann. 'I wasn't supposed to tell anyone. But Fabian hasn't got out of bed for three days.'

'Three days!' said Mannstein, beginning to rise from his seat.

'No, Doctor. He's not ill. I don't really know what's wrong with him. He came back late from the Derby Castle event, and hasn't got out of bed since. I asked him if I should call for you, Doctor, and he told me no. He told me he didn't want to see anyone.'

'Has he eaten?'

Kaufmann shook his head.

Dr Mannstein continued to rise. 'I'm going to see him now.'

'But you'll get me into trouble!'

'Kaufmann,' said Weber, rising as well. 'How frightened can you be of a man who hasn't eaten for three days? He'll get out of bed to punch you and faint!'

'Hold on, where are *you* going?'

'To your room. I've done a bust of this man, for God's sake; that makes him one of my children!'

Kaufmann watched them leave, fighting their way through the steady stream of men entering the café. He sat for a short time on his own, and then, with a sigh, drew two notes of camp currency out of his pocket, and threw them onto the table.

By the time Kaufmann got back to his and Isaac's room, breathless from trying to catch up, Weber and Mannstein were already by Isaac's bed. Weber was manically throwing off the blankets and pulling up the sheets and pillows, in a frenetic mock-search. 'Fabian! Fabian!' he was shouting.

'Looks like he decided to get up,' said Dr Mannstein.

June Murray had lived her life in mainly male environments, and now, as she sat on the leather lid of her father's old Cogswell & Harrison suitcase, she began to wonder if it had rubbed off on her in unexpected ways. She was sure that, as a girl, she had been good at packing clothes. She remembered, in fact, spending hours packing and unpacking a miniature suitcase that her aunt Dorothy had bought her, learning even at the age of three the basics of keeping garments flat and maximising space. But somehow or other, along the road to adulthood, she had lost the folding gene; or rather, perhaps, acquired the male lack of it. Her mother had helped her to pack this case, and when she had left Bewdley there must have been at least an inch of space between the top layer of clothes and the lid. Now her full weight – admittedly, not much more than eight stone – was unable to crush the three sweaters bundled up above the rest of her clothes to a level that would allow her to shut it. She had moved the case onto her bed, and was sitting on it there; but every time she bent over to flick the locks, the clothes inside would respond to the shift in weight by springing up half an inch, and the latch would no longer align with the clasp.

'Bugger!' she said, bent double, crouching, her forehead touching the too-thin blanket.

She checked her watch; the taxi to take her to the ferry would be coming in twenty minutes. She was keen not to miss it; the service had just restarted following a forty-eight-hour cancellation of all passenger boats to the mainland because of suspected U-boat activity in the Irish Sea. Her stay on this island had gone on longer, much longer than she had expected.

'Perhaps I can help?' said a voice, in German.

June recognised it immediately, and thought about keeping her head down until he had gone, but then her calves began to hurt. She unfurled her neck. Isaac, framed by the door, which she had left open to ease her passage down the stairs with the case, looked crazy: he was unshaven, his hair was sticking up on the sides of his head in horns of black, and he was wearing his jacket buttoned up over what appeared to be a pyjama top. His face looked calm, though, and his voice had been measured.

'I don't know if you can,' she said, trying to muster as much hauteur as this position allowed.

'Well, I've lost a bit since I've been interned, but I still think our combined weight will close it.'

She put her hands together in her lap, trying to consider what a normal woman would do under these circumstances. Refuse to talk to him, she supposed. But it was no use giving him the cold shoulder if she couldn't actually leave – you have to be able, in such situations, to play the trump card of an exit, the dignity of which would be much lessened by all her underclothes falling out of the suitcase. 'All right. Come and lend me your' – she wanted to say 'behind' but – quite apart from the unladylike diction – she was not prepared as yet to grant him the complete let-off of playfulness;

then 'body' glanced through her mind, but that also felt not entirely appropriate, so eventually she just settled, weakly, for 'weight.'

He nodded, took off his jacket – she had been right, he was wearing a pyjama top underneath – and came over. He hoisted himself onto the narrow bed, half standing on it next to her, and then turned round and gingerly crouched on the suitcase lid. June was unable to keep from her mind the idea that she was getting a view of him from a vantage point not unlike that from the side of the toilet bowl. It made her smile, which, as he sat down, he noticed, and smiled too. She looked away, frustrated: it was too early for the mood to break; too early for these making-up larks. He had to earn it: first the pain and the tears and the shouting; then the smiles.

'Bounce,' he said.

'Pardon me?'

'Bounce.' He moved himself up and down in demonstration. 'Together with me, after three. One, two' – they raised their haunches as one – 'three!' And they came down simultaneously. Isaac threw his hands at the locks, and, with some small adjustments of his fingers, flicked the clasps into place.

The moment of lightness passed, and the atmosphere became colder between them. It occurred to June that he had not said, as a hero might in a film, 'Unpack your suitcase, you're not going anywhere.'

Getting off the bed was awkward. Isaac moved first, and then held his hand out to June, who, without ostentation, refused it, levering herself onto the floor with a quiet dignity. There was a point when they were standing together in the middle of her small room, somewhere the two of them had never been before; without the benefit of normal lovers' geography, neither of them knew where to stand.

'Would you like to sit down?' she said, eventually, gesturing to the one seat in the room, a hard-back wooden chair reminiscent of Van Gogh's.

'Thank you,' he said, grateful at least that she had not simply asked him to leave, and went to take it.

She remained standing. 'I can get them to send up some tea, if you would like?'

'No, thank you. June—'

She heard his urgency, and wanted, just for a moment, to postpone it. 'Isaac. How did you get in here?'

He started, drawn back from his speech. 'I . . .' he began, and then looked stumped, as if he genuinely could not remember. Something about that made her heart turn over. 'Oh! Yes. I climbed over the wire.'

'You did what?'

Seemingly trying to follow the thread of his own story, Isaac pulled up the sleeves of his jacket and looked at the underside of his arms. They were striped, as if clawed by a tiger, four lengthy but peculiarly neat lines of blood on each, as though underneath the pyjamas he had matching skin.

'Oh my God . . . Isaac . . .'

'It's fine, just grazes.'

But she was already walking over to the tiny sink in the corner of the room. He watched her rummage around in a washbag and produce – where did women get access to these things? – some cotton wool, which she ran under the tap: he saw the white fleecy ball turn grey and sopping in her fingers. When she returned, having pulled up his sleeves in an alarmingly efficient nursing manner, the coldness of the damp wool, as she gently wiped down his wounds, was bracing.

'What were you thinking about?'

'When?'

'When you climbed over the wire!'

Isaac's brow furrowed, and his lips pursed, for all the world like a man who does not know the answer to such a question. And the truth was, he had not been thinking about anything. He had just been impelled up and over by a need to explain himself – to explain what he had done and what he intended to do now – to June.

'What if you'd been seen? Caught?' *Shot* seemed to hang in the air for a second, although both of them knew that, while all the sentries carried rifles, no internee had so far been fired at in anger.

'Yes. I know. I wasn't worried about that.'

'Why?'

'Because I've decided to take my punishment, anyway. I'm going to go on one of the boats.'

'You're . . .' said June. Her hand, on its way up his arm, stopped; he could feel the water from the ball seeping into a tiny pool. 'Excuse me? You're going on the transports?'

'You know about them?'

'Yes.'

Not only did she know about them; she had already had a long argument with Lieutenant Colonel Rutter about them. In her last meeting with him, which she had assumed would involve nothing more than a polite farewell, she was surprised to find his attitude much changed – and not just towards her. His stance on the internees had hardened again. It was clear that, for him, the Derby Castle event had been something of an experiment in leniency – an experiment that had most demonstrably failed. And so, following the assassination attempt, he had settled, with some comfort, back into the hair shirt of strict military conduct. Nothing she could say could move him (in truth, she got the impression he partly held her to blame for the whole incident). Isaac was right, therefore: although the transports to Canada and Australia were primarily a government directive to cope with overcrowding on the island, to Rutter they represented a well-timed opportunity for punishment – or rather, an opportunity to demonstrate the capacity of the island authorities to inflict punishment if necessary.

'I don't understand. The list of internees going hasn't been drawn up yet.'

'I'm going to volunteer to go.' He said it brightly, like men must have done when talking of their intention to sign up at the start of the Great War.

'What? Why?'

Isaac took a deep breath. He was finding it somewhat hard to explain himself, because, after lying in bed for three days, a switch had been thrown in his mind, a switch that made him feel that he was not merely clinging on like a desperate, untrained rodeo rider to the wild horse of his life, but was following a pre-planned course: his destiny, in other words. And when a man believes he is following a destiny, it becomes difficult for him to accept that everyone is not already aware of their place within it. So a part of him had turned intensely solipsistic, had become convinced that she must already know about his situation. He knew that she did not know, but somehow felt none the less that he was going over old ground.

'The assassination attempt on Bauermann. On the Nazi?'

'Yes, on the night of Derby Castle. I know about it.'

'I was involved in it.'

June stood, and turned away from him. The steady draught of December through the stubborn gap in the window was enhanced on her skin by the cold tingle of creeping dread. 'I see.'

'I was supposed to be the lookout. But' – he faltered, then realised that the truth was simple – 'I was asleep.'

She nodded, one measured movement followed by another; her head felt freighted down with this information. A moment ago, she was a woman with much that set her apart – a mission towards the truth, a sprouting love for a refugee, a high and determined independence – but now she was something else: someone whose actions had made a difference in time, someone with a small part in history. History, of course, is a single and rigorously unbending narrative, but an individual's involvement in it is strewn with alternative scenarios, and these ran through June's head immediately as a series of *ifs*: *if* I had not gone outside Derby Castle with Isaac; *if* I had not kissed him; *if* I had insisted it go no further; *if* we had never met . . . What? A Nazi internee would be dead, and the perpetrators unpunished. Is that what she wanted? Did she even know enough about the truth to know for certain that that was just? What truth would make it just?

Isaac was continuing: 'Well, I wasn't asleep the whole time. I was just late, because I was asleep. I got there a few minutes late. I thought it was fine, but it wasn't. It was too late.' He spoke in short sentences, like a child explaining himself. He was surprised – because he thought he had moved on – to feel tears pricking behind his eyes. 'But the British soldiers didn't see me. I hid until they were gone. That's why I was . . .' He stopped, wondering if he should get up and put his hand on her shoulder to turn her round, so that he did not have to say these things to her back; although he was always enticed by the sight of a woman's back, trembling with the potential of beauty. He felt a keen urge to run his hand down it, to remind his palm of its divine, elongated

S. 'That's why I wasn't there, on the cliffs. When you woke up.'

When you woke up. He and she both felt what was not being said, the fact of elision; it was palpable, an absence that has become a presence, like a ghost become visible. One day, men and women will not have to talk like this, thought Isaac.

'Yes,' she said, with some irritation. During the last three days she had spent much time going over her feelings about Isaac, about what had happened between the two of them. She had, initially, felt simply shabby about the whole thing, unprofessional, of course, but also deeply sorry: sorry for Lulu and Bekka in a way that – perhaps because she was older, perhaps because she knew what they had been through – she had never been for the family of the married lecturer at Goldsmiths'. There is only so much sorrow, however, that can be felt for people one has never met – sorrow needs an image in the mind, an objective correlative – and, as the days passed, and no word came from the camp behind the barbed wire outside her window, shame turned to anger, a well-trodden anger. For all her modernity – and this was galling to her – she had found it difficult not to feel straightforwardly betrayed, not to feel her anger taking a tired, familiar shape, moulding itself around all the old tropes of a woman used. The only difference, perhaps – and she clung to this – was the existence of a civic component to her rage. *How dare he?*, in other words, was augmented by *Doesn't he realise the importance of what I'm doing here?* She was putting her job on the line by becoming 'involved' (the phrase that, at this stage, she preferred in her own head) with an internee. Most importantly, all her work – work she was doing on their behalf, on *his* behalf! – would be discredited. She knew, of course, that these were reasons to be angry with herself rather than him – if she had been so concerned about the dangers to her work, the easy thing to have done would have been not to become involved – but (and here, the logic, she knew, was entirely feminine) somehow, if it was love, if it was real, then perhaps it was worth the risk. If it was not – if it had been, as she had concluded with a shudder, simply a man scratching the itch of his lust on her – then she had a right to be angry, because she had been tricked.

Now, though, all this internal debate was rendered, at a stroke, meaningless. Her irritation was a symptom of her annoyance with herself for having spent so long on what suddenly seemed like girlish mooning about it all. The introduction of murder plots and resistance groups and revenge into the mix hardened everything – it rendered what she had imagined was primarily an emotional issue political. The civic element was no longer a component, but *everything*, and the stakes were desperately raised. Now that the man she was involved with was not only a refugee and an internee, but an accomplice to an assassination attempt – God: it was not just her work on the line, but could well be her freedom. Her *life*.

'Why didn't you tell me?' she said, turning round at last. The caw of the seagulls passing her window had seemed, for a second, to be laughter, callous laughter, directed at her. Her expression was fierce, a fierce mixture of rage and sadness and thwarted love.

'When?'

'On that night! The night of Derby Castle!'

Isaac's face went pleading. 'No, but when? When specifically?' He got up from the chair and went towards her. 'When we were talking in the booth – surrounded by others? When we went outside, and had only one thing on both our minds?' She flushed, but her embarrassment vanished in a puff of internal smoke when he added: 'When we were *dancing*?'

Then, all she wanted to do was cry: cry and remember. There was a silence while Isaac's questions went unanswered, or, at least, as much silence as the sea affords: its roaring breath continued undiminished, unconcerned by this or any other human drama. They were standing only about a foot apart, but it felt as if they were on either sides of an abyss; as if an earthquake had split the floor of the Douglas Arms, and the fault line, the zigzag crack itself, lay between them. Eventually, she crossed her arms, and, trying to find a businesslike voice, said: 'Why would you want to get involved,' the phrase meant something else to her now, 'in a murder?'

Isaac looked away. 'You've been doing the interviews,' he said. 'You know what *they*'ve been doing to *us*.'

She nodded, pursing her lips. Although this was plausible, something about it was not quite right. It was correct – justified, noble even – but at the same time, it was glib. It was the response of a simpler man: it missed out parts of himself. 'Is that it?' she said. 'Really?'

Isaac looked back to her searching eyes and felt the bricks he had placed inside himself crumble. This was too difficult to explain. It had to do with communism, with his father, with proving himself, with the loss of Germany, and, most fundamentally, with finding out – *finding out what?* he thought now – about Douglas Lean and Lulu. He could not put it all into words. Instead, he said, carving each word out of himself, 'I had to act.' *Action*: it was what had always been missing. Some *doing*, something physical, that would use up all the terrible mental energy thrown up by the times. 'I couldn't—' he continued, but then stopped, the phrase 'I couldn't just sit and watch' dying on his lips, as indeed that was all that had been asked of him – that, in a nutshell, was to have been his action – and he had failed in it. He looked down, and for a second seemed so broken that she decided not to push him any further on this.

'And now . . . you're going? To Canada or Australia?'

'Yes.' He was still looking down.

She wanted to take his chin in her finger and thumb and force his face up to meet her eyes, like her mother used to do to her when she was caught misbehaving. 'How does that help anything?'

He looked up. 'I don't know. It's what feels right.'

'*Feels* right? What kind of talk is that?'

'I'm going to try to take Waldstein's place.'

'Who's Waldstein?'

'The one who organised the assassination attempt.' The one who had also organised, from his cell in Peel Camp, the placing of a piece of paper underneath Isaac's door earlier today, a copy of the notice presently causing such a commotion in Fritz Strang's café, inscribed with the message '*Danke schön, Verräter*'. It was this that had fractured the virtually comatose state Isaac had been in since Sunday night; this which had forced him out of bed and into decision. 'I intend to go on the transports instead of him.'

June checked her watch. Ten minutes now, before the taxi. The set of his face, ready and determined, annoyed her, an odd, scratchy feeling, such as a wife might feel seeing a look come over her husband's face for the thousandth time. 'Don't be so stupid, Isaac. How are you going to do that? If you tell them that you were the lookout on the assassination attempt, they'll just deport you as well. They won't let him off because of it. It's not a straight swap!'

He looked rather thrown by this, and it took a little while for him to absorb it into his idea of his destiny. 'Well, then, I shall take his place surreptitiously. The British never pay that much attention to us as individuals. I'll go to him and offer to disguise myself as him, and get on the boat that way.'

She looked at him, her eyes narrowing, with a new level of concern. 'Have you gone mad?'

For a moment, he considered just saying, *yes*.

'The British are keeping all those they captured in the assassination attempt in cells at Peel. Apart from occasional supervised visits, they're in solitary confinement. Come transportation day, the rest of you might be loaded onto the boats like cattle, but Rutter and his soldiers will be watching those four men like hawks.'

As she was speaking, the certainty and self-belief seemed to drain from him. Or rather, the assumption, which his new-found idea of destiny had given him, of maturity; that was what seemed to fade. It was as if, with every word she spoke, he grew a year younger, as if her voice carried on its breath the elixir of youth, and he was taking in too much, he was overdosing. By the end he looked so much like a little boy lost, June expected him to grow flannel shorts and a cap.

'I don't care!' he shouted, his face flailing. 'I don't care how difficult it is! I'm going. Even if I can't take Waldstein's place, I'm going. It's what I have to do!' He paused for breath, and to lower his voice. 'Oh, June. You don't know . . . you don't know . . .'

'What don't I know, Isaac?' she said, softly.

The guilt, he thought. *You don't know the guilt.* Eating away at him, like maggots on a corpse: he had not realised that remorse, which sounds like such a soft emotion, could be so painful. There was so much of it: guilt about his father, guilt about his mother, guilt about Waldstein, guilt about his religion, guilt about June, and guilt – *guilt, guilt, guilt*, if he said it often enough, could it become meaningless? – about Lulu, whose last letter he had read this morning.

And when a man is overcome with guilt, especially a man who has recently lost his faith in thought and finds his only outlet in action, it can create in him the feeling that his one option is flight; that the only answer is distance, is getting far, far, away.

June watched as tears fell copiously from Isaac's eyes. She could not tell if he even knew they were falling. It felt a strange question for her to ask, but it was the one that came tumbling next out of her lips. 'What about your wife? Your baby?'

He shook his head. 'What difference does it make being four thousand miles away from them instead of four hundred?' A considerable difference, in fact, he knew; but that difference, at this time, was exactly what he wanted.

'What about *me*?'

She moved towards him as she said it. It was a movement without aggression – neither psychological nor sexual – but, none the less, Isaac felt his feelings for her chipping away at his resolve. He had not realised that the presence of her body at close quarters would have such an effect, because he thought he held it in his memory: he thought he remembered its effect, had gauged its power, could handle it, however strong. But he had misjudged. Desire, at this stage in a man's and woman's physical knowledge of each other, wishes – frantically – to be *reminded* of its object. It was so powerful, he felt his grip on his destiny loosen. He had not bargained for how much her body would disturb his purpose; how much desire breaks down high purpose; breaks it down and converts it to secret purpose.

'I don't know, June.' He put his arms out, as if to clasp his hands to her shoulders, and then let them fall by his side. 'I wouldn't know anyway, even without all' – he looked around them, trying to take in the extremes of their environment – 'this. Without being here, or without the assassination attempt, or being transported to Canada. Even if all that weren't in the equation, I wouldn't know. We're supposed to, aren't we? Know what we want. Even if we don't know anything else, we're supposed to know that.' He shook his head. His crying had stopped; something of himself had been recovered. 'But I don't. Not any more. You know what Jews were robbed of, in Germany, along with their jobs and their money and

343

their citizenship? Choice. *Choice.* And it's a basic assumption, now, choice. It's there with freedom and democracy and . . . excuse the politics, but: choice is what capitalism has taught us all to expect. The strange thing, though, at some level is that . . . you get used to it, living without choice. There's a strange comfort to knowing that the only choices you have to make are about whether to eat or whether to starve; whether to cover your head or your body when boots are raining in on you from all sides; whether to live or whether to die. These aren't choices. They're imperatives. And it's a relief. It's life without hesitation.'

June backed away. She was almost smiling. 'You always were one for long speeches.'

Isaac did his best to return her smile. He knew there was some truth in her implication: that in a moment of emotional crisis he had reached for the manifesto; that the Marxist in him could always pinpoint a larger context, and here had done so, found a social analysis to exempt him, a historical and political (rather than personal) reason why he could not make a decision. But he also knew there was some truth in what he had said. The one did not cancel out the other.

'So that's what you want, then? An escape? A getaway? Rather that than have to make a choice?'

He did not answer. She was putting on her gloves, black suede with piping on the fingers. Then, she was going over to the bed and grasping the handle of her suitcase.

'What are you doing?'

She gave him a questioning look. 'The taxi will be here in about five minutes.'

'Taxi?'

'I'm going.'

'*Going?* Back to the mainland?'

'Yes, Isaac. Back home, to be more exact. Back to the Ministry of Information. I would have gone two days ago if the ferries had been running.'

Despite the conviction that he had come here to say goodbye – and one more thing – the fact of goodbye, and particularly her ease with it, rocked him. *The certainty of women,* he thought. 'Oh, I thought . . .'

344

'What?'

'That we would have more time.'

She looked at him directly, but tightened her grip on the suitcase handle. 'More time to do what?'

He shifted from foot to foot. 'To . . . talk. To sort things out.' *To make everything all right*, he wanted to say, and felt inside himself the peculiar realisation that, however much he believed in it, he was not in fact suited to permanent revolution.

She let go of the suitcase, and approached him once more. This time her movement did contain some aggression, some speed. 'Listen, Isaac. I'm not a nineteen-year-old. Neither, despite the way you sometimes talk, are you. We shared a night together. Not even a night, just some small time during one night.' She had been holding back, but her anger was fuelling her now, the way it did with the stupid bureaucrats and the stupid soldiers. 'Our bodies touched. I might, at the time, have thought it meant something more. So might you have. But it seems it isn't going to. Well, never mind.' She appeared to rise up, so that her eyes were in line with his; when she spoke, her voice had the clarity of crystal. '*It happens in wartime.*' He looked shocked, and not a little frightened. 'I'll thank you to keep it quiet if possible. It won't help either of us for it to become gossip among the soldiers here.'

He opened his mouth in outrage. 'I would never—'

She shrugged. 'I don't know what you would and wouldn't do. I hardly know you.' She walked back towards the bed.

A horn sounded from outside, comical among the cry of the gulls, like someone doing a sarcastic gull impression. She glanced through the glass, and her face registered the presence of the taxi.

'Wait,' said Isaac, rushing over to her, grasping her shoulder just as she grasped the suitcase again.

'Why?'

'It did mean something. You know it did.'

'I said it might have done. It doesn't make any difference now. You're married. And you're going to the other side of the world. And I've got more important things to do than have this conversation.'

His face screwed up. 'I don't agree.'

'What?'

'I don't agree that it doesn't make any difference. *Yes*, I'm married; *yes*, I've got a child; *yes*, I'm going away.' He hit each '*ja*' like a hammer. '*Yes*, we don't know each other properly and I'm a Jew and you're a Christian and I'm German and you're English and I'm interned and you're free. *Yes*. And *yes*, there's a war. So we've got a lot of things in our way, things in our way that mean . . . that probably mean that' – and he paused, a split-second, but there was no point in not naming the shuddering word now – 'our love has got no future. But just because something has no future, that doesn't render it meaningless.'

'Doesn't it?' she said, her voice thin through a closing throat.

'God, June. The Jews in Europe may have no future. But they still existed, once.'

A crack of laughter burst through her sadness at the ridiculousness of the comparison: their *love* – that was what he had called it – was such a tiny molehill on this terrible mountain of history. And yet, the laughter only qualified the tears, dissolving in them. There was something appropriate, too, about his words. That was what history was: the net in which we are all caught, struggling for breath.

She let go of the suitcase handle. Her features cleared, and, in the way they did, suddenly made sense – freed of anger and too much thought, her face offered itself up simply as something Isaac desperately wanted to kiss, or at least touch. But it was she who touched him, running one gloved hand down his cheek, from temple to mouth. If this was to be the last contact they would have, he wished – like a cactus wishes for rain, a moth light – that she would take the glove off, so at least there would be no barrier between his skin and hers, at least one skein of his face would bear a trace of her cells for ever.

But she didn't. With a smile that gave him up, she withdrew her hand. It seemed that, between him and June, there would always be barriers. The horn of the taxi sounded again, more insistent this time. She turned towards the sea, and light flooded her face: Isaac felt as if all the world were pouring through the gap in the window, drowning them.

'I must go,' she said.

'Just stay for a little while longer. There's one more thing I have to say.'

'Isaac, the taxi is here, and the ferry leaves at half-past.'

'You can catch the next one.'

'Yes, and miss my connecting train.' But her voice was not harsh. 'And we've said what we need to say, haven't we? What else is there to say? Apart from "goodbye" . . .'

Isaac breathed in. For the hundredth – the millionth – time, he felt the salt settle in his lungs. 'I want to do my interview again,' he said.

There was a minute pause, a tiny drop in time. Then, June nodded. Isaac put his red-lined arms on the white wood, and, with one strong, clean movement, shut the window.

Alfred 'Chips' Bassett was not in an especially good mood. He knew that it always took a while for the Ministry of Information to get back up to speed following the Christmas break, but he had imagined it might be different during wartime. It had, in fact, been a little different last year, with Christmas coming so soon after the outbreak of war: then, it was considered so important to keep the British public convinced of the necessity of war that they had carried on pumping out propaganda all through December and into the new year, which meant the unprecedented spectacle of Ministry officials working on Christmas Day itself, anti-Hitler posters and cartoons strung around the offices beside tinsel and trees.

More importantly, the lack of a break had meant that, tired though they may have been, there was no moment of mass slug-gishness. Bassett was not a believer in the idea that holidays recharged the batteries; not, at least, the batteries of the British worker. Rather, he felt that all holidays did was drop the scales from their eyes, alerting them to the fact that work, the whole idea of it, was something of a myth – was, in truth, simply a long sen-tence foisted upon their lives – and they normally arrived back at it with an air of bemusement as to why they were doing this at all, which would take some days to disperse. This year, 1940–1, the government had decided, on the basis that a break would be good for morale, that the Ministry could be run over the Christmas period with only a skeleton staff. Today was 6 January; the break was over; his and all the other major departments had been up and running for forty-eight hours; and yet, at 9.57 a.m., he was still waiting for Emily to bring him a cup of coffee, and for Henderson to arrive with his schedule for the day.

He was just about to walk out and berate Emily when there was a knock on his door. He leant back on his ox-blood chair, and tried to assume an air of casual indifference. 'Come!'

The door opened, and round the side of the frame appeared not the curved form of Emily, breasts first, but the face of a young woman, a face he vaguely recognised.

'Minister?'

'Yes?'

'It's Murray, sir. June Murray. I work in SO1. I came to see you last year, about a memo . . .' She trailed off.

'Yes, of course, I remember,' said Bassett, although he did not.

'May I come in?'

'Well . . .' Bassett did not know what to say. Without Nigel Henderson's schedule, he was not sure whether or not he actually had an appointment to see this woman. He was loath, however, to admit that he was not sure about that. 'Yes.'

'Thank you . . .' June walked into the office, carrying a black leather portfolio; the drift of her body across his eyes put Bassett's mind at rest that, at least on one level, it had been the right decision to let her enter.

'Do sit down.'

'Thank you.'

He felt the settle of her into the opposite chair, the give of the red leather. She was resting the portfolio on tightly drawn-together knees.

'It's very kind of you to see me at such short notice.'

'No trouble at all,' he replied, giving her something of a polite, encouraging smile, although her words had confused him further, making him still more uncertain as to whether he was supposed to be seeing this woman. 'Short notice': did that mean the meeting had been arranged very recently, or that her knock on the door was entirely unscheduled?

'You mentioned last time we met . . . something about a memo . . . ?'

'Yes sir. INF 1/251. The one about Nazi atrocity stories . . . and Jews.'

Bassett's face cleared, as the light of recognition burnt through the mist of memory. 'Oh yes! From SO1! I remember now.' The olive skin, the dark eyes. He'd thought about her later that same afternoon in fact, upstairs at the Coach and Horses, with Emily.

Time was, with Diana, he'd think of Emily. 'You were very upset about that bit about "indisputable innocence", wasn't it?'

'Well . . . I don't know about "upset", sir. I was concerned about it. About the Ministry's position.'

'Yes, of course.' There was a pause. Bassett looked over at the clock: three minutes past ten. Its tick was amplified through the solid marble of the mantelpiece it sat upon. Where on earth was Henderson? He felt embarrassed, because he presumed her silence to mean that she expected him to know the subject of the meeting, and was waiting for him to begin. 'Of course,' continued Bassett, trying to dispel the awkwardness, although feeling immediately that he should not have repeated the phrase, 'the Ministry's position on that may be shifting. Some of the reports we have had coming out of Germany and occupied Europe recently . . .'

Her face immediately became animated: it seemed to flush – he saw the olive go red – not out of embarrassment, but excitement. 'Oh, good. Good. Well, that's exactly why I wanted to come and see you, sir.'

'Right. Well. Yes. Of course.' Stop saying, 'of course', you old fool. 'Although,' he continued, feeling a surge of panic, 'I don't want to overstate the matter. So far there's been no actual directive to change Ministry policy. We would have to be absolutely sure before . . .' He waved a hand in front of his face, indicative of their shared understanding of the matter, a gesture that rheumatism robbed of all looseness.

She nodded, and opened the portfolio. Bassett noticed the movement apart of the knees, the creation of the small valley in her skirt.

'Yes, sir. I understand. But that's my point. I've compiled a report, sir. A dossier. About that very subject.'

'The Nazis' treatment of the Jews?'

'Yes, sir.'

He felt an inner tightening; perhaps he had allowed this woman too much latitude simply because of the richness of her skin. 'We have seen many such dossiers already, though, Miss Murray.'

'I know, sir. But this one is made up entirely of eyewitness reports. They haven't been translated and smuggled into this country by the Polish Resistance, either. These are not copies of documents that have landed on Ministry desks. They haven't come from lobbyists with an axe to grind. They are all' – she seemed unsure of how to put this: her lips pursed, then relaxed – 'from the horses' mouths.'

'Which horses?' asked Bassett. 'What do you mean?'

June formed her fingers into a steeple and pressed it to her mouth. She looked into Bassett's maudlin eyes and was glad, at least, that she had found him alone: the admission she was about to make was not one that she would have expected Nigel Henderson to forgive. 'Towards the end of last year, sir, I went to the Isle of Man to speak to the men and women interned there.'

'You did?'

'Yes, sir. Lieutenant Colonel Rutter very kindly gave me permission to interview a selection of internees. I asked them about their experiences at the hands of the Nazis. Some also told me about the suffering of others – friends, family members – who have not been lucky enough to make it out of Germany.'

Bassett frowned, making what hair was left on his crown form the sternest of widow's peaks. 'This was an official Ministry assignment? I wasn't aware of . . .'

'No, sir. I did it off my own bat.'

'Ah.' Alfred Bassett reached into the side pocket of his Henry Poole suit, and took out his pen, a Parker 95 with a rolled-gold nib, and, flicking over a leaf of the creamy paper pad that always lay centred on his leather-covered desk – a flicking back of which leaf would have revealed the beginnings of a new love-letter to his wife – he wrote, on the fat, buffered new page, the words 'June Murray', followed by a looping question mark. 'I see.' He underlined the question mark twice.

'Mr Bassett, sir.' Her voice rose, but her edge of desperation remained contained. 'I know I've gone against Ministry protocol . . .'

'I think perhaps that is putting it mildly, Miss Murray. This sounds to me completely unacceptable behaviour. You are a . . . What *is* your post exactly?'

'I'm a translator, sir. In Special Operations.'

'A *translator*. I see. And were you translating from German in the Isle of Man?'

'Yes, sir. Mainly. Although a number of the internees already speak very good English.'

'No doubt. But, as far as I understand it, your job does not involve going out and about in order to translate the stories of whichever friendly enemy alien you feel like listening to. It involves working on the material you are given, and then handing it back to your superiors. Does it not?'

June looked down. She had expected to be told off, and more or less like this, in the public-school style. It did not sway her from her purpose. 'Sir,' she said, looking up, 'I understand that I have stepped beyond the boundaries of my position. I also understand that in our last meeting, you made it clear that, as far as this Ministry was concerned, memo INF 1/251 was binding.'

'Well, I'm glad for your self-awareness at least.'

'I understand that a project such as this dossier' – she placed both her hands flat upon it, the fingers spread – 'is not in my remit, and the only way I could get such a thing off the ground, officially, would be to submit it as a suggestion for the consideration of the head of the SO1. But the thing is, sir' – and here, Bassett thought he saw her pupils, already dark, turn black, a change in them that bordered on the feral – 'there isn't time for all that. There isn't time for *suggestions* and *considerations* and *meetings* and *discussions* at an *executive* or a *parliamentary* level.'

'Miss Murray. I don't like your—' tone, he was going to say, and it was true, he didn't: she wasn't spitting out the words, but she may as well have been, infused as they were with contempt.

'We need to tell people what's happening, Mr Bassett. I came to work for the Ministry of Information. I thought what we're supposed to do here was to give the British people information.' She shook her head, making her hair swing. 'We don't. We don't inform the public; we decide what information we want them to have.' She took a breath, not long enough for him to interrupt. 'Well,' she continued, holding up her portfolio, '*this* is the information. It's the only information. And there isn't time for any more debate as to whether or not we think they need to have it. People are being killed, Mr Bassett.'

'I know, Miss Murray. There's a war on.'

'Not as you imagine it,' said June, with such intensity – there seemed to be a full stop between every word, to drive each one home – that even Bassett's all-encompassing complacency was, for the moment, shaken. 'The gentleman's war – the one that you thought you fought last time – however wrong it was then, this time . . . this time the whole idea is an *aberration*. This is not about fighting the fair fight. It's not the Queensberry Rules. The German state is setting about the systematic destruction of thousands, perhaps millions, of innocent, defenceless men, women and children. This' – she held up her portfolio again, the leather close to his eyes: he could see its black grain wrinkling – 'is not a war. It's a mass execution.' She put the portfolio back down on her knees. There was a long, ticking silence before she said: '*Sir*.'

Bassett leant back in his chair, and sighed. He heard the slow tut-tut-tut of rain beginning to hit his wide river-overlooking window. His could feel it, the liquid sensation of his stiff old heart loosening. He was a soldier, but also a romantic, a combination that finds it difficult to resist passion and bravery in the service of a cause, however misguided. Perhaps he should look at her dossier, he thought. He had no idea why she was so bothered about the Jews, but, dimly, he knew there must be some validity in such commitment. To take such risks, in full awareness of the consequences, and then to come to him and admit it – unapologetically . . . Well: it took some guts. Yes. It took some guts.

She saw the map of his face change, the many lines undulating like the contours of a high hill, from condescension to respect; she saw him hold out his hand – she saw the lines on his palm, the crazy, antique grid of flesh – and his mouth begin to form the sentence 'All right, I will look at your dossier'. She saw the index finger lift, ready to qualify the offer, to underlay it with a 'no-promises' clause. She felt time open, for a split-second, to receive her. And then the door crashed against the square-panelled wall, and Nigel Henderson burst into the room at full pelt.

'Minister!' he said, and then, curtailing himself: 'Excuse me. I didn't realise you were in a meeting.'

'That's quite all right, Henderson,' said Bassett, although he was irritated by his parliamentary secretary's failure to knock. 'You remember Miss Murray . . . June Murray . . . from SO1, of course?'

The Minister of Information had deliberately given rather little of it – information, that is – away in this description, childishly hoping to catch out Henderson. However, he had underestimated his junior.

'Miss Murray. A pleasure to see you again. I wasn't aware of your appointment with the minister today . . .'

'No, sir. I didn't have one. I just came by in order to try to organise a time to see Mr Bassett – and then when there was no one in the ante-room, I chanced a knock on the door . . .'

Henderson looked at Bassett, who raised his eyes to heaven and said, 'Emily appears to be still sleeping off Christmas . . .'

'So it would seem.' He shuffled on the spot, caught for a second between his overweening sense of etiquette and the urgency of his news. 'Minister, I apologise for my own lateness this morning, but I have received a telegram from the Admiralty of the utmost importance . . .'

Bassett nodded. 'I do apologise, Miss Murray. Perhaps we can continue this discussion at a later date . . .' He said it with some kindness in his voice, trying to make it clear that he would not, for the moment at least, be following up on her various breaches of protocol.

'I quite understand, sir.' She rose to leave, clutching the portfolio to her side.

'No, wait a moment,' said Henderson. 'I think – if you'll permit me, Minister – it might be politic for Miss Murray to stay for a second. She could take this news back to Special Operations and see what they make of it.'

Bassett looked a little surprised, but motioned for June to stay. She retook her seat.

'Well, come on then, man. What is it?' said Bassett.

Henderson took a piece of folded paper from the top pocket of his jacket, and laid it on the minister's desk. June could see the crown, the symbol of the Post Office telegram. Bassett unfurled it and stood back. The whole action had something medieval about it: a nobleman presenting the parchment of the Magna Carta to the king. Bassett opened a side drawer of the desk and took out a pair of glasses, which he perched with elaborate care on the bridge of his nose. What effect they had on his eyesight was difficult to ascertain, as he still had to bring his squinting eyes very close to the paper in order to read it.

'06.47. Douglas. U-boats 47° east, 3° west, Malin Head. Engaged British cruise liner. Struck amidships. Sunk without trace.' He looked up, and removed his glasses, although his face retained more than a trace of the squint. 'Well, we'll suppress it, I suppose . . .'

'No, Minister. We shan't suppress it. Because it turns out that this particular ship is—'

June interrupted, the words sounding louder in her mind than the beating of the blood in her suddenly sick heart: 'The SS *Apollo Rising*?' Desperately, she still framed it as a question.

Henderson turned to her, his head-boy features registering some shock and not a little annoyance at being upstaged. 'How did you know that?'

She tried to form an answer; none came. She shook her head and looked down.

'Excuse me, you two, but one of us in here – the one who runs this office, in fact – remains baffled.' Bassett was sitting back in his chair with his arms folded.

'Do excuse me, Minister,' said Henderson, his eyes still resting suspiciously on June's bowed crown. 'The SS *Apollo Rising* is the first of the boats to leave the Isle of Man, transporting nearly seven hundred of the enemy aliens interned there to the colonies. It was on its way to Newfoundland.'

Bassett's eyes now also went to June. From his seated position, her face looked religious, downcast and set like marble. 'I see.'

There was a pause, during which Nigel Henderson looked between the two of them, his mouth slightly open, his expression that of a man who cannot believe that the next conclusions are not apparent to everyone. 'So . . .' he said, picking up the telegram from Bassett's desk, and holding it aloft, making him look somewhat absurdly like the previous prime minister arriving back from Berlin, 'the Germans have handed us a propaganda victory! They've sunk a ship on which the passengers were their own people! The

Germans have killed a whole boat full of Germans! And a few Italians, but they're on the same side! What do you think of that, Miss Murray?'

She looked up. Her face was blank. She thought about it, of course: painstakingly explaining to him how wrong he was, how, to the Nazis, these were not Germans who had drowned, but the exact opposite: anti-Germans. It was only us, the British, who persisted, correctly – but, in the context of the war, disastrously – to see them still as German. June Murray thought about it, but she realised, even as the arguments ran through her head, that the wall of illogic which supported Henderson's celebratory mood was so deeply founded on earth of wilful ignorance that there was no point; nothing had ever been so pointless. She realised, too, that soon these men's patience with her would evaporate; her time with them was limited, and there was still a worthwhile question, the *only* worthwhile one, to be asked. Her voice, when it emerged, was muted. 'Were there any survivors?'

Henderson's grin held, although seemed to tighten. 'Survivors? I . . .'

'No survivors predicted,' said Bassett, reading from the telegram again. He looked up at her, and removed his glasses. His bloodshot eyes were sad, and seemed to be attempting to communicate to her that he had tried, for a moment, to spare her this information. 'They will be searching, of course . . .'

'Not while U-boats are present in the water, sir,' said Henderson. 'Anyway,' he continued, with some irritation, 'we need to get this to the newspapers as soon as possible! That, Miss Murray, is why I wanted you to stay. Go back to Special Operations. Let everyone in your department know what's happened. Then, let's keep track of the German press and find out what their reports say: no doubt they'll be trumpeting the sinking of a British ship far and wide. That'll make it all the sweeter when they find out the truth. I look forward to your translations of that!'

Henderson continued, speaking and speaking, the same words coming up again and again – *truth, German, propaganda, ship, British, news, killed, victory* – but, to June, the meanings were getting lost. His voice had become to her as a strange animal song, like the cry of a whale or dolphin or furious bird, rising and falling in pitch, emotion and excitement, but moving further and further from sense. She wondered if looking at him would help – she knew that watching a man's lips move can help the listener understand what is being said – but when she raised her face, something – perhaps a desire for neither of the men in the room to see it running with tears – propelled her to look away, towards the window, where the rain had stopped momentarily. Releasing some of their water had thinned the solid clouds, and, as the sun burst through, she could see the shaft of light moving over London, turning its grey expanse gold. Henderson was still talking, interrupted occasionally by Bassett's different but also incomprehensible note, as she rose and walked towards the window. She wondered what it would take to open it; whether it could be opened as easily as Isaac had shut the one in her room at the Douglas Arms; and if, once opened, she might be able to hurl her portfolio, now held in her right hand, like a discus across the Thames, rising to the sky, to the sun, and then falling into the river near the far bank. She wondered how long it would float, bobbing on the current like a small black raft, before the muddy water would seep in through the buckles and the paper inside would thicken with moisture; how long before it became so heavy that it would sink, see-sawing down into the depths, past the polluted fish and the rusty chains and the greening wood and the endless flotsam and jetsam of the drowned.

Not long: she would have liked more time. It would have been better to throw it out to sea, because, she remembered, salt water has a greater density than fresh, and buoys objects up on it for longer. But this had often confused her, as the river and the sea are conjoined, and she had always wondered at which point the salt dissolves, dissolves like dreams into the walls of the land.

PART FOUR

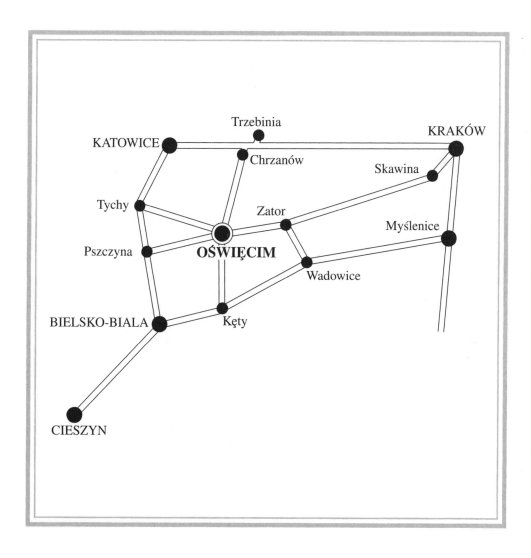

Oświęcim, 2000

Colony	Number of Jewish-German Refugees Willing to Accept
Barbados	None
British Guiana	None
British Honduras	Possible opening for one veterinary surgeon
Ceylon	None
Cyprus	No prospects, except a few butchers with capital above £500
Fiji	Openings only for photographers, opticians and oculists with substantial capital
Hong Kong	None
Jamaica	No possibilities
Malaya	No possibilities
Mauritius	No possibilities
Nyasaland	Few, if any
Rhodesia	Five hundred families on a subsistence basis, with pre-arranged finance
Trinidad	Possible openings for two refugees, but note: the Chamber of Commerce is strongly opposed to the encouragement of Jewish refugees in the country
Zanzibar	None – there might be an opening for a German-Jewish dentist later, but at the present time the atmosphere is not favourable

Memorandum of Commonwealth Instructions for the UK Delegation to the Evian Conference on Emigration from Germany, 6 July 1938

'The whole world is a very narrow bridge: the main thing is not be afraid'

Rabbi Nachman of Breslov

Coming onto the platform at the top of the aeroplane steps, the biting wind reminded Isaac Fabian that this was not a holiday trip. He had, as Bekka had predicted – not so much predicted, in fact, as promised, in order to stop him grumbling about exhaustion during the 6 a.m. check-in at Gatwick – fallen asleep during the flight, and found himself dreaming about a trip to St Lucia that he and Lulu had taken in 1979, the last holiday they had before she became ill. With hindsight, Isaac often thought he perhaps had, at the time, some mystical intimation of the cancer lying as yet unborn in her womb, because he had really splashed out on that holiday, paying a seventy-five-pound supplement to fly business class, and choosing a four- rather than a three-star hotel, with an en-suite bathroom and a balcony, from which, with some craning of the neck, they could see the sea. Oddly, the dream had not distorted, or rewritten the memory of the holiday especially. Rather, it had focused on a tiny part of it, playing and replaying onto the screen of his sleeping mind the film of their arrival at the tiny international airport: the palms, the glittering blue, her hand squeezing his hard as they landed, perhaps from fear but also from hope, the hope that for these two weeks at least, they might be happy.

And so it was that, even though he knew – from his daughter's grey hair, cut in that cropped way that didn't suit her; from the liver-spots on the backs of his hands, no longer excusable as freckles; from his filmy, cataract-fogged vision; from the tiny pains in his feet, his bowels, his joints, his lower back, and in places where pain should not even be possible (the corners of his eyes, the base of his Adam's apple); even from the fact of confusion itself, from the fact that it was taking him so long to realise when it was and where he was – that he was old, much older than he had been in 1979, and so could not possibly be in St Lucia, somehow, when he stepped off the plane, he was still expecting that sweet shock of holiday, that moment when you move from the cold, compressed air of the flight chamber to the thick, soft wall of heat coming up from Caribbean or Mediterranean tarmac, a moment which always carries with it a whiff of wonder, of unbelief that you have indeed travelled from one climate to another. He stood there, on top of the aeroplane steps, and let the chill eastern wind blow through the sleeves of his dark brown Marks & Spencer suit – making him look, from a distance, like some imagined flag of old age, violently flapping – and waken him to the reality: it was 2000, he was eighty-six, a widower, and he had come, on this freezing February day, with his ageing daughter, to Kraków, in Poland, for a day-trip to Auschwitz.

'Are you all right, Dad?' said Bekka, straightening up, with some difficulty, as she emerged through the plane's door.

Through the thick lenses of his tortoiseshell glasses, Isaac saw her face rise to meet his, and, for the millionth time since middle age, marvelled with internal horror at how much the human face ages outdoors. Even the strip light of the aeroplane, which had thrown its harsh, fluorescent rays on her as if trying to drag her skin down with them, could not compare with the visual impact on his sixty-one-year-old daughter's face of this white-grey Polish sky, revealing it to be virtually agricultural, dug through with troughs and pits and raised mounds and exposed roots. He looked at the cracked earth of his daughter's face, and wondered what in God's name this light must make *him* look like. 'I'm fine, Bekka. Fuss *nicht*.'

Bekka handed him his briefcase, and his walking stick, which she had retrieved from the overhead locker, knowing he would forget it, and raised her eyes to heaven. Her solicitousness towards her father was always rewarded with this, these days, some half-German, half-English put-down. His language seemed to be regressing, she thought, as he approached the deeper recesses of age, more and more German coming back, like the return of something repressed, into his vocabulary.

They walked down the steps together. Despite his irritable insistence on being fine, he automatically accepted her arm on his, to provide an equivalent steadying on his left side to the stick on his right. The thrashing of his suit eased to a flutter as they descended, and Bekka felt her heart tweak at the sight: they had been told by the organisers of the trip – a Holocaust educational body, based in London – that warm, robust clothing was best, and therefore she had suggested various big jumpers and weatherproofs, but her father had been firm that, for Auschwitz, a certain formality must be observed. His only other suit, a black one, they had agreed was too funereal – an odd decision, perhaps, as they were dressing to visit the world's most funereal place, the site of the largest cremation in history – but still it seemed wrong, somehow, so obviously to call attention to the dead: at once too obvious and too inadequate. Then, once he had decided on the brown Marks & Spencer, he stubbornly refused to wear a coat over it, insisting, as he always did, that the point of wearing a suit was lost if you covered it with a big overcoat. She was pleased, at least, as she zipped up her own navy fleece, that he had taken her advice to wear thermal underwear beneath it. Spooning him into the tight, white long-johns and vest this morning, she had been amazed that, even though the flesh on his bones was now very thin, it was also slack enough to ruck up at the cuffs, as if it was another layer of material he was untidily wearing underneath.

The next aeroplane came in to land as they approached the undersized terminal building, and Isaac's eyes followed its path, causing a new bubble of pain to pop in the crick of his neck. He watched the wheels descend painfully from the body, like the crooked legs of a pterodactyl, and wondered when he had lost his phobia about flying. Originally, it had been a phobia about all travelling, or at least all travelling across water, which had set in soon after he had been lifted from the ice-cold waves of the Irish Sea. That itself he remembered only in fragments: he remembered sleeping, with many others, on the wooden floor of a large room that tipped diagonally with the movement of the ship – a ballroom, he thought, but maybe he had got that confused with somewhere else; he remembered being woken with a large crash, and a chandelier dropping ten feet away, smashing in sparkles like a beautiful bomb; all other lights going out; and then, mass panic spreading across the ship like volcanic lava. From there to the point of his rescue was muffled in his memory. He knew that the British had not provided enough lifeboats for all the internees, and the first six had gone overboard immediately, filled with soldiers, but he was not sure he knew it from his own experience or from hearing about it afterwards, like when your own memory gets mixed up with photographs. He did remember a fall through the air, clinging on to a makeshift raft, down past the vast, upturning hull of the *Apollo Rising*; and he remembered the raft splitting in two on hitting the sea – who knew that water could be so hard, that it could destroy wood on impact? Lastly, he had a faint, concealed – as if his mind had bricked it up – memory – no, not a memory, not a *pictorial* recollection, but rather a reverberation of a feeling, a sensation-trace – of intense cold, which would sometimes return, enough to make him shiver, when he was confronted with the smell of the sea or of smoke or of spilt oil. Then blank. His next clear memory was of lining up, in some hastily requisitioned warehouse on the eastern Irish coast, to receive a cup of tepid tea; and being told, as he drank it, that as soon as they were judged to have recovered, the British were going to put the surviving internees back on another boat to the colonies.

The travel phobia had worked in his favour, initially, since when he was assigned a place on HMS *Aurora* two weeks after his return to Douglas, his reaction was so violent – his body grew a hundred sores, and he had the first inkling of the psoriasis that was to trouble him on and off for the rest of his life – that he was rushed straight to the camp infirmary, where he remained until the day after the boat sailed. At which point his skin miraculously healed, he was discharged, and at the same time informed that a date had been set for his release from internment. It turned out that Lulu, rather than wallowing in despair following the Douglas Lean debacle, had gone to King's College and found Jimmy Bailey, who was more than prepared, give or take the odd spelling mistake and grammatical error, to write the third testimonial on Isaac's behalf. When Lulu wrote to tell him of this, Isaac felt ashamed, realising that, for all his abstract faith in the proletariat, a certain submerged snobbery had blocked him from thinking of Jimmy earlier.

After that initial, unexpected silver lining, however, the travel phobia caused nothing but trouble. Even the trip back to the mainland from the Isle of Man, no more than a two-hour sea passage, filled him with the most acute dread: waiting for the ferry on the jetty at Douglas, he vomited into the sea with more noise and fury than most men would have aboard a boat pitching and tossing on waves black with storm.

Of course, they had very little money after the war, until the reparations started coming through in the mid-sixties, so holidays abroad were not really an option anyway; but, for years, even the sight of a boat or an aeroplane was enough to strike fear into his soul. When Lulu returned to Germany in 1947 for a month, paid for by her parents, he pleaded that it was too soon, that the scars still needed time to heal, but in reality he was just terrified of the flight.

And then, round about 1967 or 1968, after he had banked the first of the reparations cheques, and a small amount of cash had started to come in from the publishing house – ironically, given the times, just as he started to move away from underground and political writing and towards fiction – he was walking past a travel agent's in Swiss Cottage, on his way to the Cosmo restaurant, when he saw an advert for a package holiday to New York. Decades of the phobia had trained his brain to ignore the windows of travel agencies, and so he was surprised at himself for stopping and looking in; and then more surprised to find himself gazing for a long while into the blue and steel of the poster, until he remembered something. *They were supposed to have gone there.* When they arrived in England, he and Lulu were intending to travel on to America. In fact – and he saw in his mind the bold print on the brown card – it was a condition stamped onto their entry visas. It was peculiar: the memory appeared in his mind with the *ping!* of a small piece of forgetfulness recovered, not with a momentous crash, more suitable perhaps to the realisation that, had war not broken out and prevented their onward journey, his whole life would have been different.

And so he went in and bought them two tickets; he considered buying one for Bekka as well, but since she had come back from university, her attitude to her parents seemed to have cooled rather, and he felt a bit of a foolish old father – not for the last time – for imagining she would still want to go on holiday with them. They were not, of course, one-way tickets: he did not present them later to his wife, back at their tiny flat off the Finchley Road, as a plan to emigrate, a quarter-century too late. It was only a two-week package, £120 with accommodation included – while at the travel agent's, he had, in a mad moment, heady with triumph over his own fear, asked how much it would cost to get there by boat, but it was much more expensive and would have taken far longer out of their lives – but still, there was a sense that here in their lives was a moment. Lulu cried – tears that were at least nearly those of joy – and, as he held her shaking form, Isaac knew, hazily, that she was crying because this, at last, was their little liberation; that, until he had come through the door with these tickets, they were still, to some extent, refugees, because the primary condition of the refugee is that he is not in control of his own movement across the world.

'Was the flight OK for you?' asked Bekka. They were in the queue for passport control. Isaac had just felt his heart – an organ which he imagined as crusted-over inside his chest – sag, as he fumbled within his jacket pocket in search of his passport: it wasn't there, but then he remembered Bekka had taken all the tickets and passports, and yes, as he turned to face her, there it was in her hand, her hand with its sharp metacarpi poking through the thin skin like the ribs of a tiny dead bird. As he took it, he could not help but feel a momentary thrill in his possession of the slim red book, with its lion and unicorn dancing around the *Honi Soit qui Mal y Pense* crown. He had been granted British citizenship in 1949, but a part of him could still hardly believe it, that he was British, a nation he had virtually never thought about when he was growing up, his idealistic gaze turned as it was almost entirely towards the East. He remembered having a vague sense that they were a race of people who rarely washed, whose intelligence level was generally low, and who were incorrectly smug about the superiority of their sense of humour. Time had taught him that the first two assumptions were wrong, but also that there was a sweet stability about the country, a reasonableness and humanity that made him, in his secret self, proud to be British; which did not prevent him from insisting,

368

to whoever might be prepared to listen, that Shakespeare was actually better once translated into German.

'I preferred the hardback version,' he said.

'Of what?'

'The passport,' he said. 'It was less easy to lose.' And felt more *offensichtlich* – palpable – in the hand, he thought. More real; more difficult for anyone to take away.

'Dad, is your hearing aid on?'

'*Was?*' It wasn't, he had turned it off during the flight: the constant hum of the engine combined with a hundred conversations turned aeroplane sound into white noise in his ear.

'I asked you how the flight was for you.'

'*Ja*. I heard you. Yes, it was fine.'

The couple in front, young and married, went forward together to present their passports to the official in the booth; the husband was sent back behind the white waiting line. His wife laughingly waved at him as she went through, pretending to run away.

'Only you seemed frightened when we landed.'

'I did?'

The passport official, a mustachioed man in a dark green uniform, nodded for Isaac to come forward. He opened his passport at his photograph. It had been taken about six years ago. Half a dozen years younger than now, he thought, and yet he could hardly recognise this ancient, with his few thin wisps of white hair and enormous, hanging jowls.

'Yes,' continued Bekka, raising her voice so that he could hear as he moved away. 'You reached for my hand as we came down. And squeezed it hard.'

Isaac felt himself flush with embarrassed heat, and a stab of hatred for Bekka went through his chest: why couldn't she have waited until they were past passport control, so she would not have had to shout? It was so typical of her, she never understood when it was appropriate to be silent. None the less, it made him wonder. Had he held her hand? He had been dreaming that Lulu had taken his, but perhaps the dream had just merged with the reality, as they seemed to increasingly these days. Well, she might be right. He knew he did still feel anxious on aeroplanes when they took off and landed, but no longer because of his phobia; simply because he did not want to die. He looked once more at his picture and thought: I am so old, and yet still I don't want to die.

He handed over his passport, and saw the official's eyes go down and then up again to check his face. Isaac tried to compose his features into neutral – his old features, he could feel every movement of every line – but it was hard, because a part of him felt instantly, autonomically, scared. Old habits, he thought.

The day-trip to Auschwitz had been Bekka's idea. She was becoming, in her old age – *her* old age! – more and more Jewish, Isaac thought. It was as if, since Lulu had died, the Christian part of her had started to decay; or maybe it was just that she was doing that thing that people do of becoming more religious as they grow closer to death, and, for some reason, she had focused all that on her Jewish half. This hedging of life's bets had not overtaken Isaac. Although he had stopped paying membership fees to the Communist Party in 1975, he still believed that religion was indeed the opiate of the people, that if triangles ruled the world they would believe in a three-sided God and so on. Also, emotionally, he felt that it would constitute an obscure betrayal of his dead wife to, at this late stage, re-embrace Judaism – it was only by renouncing his father's religion that he had been able to marry Lulu, and somehow, by continuing to renounce it, he preserved a fragment of their marriage. This was important to Isaac, who had betrayed his wife once, and had vowed – however irreligiously – never to do so again.

Outside the terminal, they and other members of the group going to Auschwitz were directed towards two large coaches, throbbing as if shivering with the cold. It turned out that most of the people on this particular trip were teachers from the Kent area: one of the representatives of the Holocaust educational body, a young woman with her hair tied back in a severe bun, explained to Bekka that their trips tended now to be organised through education authorities, and that therefore most visitors to the museum – that was what she called it – were no longer Jews in search of their lost roots, but rather entire staff-rooms sent out to research the

Holocaust section of their curriculum. This made Isaac feel disgruntled as he walked arthritically down the coach aisle: passing a series of bright red British faces, he felt more than ever that this excursion was exactly what it was, a day-trip; something you associate, especially once you're sitting in a coach full of people from Kent, with going to Margate or Clacton, not Auschwitz. As he settled carefully into the scratchy seat, he wondered briefly whether there would be a stop for ice-creams and fizzy drinks.

'Don't be such a curmudgeon, Dad,' said Bekka, settling herself next to him.

'A what?'

'A grumpy, bad-tempered old man.'

'I have not said a thing!'

'It's written all over your face,' she said, smiling, the lines on the edges of her face meeting, circling it in age.

She had lost weight as she'd grown older. Isaac could never understand why women did that, especially Bekka – such a feminist, but still frightened of fat.

'That's just what I look like now,' he replied. 'You'll see. Once you get past seventy-five, your face looks always cross. You can't help it. Besides, at my age, what's not to be grumpy about?'

The coach driver, a fat man in a flat cap, with an extremely pre-glasnost air about him, shut the door with a hydraulic hiss, and the coach began to move off, following its lumbering partner out of the terminal.

'Do you want me to put that up top?' asked Bekka, pointing to Isaac's briefcase. It was a brown schoolboy's thing, with the leather fraying at every buckle, and she had no idea what old man's eccentricity had led to him bringing it; she had bought him a perfectly good overnight bag for his eighty-fifth birthday but never seen him use it.

'No, thank you.'

'You sure? It's quite a long journey. Over an hour.'

'You already told me that, in the airport. When you asked me if I needed to go to the toilet. Really, Bekka, I know I am old, but you don't have to make me feel like *I'm* the child.'

She looked away, hurt, and Isaac instantly knew that though he had not meant to draw attention to the fact that Rebekka did not have children, she had taken it that way.

'Did you want to stop in duty free?' she asked.

'Not especially. I don't think I want to carry a case of brandy around Auschwitz.'

'You could leave it on the bus.'

Isaac looked out of the window. She had paid for them to spend the previous night at the Gatwick Hilton, to avoid having to catch a train to London from Cambridge at some unearthly time in the morning, but her budget for the whole trip could not go above five hundred pounds, which had led to the peculiar spectacle of aged father and daughter – assumed by the hotel reception, of course, due to the licence that our culture awards old men, to be aged husband and wife – bedding down in the one room, thankfully containing twin beds. It was the first time that he had, even in the literal sense, slept with a woman for fifteen years. Prior to undressing she had turned out the light, but he still saw her white night-dress ride up as she climbed awkwardly into bed, exposing her matchstick-thin thighs. It had put through him the most confusing welter of feelings: ashamed, for looking at all; furious, that he would never again see or touch a naked woman in the flesh, even flesh as pitted as this; pity, for her, and the ruin of her body, a fact which he knew made her continuing loneliness as inevitable as his own. And underneath all that, he felt pierced to his core with sadness that he had missed nearly a year of this skin when it was new and it would not have been perverse to feel it resting against his own, a year of having his baby child brought into their bed by Lulu in the early morning because of something called internment.

'I might buy a few things on the way back,' said Bekka, even though her father was continuing to look out of the window. 'I saw some nice-looking bottles of red as we went through. I thought I might buy some to lay down for a few years.'

Isaac nodded, without looking back at her, absorbing the blow, this reference to the immediate future. Everywhere he went, every day, there were a hundred moments like this, casual allusions, plans, predictions, estimates, which cut him to the quick. The passing of the millennium had only made it worse, with its sense of an end of an era, self-evidently his. He wondered if, unconsciously, she had meant it to hurt, in revenge for his remark about not being the child; if she knew how hard it was for him to accept that, even if the laying-down period was relatively short, he was unlikely to be around to feel the taste of that well-aged wine on his tongue.

The coach heaved itself out of the airport grounds, and onto an endless wasteland of roadworks, towards the motorway leading west. Isaac thought how strange it was that, most of his life, he had been a communist and yet he had never been to a communist country; and now here he was, and it wasn't communist any more. You wouldn't know it, though, from this abrasively industrial landscape, easily mistakable as some infinitely ongoing Stalinist project, some five-hundred-year plan. But on the aeroplane, he had glanced at Bekka's *Guide to Kraków* – the buying of which had created in him a spasm of irritation, redolent as it was of her always doomed hopefulness, because they both knew there would be no time to go into the city – and what had caught his eye in the glossy colour photographs of the Old Square was not the sixteenth-century Cloth Hall that runs down its centre, nor the Gothic thirteenth-century Town Hall tower that rises above it, but the shops occupying the ground floors of all the grand buildings – Diesel, Starbucks, the Body Shop, French Connection, Virgin Records, Robot, Toni & Guy, Sunglass Hut. Isaac could not tell whether the cold stab of alienation he felt looking at these names emblazoned all over the page was because it reinforced for him how absolute was the conquest of capitalism, or because he knew he would never in this life go into any of them.

Approaching the slip road for the motorway, Isaac saw a signpost marked 'Oświęcim', which the driver followed. He thought how valuable linguistic difference was; how useful that it did not say 'Auschwitz', that whatever happened in the rest of history, a sign pointing the way to Auschwitz is a sign pointing to a road that drivers would always hesitate to take. He turned up the volume on his hearing aid slightly; it gave off a small sigh of feedback, as ever, before letting in sound.

'. . . well, I don't envy you in religious studies,' he heard a woman in the seats in front of them say. 'Isn't it the last thing kids today are interested in?'

'Yes, absolutely,' replied a tremulous male voice. '*But*, I did get them quite interested yesterday. This new theory I put to them, to explain the divinity of Jesus . . .'

'Oh yes?'

'Yes. Very modern. Uses the language of psychoanalysis to try to explain the concept of Jesus as God and man, as Word made Flesh.'

'Right . . .' Isaac could hear a sliver of boredom in the woman's voice.

'What you have to imagine – this is what I said – obviously it's all nicked, a sermon from our local trendy vicar – is that the conscious part of Jesus's mind was human. That was like any man's. But the unconscious was divine. Jesus's unconscious was, as it were, made up of pure Holy Spirit.'

A tapping sound pulled his attention away; he looked round to see Bekka typing on her laptop computer.

'What are you doing?'

She continued to look at the screen. 'I'm just checking the information I downloaded about the camp.'

Isaac grunted his acknowledgement of this, but felt again somehow reprimanded, knowing that she knew he didn't understand anything about computers or the Internet. It was admirable in Bekka that, at sixty-one, she did, but she had always been fairly state of the art with gadgets and devices; it was part of her feminism, a refusal to accept that women are less capable with technology. It was she who had found the websites which claimed to document the names of concentration-camp inmates. She had found the name Fabian in a number of these – it was a fairly common German-Jewish surname – but, none the less, had become convinced that it was Auschwitz where her grandfather, Isaac's father, was murdered, because it was only in the Auschwitz section that her most reliable website, www.jewishgen.com had thrown up an 'I' initial to go along with the family name. When she had shown Isaac, it had shocked him at first, not because it made his father's death more real, or confirmed the suspicion of how his life had ended, but because for a second his old brain had read it as his own name, and he felt a weird trill of fear, as if reading of his own death, before in the next second the reality of how it very easily *could* have been his own name hit him as hard as it had ever done.

The date of entry to the camp was recorded – 10.11.41 – and the date of death – 12.02.42. Isaac had begun to make the calculation of time in his head, but he was never good at mental arithmetic, even when his brain felt, as it once did, freshly minted, teeming with thought. Although, perhaps it wasn't simply the mental effort, but also the psychological effort of imagining that time – the smallness of it at once appalling and at the same time blessed, because the best thing he could hope for his poor, lost father once behind those gates was an early death. Still staring at those numbers next to 'I. Fabian' on the backlit screen, he heard Bekka saying that if it was true that Isidor had died in Auschwitz, then it was more than likely, given the Nazis' tendency only to split up families at the point of selection for the gas chambers, that his mother and four sisters had been killed there, too. Next thing he knew, she was saying they must go, and Isaac had been caught between all the reasons to say no – he was too old to fly to Poland; it would be too depressing; the website information was too inconclusive – and the strongest pull not only to say yes, but to pack a bag and catch a plane immediately. He had still been in that quandary two days later, when Bekka called and said she had been in touch with an organisation in London and they were going together on a day-trip. The certainty of women, he thought, without being able to remember when he had thought it before.

'I'm not sure it is healthy for you to spend so much time looking at such things,' he said, pointing at her laptop.

'Computer screens?'

'No. Although yes: I read somewhere in the paper that was bad, too. But I meant . . . those – what do you call them? Web-places?'

'Sites. Websites,' she replied, making a point of stressing the 'W' to oppose his increasing tendency to pronounce the letter as a 'V'.

'*Ja*. Websites about the Holocaust. It's not good for your head.'

'You're right. But we've had this discussion already, Dad.'

Had they? A surge of panic went through him, as always when anyone said anything like this, at the thought that he must have Alzheimer's.

'I'm not reading them to find out about the Holocaust. I just want to find out about our family.'

Isaac shrugged. 'Since when such a big interest?'

Bekka looked away from the screen. He saw her top teeth bite gently into her lower lip in thought, an action which since her childhood had always made his soul flood towards her. 'I don't know. Just gradually, as I've got older. Although when I was about nineteen, I remember asking Mum . . . I was going to ask you but I thought it might upset you . . . asking her why we had so few relatives – so few aunts and uncles and cousins.'

'You had some on her side.'

'Well, so you told me, but we never saw them, did we? Anyway, she said . . .' she smiled mournfully as the memory came to her, 'she said: "You'll have to ask Mr Hitler about that." And that was all she said, and I didn't really ask her anything else. But I suppose I must have been interested even then.' Her smile became lighter. 'I always remembered that, because when *Dad's Army* started they had that song – "Who Do You Think You Are Kidding, Mr Hitler?" – and it always reminded me of her saying that. You remember *Dad's Army*, don't you?'

'Of course.' *My God*, she *thought he had Alzheimer's now: she was checking!* It was a funny show, he remembered, although he'd always found it difficult to laugh at the opening credits, with their arrows jutting frantically at the northern coast of France.

Bekka tapped a few more keys, and then shut down the laptop. 'You know, Dad, there's lots of these types of trips you can do now. Especially since the Wall came down. Companies specialise in helping people to trace their families . . .' She waited for a response from Isaac, but none came. 'You can go everywhere now. Lithuania, Estonia . . . On the Net I found one tour group that runs a trip to Kaliningrad.'

Isaac ran a hand across his face. He had shaved this morning, before dawn, out of the same impulse for propriety that had made him wear a suit, but already he could feel a gritty strip of white stubble on his chin. It amazed him that anything could still grow out of his body, out of his grey, barren skin. 'Bekka,' he said, trying to sound resigned rather than annoyed, 'I'm too old to be doing so

376

much travelling. And besides, what would I want to go to Kaliningrad for? Have you seen photographs of what it looks like now?' Pictures swam into his mind from a book Lulu had bought him for his sixty-second birthday: his university town, his Cambridge, covered over with concrete – a dumped city, dusted with tower-blocks and tenements, the arse-end of the old Soviet Union. 'It is good the Russians changed the name because Königsberg – truly, it does not exist any more. It was destroyed, razed to the ground – first by the British then by the Red Army.' So many name changes: Kaiser Wilhelm Platz had been changed to Adolf Hitler Platz and then to Lenin Platz; Königstrasse to Hermann Goering Strasse to Frunze Street, after the Red Army general, Mikhail Frunze. Was there anywhere else in the world whose history was so burnt into its streets? 'Do you know it used to have seven bridges?'

'Yes. Of course. You've told me many times.'

Have I? 'Yes, well. Now, only two of the seven survive! Two!'

'That would make it difficult to retrace the steps of Opa's walk, I admit . . .'

Isaac stared at her. 'I told you about that, as well?'

Bekka's smile grew fond. 'Yes, Dad. When I was a little girl. I loved to hear about it. I've never told you this, but always after that – still now even – when I walk across a bridge, I try to think about something bad I've done.'

'Bad?'

'Well, not properly bad. Just selfish, or bad-tempered, or whatever . . .' She looked away, her teeth returning to her lower lip in embarrassment at this little confession.

'And . . . ?'

'Well, I do what Opa would have done. I think about the bad bit of behaviour and then, in my mind, I say sorry about it, and then I think of the badness flowing out of me and into the water underneath the bridge.'

Isaac felt wonderment well up in him on hearing this. An image of his father rose in his mind, still walking, crossing water, smiling as sin fell from him – but before he could let it loose, a crackly voice said: 'Ladies and gentlemen!' They both looked up to see a young, fresh-faced woman in a puffy yellow anorak, standing near the front of the coach, holding a microphone. 'Welcome to Poland. We know you are here for today just in order to go to the Holocaust Memorial Museum at Oświęcim, but we hope that one day you will come back to see some more of the country. There is more to Poland than just concentration camps!' She said this with a beaming smile. Isaac and Bekka looked at each other, and, for the first time since they'd set out this morning, laughed, together. 'You will have noticed on the side of our coach the white eagle, the symbol of our country . . .' continued the young woman.

Isaac drew his briefcase further up his sunken body, towards his chest, as if it were a blanket, and let the litany of facts and figures about the exemplary history of Poland lull him to sleep.

He was awoken, three-quarters of an hour later, by a rustling sound and an unidentifiable smell in his nostrils. Blinking sleep out of his eyes, he saw that Bekka had taken out her Tupperware box and was unravelling the foil off her packed lunch. He checked his watch: ten-past ten. 'It's a bit early for that, isn't it?' he said, although his own stomach was rumbling. They had been too early for the full breakfast at the Gatwick Hilton, so she had ordered a continental, without realising that croissants were a virtual impossibility for him, the flakes invariably clogging his dentures.

She put a leaf of something green in her mouth, and dusted her fingers. 'No, Dad. While you were asleep the lady from the Holocaust educational trust got up and said that we should have something to eat now, because there won't be a proper break for lunch. She said there might be a little time between Auschwitz One and Birkenau, but it might be best to have something now.'

Isaac frowned: he found himself wanting to say how it was surprising that, by now, there wasn't a café there.

'I got yours out, too,' she said, holding forward another box. She removed the lid before handing it to him, knowing it would be too much for his arthritic fingers. He looked down: some off-white circles, two pickled cucumbers, a banana. 'No bread?' he said.

'No, Dad. I've told you. I'm on a no-wheat, non-dairy diet.'

'*I'm* not . . .'

'Yes, well. I didn't have any bread in when I made the lunches. I'm *sorry*.'

Isaac placed the box on top of his briefcase, and held up one of the off-white circles. 'What's this?'

'Quorn.'

'*Was?*'

'Quorn. It's a meat substitute. *Dad*. Don't look at me like that. You know I've been a vegetarian for years.'

He nodded, as if he did know, and did his best to appear grateful. Forcing the Quorn's bland non-flesh down – it tasted more dead than anything he'd ever had in his mouth that had actually been killed – he repressed the urge to have a go at her for the way in which she fitted her own stereotype so well. Lulu and Isaac had never had any more children. Their economic circumstances made it impossible in the years following the war, and by the time those circumstances had changed, it was too late. When the emotional waters flowing between him and his wife began to freeze, Isaac had poured much of himself into Bekka, and with hindsight he could see what had happened: his radicalism had mutated in her, his Politics into her politics. What communism had been for him, feminism, and its attendant life-choices, became for her; and in the 1970s, having spent most of the sixties running a long and damaging gauntlet of non-committal men, she had announced herself to be a lesbian. Isaac found it completely impossible to understand how one's sexual orientation could be determined politically, as Bekka's clearly had been, and had viewed this, and all her subsequent attempts at self-determination – whether it be becoming a vegetarian or an extreme Kleinian in her own psychotherapeutic practice – with a jaundiced eye.

The urge left him. He'd always found it difficult not to goad her about her beliefs, but he was improving, discovering, incredibly, that although everything about the body hardens as you age, the same is not entirely true of the self. Last night, on the train out to Gatwick, he had read something in the paper about 'post-feminism', and managed to stop himself asking her in mock-innocence what that meant. In truth, he didn't really know what the phrase signified, but he was aware – just from the

379

pseudo-pornographic pictures of women on the street and on the television – that her battle, like his, had been lost; and that all these other -isms that she attached herself to now were simply an attempt to claim some part of some radical ground somewhere, without which she felt bereft.

He looked out of the window. They had left the motorway, and were travelling at speed through the Polish countryside. There appeared to be no villages; just a series of red-roofed, modern houses backing on to large squares of land. Crossing a small bridge, Isaac noticed a disused railway track, and wondered immediately if it had originally led to the concentration camp. It occurred to him that this could be applied country-wide: that it might not be possible to use the Polish rail system at all without wondering whether these tracks at some point carried cattle-trucks not just to Auschwitz, but also to Sobibor, Belzec, Chelmno, Majdanek and Treblinka.

Then, just as the first real chill, the first real sense of where he was going, settled upon him, the houses grew closer together, and a sign appeared, at the outskirts of the town: Oświęcim. His mind ran through a few attempts to imagine how it might be pronounced; they all sounded very different from Auschwitz. On the left-hand side of the coach, a set of tower-blocks rose with all the grey hugeness of communist architecture. As they ploughed further into the town, it became clear to Isaac that Oświęcim had not undergone the radical capitalist makeover awarded to Kraków, and no doubt most of the other cities in Poland. This did not inspire him. He did not ride through the town, on his concentration-camp coach, energised by the notion that Oświęcim represented some kind of surviving outpost of communism in all its aesthetic masochism. He knew why money had not flooded here: the shadow of Auschwitz–Birkenau had fallen long over the stark industrial hamlet, freezing it economically; the many tourists who arrived here throughout the year came, as they were about to do, for the day, and spent no money anywhere else apart from the camp bookshop.

As if in confirmation of this, the coach stopped at some traffic lights opposite the one hotel Isaac had seen so far. It was an

380

extraordinary building, intense in its ugliness, one enormous breezeblock of concrete mounted on another. Above the highest of the rows of pencil-thin windows which denoted the rooms – How nasty must they be, thought Isaac – had been placed a banner, emblazoned with the legend 'Hotel Glob'. He spoke no Polish – for all he knew, 'Glob' might mean butterfly – but in his mind, the word, at once absurd and dead, was onomatopoeic of not just the hotel but the entire town.

The coach made its way through the dank centre and out towards the far end of the town. The young Polish woman in the yellow anorak was again holding her microphone, and now telling the travellers specifically about 'The Museum': about how it was on the curriculum for Polish schoolchildren to visit it; about how, since democracy had come to Poland, the emphasis in the guided tours was on how ethnic minorities, especially Jews, had been murdered there, whereas previously the communists had insisted that it be described as a place of solely Polish tragedy; about how they were going to split up into ten different groups; about how there was only a toilet at the entrance gate, so to go as soon as the coach stopped; about how it was almost a mile from Auschwitz 1 to Birkenau, so they would be coming back to the coach if people wanted to leave their things. And she told them to watch out, on that mile journey, for the disused warehouse which the German chemical manufacturers I. G. Farben had used during the war as a factory employing slave labour from the concentration camp. Isaac had read about I. G. Farben: as well as employing slave labour, one of their subsidiary companies made Zyklon B. He felt a strange sensation when she said the name, because it was a nostalgic feeling, but not a pleasant one: he felt the nostalgia of anger. The thought of I. G. Farben, and all its multinational offshoots still functioning – Bosch, Agfa, Bayer, Hoechst – made his communist blood, which so long ago had stopped simmering, boil.

The coach made a right turn, and he was surprised to feel it slow down to park; still more surprised when it stopped and everyone started getting off. He looked out, and could hardly believe that this mundane, municipal-looking space was the entrance to the killing fields. 'We are here?'

'Yes, Dad,' said Bekka, taking the still-open Tupperware box from his lap.

'Thank you for lunch,' he said, trying his best; trying his very best.

She looked at him, searching for traces of sarcasm. On seeing none, she smiled, revealing her most precious prize, her teeth – still a full set, and relatively unyellowed – and said: 'My pleasure, Dad. At least it was kosher. I felt that was appropriate.' She got up, to look for his stick in the luggage rack.

Perhaps, Isaac thought, *but I shouldn't think anyone here ever insisted on a no-wheat, non-dairy diet*. Then he realised from his daughter's furious expression that he had said it out loud, something which was happening more and more these days.

Outside, in the car park, it seemed to be colder than when they'd boarded the bus; even Isaac, for all the concrete in which his ways were set, wished he had brought an overcoat. The whole idea of this trip suddenly seemed designed only to create for him the maximum psychological and physical discomfort. He looked out to the road and for a second wondered about making a run – or rather, a very slow walk – for it, but saw only a sign for the local youth hostel, one of whose graphics was a cartoon of a man having a shower. It made him suppress, guiltily, a grim smile, but at the same time settled his nerves; it was one of his defences, and a fair one at that, the blackly comic response. Thank you God, he thought, for making it quite such an ice-cold day, which was how latterly he had begun to talk to the God in which he did not believe. Not in prayer – not the murmur or song of constant praise, intermingled with some plea, some petition – but always in anger: when the petty pains of his world and body grew too much, he would, in his mind, speak to the Lord, thanking Him for making his life just that bit more difficult than it already was. It *was* a prayer, in fact, but a sarcastic one.

They were assigned to Group 7; this meant a new guide, an older Polish woman who held the number 7 up on a small placard, and who, on introducing herself, said that she had worked as a guide at the museum for over twenty years, which seemed to Isaac an incredibly long time to be relaying the kind of information she must have to every day without having a nervous breakdown. She reiterated to the group that there were no toilets inside the camp, and so everyone who wanted to go should go now. Bekka looked at Isaac expectantly.

'*Was?*' he asked.

'Dad. You must go. You know what your bladder's like. We'll just get in and you'll want to go straight away.'

He glanced over to the line of tour-party members filing towards the administration building which housed the bookshop and the ticket office. Had that been built by Nazis, too? he wondered. They were pounding, easily, with untroubled legs, down some stairs towards the toilets, and Isaac made one of the many lesser-of-two-evils calculations regarding his comfort that he made every day, every five minutes; he did not, at present, need to go to the toilet, and even though he knew Bekka was right about him needing to go *soon*, he also had to consider that it was going to be a day of solid standing up and walking, and to begin that by going up and down a set of stairs was unconscionable. 'I am fine. Really. I have not drunk much today, so I think it will be OK.' His eyes went plaintive. 'I cannot force it.'

She made a face, twisting down the edges of her mouth, making Isaac's skin tingle; he hated that expression as much as he loved the one where she put her teeth on her lower lip. 'Well, it's up to you. But I'm not coming all the way back out here with you when you need to go, I warn you now.'

Isaac nodded, not wishing to reiterate the fact that he was not a child.

'I'm going to go, so I'll see you back out here. Don't wander off.'

He watched her go, the walk contradictory from the back, her frame skeletal but her movement bulky; perhaps it was just that she was annoyed, generating a heaviness in her step. Disregarding her request, he moved away almost instantly, curious to see what there was to see. He walked along a path by the side of the building, rounded a corner away from the main bulk of tourists, and there it was, only about fifty yards away, visible to his ageing eyes with a squint: the proper entrance, to Auschwitz 1, the gate above which, carved in iron, hung '*Arbeit Macht Frei*'. Isaac felt a weird thrill, the same thrill he had felt twenty years before on visiting the Leaning Tower of Pisa: the simple thrill of seeing a famous monument, of seeing that history lives, even history off the leash like this. It made him feel guilty again, because it was a sort of pleasure, and he felt he should be feeling only horror.

There was a bench by the side of the path. Gingerly, hearing in his inner ear the sandy crunch of his bones, he sat down and wondered why this particular Nazi lie, 'work liberates', should continue to be accepted by the world. Most people still spent the greater part of their adult lives in jobs that, to a greater or lesser extent, they hated, under the illusion that somehow this work will lead to some greater freedom for them in the future. The Red Army servicemen who passed through this gate fifty-five years ago – exactly the people whom Isaac might have believed at one time to be the bearers of a new message – had liberated humanity from the camp but not from the slogan.

The first group from his trip passed by, the buzz of chat that had been apparent on the coach gone in the face of mass trepidation as they approached the gate. He sighed, knowing that Bekka would be back from the toilet soon, having meticulously handed over some sisterly change to the Polish crone who would undoubtedly be sitting outside the cubicle area, and Group 7 would be wanting to move off. She would be angry again with him, but it could not be helped: there was something he had to do. Auschwitz could wait: the black-and-white photographs of children with their hands up, of rabbis having their locks cut at gunpoint, of women hurrying with their shawls; the urn in front of which you would have to stand for two years if you were to give a minute's remembrance for every prisoner who was killed; the rooms full of hair and shoes and suitcases, like art installations except chock-full rather than empty of meaning; the tracks of Birkenau; the sheds where they kept the stolen coats and furs and perfumes and leathers, called, so heartbreakingly, so hopeful of the new, *Canada*. It could all wait. He picked his briefcase up off the gravel, and placed it on his lap. His fingers flapped at the buckles, with some pain; eventually, it opened, and from its dusty interior he drew out an A4 sepia envelope, marked with the stamp of Berman, Goddard

& Whitney, the legal firm responsible for the division of the estate of June Murray.

He had thought of her many times, of course, in sixty years; although he had never seen her again, and wondered how she would have known that he was still alive – even how she knew that he had not drowned in the Irish Sea in 1941. But, he supposed, lawyers have a way of discovering things: perhaps she told them that if he was alive to get it to him; if not, to destroy it.

He may never have seen her again, but she had always been with him. Not really in the romantic sense – it wasn't that he held his love for June inside his breast for fifty years like a secret and constantly burning flame – but in terms of the impact on his marriage. It was never entirely clear to their friends what happened to Isaac and Lulu as the years went on; it was never entirely clear to Isaac and Lulu either, although he at least had some idea. He had never (so many 'nevers', he noticed, hung now around his thoughts) told Lulu about June, but still there had been a shift, an accommodation, in their relationship, once he returned to Cambridge from the Isle of Man; it was as if they had moved slightly out of each other's focus. He had been surprised that he had not told her, in fact, as he had always thought of himself as compulsively honest, unable to restrain, in the presence of those closest to him, his deep confessional drive. But he had come back from his drenching in the Irish Sea baptised, as it were, into a different way of being. Something was washed away in those freezing waves, and it would be difficult to find a better word for what that was than innocence: the same innocence that Lulu had found it difficult to explain to Douglas Lean over vegetable pie and lamb casserole at Joshua Taylor's. He had returned to their one room at Mrs Fricker's, and even in the midst of the tears and the joy and the embracing and the holding up to his face of Bekka, he could feel within himself a stone block of pragmatism, which he would hold on to in order to preserve this marriage, whatever the consequences.

These were the consequences. Lulu knew that something had changed in Isaac, and even though she did not know why that was, she felt obscurely cheated, having been through so much and waited so long for him, and here he was: changed. It wasn't so big a change, on the surface, or possibly not even below, but the soul is like the face in that respect – it takes only a tiny rearrangement for the brain of the other to compute that this must be a different person. In her dreams immediately following his return, she found herself often back at the Guildhall, with Rear-Admiral Holloway, arguing that some bureaucratic error must have been made, that due to a mix-up they had released the wrong internee, only for Isaac to come and drag her away just as she was getting to her conclusive proof (what exactly that was would always fade from memory as soon as she awoke). She was upset with herself for these feelings, thinking it was ungenerous of her, that people did change and that was part of the experience of marriage; but, of course, the way marriage works, on the rare occasions that it does, is by making change incremental. In the normal run of events, each partner gradually acclimatises to change in the other, which creates (so the theory goes) acceptance. There was no gradation to Isaac's change; it shocked Lulu, like waking up and discovering that overnight he had grown much older. It made her realise, as well, how much love turns on a sixpence, because here he was, the same face, the same voice, the same mannerisms, the same ideas, and yet this one thing about him, this fraction of his being – this innocence – had gone; and that made all the difference. Love is a micro-system; it does not see the bigger picture.

This lack of love, or rather this change in the weather of their love, did not mean, as our myths demand, that their marriage was a wasteland. We have replaced God in our culture with Love, and the happy marriage is its holy grail, but in fact there is almost no chance of Love, as we are told to believe in it, surviving any lifelong sexual relationship. What survives is compromise, and they both made those. Isaac, especially, could be said to have taken well to the element of unhappiness in their marriage, because he did not replace innocence in himself with cynicism, as might be expected, but rather with that more post-revolutionary virtue, stoicism. As such, a certain expectation of sadness – a certain amount of something that had to be *borne* – was fitting. He was even able to add to this blend of sadness and stoicism a twist of grim humour, particularly in latter years, when the memory of what had happened on the Isle of Man had faded, and with it the need for self-flagellation.

To some extent, their closest years, post-war, were after Lulu had become ill. It is said that the only people who flourished in concentration camps were depressives, because they felt at home there, finally in an environment that fitted with their internal lives, and, in this sense, cancer was their concentration camp. Not that, individually, Isaac and Lulu were depressives, but their marriage was depressed, and what cancer provided was a focus for their unhappiness which was not each other. It let them – especially Isaac – off the hook for their unhappiness. Freed of the oppressive guilt that he had carried around unwittingly for years, he found himself able to care for her, as she grew gradually weaker, with a weightless heart, which he allowed to fill up slowly with the non-toxic sadness of loss. On her deathbed, on the point of their final separation, they seemed to have rediscovered whatever it was that had first brought them together. They kissed, and the connection between them felt total again, as real as the plastic tubes which, to Bekka, standing at the end of the bed, seemed to be running between their faces.

Which is not to say that he had not wondered, and wondered still even now, about June Murray. He had wondered, as all men do, what if? He knew nothing about her: he did not know that she had married, three years after the war, a man who had done cartoons at the Ministry of Information; nor that she had wanted to continue her career, and had talked for a while about getting a job as a foreign correspondent in Berlin for a national newspaper, but the birth of two children soon put paid to that; nor that she had painfully divorced in 1957, after discovering her husband in bed with their nanny; nor that she took the then unusual step of reverting to her maiden name, and spent the rest of her working life on the staff of a global merchant bank, eventually rising to become its chief translator. The one thing he did know about her was that she had just died: two months ago, in Provence. These facts were related in the stark and businesslike letter from Berman, Goddard & Whitney.

His first thought was: so she was alive, for fifteen years, after

387

Lulu had died. It had occurred to him – in truth, even before Lulu died, even in the midst of painstakingly, through morphine injections and bedbaths, retracing his love for his wife – that her death would leave him free to find June. But it had occurred to him in a distant, hypothetical way, the mind throwing up options the way it does, long after the possibility of pursuing those options is closed. He was already an old man, in his late sixties, when Lulu died; June, if alive, would be over seventy. Some fictions would have had him believe that there is nothing unseemly about a man of his age chasing a woman three years older across the world in order to release a love that had been caught in the net of circumstance half a century earlier. Isaac knew that was incorrect. For a start, on the most base level, the gradation effect of marriage may have worked as regards his and Lulu's own ageing – he had somehow managed still to see in her, even when ageing's ravaging effect was accelerated by cancer, the face of the woman he had married – but when he looked around and saw other women of his own age, he still thought, as he had done when Dr Mannstein had shown him the photograph of Irma on the short march up to Derby Castle: how does love get here? The fact that he was himself *there* – or past *there* now – made no difference. He never had any thought of remarrying after Lulu's death, because he could not countenance the idea of living with a woman half his age; and women of his own age looked like men. He knew how it was supposed to work – as he was older, he was supposed to find older women attractive – but this turned out to be nonsense: eyes are the only part of the face that don't age, and neither do the eyes' demands.

He had no wish, therefore, to find June only to be horrified by her; and this was without taking into account the possibility that she may be married, crippled, dead, or horrified by *him*. There were other, less brutal, reasons: a part of him saw it as a further betrayal of Lulu now to pursue June – just as it would be to re-embrace religion – and if he was prepared to renounce the hope of eternal life for his late wife, he was happy to renounce the possibility of five to ten years of sexless companionship with another woman. Another, contradictory, part of him wished to preserve June and his liaison with her as it was lit, golden in his memory – a man in his dotage will guard and tend his erotic adventures like pet doves or pigeons, and Isaac only really had the one.

'*The last will and testament of our client, June Murray,*' the letter, which was addressed to him, said – June: it was an old lady's name now, wasn't it? Like Maureen or Vera – '*who died on 14 December 1999, in Aix-en-Provence, contained a provision that the enclosed document, which has remained sealed in our offices according to her express wishes, be passed on to you. The document is yours to do with as you wish. If, however, for any reason you do not wish to receive this document, the wish of our client was that you return it to these offices for safekeeping.*'

Isaac had known instantly what the enclosed document was. He could remember speaking the words that he knew would be written on it; remember her scribbling them down in frantic sweeps on a notepad; remember the draughty room, the cuts on his arms, the persistent honking of the taxi outside. He would say he could remember it as if it were yesterday, were it not for the fact that yesterday was far harder to recall.

He had put off reading it for two days, and then Bekka had booked the trip to Auschwitz; and he had thought, Well, perhaps it's appropriate if I take it and read it there. Now, he wondered if that had been a mistake – he had enough stuff to deal with today, here, just looking at this gate, not even going inside, without this on top. He was about to put it all back into the briefcase when suddenly the realisation came to him that putting it off – putting *anything* off – was a luxury he could no longer afford. He placed his index finger, perfectly bent by arthritis for the job, into the lip of the envelope and tore sideways, revealing inside four pages frayed and yellowed by the time he no longer had.

```
Q: Could you begin by telling me your name and age?

A: Isaac Fabian. I'm twenty-seven.

Q: And where are you from, originally?

A: Königsberg, in East Prussia.

(There is a pause.)

Q: Now, I have interviewed you once before. Can you
explain why you have specifically asked to be
interviewed again?
```

A: Because when I spoke to you before I didn't tell you everything I knew. Everything I'd seen.

Q: Why?

A: I wasn't sure it was the right thing to do. I did not ... I didn't fully grasp the nature of your project. So, I suppose, I didn't trust you completely.

Q: And now you do?

(There is a pause.)

A: Yes.

(There is a pause.)

Q: In your previous interview, which I have in front of me, you spoke of your arrest after Kristallnacht. About meeting your father, whom you were certain had been maltreated, in the police cell.

A: Yes.

Q: Would you like to expand on that?

(There is a pause. Interviewee nodded.)

A: After my arrest, I was put onto a train, with all the other people in that cell.

Q: Including your father?

A: No. I think I said, he was taken away earlier. No, it was all of those left at the end of the two days I was kept there, about thirty-five of us. We were all taken to the train station in an armoured car ...

Q: Thirty-five of you in one car?

A: (Laughing) That was nothing. When we got to Königsberg station, there about seven hundred Jews there, all men ...

Q: No women or children?

(There is a pause.)

A: Not there. Later there were some.

Q: Sorry. Go on.

A: They put us on the train. It was a freight train. They put all seven hundred of us in three carriages. There were no seats: we were just crammed together, like sardines. It was hard to breathe. There were no toilets either, so men just went – I'm sorry to have to

say this – just went there and then when they needed
to. By the end of two days ...

Q: You were in there for two days?

A: Yes. About. It's difficult to tell, because of
course we couldn't see day or night, except through the
slats in the wood. So, what I was saying was: by the
end of two days, it stank in there.

Q: What about food and water?

A: They gave us none.

(There is a pause.)

Q: So ...

A: Some of the older men were dead on arrival. One of
them, I was standing crushed up against, he died quite
soon, I think, because I felt him become heavier,
although he did not fall over because we were so packed
in there that the rest of us were holding up his
corpse.

Q: Can I just go back on something? These seven
hundred men. Did you know them?

A: I knew a few of them. They were all members of the
Jewish community.

Q: Were any of them criminals, as far as you knew?

A: None that I was aware of.

(There is a pause.)

Q: Political activists? Communists?

A: None.

Q: I see. Please go on.

A: Well, eventually, after these two days, the train
stopped, and the doors were opened. It was chaos – it
is very hard to see straight away after two days in the
dark – and all these SS men are there shouting, telling
us to get off. And you know, it's very hard to move as
well, but if anyone took any time getting down from the
train, he would be hit with a club or a whip. There was
a rabbi ... he must have been about sixty-odd ... anyway,
he was taking a long time getting down, so I reached up
to him to give him my hand, but then I felt this pain

391

across my back, and that was a whip. Then two SS men
got up into the truck and picked up the rabbi and threw
him out, so he landed face down in the dirt.

(There is a pause.)

Q: Where had you been taken?

A: Sachsenhausen.

Q: Where is that?

A: It's about forty-five miles north of Berlin.

Q: Then what happened?

A: There was so much shouting ... eventually, the ones
who were still standing formed into a group, and the SS
men marched us to the camp. They took us to some
building - it was like a stable or something - and we
were forced to hand over all our money and belongings.
Then we had to strip, and stand against the wall.
Hundreds of us, standing there naked. They showered us
with cold water, and then handed out our uniforms,
these striped sacks we all had to wear, with yellow
stars on them. Then, finally, we were led to these
barracks, where we were allowed to sleep on some bunks
covered in straw.

(There is a pause.)

A: Anyway, I don't want to tell you everything that
happened from the moment I got there to the moment I
got out. I just want to give you a sense of what was
happening there, and is still happening there ...

Q: Yes.

A: Every day, we had to get up at three in the
morning, and carry stones.

Q: Stones?

A: Yes. Big stones and rocks. Carry them from one
ditch to another. It was maybe some sort of road-
building, but it just seemed designed to destroy us
physically as quickly as possible. You were given
for breakfast a piece of bread with something that
pretended to be margarine on it, and a cup of black
water that pretended to be coffee, and then you worked

392

on that from three in the morning until six o'clock at night.

Q: What about lunch?

A: There was no lunch. We had to survive on the bread. For supper after work there was soup, one bowl. And that was water with some potato skins in it. Anyway, if, because you were tired or whatever, you dropped the stone you were carrying, you were beaten. Some men were shot.

Q: In cold blood? For dropping the stones?

A: Yes.

Q: You saw that?

A: Many times. And not just for dropping stones. Any offence was punishable by death. Coughing too loudly. Falling asleep while working. Having lice. Having diarrhoea. Some were not shot straight away, of course.

Q: No?

A: No, they were tortured. They had a post in the main courtyard where they would place a man on his back, hanging there, without his hands and legs touching the ground. If he rolled off he would be shot. I saw that happen to a friend of mine, from Königsberg. Eventually, he broke his back.

Q: What was his offence?

A: An SS officer dropped some money, change out of his pocket. He bent down to pick it up. He was going to give it back to him – why not, if you were caught with money, you would be shot anyway? – but the SS man decided he was trying to steal it.

Q: What else have you seen?

A: Other things too horrible ...

Q: You must tell me. Please.

(There is a pause.)

A: A rabbi forced to clean the shit from the toilets with his bare hands. Men starved to death in cells so small they can't even stand up. A man whose fingers were broken, one by one, for not making up his bed. A

393

man forced to lie naked on the ground while three SS men jumped up and down on his stomach. But this is not the point.

Q: It isn't?

A: No. These random acts are only the tip of the iceberg. They aren't the central project of the Nazis. They are planning something much more ... much more ... systematic.

Q: How do you know?

A: Because I saw the start of it. I was in Sachsenhausen for three months. At the end of it, the commandant in charge of our block used to come in and read out a list of names: at first ten or so every week, then twenty. By the time I was released it was fifty. He said they were required for 'special work'; but they never came back.

Q: You're suggesting they were killed?

A: I said they never came back. Remember, fifty a week from each block – that's five hundred men a week from the whole camp. They can't just disappear.

Q: Well, they might have been transported elsewhere. Or released.

A: They weren't.

Q: How do you know?

(There is a pause.)

A: The stone-carrying that I was assigned to, it used to go on about a mile outside the camp. Now, one of the SS in charge of the labour-force, he smoked a lot: I remember, he used to chain-smoke forty, maybe fifty, cigarettes a day. This one day, he ran out. So suddenly, he drags me out of the ditch I was working in, and tells me to run back to the camp: there is a packing shed just outside the wire, where he has left his cigarettes. Now he knows that I could be shot on sight by the sentries for approaching the camp separate from the work group, but he didn't care – he would have just carried on sending prisoners back until one of

394

them wasn't killed, and brought back his cigarettes. He also tells me not to bother to try to escape as, if I'm not back in fifteen minutes, he will raise the alarm. Which means I have to run. Doesn't matter that I'm already completely exhausted. I thought about trying to escape despite what he said, but I'm so tired that I know I wouldn't get far. Anyway, about half a mile from Sachsenhausen there is a wood. And as I'm running on the road beside the wood, I hear shooting. So now I've been going for about six or seven minutes, and I'm worried about getting to the camp and back in time, and so I try to ignore it, but then I hear some screaming as well, and I can't ... I have to see what it is. So I run into the woods and follow the sound. It gets easier as I get closer, because of the sound, obviously, but also because of the smell.

Q: The smell?

A: Burning. Like meat.

(There is a pause.)

A: After about fifty yards' running, the trees began to be less close together and up ahead I could see a clearing, and the backs of some SS men. I threw myself on the ground, and crawled the rest of the way. I could hear a volley of gunshots, about every thirty seconds. Then some shouting, then more gunshots. At the edge of the clearing, I hid behind a tree, and poked my head round. I was terrified they would see me.

(There is a pause.)

A: This is what I saw. There was one group of people – about two hundred of them – men, women and children – lined up a small way from the centre of the clearing. The first thing I noticed was that they were naked.

Q: Naked?

A: Yes. Everybody, completely stripped, trying to use their hands to cover themselves. There was a pile of clothes at the edge of the clearing, and that was what

the SS men who had their backs to me were doing,
sorting through the clothing.

Q: Where were the women and children from?

A: Ravensbrück, I think. It is near by.

Q: Please go on.

A: There was another group of SS men standing back
from the main group of naked people, with rifles. And
one officer, a Sturmbannführer (lieutenant) whom I'd
seen in the camp many times, was shouting at them to
come forward, ten at a time. So they did. The men.
The women, holding the children's hands. Without
resistance, without screaming: all I could hear was the
occasional distant sobbing, and one or two prayers.
Mostly, though, silent. They came and stood in the
centre of the clearing, and then I realised that behind
them was a pit, and in the pit there was a massive fire
burning. It was the fire in which the bodies that had
already been shot were burning. That was the smell of
burning flesh. They made them stand with their backs to
this fire, although some of them turned round to look
into it. And then the officer gave the order to fire.
And they fell, some of them straight into the pit,
others just to their knees: the SS men had to come and
kick them in, shielding their faces from the heat. I
saw them shoot two groups of ten. Then I turned and
ran.

(There is a pause.)

Q: Did you not think then of escaping? After what
you'd seen?

A: No. I didn't think of anything. My mind was blank.
I was like a machine ... I just did what I was told: I
ran back to the camp.

Q: What happened when you got there?

A: Nothing. The massacre saved my life, I think.
There were fewer SS on duty patrolling the outskirts of
the camp than usual – besides those in the woods, all
the ones who led the work groups were out – and so I

managed to slip into the packing shed quite easily. I found the cigarettes and ran back. I'd been gone only twenty minutes all told, and he was so pleased to have his cigarettes, I got away with just a knock on the head from his rifle butt.

(There is a pause.)

Q: When were you released from Sachsenhausen?

A: February 1939.

Q: Why did they let you go?

A: Some of us, before we were arrested, had put in applications to emigrate. In January 1939 the Nazis passed a decree allowing out all Jews detained in camps who held visas or were waiting to receive them.

(There is a pause.)

A: And so now I live here, in Britain, with this knowledge, that this is what these camps – these camps where my father and my mother and my sisters, who are not here with me in Britain, must have been sent – this is what they are for: death. And what I've told you happened nearly two years ago. Then it was just Germany. Now you must multiply that across the face of Europe. The numbers I have told you – they are nothing, tiny fractions. Soon they will find new ways of killing, quicker, more efficient, less messy. I know Germans: I am one. We have a will to improve. They will improve their methods of murder. They may already have done so.

(There is a pause.)

Q: Is there anything else you wish to tell me?

A: Is there anything else you need to know?

(There is a pause.)

Q: No. Thank you.

Isaac looked up, and opened his mouth, his creaking ribs expanding with long, deep breaths of Auschwitz air: it felt like swallowing huge gulps of sadness. His chest was tight, as if at some point while reading the document he had forgotten to breathe. About halfway

397

through it, he had felt his heart, his old, encrusted, rusty pump, begin to beat faster, and had thought: Ah – how ironic, God, if it kills me; how wonderfully that would suit Your mysterious purpose. For a second, he couldn't look at the gate and its inscription, and so turned away, to see Bekka marching towards him as fast as she could, a furious expression on her face.

He knew why it had caused his heart to beat faster: because reading it had made him feel frightened. Not because of the horrific descriptions; not because of the memory of mass murder. The fear was the fear that an errant schoolboy feels when the evidence looms; the fear of the man who knows he is about to be caught lying. There, beyond the gate, somewhere in the museum, with its exhibitions and photographs and statistics placed upon its walls, would be the proof.

Because Isaac's testimony to June Murray had not been true. Well. That is incorrect. It was all true. But it was also all lies.

Isaac Fabian was arrested by the Königsberg police after Kristallnacht. He was placed in a cell for two days, and indeed marked down for transportation to Sachsenhausen; but he never went. He never went because Lulu's family, who had not spoken to him since their marriage, intervened, with bribes and political entreaties and veiled threats of social retribution. It stretched her father's friendship with the Königsberg Chief of Police as far as it could go, but it did not break it. When Lulu came to fetch him, for a moment, having realised in the lobby of the police station the cause of his release, he pulled away and demanded to be sent back to the cells; but her face was so full of fear that his heroics, shaky in truth as they were, disintegrated. They returned to their small apartment in Kantstrasse and began – against the wishes of her parents, to whom they were beholden – to make plans to emigrate.

He found it difficult, now, to touch the feeling behind the words in front of his eyes. He knew what it had been, but to think of it here, looking at his fingers, which had touched her body, so ruined they could hardly hold the page on which the words were written, it seemed absurd. It had been love: love had been his motivation. He had known what she had wanted, what she desperately needed for her dossier – some corroboration, some excessively painful eye-witness evidence – and so he had given it to her. It was his gift, written in blood. For a moment, he touched it again, deep, deep down in the buried chest of himself, the reality of what he had felt for June Murray, and was bewildered, bereft, as once before, by the knowledge that this feeling would never come again.

The story he had told was cobbled together from terrors, bits and pieces he had heard from Communist Party members, from other internees, from fearful rumours fizzing around the Jewish community in Königsberg, from anti-Nazi pamphlets, and, primarily, from Rainer Waldstein. At some level, he was assuaging his guilt towards him as much as towards her – because Waldstein *had* been transported, after arrest in Berlin, to Sachsenhausen, and *had* told him about seeing a massacre. And Isaac had not been certain whether to believe him at the time, because the man was so full of dark imaginings. But once in June's room at the Douglas Arms, having made the decision to tell the story that Waldstein, in his twisted way, refused to, Isaac found himself utterly believing it. In fact, reading this document now, amazed at his own tone, how convincing it was, he realised that, although the starting point for doing this – this *intensely* complicated thing – may have been love, something else, while he was speaking, had got caught up in it: the need, the desperate need, for what he was saying to be heard. As the words had poured out of his mouth, Isaac, a man who was never good at acting, who hated moving an iota away from himself, found that the need for this to be known had seemed to inhabit him. He had been possessed by it, enough to feel that it *was* his story, his testimony. He had felt on his face the heat from the pit and smelt in his nostrils the stench of burning flesh. Looking back now, he was almost moved, for a moment, to renounce a life of materialism and believe that some angel – of truth or, perhaps, of death – had slipped momentarily into his soul.

Or perhaps that was all rubbish, he thought, clicking back into himself. Perhaps all he had done was say the most unbelievable things he could think of: who knew that they would turn out to be true? He wondered, trying to piece together his own motivation, if all of it was subconsciously related to the need to suffer: he had read many times of Holocaust survivors feeling guilty that they had not died. Perhaps, in these words, there was an element of the internee, with his B & Bs, and his recitals, and his ersatz Viennese cafés, and his ballroom dancing, feeling guilty that he had not been placed in a concentration camp.

He flicked his eyes quickly back over the document. He had always been a speedy reader, and found that this was possibly his only physical attribute that had not deteriorated in old age – the only bodily movement, his eyes across the page, that had not slowed down. On a second, more detached, reading, he felt less convinced: he felt he had heard all this before, that it was too standard a Holocaust story, clichéd even, or at least not entirely felt, not entirely real. He could not determine whether this was because time had rendered its narrative too familiar, or because it *wasn't* entirely felt, or entirely real.

All truth; all lies. Had June known? Not consciously, Isaac thought: her desire to hold in her hand an account of genuine atrocity may have overridden her judgement, but not her truth-telling essence. He wondered if she had come to realise it at a later date, but again he thought not – he felt the act of sending the document back to him after her death was not a reprimand, but a remembrance; of their love, perhaps, or simply of their attempt to make a difference. Although he *had* noticed, on a second reading, a tiny lie of June's, where she had asked him if any of the men lined up on the platform at Königsberg station were communists, and he had answered, 'None.' In fact, he had answered, 'None, except for me . . .' – he remembered smiling at her when he had said it – and she had deleted that when she had typed up the interview, presumably because she had not wanted Isaac's testimony to be prejudiced in the eyes of her superiors because of his political affiliations. This lie, this small shift, made him feel less ashamed of what he had done. The truth, he knew, more than ever, was always complex; but there are times when it needs to be made simple.

Now, however, in the year 2000, was not that time. He looked away from his puffing daughter and back towards the gates. Now, there were people out there who were saying that all this never happened; so now, this document he had in his hands was dangerous. It

400

contained, he knew, flaws: the freight trains took thirty hours, not two days, to reach Sachsenhausen from Königsberg; 430 Königsbergers, not 700, were on those trains, which included many others from surrounding areas, too; and, most significantly, the women's camp at Ravensbruck, although built by men from Sachsenhausen, did not start admitting prisoners until later in 1939 – the women and children had been an addition to Waldstein's account that Isaac had included on June's prompting. What did it matter? By the end of the war, 300,000 men had been killed at Sachsenhausen and 70,000 women at Ravensbruck. But he knew that it *did* matter; he knew that it was part of his responsibility to make the unbelievable undeniable. If June's legacy were to get into the wrong hands, some *arschloch* historian would seize upon it as evidence of larger-scale falsification. How ridiculous, he thought, and suddenly despaired. If it never happened, *where is my mother? Where is my father?* in his head addressing God, or David Irving.

'What are you saying, Dad?' asked an exasperated and breathless Bekka, and he realised that once again he had been speaking his thoughts aloud. She had finally reached his bench, and was holding on to the side of it to steady herself.

He used the moment to slide the document underneath his briefcase. 'Nothing.'

'Why did you move from where I told you to stay? Our group's already gone in! We're going to have to catch them up!'

'I'm sorry . . .' he said.

She started: her father hardly ever apologised for his behaviour any more, certainly not to her. She looked at him more closely, noticing that he had removed his glasses: were those *tears* in his eyes, or just the mistiness of an old man's corneas? 'Are you OK, Dad?'

'Yes. I'm OK.' He looked up at her. 'Fuss *nicht*,' he said again, although much less snappily than when they had got off the aeroplane.

She sat down on the bench beside him. For the first time, it occurred to her that it might be difficult for him to walk through the gates opposite. Well, it had occurred to her, she thought, when she first booked the trip, but only in an abstract way; she was so used to his stoicism now that the idea of anything making him

401

actually crumble seemed impossible. 'We don't have to go in if you don't want to,' she said, putting a hand on his shoulder.

'No, it's fine, Bekka. We've come all this way. And besides, I want to. Just give me a minute.'

She nodded. They sat. Another group of tourists, mainly teenagers, went through the gates opposite. Isaac noticed that this group *were* Jewish: all the boys were wearing yarmulkes. An old phrase came to his mind: *How odd of God to choose the Jews.* No, he thought, how odd of the Jews to choose God; how odd of them to invent Him for Man, and then with Marx, with Freud, with Einstein, to drive Man from Him.

'Oh!' said Bekka, rummaging in the pocket of her fleece. 'I nearly forgot. The woman from the Holocaust educational trust showed me this. She let me bring it to show you.' She held out her palm; resting on it was what looked to him like a small silver box.

'*Was ist?*'

'It's a digital camera,' she said, smiling. 'It's got some pictures on it from last time she was here.'

Isaac frowned: he did not really approve of the idea of people taking pictures at Auschwitz – it was a horror of the world, not a wonder – and had barred Bekka from bringing her camera. Was she trying to make a point? 'What about it?'

Bekka held it up. Set into the back was a small frame, with a picture inside it, a shot of some bricks in a pit, like a dump or something. It was so small it was difficult to see clearly, even with his glasses back on.

'It's the site of the gas chambers.'

Nice, Isaac found himself unable not to think.

'We go there at the end of the day. But . . . can't you see?'

'*Was?*'

'The stars . . .'

He looked again, squinting; the picture was so tiny. *The stars?* Gently, Bekka brought her thumb onto the back of the camera, and pressed a button that zoomed the picture closer to the eye. Then he saw them: dotted around the frame, little snowdrops of light, glowing white against the brick and the brown grass.

'*Ja*, I see them now. What are they?'

'Well, it was drizzling, so she says it was just the reflections of the light from her flash on the raindrops. But there's something beautiful about it, don't you think?'

Perhaps the thing that had been most eroded in Isaac by experience was sentimentality; perhaps it is the thing that experience most erodes in everyone. But as he looked, he felt his soul being drawn into the minuscule window on the back of the camera as if by some other button, on some other, bigger machine; and, for a second, he allowed sentiment to wash over him, and believe what he knew Bekka wanted him to believe, what she herself wanted to believe – that maybe this was where his mother and father were, two of these tiny stars dancing across the face of Death.

He let the tears that had been building up in his eyes for some time fall down his face. Bekka saw them and did not know what to say: she was of a generation and a type that thought it was good to cry, and particularly good that men should cry, but still – there is something about your father crying that will always be unwatchable.

'Oh, Dad . . . I'm sorry . . .'

'Fuss *nicht*,' he said, for the third time that day, and smiled, wiping his eyes with his hand. He leant over and surprised his daughter, even more than he had done with his apology, by kissing her gently on her softly wrinkled cheek. He looked at her startled face, and realised that he was wrong: her short hair *did* suit her. At least she'd chosen a style that challenged her age, instead of submitting to it; at least she hadn't gone for that standing wavy block which most women thought they legally had to ask the hairdresser for after the age of fifty. It made her look like a lesbian, of course, but that was just another way of saying she looked like a radical; of saying she looked like his daughter. 'How much is the trip to Kaliningrad?' he asked.

Bekka looked to him, shocked. 'I don't remember. About three hundred and fifty pounds per person, I think. It's a four-day trip.'

'OK,' said Isaac, standing up. 'Let's talk about it on the way home.' He turned, and walked away at some pace, his stick tapping on the gravel.

Bemused, but feeling lighter of heart than she had, Bekka rose and followed him towards the gates of the camp. There was a rubbish bin on the left-hand side of the path, and, as Isaac Fabian passed, he dropped what looked like a bundle of paper into it. His daughter was curious enough to want to stop and look in, but they were late, and she thought it best just to keep moving.

POSTSCRIPT

This novel is a collage of fact and fiction. The basic background – the classification of German refugees by tribunal, their internment on the Isle of Man in 1940, and so on – is all true. Other details have been changed to serve the purpose of the narrative: there was a ship with many refugees on board which was sunk by a U-boat, but it was called the *Arandora Star*, not the *Apollo Rising*, and it sailed in July 1940, not January 1941. Similarly, there is an electric train that tracks the coast of the Isle of Man, but it does not go all the way to Port St Mary. There are many other small changes to historical truth. The Ministry of Information memorandum, INF 1/251, however, is a genuine document, and the rendering of it in these pages is verbatim.

ACKNOWLEDGEMENTS

Many people helped with the research towards this book. I'd like to thank specifically Karen Pollock, Greville Janner and everyone else at the Holocaust Educational Trust; the staff at the Jewish Museum in Camden; the Association of Jewish Refugees, and anyone who got in touch with me via their website; all the people I met while researching on the Isle of Man; Ray Fromm, who sent me a video of the film *The Dunera Boys*; my mother, Sarah Fabian-Baddiel for providing me with the letters my grandfather wrote while interned and Canan Gündüz for translating them.

I am also indebted to the few historical texts that cover the internment of refugees on the Isle of Man during the Second World War, notably Connery Chappell's *Island of Barbed Wire*, Peter and Levi Gillman's *Collar the Lot: How Britain Interned and Expelled its Wartime Refugees*, and David Cesearani and Tony Kushner's, *The Internment of Aliens in Twentieth-century Britain*. A contemporary text which led to the first questions in the Commons about the justice of internment, François Lafitte's *The Internment of Aliens*, published in 1940, is still exemplary. Fred Uhlman's biography, *The Making of an Englishman*, was also very useful.

For generally providing assistance, sometimes with the book and sometimes with my life, I'd like to thank Dmitri Vigneswaren, Alison Carpenter, Katherine Grimond, Rose Lattuga, Pini Dunner, and his grandfather, particularly for telling me about the rabbinical beans, and Jon Thoday.

Thanks also, for invaluable help and support, to my editors, Ursula Mackenzie and Richard Beswick at Time Warner; to my copy-editor, Sarah Shrubb, especially for finally conceding that Indian summer, whatever people may think, is indeed a period that begins in November; and to my literary agent, Georgia Garrett, for work on this book far above and beyond the call of agency.

For less formal editorial advice, I'd also like to thank Russell Celyn-Jones, Lisa Jardine, Peter Bradshaw, Frank Skinner, and the late, much-missed, Deborah Keily. Similar advice was also offered by my partner Morwenna Banks, but it represents such a tiny fraction of her general support, help, love and good works while I was writing this book that I feel no thanks will ever be enough.

I'd also like to thank Dolly Banks-Baddiel, not really for helping in any way, but for providing a reason to keep going.